Tess turned and sent him a blinding smile . . .

❦

Their eyes met across the room and time stood still, the world falling away, until there were just the two of them staring mesmerized at each other.

Tess could not have moved if her life depended upon it. As if waking from a long and terrible dream to find herself safe and cherished, she stared at his face, taking in the striking sweep of his heavy black brows, the high cheekbones, and the bold jut of his nose. It was an arrogant face, a hard face, but it was those large, thickly lashed eyes, eyes of compelling blackness that made him such a handsome man.

Her eyes dropped to his lips. Like one in a trance, she began to drift slowly toward him.

As transfixed as she, Nicolas met her in the middle of the room, his arms sweeping her into a powerful embrace. Drowning in the sweetness he found, he pulled her closer. The soft brush of her body against his was utter magic . . .

❦❦❦

D0123621

W9-BQI-563

SHIRLEE BUSBEE

Lovers Forever

WARNER®
VISION
BOOKS

A Time Warner Company

WARNER BOOKS EDITION

Cover design by Diane Luger
Heart illustration by Danilo Ducak
Hand lettering by Carol Dallacroce

Warner Vision® is a registered trademark of Warner Books, Inc.

Warner Books, Inc.
1271 Avenue of the Americas
New York, NY 10020

Visit our web site at
http://pathfinder.com/twep

Ⓦ A Time Warner Company

Printed in the United States of America

First Printing: May, 1996

10 9 8 7 6 5 4 3 2

For my dear, departed Tom's wonderful mother, Beatrice Huff, who consoles and cajoles me, commiserates and cheers me, and is my most delightful friend.

And, Edwin and Nancy Busbee, a pair of my favorite in-laws, who share their love of fine restaurants and good food with us and with whom we've shared the occasional "four-bottle" dinner.

And, of course, the best proofreader, the most excellent soundingboard, and the best husband of all, Howard.

Chapter One

"*D*id you see that gown? And to wear it to Lady Oakhurst's charity bazaar of all places! It was a shock, I can tell you, when I first laid eyes on it—cut so low, I didn't know where to look! And the color! As close to orange as I ever hope to see! You'd think at *her* age—why, she must be at *least* five years older than I, and I am not considered a green girl any longer—that she'd know better." Hester Mandeville, her lively face full of outrage, barely paused for breath before she went on in heated accents, "Her brother, Randal, not dead a year and Athena is already flaunting herself in a garment that I would not hesitate to stigmatize as fast!"

It was a summation that would have done a woman twice her age proud, but Hester's comment lost much of its moralizing impact by being uttered with a note of such open envy that her niece, Tess, had to choke back a gurgle of laughter. While Tess had been startled to see Lady Athena, the earl of Sherbourne's older sister, wearing "colors" before the year of mourning was up, the gown hadn't been quite that bad. It had been cut rather daringly, it was true, but the shade had been more of a rich antique gold than orange!

Sending her pretty aunt, normally the most tolerant of creatures, a look of affectionate amusement, Tess murmured, "But aren't we also beginning to wear some color again? You can't have forgotten," Tess went on with a sudden catch in her throat, "that Sidney died just eleven days after Lord Sherbourne."

Moral outrage over Athena Talmage's clothes was instantly suspended as both women were assailed by a wave of grief. Each dabbed at the corner of her eye with a handkerchief. Hester said fiercely, "Those wretched Talmages! There was no excuse for that wicked, wicked duel! It was done out of spite! Randal knew that Sidney was no swordsman. . . ." A tight, unhappy smile curved Hester's soft mouth. "It must," she added in a husky voice, "have come as a most unwelcome shock to the great earl of Sherbourne that my brother was not quite the novice with the blade that he had supposed." She took a shaky breath and blurted out, "I'm glad Sidney was able to kill him first. And I don't care if I am being uncharitable!"

For several seconds there was silence in the well-sprung coach as it bowled smoothly along the road toward Mandeville Manor, the home of the two ladies. Ordinarily it was a pleasant, if longish, ride from the small town of Hythe, on the coast of Kent, to the gracious welcome of Mandeville Manor, some twenty miles inland. Ordinarily, too, the women would have enjoyed the lovely October day—the sky was a brilliant blue with only a few clouds on the horizon, the sun still warm, the leaves of the oaks and beeches barely revealing a hint of the brilliant color they would display in another month. But neither lady was aware of the passing countryside—each was remembering the terrible tragedy that had shaken the very foundations of their comfortable life some ten months ago.

Staring blindly out the coach window, Tess felt the tears filling her eyes and she took a deep steadying breath, willing herself not to cry. Oh, but it was hard! She had adored her uncle. Sidney, the fifth Baron Mandeville, had been a high-spirited, sunny-faced individual, a handsome man with a merry charm. He'd always had a smile and a kind word for nearly everyone, and despite the fact that he had been a reckless gambler who had helped bring the family closer to ruin, Tess's deep affection for him had not lessened.

Tess's mother had died a few weeks after her birth some twenty-one years ago, and her father had lost his life in a hunting accident before she was four years old, so she had no clear memory of either of her parents. Before she had even been old enough to realize the tragedy that had struck her at such a young age, her father's sister, Hester, and his brother, Sidney, had ably filled the breach, showering her with warm, unstinting affection. Tess hadn't viewed her late father's siblings as parents precisely. Sidney had been only twelve years her senior, while Hester, seventeen years older than Tess, was a mature thirty-eight. Yet no one seeing her aunt's lovely, laughing face and slim form could possibly think of Hester Mandeville as matronly!

Tess sighed heavily as she continued to stare out the coach window, an errant shaft of sunlight suddenly turning a stray curl of hair from beneath her silk bonnet to flame. The death of her uncle Sidney had been doubly tragic—not only had she lost the nearest thing to a father she had ever possessed, but Sidney's death had brought the despicable Avery Mandeville on the scene and *everything* had changed!

Her generous lips thinned. She didn't really begrudge Avery his inheritance; she didn't mind so very much that Mandeville Manor and its broad acres were now his and that she and her aunt lived in their old home at his sufferance; she didn't even mind that he was constantly in and out of the manor, dividing his time between it and the London town house—they *were* his by law, after all. What she minded, and what brought a militant sparkle to her striking violet eyes, was his persistent and decidedly unwelcome pursuit of her hand!

At twenty-one, Tess Mandeville was an arrestingly beautiful young woman. Her rich red hair and black-lashed violet eyes were a stunning combination, and with her delicately sculpted features and trim, lithe body she was undeniably a tempting bundle of femininity. She was also, from her mother's side of the family, a sizable heiress, and while she suspected that Avery had no objection to her comely form, she was more than certain that it was her fortune that interested him the most!

It was common knowledge these days that the Mandeville fortune was sadly in need of repair and that poor Sidney had been haphazardly looking for an heiress to marry before his untimely death. The Mandevilles were not destitute by any means. They could, with a few economies, easily maintain a comfortable way of life; but they certainly could no longer spend money without thought of the future. Receiving word of Sidney's death, Avery, the newest heir to the barony and a distant cousin, had immediately resigned his captaincy in the infantry and returned to England, eager to claim his title and fortune. Upon his arrival from the continent, where he had been fighting under Sir Arthur Wellesley against Napoleon's troops on the Iberian peninsula, he had been greatly displeased to learn that while he could now style himself Baron Mandeville and claim the elegant rooms of Mandeville Manor and the equally sumptuous rooms of the London town house, there was very little ready money with which to support the luxurious lifestyle he felt was his due. It had been swiftly borne upon the new baron that marriage to an heiress was definitely needed. And who should be there right beneath his nose but Tess . . . lovely, unmarried, and so very suitable for his needs. Tess with her greed-inspiring fortune, at present and until she either married or attained the grand age of twenty-five held in trust for her—and excellently guarded from scheming individuals—by one of her mother's younger brothers, Lord Rockwell.

A little smile suddenly flashed across her expressive face. Tess may have lost her parents at an early age, but happily she had been blessed with caring relatives on both sides of her family. Not only had she enjoyed the unstinting affection of Hester and Sidney, but she was also, albeit carelessly, doted upon by her mother's two brothers. Thomas, the current Lord Rockwell, and Alexander, as handsome and as charming a rogue as one would ever meet. Tess seldom saw either of her maternal uncles, which was hardly surprising since Thomas and Alexander were several years her senior and both were well-known, much-in-demand men about town who seldom strayed from the wickedly exciting environs of London. It was true she was infrequently in their company, but she was always aware of their affectionate concern for her.

Her gaze narrowed. A letter from her, containing just a hint of the new Baron Mandeville's increasingly distasteful wooing, and she knew her tall, broad-shouldered uncles would swoop down from London and with brutal efficiency teach Avery a much needed lesson.

Catching a glimpse of the fierce sparkle in her niece's eyes, Hester asked, "What makes you look so, my dear?"

Smiling across at her aunt, Tess said lightly, "I was just imagining the expression on Avery's face if Thomas and Alexander were to pay him a visit."

A hint of color surged inexplicably into Hester's cheeks, but her voice was determinedly casual as she said, "I'm certain that Alexander wouldn't hesitate a moment to take him to task if you breathed just the merest hint of your difficulties with Avery. Alexander is the kindest, most considerate gentleman I know, and he simply would not allow you to be badgered—especially by the likes of Avery! Both of your uncles are very protective of you and rightly so." She smiled faintly. "Their interest would certainly put Avery on the horns of a dilemma, wouldn't it? He wouldn't know whether to fawn upon them, hoping to gain their good graces, or whether to puff with outrage that they suspect him of ungentlemanly activities." Hester's smile faded and she asked quietly, "Has he been particularly unpleasant? Shall I speak to him?"

Tess shook her head. "No, you know we dare not do anything that might impel Avery to demand that we leave Mandeville Manor—Aunt Meg would be devastated."

Since Sidney's death it was a complicated situation in which Tess found herself. Actually, her situation wasn't terri-

ble at all; she was the possessor of a fortune and two fond uncles who would move heaven and earth to keep her happy—
she could escape from Mandeville Manor any time she chose
to. It was Hester's fate and that of her great-aunt Margaret that
kept Tess chained to the manor house in which she had been
born.

It was odd, Tess thought, how many of the troubles of the
Mandeville family seemed to go back almost seventy years
ago, to the 1740s, to Gregory, her great-grandfather, and his
despicable abduction of Benedict Talmage's bride-to-be, the
Dalby heiress. Theresa Dalby had possessed the red hair and
violet eyes that Tess herself had inherited. A tremor of unease
suddenly quivered through her as she wondered if she might
share her great-grandmother's fate—marriage to a man she
did not love.

It was an old, sad tale. Once upon a time there had lived in
amiable harmony, as neighbors and friends, the Talmage family, earls of Sherbourne; the barons of Mandeville; and the
Dalbys. While the Dalbys could not style themselves as lords
of the realm, they were of aristocratic birth and breeding and
possessed an immense fortune. The last holder of the Dalby
name had been knighted and so could call himself *Sir* Arthur
Dalby. It was Sir Arthur's only child and heiress, she of the
flame red hair and dancing violet eyes, who had been Tess's
great-grandmother and for whom she had been named. The
Dalby lands had been situated between the Sherbourne and
Mandeville estates, and when it became obvious that Theresa
would be the last Dalby and would inherit everything, it wasn't
so surprising that the earl of Sherbourne and Baron Mandeville should cast appraising gazes in that direction. Especially
so, since each man had an unmarried son . . . a son who as
Theresa's husband would gain all those broad acres and all
the immense wealth of the Dalby fortune.

An intense rivalry broke out between the earl of Sherbourne's heir, Benedict, and Baron Mandeville's eldest son,
Gregory, as both men competed furiously for the hand of the

heiress. It had seemed, when Theresa's betrothal had eventually been announced, that Benedict had won the contest and that Gregory would have to retire gracefully from the fray. Unfortunately, Gregory Mandeville was *not* a gracious loser; barely a week before Theresa Dalby's marriage to Benedict Talmage was to take place, Gregory cravenly abducted her from her home.

Despite the Dalby fortune, it had been a love-match between Benedict and Theresa. By stealing his hated rival's bride-to-be, Gregory had not only struck a powerful blow to Benedict's pride, but he had also grievously wounded his heart. Painfully aware of what means Gregory would use to force Theresa's compliance, Benedict searched frantically from one end of England to the other, knowing that when he found the pair that he would be too late to prevent the unthinkable—Theresa's brutal ravishment by Gregory. Benedict's unceasing, desperate quest came to naught. It was not until nearly a year later that Gregory dared return to Mandeville Manor with his new wife *and* their newborn son.

Gregory certainly hadn't taken any chances, Tess thought with a grimace of distaste. Not only had he abducted another man's bride, but he had kept her well hidden until she was not only pregnant by him, but had borne his child. A wave of pity swept through her as she imagined Theresa's anguish. Abducted, raped, and forced to bear the child of a man she loathed.

"Do you think that Great-Grandmother Theresa ever felt anything but hatred and disgust for him?" Tess suddenly asked Hester.

Understandably confused by the question, Hester blinked at Tess, obviously attempting to gather her thoughts. "Are you referring to Gregory and Theresa?" At Tess's quick nod, Hester shrugged. "I don't know. I mean, it's not as if it were something I could ask her about, was it?"

Tess's mouth twisted. "I suppose not. I've just always wondered how she coped. It must have been horrible for her."

Perfectly willing to discuss the matter, but totally mystified about why Tess should be interested in something that had happened so long ago, Hester said quietly, "Well, she didn't have to cope for very long—remember, she and Benedict disappeared together three or four years later."

A dark look on her face, Tess muttered, "I know, but before *that* she had to endure Great-Grandfather *and,* don't forget, watch the man she really loved marry another. They both must have been utterly miserable—she married to a black-hearted scoundrel and Benedict finally forced to marry for the sake of his title. It must have been bitterly heartrending for her when Benedict's son was born. I don't doubt that every time she looked at her own son she didn't think that, except for dear Gregory's perfidious actions, the baby would have been hers and Benedict's."

"It happened a long time ago, Tess. Why are you brooding on it now?"

"I don't know," Tess answered truthfully. "I suppose it has to do with the fact that everyone says I look so much like her—even *I* can see the resemblance between myself and the portrait of her in the gallery. But it's not just the hair and eyes or even the shape of my face . . . it's something inside of me—there are times I feel such affinity with her—almost as if I can feel every emotion she felt." Her mouth set in grim lines. "And I know she hated my great-grandfather with every bone and fiber of her being! I just hope that she and Benedict had a long happy life together when they finally ran away."

"Well, Gregory certainly had a *long* life after she deserted him—and I find it ironic that he outlived not only their son, Richard, but one of his grandsons as well—your father, Edward. Ninety is a vast age, but I doubt he enjoyed very many of those added years."

"He may not have enjoyed them, but I suspect he was thoroughly enraged when he realized that he was dying." Tess shook her head. "He was such a despotic presence, even though he's been dead for over two years now, that sometimes when I walk into the blue salon, I expect to find him sitting there glaring at me."

Hester's soft mouth thinned. "I know it is unkind to speak poorly of the dead, but he was such a devil! He was most unkind to you, Tess, no doubt because of your resemblance to Theresa."

"Clearly he hadn't the least feeling of affection for any of his family. You'd think he'd have left his own sister better provided for, and as for you . . . well, I think he was still punishing you for not finding a wealthy husband, and that's why he made such a shabby provision for you in his will. He *wanted* you and Margaret to know that he didn't give a farthing about your future!"

Hester averted her face, and Tess could have bitten her tongue off. Hester had never said anything directly, but Tess knew that in the past there was someone her aunt had loved or was still in love with, and that her lack of fortune or his had something to do with Hester's unmarried state.

Tess was frantically seeking some way to change the topic when Hester began to speak. Her voice constricted, she got out, "Grandfather couldn't have known that Sidney would die so young. He knew Sidney would take care of Aunt Meg for the rest of her life. And as for me . . ." She smiled painfully, "I never was a particular favorite of his anyway."

"Are you defending him?" Tess demanded, outraged, her violet eyes nearly purple with anger. "You just said he was a devil! And as for *your* not being a particular favorite of his . . ." Tess suddenly grinned. "Oh, but wasn't he furious that his only great-grandchild should turn out to be a mere girl?"

Hester smiled wryly. "Indeed he was. I can remember the day you were born—he took it as a personal affront that your poor father and mother had produced only a puny female. I can still recall his ranting and raving as he stormed through the manor. He was absolutely livid. Claimed your dear mother had done it on purpose, just to spite him. Swore he'd find a way to prevent your father from inheriting the title if the next child wasn't a boy!" Hester shook her head. "I wonder, when your father died just a few years later, if he didn't regret his hasty words." She grimaced and added, "Probably not. He always seemed to believe that he could arrange things precisely as he wanted."

Everything Hester said was true. Tess had grown up under the malevolent eye of her great-grandfather, and during his lifetime, not a day had gone by that she hadn't been reminded that she should have been a boy or that she looked like the wife who had deserted him and vanished with another man. It hadn't sat well with Gregory, either, that she was an heiress in her own right and her fortune was safely in the hands of her uncle, where he could not get his grasping hands on it.

Gregory might not have known Sidney would die so improvidently, Tess conceded grimly, but he certainly had known that by not setting aside a decent amount in his will for Margaret and Hester, he was condemning them to a miserable existence if something *did* happen to Sidney. She would concede that by the time he died Gregory didn't have a grand fortune to command any longer, but from what remained, he could have settled enough money on each of his female dependents to insure them an independence—even if only a frugal one.

Which brought Tess back to her dilemma. Her own fortune was secure, but Margaret and Hester were at the mercy of the new Baron Mandeville for the roof over their heads and the very food they ate. Tess would have gladly expended a portion of her own impressive fortune on her aunt and great-aunt, but both ladies were loath to take advantage of her sincere offer. Despite several long conversations, usually when Avery had done something especially upsetting, Tess couldn't seem to make them understand that allowing her to provide for them would be no different from allowing Avery to see to their care. But both ladies were horrified at the idea of Tess using her fortune to take care of them—they were Mandevilles! It was up to Avery to see to their care. In some convoluted manner that made absolutely no sense to Tess, they felt that it would be unfair to her, that they would be taking undue advantage of her, if they allowed her to settle a reasonable sum on them.

Tess sighed heavily. Unless or until events became absolutely unbearable at Mandeville Manor, neither of the two women dearest to her in the world was willing even to hear of using Tess's money for their own benefit. In the meantime, in spite of Avery's odious attentions, and the possible danger to herself should he decide to follow Gregory's methods of obtaining a fortune, it was unthinkable that she simply abandon Hester and Aunt Meg to the indifferent care of that smarmy toad Avery! Which meant, Tess admitted uneasily, she had to stay at Mandeville Manor and helplessly watch over Hester and Aunt Meg like a hen with two chicks confronted by a rapacious tomcat!

A few minutes later Hester broke the thick silence by asking curiously, "Why were you thinking about the old scandal? Gregory's abduction of Theresa and her later disappearance with Benedict Talmage occurred decades ago. What made you think of them now?"

Tess shrugged. "I guess I had been thinking about the way things have turned out—Sidney's death and how if Gregory hadn't acted so despicably, there wouldn't be such enmity between ourselves and the earls of Sherbourne. Of course Gregory still would have been a spendthrift and wasted most of the money. So the Mandevilles would still probably have ended up in need of *another* heiress with which to repair their fortunes."

Hester shot her a look. "Are you certain that Avery hasn't been annoying you?"

"Oh, perhaps, a little." She glanced slyly at her aunt. "If you and Auntie Meg would let me set you up in a tidy little house near Hythe, I wouldn't have to endure his company at all!"

Hester looked distressed. "He *has* been pestering you!" Leaning forward, she said earnestly, "You don't have to stay, darling. You know your uncles would be most happy if you went to London or to Lord Rockwell's estate in Cornwall to live. And though we would miss you like the very devil, Meg and I would do fine. . . ." She took a deep breath and blurted out, "And if he decides to cast us out of the house or he becomes too obnoxious for us to bear, we will let you buy us that little house!"

"But not until then?"

"Oh, Tess! You are the sweetest child in nature, but you know that we cannot. It would not be right!"

Seeing the worry in her aunt's eyes, Tess put on a sunny expression and said lightly, "Well, I don't think I'd be happy in London, and as for Cornwall, I'd much rather be right here with you—even if it means putting up with Avery!"

The coach slowed and a moment later they were traveling down the elm-lined drive that led to Mandeville Manor. The manor itself appeared shortly, an elegant half-timbered house built in Elizabethan times. Dark green ivy pressed itself to the sides of the building and softened the outlines of the many dormers in the tiled roof; the lattice-worked windows gleamed in the fading sunlight. With a flourish the carriage swept around the shrub-lined circular drive, and the coachman brought the horses to a stop at the base of the broad steps that led to the massive double entrance doors.

The horses had barely been pulled to a stop before one of the carved oak doors was thrown open and a tall man in buff breeches and a form-fitting coat of bottle green came strolling down the stone steps to meet the ladies. The gentleman, Avery Mandeville, the sixth Baron Mandeville, was without a doubt an attractive male, possessed of a well-made body with broad shoulders and slim hips; and the fact that he had been a military man before inheriting the title was obvious in the way he carried himself, his back ramrod straight, his head high. He far more resembled his third cousin, Gregory, than had any of

Gregory's immediate offspring, having inherited Gregory's notable thick blond hair and icy blue eyes as well as the handsomeness that ran in the family.

In fact, watching his approach, Tess thought that he could have been her great-grandfather at the same age. A shiver went through her. The knowledge that she bore a striking re- ' semblance to Theresa and that Avery's features were uncannily those of Gregory's made her distinctly uneasy. While the situation was different, she couldn't help wondering, since fate seemed to have assembled a pair of copies of the original players in herself and Avery, if history wasn't going to repeat itself.

Deliberately she shook off her unpleasant musings. It couldn't happen again—she'd never marry Avery, no matter *what* he did! She was far more likely to take a dagger to him if he ever laid a hand on her. As for her being desperately in love with a descendant of the earl of Sherbourne, the whole idea was ludicrous! She'd never met Randal Talmage's youngest brother, the latest earl of Sherbourne, nor did she even know his name. Love an unknown stranger indeed!

Chapter Two

*A*very reached the coach and solicitously helped Hester down from the vehicle. Kissing her hand, he murmured, "Ah, dear cousin Hetty, I *do* wish when you want to use the carriage that you would inform me first. What would have happened if *I* had needed the coach this afternoon?"

Hester's cheeks burned with embarrassment, and she began to apologize most profusely, but Avery gently waved aside her words. "Oh, don't let it concern you. Just remember in the future to let me know of your plans. And now let us talk of other things—can it be that during the brief hours you have been away from Mandeville that you have grown even more lovely?"

Flustered, Hester stammered out some polite reply and threw Tess a beseeching glance. Correctly interpreting Hester's look as a plea not to annoy him, Tess bit back the tart words that threatened to escape at his antics. Ignoring Avery's outstretched hands as he turned to help her from the carriage, she nimbly alighted unaided.

A glitter of annoyance in his blue eyes, Avery drawled, "Such independence! It is obvious that you have been vastly spoiled by your aunts. No doubt you need a husband to teach you some manners! Will you at least allow me the pleasure of escorting you to the house?"

Tess looked consideringly from him to the short distance to the front door. "Oh, do you think I might be in danger?" she asked innocently. "That something dreadful might happen to me in the few seconds it will take to mount the steps and go inside?"

His handsome features tightened. "Don't be ridiculous! I was merely being polite."

Brushing past him, Tess said airily, "Well, I'm certainly glad we have resolved this particular little misunderstanding. Now if you'll excuse me . . ."

Tess hurried into the house, not even waiting to see if Hester had followed her. Reaching the relative safety of her own rooms, she tossed aside her frivolous bonnet and ran her fingers through her tangled ringlets. She had been, she admitted guiltily, beastly to Avery, but she just couldn't seem to help herself. He grated on her nerves, and there was just something about him that made her jumpy and waspish and not at all her usual sunny self. Besides, she didn't like the way he treated Aunt Meg and Hester—arrogant one minute and in the next leaking oily charm all over them, much as he had just behaved with Hester a few minutes ago. He toys with them, Tess thought angrily, like a big, sleek cat with a pair of mice. Showing his claws, then retracting them. Always making them aware of the power he holds over them. Never letting them feel totally at ease.

With an irritable flounce, she turned away and began to shrug out of her travel-rumpled gown. She had just tossed the plum-colored gown onto the plump featherbed and was tying the sash of an apple green silk wrapper around her slender waist when the door to her room was thrown open. In outraged astonishment she stared as Avery calmly entered her room and shut the door firmly behind him.

"How dare you!" Tess began, her violet eyes flashing with temper. "Get out of my room this instant!"

Avery leaned back against the door and said bluntly, "I think you forget that this is *my* house now and that as lord and owner, I can go anywhere, anytime I please."

"In that case," Tess fairly snarled, "I shall remove myself from *your* house this very instant! If you shall be so good as to let John Coachman know that I shall be needing the carriage, I won't remain a second longer than is necessary to pack my belongings and leave for London. My uncles will be delighted to see me!"

"Hmm. Well, that does present a problem, doesn't it?" Avery drawled languidly. "You forget John is *my* servant and that the horses and coach are also mine." His cold blue eyes met hers. "And it so happens that I don't want to send them out again today. As a matter of fact, I have given all of the servants a few days off."

Tess took a deep, fortifying breath, her mind racing. The unexpected news that all the servants were gone was not encouraging. She knew that Avery was not happy with her open aversion to his suit, but surely he wouldn't be bold enough to attempt to force his attentions on her? Just his presence in her room like this was dangerous and could have ruinous repercussions. Every minute he remained here increased the danger. Her jaw set. "I think it is time that we had some clear understanding between us. I don't know what you believe you are accomplishing by these tactics, but I do not intend to let you compromise me. So if you do not get out of my room within the next two seconds, decorum be damned! I shall scream and scream for so long and so loudly that they will no doubt hear me in Canterbury!"

He smiled, and something in that smile suddenly made Tess frightened. "Go ahead," he drawled. "I wonder what everyone will think when they discover us alone together in your bedchamber and you in such a charming state of dishabille?"

Tess was not noted for cool temperance. With a soft growl of fury, she snatched up a handsome silver candelabra and flung it at his head. He moved at the last second, and the candelabra crashed against the door with an explosive bang. Bosom heaving, she faced him across the short distance that separated them.

"Let them find us!" she said rashly. "I'd rather live with a ruined reputation and be the object of scandalous gossip for the rest of my life than allow myself to be tied to an unprincipled rogue like you!"

Avery regarded her thoughtfully for a long, unnerving moment, his handsome face revealing nothing. Then he shrugged and murmured, "I was hoping you'd be sensible about this and realize that marriage to me is your fate, but I can see that you are going to be difficult. So be it." He shot her a derisive glance. "I wonder if you'll be as proud and confident of facing the resulting furor once it is learned that we have spent the night alone together . . . that I have availed myself of all your lovely charms?"

In dumbfounded fury, Tess stared at him, hardly able to credit that he was brazenly admitting that he planned to force her into marriage the same way her great-grandfather had forced Theresa. However, before she could give tongue to the hot words that crowded her throat, Avery sketched her an infuriatingly polite little bow and left her room, shutting the door ever so quietly behind him. With something akin to horror she heard the key turn in the lock and then the muted sounds of his departure.

He wouldn't dare, she thought incredulously. He couldn't possibly believe that he could get away with it!

She flung herself against the door and tried the knob. In growing consternation, she watched as it turned uselessly in her hand. Like a wild animal caught in a trap, she beat her fists against the unyielding wood, hoping that someone would hear her. Sobbing as much in anger as fear, she continued to beat against the door, calling out urgently for someone to free her.

It was to no avail. No one came in answer to her desperate shouts. What Avery had told the servants or how he could keep her aunts at bay, she didn't know, but for the moment it appeared that he had matters well in hand. She was locked in her own room—the prisoner of a man she despised. . . . Filled with despair, she sank to the floor at the base of the door. Good God! What was she to do?

Reminding herself that letting fear overrule her common sense would be fatal, she took a few calming breaths and rose to her feet. Avery was not going to win. Her chin set at a determined angle, she crossed to a damask-covered slipper chair by her bed. She had to think.

She sat there for a long, long time, unaware of the falling darkness around her, unaware of the swiftly passing time, her thoughts churning wildly. She had known that Avery was dangerous, but she had not expected him to act so precipitously or so brazenly. She frowned. Something must have happened while she and Hester were gone this afternoon, something to put the wind up him and force him into taking such risky action. But what could it have been?

Absently her gaze traveled over her bedchamber, done up fashionably in her favorite shades of rose and cream, while she considered various possibilities. Almost by accident her eyes fell on the small silver salver sitting on the edge of her satinwood dressing table and the envelope that lay within it.

As she sprang up from her chair, she suddenly became aware of the evening gloom that permeated the room. Grumbling to herself, she found the matching candelabra that she had earlier thrown at Avery and lit it. Carrying the light, she walked over to the dressing table and snatched up the envelope, noticing angrily in the flickering candlelight that Lord Rockwell's seal had been broken and not very cleverly repaired. Almost as if it didn't matter that she should know the letter from her uncle had been opened and that eyes other than hers had already read it.

Muttering an unladylike curse, Tess took out the single page and swiftly scanned the contents. Lord Rockwell must have sensed that things were not going well at Mandeville Manor, because the letter imparted the knowledge that he and her other uncle, Alexander, were coming to Kent for a visit—an extended stay. They would arrive Saturday, four days hence, and they looked forward to a long, leisurely visit with her and her aunts. Near the end of his missive, Lord Rockwell mentioned the possibility that once the visit to Mandeville had ended, all three ladies might like to travel with them to Rockwell Hall, his estate in Cornwall, where they could celebrate the holidays together.

Well, that certainly explained Avery's actions, Tess concluded glumly. Avery wasn't a stupid man, and after reading Lord Rockwell's letter, he must have realized that some news of his determined pursuit of Tess must have reached her uncles' ears and that they were coming to Mandeville Manor to see for themselves the true state of affairs. The offer for Tess and her aunts to spend Christmas at Rockwell Hall made it clear that her uncles also intended to spirit her away to what they considered a safer place.

Nibbling her full lower lip, Tess nervously paced the confines of her room. Avery must have known as soon as he had read her letter, and there was no doubt in her mind that he *had* read her letter, that there wasn't a moment to spare. That whatever plans he had for her must be completed by Saturday, when her uncles were due to arrive.

With a sense of growing panic she dashed around the room, checking to see if she had overlooked a way of escape. The narrow leaded windows that overlooked the gardens at the rear of the house did not open but only provided light, and it was a treacherously long drop from her second-story bedroom to the stone terrace below.

She swallowed. If nothing else occurred to her, she would just have to beat open the windows and take the risk of breaking her neck rather than wait tamely for Avery's reappearance. She had to escape! Hours had passed since he had locked her in her room. There was not a moment to lose!

With that in mind, she hastily fashioned a rope from the linens on her bed, then changed into a black velvet riding habit and pulled on her boots. After scooping up her jewelry box and stuffing it, along with some odd pieces of clothing, in a pillowcase, she grabbed a black cloak and took one last look around the room. There was nothing else that would be of use to her.

Darkness had fallen. The hour was not very late, but Tess was suddenly conscious of the ominous silence of the house. Ordinarily there was the bustle of the servants, the sounds of doors opening and shutting, the rattle of trays and oddments as the staff went about their tasks, but this evening all was quiet. It was as if the entire house knew what was to take place and were holding its breath . . . waiting for history to repeat itself.

History would *not* repeat itself, she promised herself fiercely. Avery would find she was made of sterner stuff than Theresa had been.

Tess set the pillowcase near the window and picked up the brass poker from near the fireplace. As she struck a mighty blow against the windowpanes, there was a loud crash; her fingers stung from the force with which the poker had connected with the window, but the glass remained undamaged.

Choking back a sob of despair, she struck again and again. She was concentrating so fiercely on smashing open the window that she almost didn't hear the turning of the key in the lock. But just as an encouraging crack appeared in one pane, that soft grating sound impinged upon her consciousness and spun her around like a tigress at bay. Heart thundering in her breast, the poker held firmly in her hand, she stood ready to do battle with the blackguard who planned her dishonor.

To her relief, it was not Avery's menacing form that appeared in the opened doorway, but those of her two aunts, their faces tense with anxiety. Aunt Meg held a warning finger to her lips as she caught sight of Tess. Hester was directly behind her, carrying a small bag and a candle.

The painful knot in her stomach that had been her constant companion since Avery had locked the door vanished, and with deep affection she stared at the two women entering the room.

Margaret Mandeville had been considered a great beauty in her day and at seventy-one was still striking, with her softly rounded chin and straight little nose. She had inherited the icy blue eyes of the Mandevilles, but there was normally such gentle humor in their depths that one soon forgot their frosty hue. Usually her expression conveyed open delight and sweet agreeability, and that made her a universal favorite of nearly everyone who met her.

It was clear Margaret took after the Mandeville side of the family, which was only natural, considering that she had been Gregory's much younger sister. Hester was clearly related to her—she had the thick fair hair of the Mandevilles but also possessed her grandmother Theresa's beautiful violet-shaded eyes.

Staring at the pair of them as they rushed up to her, Tess felt her eyes sting with tears. They had never failed her, and even now they were running a terrible risk coming to her this way. If Avery should find them . . .

"Hurry, child, we must get you away this instant," Aunt Meg said in hushed tones. "I gave him all the laudanum I had on hand in his wine at dinner, but it wasn't very much, and although he is sleeping soundly at the table at this very minute, I do not know how long we have. I dismissed that impertinent butler of his and told him Avery had given word that he wouldn't need him anymore this evening. The man couldn't very well argue with me, but he did not like it! We dare not tarry—you must be gone from here this instant. There is not a moment to lose!"

"But what . . . ? How did you . . . ?" Tess asked disjointedly, trying to grasp this unexpected change of events.

Her blue eyes smiling gently, the cloud of white hair framing her still pretty features, her great-aunt murmured, "How did we know what he planned? I suspected something was going on the minute the messenger arrived with Rockwell's letter this afternoon while you were gone. Avery glanced at it, and such a scowl marred his features! He disappeared immediately into the library, and when he came out several minutes later and dismissed all the servants, except those two rascally creatures he brought with him from the continent, I just knew he was up to no good! But I couldn't decide what it could be, until he sent Lowell upstairs to put the letter in your room and I spied your uncle's handwriting on it when we passed on the stairs. When I realized that he had read your letter from Rockwell, it wasn't hard to figure out." Aunt Meg suddenly flushed. "After Lowell had come back down, I slipped upstairs and into your room and, I'm ashamed to admit it, child, read Rockwell's letter, too, but only after I saw that Avery had opened it—I never meant to snoop! Once I learned that Rockwell was coming, I knew that Avery would be forced to act immediately if he didn't want you and your fortune to escape from him." Contritely she added, "I know he is an unpleasant man, but I never really thought he would go this far. I'm sorry, my dear, that I didn't realize the danger. I would never have put you at risk, if I'd even suspected for a moment that he was of the same monstrous stripe as my late brother."

"But what about you?" Tess asked worriedly. "Once he awakes and finds me gone he's going to know that you helped me—I cannot leave you here alone with him!"

"Do not worry about us," Aunt Meg said firmly. "You are the one in the most pressing danger. He may suspect our part in your escape, but he cannot prove anything without admitting his own cold-blooded plan."

Hester agreed. "Tess, he is no doubt going to wake up with a terrible head later, and if Aunt Meg and I greet whatever tack he tries with us with wide-eyed innocence, he is probably not going to believe that we were able to plumb his plans or that we would drug him, steal his key, and set you free." Hester smiled deprecatingly. "Look at us—would you suspect us of such nefarious activities?"

Despite the gravity of the situation, Tess had to smother a chuckle. Two more unlikely miscreants would be hard to find. Both her great-aunt and her aunt were, like herself, small women, finely made with daintily shaped figures. Neither woman was any longer in the first blush of youth, and with their gentle manners, Aunt Meg's fluffy white hair, and Hester's clear, candid violet eyes, it would be hard to think them guilty of anything more serious than napping through vespers!

Choking back a sob mingled with laughter and despair, Tess shook her head. "No, and I'm quite certain that you would be able to pull the wool over most people's eyes, but . . ."

Aunt Meg clucked her tongue. "Stop it! We are not in danger—you are." Sending her great-niece a look of mock severity, she said firmly, "If you are really worried about us, you will leave immediately. The sooner you are gone, the sooner we can return to Avery the key to your room and remove ourselves to the safety of our rooms—where that monster will find us soundly asleep when he finally does awaken."

Not giving Tess a chance to argue, Hester thrust the small bag she was carrying into her hand and said, "We gathered up all our ready money and packed some cold meat and cheese for your journey. Once Aunt Meg informed me about the contents of the letter—we didn't have much time to plan things." Hester took a deep breath. "You must get away from here at once!"

Still Tess hesitated, unwilling to leave the other two. A stubborn expression on her face, she demanded, "Why can't you come with me? You know my uncles will welcome you and protect you from Avery."

Aunt Meg pursed her lips. "And how do you expect us to come with you? I'm sure that between us we could harness the horses to the coach and, more than likely, manage to drive the vehicle, but we would have to stick to the main roads and we would be traveling much slower than a horse and rider. Should Avery attempt to find you, people are more likely to remember a coach than a lone rider." She sent Tess a kind look. "My dear, it has been a number of years since we have done any serious riding. We would only imperil your escape."

"She's right, and you know it Tess," Hester added grimly. "You have to go alone. And if we are not to come to grief, you must leave now!"

For a second longer, Tess stood there. Then, the bag Hester had thrust at her in one hand and the pillowcase containing her jewelry box in the other, she flung her arms first around Aunt Meg, then Hester, and muttered, "I'll be back for you! I will not desert you to Avery's care."

"Of course you won't," Aunt Meg said soothingly. "Now *go*!"

Without a backward glance, Tess left the room, running down the wide hallway. Her eyes half blinded by the unshed tears that shimmered in their depths, her ears alert to any sound of danger, she swiftly made her way to the rear of the house, to the long gallery that ran across the back of one entire wing. Off the gallery there was a large balcony with a stone staircase curving grandly down to the terrace below; this seemed her safest choice for escaping unseen by either of the two remaining house servants.

Breathless, her heart thumping madly in her breast, Tess finally made it to the gallery. Stopping for a moment, she glanced around nervously, the silence of the house unnerving, and again she was struck by the uneasy sensation that the house itself seemed to be holding its breath, waiting . . . waiting . . .

Tess shook off her fears and took a resolute step forward, wishing she had remembered earlier how spooky it was at night in this section of the house, how lonely, how deserted, how the shadows seemed to leap out at one in the flickering light from the burning candles that reposed in a pair of sconces at either end of the room.

The gallery was long and narrow, the high walls hung with portraits of the ancestors of the Mandeville family; as she moved slowly along its length, Tess felt as if the condemning gazes of all those long dead Mandevilles were burning daggers into her back. It wasn't a pleasant sensation, and she breathed a sigh of relief when she reached the far end and the light, little though it was, from the other pair of sconces. The double doors that led to the balcony were directly in front of her, and she stopped, her hand on the silver-plated doorknob, to glance across at the picture of her great-grandmother, the tragic Dalby heiress, Theresa. . . .

In the dancing shadows, it seemed to Tess that Theresa was staring directly at her. The portrait was full length and had been painted the spring of the year Theresa had disappeared with Benedict Talmage, the seventh earl of Sherbourne. Theresa had been twenty-one at the time and in the full bloom of her breathtaking beauty. She had been painted standing near a lily pond, her gown in the style of the times, yards and yards of boldly striped Spitalfields silk, her hooped skirt falling gracefully in a bell shape, her lovely flame red hair built up with plaiting and festooned with ribbons and flowers. Tess had frequently stood in front of this particular portrait, wondering what had gone on behind those sad eyes, and again she felt the link, the inexplicable link she often felt with Theresa. The power of it this night was suddenly so strong, she nearly gasped aloud.

The wide violet eyes seemed to beseech her, to beg her, to *plead* with her, not to tarry, to hurry, to run as far and as fast as she could. Tess stared, mesmerized, at the portrait; her blood seemed to pump in rhythm with the message in Theresa's eyes—run, run, *run*! And she did.

Chapter Three

Nicolas Talmage, the tenth earl of Sherbourne, tried to convince himself that he was *not* running away. But try as he might, the unpleasant suspicion that there was a strong odor of a decidedly hasty retreat about his impending departure did not sit easy with him.

Idly watching his lantern-jawed valet, Lovejoy, pack his belongings, Nicolas told himself firmly—and for perhaps the fifth time that evening—that he was merely returning to his estate in Kent to spend the winter as so many of his friends had done. With the City so thin of company, there was no reason for him to stay. He would just have to renew his quest for a bride in the spring, when a new and hopefully more appealing crop of marriage-minded females would be put forth.

Only partially satisfied with his own explanation of why he was departing so unexpectedly tomorrow afternoon for his ancestral estates, when it was well known that he had planned to stay at the Sherbourne House in Grosvenor Square until January, Nicolas picked up his goblet of port and took another sip. As his fine black eyes continued to monitor Lovejoy's deft movements around the room, he told himself again that it was just time to leave. There was no reason to stay.

The fact that he had just learned that the lovely, widowed Lady Halliwell was remaining in town through the winter did not have any bearing on his change of plans. Nor did the fact, he thought stubbornly, that she had hinted, oh so delicately, not three hours ago at Lady Grover's ball that she would not object to forming a closer alliance with him have *anything* to do with his sudden desire to return to Sherbourne Court. . . .

The truth of the matter was that he found the young woman extremely tempting—he found her so tempting, in fact, that three years previously he had taken one look at her beautiful face and had, for the first time in his life, fallen head over heels in love. He had been home, on leave, while he recuperated from a wound he had received at the Battle of Vimeiro in Portugal and had come to London with his brother, Randal, to spend a few weeks before returning to the war on the continent. It had been in the fall of 1808 at the start of the "little" season in London, and Maryanne Blanchard, as she was called then, had been only seventeen years old and already a great beauty and an accomplished flirt.

Possessing a beguiling smile, a head full of soft, fair hair, and china blue eyes along with a face to make the gods swoon, Maryanne had become the cynosure of all eyes no matter where she went that season. Nicolas found himself utterly dazzled by her.

Nicolas had left Sherbourne Court at an early age to begin his military career, and having spent several years with Sir Arthur Wellesley in India before fighting in Portugal, he was far more worldly and older than most of the young men who flocked to worship at the feet of the latest "Incomparable." But even at the grand age of twenty-nine, he had almost immediately fallen under her spell and had paid the young beauty assiduous court. It was common knowledge that her family was expecting Maryanne to marry well to retrieve the family wealth, but despite his lack of any fortune, for several weeks that fall Nicolas was the odds-on favorite for the hand of the fair Blanchard. When it appeared that the Beauty seemed to be found most frequently in his company, the wagering on his chances of success reached a fevered pitch in the various gentlemen's clubs about the city.

At that time, Nicolas had possessed neither fortune nor title, as the youngest and second son of Lord Sherbourne, and a military career was all that had been open to him—a life in the clergy, frequently the other career for second sons, had not even been considered. But if Nicolas had lacked a fortune, he had been blessed with charm aplenty and as handsome and manly a face and form as any maiden could have wished. With his black curly hair and laughing black eyes, broad shoulders, and elegantly muscled legs, it was no wonder that he was a great favorite among the ladies. The gentlemen, too, found him very agreeable company, and it was the consensus of many of Maryanne's suitors that if *someone* had to marry the Blanchard Beauty, a better candidate than Lieutenant Nicolas Talmage couldn't be found.

Unfortunately, it wasn't too long before polite society was titillated by the antics of a man older than Maryanne's own father—the notorious duke of Halliwell. Having watched the courtship of Nicolas and Maryanne for some weeks with cynical, calculating eyes, the duke finally decided to put an end to the nonsense. Halliwell let it be known, and not too discreetly, that since the time of mourning for his late wife, a poor downtrodden creature known more for her wealth and breeding than her beauty, was over, he was looking to marry to please himself. Wealth or even breeding didn't matter so much this time, as he had already done his duty and provided for the continuation of his line with his first wife. Wealthy, powerful, and arrogant, he soon made it clear that if the Blanchard Beauty married anyone that season, it was going to be he. Sir George, Maryanne's father, immediately began to be seen quite frequently in the company of Lord Halliwell. When it was learned that the Beauty and her family were to spend the Christmas holidays at the duke's palatial home in Derbyshire, the odds favoring Nicolas in the betting books changed dramatically.

Nicolas couldn't believe that he had been ousted so easily from Maryanne's affections, but all too soon it was obvious, even to him, that the Beauty had decided to marry for the wealth and power she would have as the wife of a duke rather than endure the uncertain life she would face as the wife of a mere lieutenant. He had been utterly disillusioned and certain that his heart had been shattered. It had been with a great deal of disgust that he had put London and the Blanchard Beauty behind him and returned to the war in Portugal.

Taking a long, slow sip of his port, Nicolas reflected ironically on the vagaries of fate. Who could have known that two short years later, not only would his father, Francis, have died, but that his brother would die without issue and that the once "mere" lieutenant would inherit everything—the title, the great wealth, the broad fertile acres, and one of the most notable estates in England? He smiled cynically. Or that the duke would die within eighteen months of his marriage to the lovely Maryanne?

Upon her stepson's inheritance of the title and all the vast wealth of the Halliwells, Maryanne had been politely removed from Halliwell House and banished to the far less magnificent Dower House. Fortunately, she had a generous settlement and spent most of her time in London, living in the imposing town house the old duke had bestowed upon her when they had married. Not yet twenty-one, at the height of her beauty and charm, possessed now of her own respectable fortune, she was once again, not surprisingly, surrounded by a court of eager admirers and suitors.

But *I* ain't among them! Nicolas thought sourly as he tossed off the last of his wine. Thinking of the lonely, bitter nights he had spent upon his return to Portugal three years ago, drowning his sorrows in far too many nights of hard drinking and taking foolhardy risks with his life in battle as he tried to forget a particular pair of china blue eyes, he knew he wasn't about to walk down *that* path again! Especially since he suspected that the dowager duchess of Halliwell wouldn't have wasted a second glance on him if he had returned to England as Lieutenant Nicolas Talmage instead of the earl of Sherbourne!

Regrettably, even knowing that money and a title meant more to Maryanne than an honest love, Nicolas still found her undeniably alluring. Too alluring, he admitted grimly. His dreams of late had been filled with her, and the seductive notion that he could have her this time, in his arms and in his bed, that his reluctant search for a bride to provide the necessary heirs for the Sherbourne title would be over, had begun to occur with disturbing regularity. By marrying her, he could have everything he wanted, the beautiful woman who had haunted his dreams for far too long and the wife he needed to bear his sons.

His handsome mouth twisted. If only he could pretend her marriage hadn't happened or at least forget the *reasons* she had married one of the most notorious old rakes in England. The fact that she had lain in the arms of another man didn't bother him—there was much to be said for an experienced woman—but it rankled him to know that if he married her, it would be his title and fortune that had persuaded her to accept him. He might need to get married, but he sure as hell wasn't going to be snared by a seductive, fortune-hunting little witch!

He scowled. And he was *not* running away from Lady Halliwell!

Before he could continue the fruitless argument with himself, there was a tap on the door to his bedchamber. Upon his command to enter, the door swung open to reveal the plump form of his London butler, Buffington. His bald pate gleaming in the glow from the candelabra that lit the room, his blue eyes full of discreet curiosity, Buffington bowed and proffered a silver salver.

"A gentleman caller, Your Lordship. I, ahem, took the liberty of ordering refreshments for him and showed him into the library."

Mystified by who would be calling at this time of night and who could warrant such obsequious behavior from a man freely stigmatized by Lovejoy as a "stiff-rumped old maggot," Nicolas set down his goblet and took up the small white card that lay in the center of the salver. One of his thick black brows arched as he read the name on the card. Roxbury? Now why in the deuce was that sly old rascal calling on him?

A thoughtful expression on his handsome face, Nicolas glanced across at Lovejoy, who had ceased his packing when Buffington had entered the room and was watching him expectantly. They had been together a long time—since Nicolas had joined the army and Lovejoy had come along with him as his batman—and there were few people Nicolas regarded with higher affection or respect. They had faced violent death together in India and Portugal, and upon occasion each had risked his life for the other. Consequently, Lovejoy was more than just his valet.

Meeting Lovejoy's eyes, Nicolas shook his head slightly and murmured, "It's nothing—continue as you were. I still plan for us to leave as soon as possible tomorrow afternoon."

Walking down the grand staircase, Nicolas pondered all the various reasons for a visit from the duke of Roxbury but could come up with nothing that made any sense. He hardly even knew the older man, although he knew that Roxbury and his father had been friends and that Randal had counted the duke's heir, Viscount Norwood, as one of his closest companions in debauchery. He could remember no more than a half a dozen times that he'd ever exchanged more than polite conversation with the man who was now waiting for him in his library.

It wasn't that Nicolas didn't know *of* Roxbury; everyone knew the duke of Roxbury. He was a wealthy and powerful man and a notable and admired figure about town. He was also, it was whispered, a man not to cross as well as the exquisitely delicate hand behind many a diplomatic, and sometimes not-so-diplomatic, coup. He was reputed to have tentacles in places and events where one would never expect to find a lord of the realm, and his power with those in high places was enormous—it was said that not one important event occurred in England, or anywhere else, for that matter, that Roxbury did not know about . . . or hadn't arranged. So what, Nicolas wondered, does he want with me?

Entering the library, he found the object of his speculations, a tall, silver-haired gentleman looking very elegant in a black velvet jacket and pearl gray kerseymere breeches, sipping a snifter of brandy. He appeared quite at his ease and was comfortably ensconced in a channel-backed chair near the fire in the marble-fronted fireplace against the far wall. The merrily leaping flames brought out the rich tones of the many-colored leather-bound volumes that lined the walls of the room and intensified the hues of the scarlet-and-gold Aubusson carpet that lay upon the floor.

Looking up and seeing Nicolas standing there just inside the doorway, Roxbury smiled, his deceptively sleepy gray eyes betraying nothing. "Ah, you *are* at home—your butler didn't want to commit himself when I arrived, but he very kindly saw to my comfort before he went in search of you."

Crossing the room and helping himself to some of the brandy that reposed in a crystal decanter nearby, Nicolas smiled faintly. "He is not normally quite so hospitable to strangers who come calling at this time of night."

"Hmm. I suppose not, but then I am hardly a stranger, my boy."

Sipping the brandy, Nicolas seated himself across from the duke. "Perhaps not a stranger, sir, but I must admit that I was surprised when Buffington brought your card to me. What can I do for you?"

"Hmm, I think, perhaps, it is a case of what we can do to help each other. . . ."

Nicolas looked startled. "Help each other?"

"Yes. You see, there is a little annoyance in Kent, which happens, we believe, to have its headquarters somewhere in the vicinity of Sherbourne Court. It has occurred to us that it would be convenient if we had someone in the area to investigate the situation more closely." Roxbury regarded Nicolas over the rim of his snifter. "Someone we could trust implicitly and whose sudden appearance would not arouse comment, or something even more, er, dire." His silvery hair gleaming in the candlelight, looking ever so much like a mischievous cherub, Roxbury smiled seraphically at the younger man across from him. "And who would question the return to his country estate of the newest holder of a long and illustrious title, the earl of Sherbourne?"

His thoughts racing behind the polite facade he offered to Roxbury, Nicolas stared at the amber liquor in his snifter. He suddenly wished that he knew more of Roxbury and the "we" and "us" the older man referred to so glibly. Then he shrugged. What the hell. The one sure thing that he did know about the duke was that the sly old devil had England's best interests at heart—at least what Roxbury and his friends considered England's best interests!

Deciding that he had nothing to lose by listening to the man, Nicolas sent the duke a keen glance and asked bluntly, "And what, sir, is this little 'annoyance' that you wish me to look into?"

"Oh, just a spot of smuggling," Roxbury returned lightly.

A grin split Nicolas's dark face. "Smuggling? In Kent? Sir, you know that Kent is the most notorious hotbed of smugglers in all of England! There is hardly a beach or shingle along its entire coast where smugglers don't land their goods—or hardly a night, either! And if that's not enough, it is nearly impossible to find anyone who doesn't have contact or dealings in one form or another with the smugglers—from the vicar who discovers a little cache of silk for his lady in thanks for the brazen use of his cellar, to the farmer who finds a cask or two of brandy in his barn, compliments of the smuggler who took every horse in his stables to cart the smuggled goods to London!"

His gray eyes unreadable, Roxbury lifted his snifter of fine French brandy. "Or a lord of the realm?"

Nicolas flushed. "Or a lord of the realm," he admitted reluctantly, having no real idea whether his brandy was legal or not, but suspecting the latter.

"Oh, don't look so guilty, my dear fellow! I am not accusing you of anything that half the members of the Horse Guards aren't also guilty of." He smiled. "If it shall make you feel any better, I'm quite positive that the brandy currently reposing in my own cellar did not come through the normal channels of purchase." Roxbury's face grew serious. "It is not the brandy or the French laces or silks that concerns us. It is the good English gold and information that is flowing freely between France and England—information that is being passed through the ranks of the smugglers."

"Again, sir, I don't meant to be indifferent, but the smugglers have been used for generations to send and receive information from Britain to the continent. Stopping it would be impossible."

"You're quite right. Stopping it *entirely* would be impossible." Roxbury set down his snifter. Leaning forward, his attractively lined features intent, he said, "What I'm talking about is something different from just the usual odd bits of information that filter back and forth across the channel. Some months ago, six or eight, it was noticed that something very different was afoot—there was a new and highly effective network passing along some *very* secret knowledge. It took us a while to pinpoint how the information was being passed, and we have only recently narrowed our investigation to your area, to a band or bands of smugglers working in the vicinity of the Romney Marsh."

Nicolas frowned. "Again, I have to remind you that the Romney Marsh area is rife with smugglers, who knows how many, but I can't imagine any of the usual bands of 'owlers' having access to the kind of information you're talking about. Most of them are just farmers and simple laborers seeking to add a little extra to their income. It's true that there is a violent criminal element, much like the Hawkhurst Gang of Sussex in the last century, who also ply the trade, but I don't see how any of them could be involved with highly secret material being sent to and fro." Nicolas glanced across at Roxbury. "Instead of focusing on the smugglers, who have to be simply messengers, wouldn't it be easier to discover the source? To find the man or men who are using the smugglers? With no disrespect to Your Lordship, it would seem to me to be the quickest way of stopping the flow of information."

Roxbury sat back on his chair and snorted. "Indeed it would. And don't think that we haven't been desperately trying to do just that!" He scowled. "We have. But unfortunately, our spy has been too bloody damned clever for us. To date we've learned only one thing—the name 'Mr. Brown'—and we have no idea what it means precisely. It could be a code. A password. Or the name of our spy! We have set trap after trap for the devilishly elusive 'Mr. Brown,' have followed trail after trail, but we still come up empty-handed—or with dead agents!" He sent Nicolas a considering look. "The man who was finally able to narrow down our investigation to your area was just one of the victims of our clever spy." Baldly he admitted, "We fished his body out of the channel three months ago—he'd had his throat cut. The next man we sent to the area was there only two months before we were presented with *his* body, and the latest man to dare to follow up on their information didn't last a month!"

"And this is the 'little annoyance' you want me to look into?" Nicolas asked dryly.

Roxbury smiled faintly. "Yes, I thought it might appeal to a neck-or-nothing young daredevil like yourself. Give you something to do besides sit by your fire this winter." Slyly he added, "You'd also be doing your former commander, Wellesley, a favor. Remember, he and his troops are the ones who are at grave risk as long as this damned spy is able to pass along vital information almost at will—despite our best efforts to stop him!"

Roxbury couldn't have used a more effective argument. Nicolas straightened and, meeting those watchful gray eyes, asked simply, "What do you want me to do?"

Roxbury sighed, suddenly looking all of his seventy some years of age. "We know so damned little! But we suspect a great deal. We don't even know whether our culprit is someone new to the area or whether it is someone who saw an opportunity and decided to take advantage of it. Because of the quality of the information being passed along, though, we are positive that it is no ordinary man, that it has to be someone who, without question, can rub shoulders with England's finest and those in the highest positions of trust. It would be hard to imagine," he said dryly, "an ignorant stable lad or a simple, country innkeeper having the same access to the facts that our spy does!"

"But he does use the smugglers?"

"Oh, yes, we have been able to tie the appearance of certain smuggled goods in London to the transfer of information." Roxbury looked troubled. "It is not the smugglers that we actually want—it is the man they work for. And that is where you come in—if, as we believe, he is a member of the aristocratic class, with your skill at spotting suspicious activity, we feel that you might be able to discover something for us."

"My, er, skill?" Nicolas asked with amusement, his black eyes twinkling.

Roxbury smiled faintly. "You weren't chosen *just* because you are the earl of Sherbourne and have a good reason to be in the area. Wellesley suggested you—said you'd been extremely helpful to him in the past."

Nicolas looked uncomfortable—he always did when his military exploits were mentioned. "It's true that I was able to be of some use to Sir Arthur, but that was under entirely different circumstances."

"No, it wasn't—it is *precisely* the same—Wellesley needed

information, and you went out and found it for him—any way that you could. We don't expect you to take the risks you did in India and Portugal—all we want you to do is keep your eyes and ears open, and if anything strikes you as odd or abnormal, we'd like you to discreetly investigate it." Roxbury sent him a hard look. "We don't, however, want you to tackle the fellow yourself; we just want you to give us your best guess, based on your observations, as to his identity."

"Very well. I shall do my best, but it seems a fool's errand that you are sending me on," Nicolas answered quietly, all humor gone from his face.

"I realize that, but at the moment you are our best hope." His face grim, the duke added, "Remember—fool's errand or not, be on your guard—the last two agents were tortured before they died—I wouldn't want that to happen to you."

"I see," Nicolas said slowly, an unpleasant, brassy taste in his mouth. A clean kill was one thing, torture another—in the course of his military career he'd done both, but of the two, he much preferred the clean kill. "Is there anything else I should know, sir?"

Roxbury took a sip of his brandy. Then, carefully setting down his snifter, he looked at Nicolas and said calmly, "You know, of course, that Avery Mandeville is the new baron and is living at Mandeville Manor?"

Nicolas stiffened. "Yes," he replied coolly, "I am aware that Avery is the new Baron Mandeville."

"Wellesley also mentioned the friction between the two of you. I wouldn't," Roxbury went on with a warning gleam in his gray eyes, "want you to let your enmity with him cause any, ah, distractions."

"You mean, you don't want me to follow in my brother's footsteps and challenge Lord Mandeville to a duel?"

"Is there any danger of that?"

Nicolas shrugged, but his black eyes were hard and the relaxed air about him was gone. "If it pleases you, I suppose I can restrain myself for the time being."

Watching him closely across the narrow space that divided them, Nicolas unexpectedly reminded Roxbury of nothing more than a big, black panther tensed to spring upon prey. The sudden change from smiling amiability to dangerous predator was unsettling, and Roxbury was aware that he was very glad not to be Avery Mandeville!

With a deceptively casual air that did not fool Nicolas, Roxbury asked, "Is it just the family feud, or something more?"

"Something more," Nicolas answered grimly. "While we were in Portugal, Avery seduced the daughter of my sergeant. When she became pregnant, he denied the whole affair. The girl drowned herself—her mother died trying to save her. My sergeant was overcome with grief, having lost everyone near to him, and after the funerals, he killed himself." Nicolas's face hardened. "I was away when it happened, and by the time I returned to camp, Avery had left for England . . . to inherit the title he now holds. Someday I intend for there to be a reckoning, but to date, he has managed to avoid me." Nicolas smiled thinly. "Something he won't be able to do indefinitely." Rising lithely to his feet, he gave Roxbury no opportunity for further questions. "Will that be all, sir? I do not mean to be impolite, but I plan to leave tomorrow afternoon and there is much that I must see to before I depart."

Roxbury took his dismissal in good grace—it was no more than he had expected. He allowed Nicolas to escort him out into the spacious hallway, then stopped just before the massive outer door. Looking back, he said lightly, "I suppose that I should warn you not to follow any instructions that request you to take a stroll, unarmed, after midnight, along a deserted beach?"

"I won't, sir, you can be positive of that," Nicolas responded with a grin.

"Well, then, I must be off. Good luck, young man . . . and enjoy yourself at Sherbourne Court!"

Nicolas stared thoughtfully at the mahogany door long

after Roxbury had closed it behind him. It seemed he had a legitimate reason for leaving the city after all—he could certainly put aside any feeling that he was running away from London. He would still be leaving for the environs of Kent on the morrow, but now there was an urgency about his trip that hadn't been there previously. The sooner he reached Sherbourne Court, the sooner he could start discovering Roxbury's spy. The excitement of the chase suddenly rose up within him, and with a dangerous smile on his hard lips, he bounded up the stairs.

And so it was that as Tess Mandeville rode furiously through the dark night *toward* London, Nicolas Talmage was planning shortly to be riding *away* from that same city. Inevitably, their paths crossed.

Chapter Four

———— ⟡ ————

*T*ess wasn't having an easy time of it, although in the beginning things seemed to be going just as they should. With her heart banging painfully in her chest, starting and jumping at every small sound, she had managed to saddle her favorite mount, a swift chestnut gelding with a small white star and a white hind foot named Fireball, and lead him from the stables. Mounting quickly, she took one last uncertain glance over her shoulder at the ominously quiet house. Then she dug her heels into Fireball's sleek sides and away they had flown, swallowed up in seconds by the darkness of the night.

As they careened wildly down the narrow country lanes, her heart didn't stop its mad thumping and her death grip on the reins didn't lessen until they had put several miles between themselves and Mandeville. But even then she continued to urge Fireball forward. Reaching her uncles in London was the most important thing at the moment. Once she was safely in their care, the unpleasant situation facing her aunts could be resolved. She had to reach London quickly, not only for herself but for Aunt Meg and Hetty, too. . . .

Aware that she must avoid the main roads where Avery might search for her, she had to forsake speed for concealment. She kept Fireball at a fairly swift pace, but as they switched from one narrow path to another, always heading in the direction of London, their progress was necessarily slower than she would have liked. The weather was not helpful, either—since she and Hetty had returned to Mandeville Manor that afternoon, a storm had moved in and Tess now had to contend not only with a smothering blackness, but with a driving rain as well. The only light that pierced the darkness was the occasional silver flash of lightning that snaked across the starless sky. It was not the sort of evening she would have chosen for a midnight ride.

Normally Tess considered herself a fairly confident and self-assured young woman, able to command any situation with which she was confronted, but this evening's disturbing events had badly shaken her. Raised as a proper young lady of good family, she had seldom been entirely alone. Always there had been a relative or a servant somewhere within call. As she rode down another overgrown lane, her isolation from everything she had ever known suddenly hit her.

With every mile she traveled, the fury of the storm increased, and gusty winds tore at her sodden habit and cloak. Fireball behaved badly, snorting and shying every time lightning flashed or thunder boomed in its wake. Doggedly Tess pushed onward, hoping during the illuminating streaks of lightning to catch sight of a barn or hay shed in which to seek temporary shelter.

Amid the noise and frenzy of the elements, she never heard the sounds of pursuit. When the darkly garbed figure suddenly rose up in front of Fireball, both Tess and the horse screamed in terror, and the gelding reared. Tess clung to Fireball's back, her fingers tearing at the reins that the apparition had grabbed.

As Tess and Fireball fought to escape the relentless grip on the reins, another figure appeared on their other side, and a second later Tess was swept effortlessly off the plunging horse. She struggled like a wild thing, her clenched fists beating against the powerful figure that held her. Despite her efforts she was easily subdued, as one big hand held her wrists together and a heavy arm lay against her breasts.

"Well, bugger me blind!" a coarse voice ground out near her ear. "It's a female!"

"Don't matter!" his companion replied testily. "It's the bloody horse we want! Knock the mort in the head and let's get out of here!"

Tess realized that she had fallen into the hands of a pair of smugglers procuring horses to transport their illegal goods to London. Then a flash of lightning gave her a glimpse of a third man joining the other two, a tall, slim figure wearing a many-caped greatcoat, his face and hair hidden by his hat and muffler. The stunning notion crossed her mind that she was in the presence of a gentleman.

Her suspicion was confirmed when the greatcoated figure said in a cultured voice full of ice, "You fools! I thought the point of this undertaking was to avoid detection! I'm certain there must be plenty of other horses, horses whose owners are safely asleep in their beds, that will serve our purpose. We are not so desperate that we need to attack travelers and steal their mounts!"

"It's a good horse, a blooded animal, Mr. Brown," sullenly replied the man who held a nervously dancing Fireball. "We thought it'd be good to have a fast horse, if the dragoons was to come after us."

"You *thought*," came the scathing retort. "I doubt that you are capable of even that much brain activity."

In the rainy darkness Tess could tell very little, but she suddenly had the impression that the man called Mr. Brown was looking in her direction. Instinctively she shrank against her big captor, thinking she'd rather be subject to his rough mercy than that of the "gentleman" who spoke with such open contempt to his companions.

"Well, go ahead," the arrogant voice said. "Before any more damage is done—get rid of her!"

Terrified, Tess renewed her struggles to escape. There was a wild flurry of violent motion that ended when pain suddenly exploded in the back of her head and a heavy blackness rushed up to meet her. Knocked unconscious by the man in the greatcoat, she slumped pitifully against the smuggler who had first caught her.

"You didn't have to hit the little thing that hard. You might have killed her," grumbled the big man who held her.

Lightning lit the blackness, and the man in the greatcoat stared dispassionately down into Tess's pale, lovely features. "I intended to—we don't need any witnesses, especially with you two dolts calling out my name every second! Leave her somewhere out of sight and let us be gone from here. We've wasted enough time as it is."

Lifting up Tess's limp form, the big smuggler disappeared between the hedgerows and laid her beneath a huge oak. If she was alive, he thought, she was going to have the devil's own headache when she woke.

When she finally regained consciousness many hours later, Tess felt half dead. Her head ached abominably, she was starving, her clothes clung wetly to her, and as she sat up and looked around groggily, she had absolutely no idea where she was. With a groan, she sank slowly back against the ground, wondering bitterly if she should be grateful that she was alive.

Squinting up at the gray, cloudy sky and the position of the watery sun above her, she realized that it was well past mid-day. From the appearance of the sky, she concluded gloomily that another storm was in the offing. Struggling once again into a sitting position, she tried to fight her way clear of the thick cobwebs that seemed to clog her thoughts. She glanced around again to get her bearings. The hedgerows and gently rolling, tree-dotted fields told her nothing. As she sat there, her thoughts moving sluggishly through her aching head, a tiny niggle of unease began to gnaw at her. She looked at her clothing, at the sodden black velvet habit and the crumpled black cloak, but the sight of them did nothing to still a growing sense of numbed disbelief. Not only did she not know where she was, but she had absolutely no idea who she was or how she had come to be lying here!

She closed her eyes and fought off the sheer terror that raced through her slender body. Of course, she knew who she was, she was . . . A horrible blankness filled her mind. She swallowed. Well, maybe this was just a dream—a very bad one! If she lay here quietly for a few minutes, this queer feeling of utter emptiness would pass and she'd wake up and everything would be normal. But as she lay there and the minutes passed, she came to the unpleasant conclusion that she was not asleep, had not been asleep, and that she certainly wasn't dreaming. She didn't know where she was, who she was, or how she came to be lying on the ground in the middle of the afternoon.

Her stomach rumbled loudly, reminding her that she was hungry—and that if she didn't want to spend another night in the rain, as she obviously had last night if the condition of her clothing was anything to go by, she had better get moving. Except she had no idea where she should go. . . .

After a painful struggle, she stood upright, bracing a hand against the oak tree for support. The ache in her head was excruciating, and she swayed dizzily for several seconds before the worst of the pain lessened and she was able to look around without the world tilting at an odd angle. Obviously she couldn't remain here. As she stood looking around uncertainly, hoping desperately to catch sight of something that would trigger a memory, *any* memory, she became conscious of a strong sense of urgency. To run. As far and as fast as she could.

Instinctively she began to move, fighting her way through the hedgerows to the narrow lane that lay beyond. Half staggering, half walking, she continued down the muddy road, increasingly aware that it was imperative to keep moving, that some nameless dread stalked her, and that if she did not remove herself from this vicinity immediately, she would come face to face with a nightmare worse than any she could imagine.

Tess was not the only one to awaken that Wednesday with a splitting headache. It was nearly three o'clock that same afternoon before Avery awoke from the liberal dose of laudanum the aunts had put in his wine the previous evening. His tongue thick, his head feeling as if it were going to split, he lurched from his bed and impatiently rang for Coleman, his valet.

The man presented himself promptly, a silver tray laden with various food and drink to tempt his master's appetite carried in his hands.

Clutching his aching head, Avery glared at his valet and growled, "What the hell happened last night? What sort of damnable swill did that rascal Lowell find in the cellar to serve me?"

Putting down the tray on a carved mahogany table near the silk-hung bed, Coleman replied sourly, "Don't believe it was anything that *Lowell* served you. Think something havey-cavey went on last night."

Avery's pale blue eyes kindled with wrath. "Of course! The aunts! I should have known they'd guess what I was about and try to protect their lone chick." Shrugging into his elaborately embroidered silk robe, he said tightly, "They may have been able to postpone my plans, but they will not be able to protect her indefinitely." His handsome face twisted. "And if they want a roof over their heads, they'll damn well stay out of my way!"

Coleman coughed delicately, and Avery's head swung in his direction. Not meeting his master's eyes, he said, "Um, no one but that pair of ape leaders has seen the dimber mort today. . . . They *say* she ain't feeling well and that they're the only ones she wants in her rooms." He hesitated and then muttered, "There's a horse missing from the stables—that little chestnut she always rides."

"What?" Avery ejaculated, his hands clenching into fists at his sides.

Well used to his master's rages, Coleman took a prudent step backward. Glumly he added, "Don't believe the chit is in her rooms. Think she's done a flit and the aunts are hiding it."

In one violent motion Avery swept the tray onto the floor, food, china, and glassware flying in all directions. Breathing heavily, his face almost ugly with rage, he fought to bring his temper under control. "Those conniving bitches!" he finally snarled. "If they think—" He broke off, took a deep breath, and snapped, "Find2 out more about that missing horse, *discreetly*—and tell the ladies, *all* the ladies, that I'll see them in my study within the hour. And clean up this mess and get my goddamn bath!"

Grateful to have escaped so lightly, Coleman scuttled about, swiftly cleaning up the broken crockery and remnants of food and drink. His task completed, he fairly bolted from the room, the expression on Avery's face making him distinctly uneasy.

As he paced the confines of his elegant chamber, awaiting Coleman's return, Avery's thoughts were not pleasant. He didn't doubt that his quarry had fled—nor that London was her destination. Casting a considering eye at the weather outside and seeing the dark, lowering clouds, he realized that even if he were to leave within the hour, it wasn't feasible for him to go tearing after Tess today. He did think about it, but a glance at the ormolu clock on the gray marble mantelpiece decided him against it. It was gone four o'clock, and if Tess had fled to London last night, she was already there—and out of his reach. His mouth thinned. And he had damn well better come up with a likely story to counteract the tale that she was no doubt pouring into her uncles' ears at this very moment!

The situation was desperate. Tess's story had to be refuted immediately. His finances were in utter disarray, and he faced ruin since that last trip of his to London and his heavy gaming losses. A speedy marriage to an heiress was the only thing standing between him and dun territory. His face twisted. Damn Tess! And those bloody aunts!

Suddenly his features cleared. Of course, there *was* Mr. Brown. . . . A tigerish smile curved his lips. Mr. Brown would not be happy with any new demands. But that couldn't be helped, Avery thought grimly. Mr. Brown would just have to advance him a generous sum or face the consequences. . . .

An hour later, bathed and impeccably groomed, his hasty plans to avert a catastrophe already in motion, Avery met with the aunts in his study. "Ah, ladies," he said smoothly as he entered the masculine room and shut the door firmly behind him. "I hope that you haven't been waiting long."

Uncertainty in their faces, Hetty and Meg stared at him. Despite his polite words, the barely leashed rage they saw on his face made them shrink together.

Avery smiled nastily. "And now what have I done to make you look at me that way?" he fairly purred, his blue eyes hard and ugly.

"N-n-nothing," Hetty quavered, sitting up straighter on her black leather chair. "We—we were just surprised by your peremptory demand to see us."

A slim blond brow flicked upward. "But why wouldn't I want to see you? After all, we have so much to talk about . . . don't we?"

"What do you mean?" Meg asked bluntly, holding tightly to one of Hetty's hands.

Dropping all pretense of politeness, Avery snapped, "I mean your heavy hand with whatever you put in my wine last night—and your lovely niece's *non*appearance. I do believe that my message included all the ladies."

"Tess isn't feeling well. She can't leave her bed," Hetty said.

"Is that so?"

"Yes, why would we lie?" Meg demanded gamely.

"Why indeed," Avery said dryly. Ignoring them for the moment, he crossed to the bell rope that hung against the wall and rang for a servant. Almost immediately Lowell answered the summons.

Bluntly Avery asked his butler, "Have you carried out my requests?"

A not-very-nice smile creased Lowell's dour features. "Yes, sir. I have." He glanced at the two women. "They ain't nobody in them rooms. They're empty. The chit ain't nowhere in the house or stables. She's gone."

"Ah, and have you taken care of everything else?"

Lowell nodded curtly. "Except for me and Coleman, all the servants have packed and left for the unexpected holiday you so kindly granted them."

A smile that sent chills down the backs of the two women crossed Avery's face. "Thank you, Lowell. That will be all."

Avery waited until the door had closed behind his henchman before he turned to the ladies. "And now," he said coldly, "suppose you tell me precisely what happened last night and where Tess is hidden."

Hetty met his gaze squarely. Lifting her chin, she said, "She is gone to London. To her uncles."

"I see. A rather sudden trip on her part, wasn't it?"

"Well, what did you expect?" Meg asked rashly. "You planned to dishonor her and force her to marry you! But thank the Lord, she's managed to escape you!"

"Oh, I doubt that," Avery said silkily. "What do you think the reactions of Baron Rockwell and his esteemed brother will be when I tell them that Tess and I have *already* been intimate? That this silly flight of hers is nothing more than a lovers' quarrel, hmm?"

"That's a black-hearted lie!" Hetty burst out indignantly. "Alexander would never believe you!"

"Ah, but I wonder if the rest of society would be so understanding. . . ."

In her great agitation, Hetty rose to her feet. Bosom heaving, she spat, "Alexander would never allow you to say such things. You'd find yourself on the dueling field if you dared to spread such lies!"

Avery looked bored. "But then, of course, the reason for the duel would have to be explained, wouldn't it?"

Hetty's defiance crumpled and she sat back down, her face drawn. "You wouldn't," she said shakily. "You wouldn't dare."

"Wouldn't I?" Avery replied almost cheerfully. "Oh, but I would indeed. I think that you ladies had better resign yourselves to the fact that I intend"—his eyes glittered—"for Tess to become my wife, one way or the other. . . ." He smiled at their defeated faces. "I will leave early tomorrow to call upon the baron and his brother. While I'm gone, I'm afraid you ladies will have to make do with the services of Coleman and Lowell." His voice grew hard. "You will, of course, be locked in your rooms, and I wouldn't count on anyone releasing you—Lowell and Coleman are quite capable of dealing with any intruders. You may wish me a speedy trip."

Hetty's violet eyes almost purple with rage, she rose to her feet and said fiercely, "What I wish, sir, is for you to go to the very devil!"

Unaware of the events taking place at Mandeville Manor, Tess had taken stock of her present situation and found it not exactly pleasant. Aside from the bodily discomforts—and there were many considering her condition—it was the terrifying emptiness of her mind that troubled her most. But as she walked doggedly down the lane, she realized there was quite a bit that she *did* know. She knew she was running away, and that for some reason she was to go to London. Why or whom she was to seek in London, she had no idea.

She was also aware that the clothes she wore were not the simple fabrics of a common farmer's wife or tavern maid, and after examining the softness of her hands, she concluded that she was probably a member of the aristocracy or, at the very least, a governess or lady's maid. Her habit was not new, nor were the fine leather boots on her feet, but the materials were expensive and the cut fashionable. . . . Now how did she know *that?* she wondered, a puzzled frown wrinkling her brow.

She sighed. It didn't do her much good to recognize quality when she saw it, if she couldn't even think of her own name. It suddenly occurred to her that her absence, however long it had been, would probably cause alarm. Was someone even now searching desperately for her? A father? A husband? Perhaps even a lover? And who had aroused this urge to flee? This undeniable sensation that she was in danger, that she was running away from someone? She frowned. Would it be friend or enemy who sought her out—and how would she know? It was a frightening dilemma. What if no one was looking for her? But surely, she told herself stoutly, *someone* would miss her!

A brief search of her person had turned up no reticule, no letters, not one scrap of paper or object that would give her a clue. She was also, she admitted glumly, absolutely penniless.

As the hours passed and Tess trudged unhappily along, her head ached, her feet hurt, and her stomach growled more vigorously with every step she took. The scary possibilities whirling in her brain gave her no comfort at all. Momentarily she even wondered if she were an escaped felon, but she soon dismissed the idea—she might be running away from something, but she didn't feel guilty.

As daylight began to fade, a slight intermittent drizzle became her companion and the need to find shelter became paramount. By her reckoning, she had come several miles from the area where she had first woken and she had long ago left the original country lane far behind her. Guided solely by instinct, she had taken many turns and twists in the various roads she had found. Just as the rain began in earnest, she had come upon a wider, more heavily traveled road. There was no doubt in her mind that it was the main road to London, but again, how she knew that fact she couldn't say.

In the darkness she suddenly spied a faint, twinkling light coming slowly in her direction, and with a feeling of pure fright, she dived to the edge of the road and hid in a patch of brambles. A moment later she relaxed as the object came abreast of her hiding place and she recognized the creak of a wagon and heard what was obviously a farmer intent on reaching home before the weather became any worse.

"Ach! Come along now, Dolly, girl! There's a warm barn and sweet hay for you—it's not much farther, Dolly, love."

Wishing she dared accost the friendly-sounding driver, she waited until the light from the candle lamp on his wagon had disappeared and then she climbed stiffly back to the road and continued her journey. Disheartened, hungry, and shivering, she almost didn't believe it when she came round a bend in the road and saw the lights of a tavern winking invitingly through the rain.

There it was, nestled to one side of the road, warm yellow light spilling out from its windows. This was not one of the larger inns that catered to the mail coaches and the aristocracy, but a smaller one, probably frequented by ordinary people like the farmer she had just passed. For some reason that gave her hope. She'd be safe in a place like this. . . .

Anxious to escape the increasingly ugly weather, she hurried forward, only to stop not ten feet from the main door. Her mouth drooped. She had no money. She had no name. How was she to pay for food or a room?

The distant, ominous boom of thunder decided her. Moving forward, she slipped around to the back of the building. Confronted by the stout rear door of the tavern, she stood there a moment, shivering in the rain. What was she to say? She could hardly expect an utter stranger to believe that she had just woken up with no memory. But what if they recognized her? Hope flowed through her, and she started forward eagerly, only to stop as she recalled her strong feeling that she was running away from someone. What if they did recognize her and sent word to her unknown nemesis?

A sudden flash of lightning lit the area, and she hesitated no more. She would just have to pray that she wasn't doing the wrong thing by pretending she was some poor wretched lost creature in need of help—which wasn't much of a pretense! She would simply have to throw herself on the mercy of the innkeeper and hope for the best. . . .

Tess didn't think very highly of her plan, but she didn't have any choice. Taking a deep breath, she pounded on the rear door of the tavern.

It flew open almost as if someone had been waiting for her knock. Tess stood there uncertainly, trying frantically to think of something to say as a heavyset older woman appeared in the opened doorway, peering out into the rain. Wisps of gray hair straggled out from beneath the ruffle-edge cap she wore, and a white apron was tied around her ample waist. Her full face set in lines of displeasure as she caught sight of Tess and she said in scolding tones, "Well, I must say that you took your time getting here! You're late, and I'll let you know right now that this is not behavior that we tolerate! From now on, your time is ours. We're *not* a charity house—even if my husband did agree to take you on for a few weeks while that rascally pimp of a brother of his is in Newgate. If you're going to work for us, my girl, you'll be here when you're supposed to be or it'll be back to London for you!"

Tess opened her mouth to explain the mistake, but before she could speak, the woman jerked her into the warmth and light of the kitchen.

The tavern kitchen was a comfortable room with smoke-blackened beams overhead and a scrupulously clean stone floor. Over the woman's shoulder Tess caught sight of a young girl and a small boy hard at work at the far end of the room near an open fire where a large haunch of beef turned on a spit. The heavenly smell of spices, of roasting chicken and beef, assailed her nostrils, and Tess nearly fainted from the pangs of hunger that beset her.

Eyeing Tess's slender, bedraggled form, the heavyset

woman frowned. "I always thought Tom's fancy piece was a big, strapping woman. Don't know how much work we're going to get out of you!" A nasty gleam lit the pale blue eyes. "I'll wager most of your *work* was done on your back!"

Tess stared at her openmouthed, not quite able to credit her ears. "I'm afraid that there has been a mistake. . . . I'm not—"

"Now don't start that! It don't matter to me—all I care is that there is work to be done and you were expected to be here hours ago. Now what's your name, girl? Tom didn't write much in that scribbled note he sent my husband—only that you'd be arriving tonight and we could make good use of you until he got out." Her round face split into an unpleasant smile. "*If* he gets out—it's my opinion that Tom Darley was born to hang—unlike my Henry, who's as honest and hardworking as his brother is crooked!"

Once more Tess opened her mouth to explain, but cravenly she hesitated. Looking at the innkeeper's wife, at the coarse, unfriendly features, she realized that she was unlikely to find her a sympathetic listener. The instant she declared that she was not Tom Darley's "fancy piece," she'd most likely be thrust out into the storm. Would it hurt so very much, for this one night, to pretend? To step momentarily into a ready-made identity? Just for tonight?

While Tess stood there silently turning over her extremely limited options, the innkeeper's wife said reluctantly, "I don't suppose you've had a chance to eat yet, and I'll not have it said that Sally Darley, *Mrs.* Darley to you, is a mean-spirited woman. So if you hurry, you can help yourself to some bread and cheese on the table there before I send you out front to help my husband." Glancing with disfavor at Tess's damp state, she added, "But first get out of those clothes and into something more serviceable. Don't dawdle, either! This may be your first night here at the Black Pig, but don't expect to have an easy time of it."

Tess never knew whether it was the idea of food or the thought of being out of her wet, uncomfortable clothing that finally overcame her scruples, but she suddenly said, "I'm afraid that these are the only clothes I brought with me." At Mrs. Darley's expression of astonishment, she improvised hastily, "I, er, had to leave London rather quickly. There wasn't time to, ah, pack."

Really looking at Tess for the first time, the other woman frowned. "To be sure," she said slowly, "them ain't the kind of clothes we see around here." Mrs. Darley stared at her for so long, assessing the cut and fabric of her clothes, that Tess was certain her ruse was discovered. But suddenly making a decision, the older woman said curtly, "Come along with me. There's a trunk with some old clothes our eldest daughter left behind when she got married this summer. Something in there is bound to fit you."

Gratefully, her fingers crossed against the sudden appearance of the *real* "fancy piece," Tess followed her out of the kitchen down a cramped little hall, to an equally cramped little room. A narrow bed and small washstand were the only furnishings. Inside, Mrs. Darley pulled forth a battered black trunk from beneath the bed. She dug through it swiftly, saying as she tossed garments about, "This is to be your room while you stay with us." She glanced sternly over her shoulder. "And I want to make it clear that I don't want to find you entertaining any 'gentlemen' callers in *here*. What you and the gents do upstairs is your business, but I ain't having that sort of goings on in *my* part of this establishment! No matter what Henry says about it being good for business!"

It suddenly dawned on Tess that Mrs. Darley wasn't normally an unkind person, but that the innkeeper's wife thoroughly disapproved of her supposed profession. "Mrs. Darley," Tess began softly, "I'm not really—" She stopped abruptly. How did she know she wasn't precisely the kind of creature Mrs. Darley had intimated she was? She swallowed painfully. A dashing highflier kept by some town buck could be an answer to her identity that she hadn't even considered!

"I told you it don't matter!" Mrs. Darley returned stiffly,

turning around to face Tess. "Here," she added, "this should fit you." She thrust a worn, pale pink muslin gown into Tess's hands. "Use whatever you like from the trunk, but don't waste any time getting changed. You can find your way back to the kitchen."

Dazedly Tess stared at the door that shut firmly behind Mrs. Darley's bulky figure. Was she doing the right thing? Deciding that she really didn't have any choice, she stripped off the clinging habit and slipped into the old muslin gown. It was a little big, but the soft worn, *dry* material felt wonderful against her chilled body. A further search of the trunk revealed an old pair of jean half-boots, which she found, to her great pleasure, fit her almost to perfection. She took a moment to braid her wildly curling hair and tie the end with a scrap of green ribbon she found in the bottom of the trunk.

Nervously smoothing down her gown, she hesitated a moment longer. Perhaps she had misjudged Mrs. Darley; perhaps if she went to the kitchen and explained? Explained what? she wondered miserably.

Tess was touched when she reached the kitchen to find that Mrs. Darley had prepared for her not only a plate of cheese and bread, but also a large slice of rare roast beef and a flagon of dark foamy beer. Mrs. Darley was not in evidence, although the young girl and boy smiled shyly at her. Seating herself at the scrubbed oak table, Tess fairly wolfed down her food. It was only when she pushed aside her plate that the girl sidled up to her and said softly, "Don't mind the missus—she has a mean tongue, but give her fair work and she'll treat you fair. It's the master to be careful of—*he's* a hard'un!"

Mrs. Darley came sailing in as Tess rose from the table. She stopped abruptly, staring at Tess, her mouth thinning. "Well, I must say that you don't look like a fancy piece in that garb. Just as well—the Black Pig is a respectable tavern, and I don't approve of the goings-on that *some* people claim will help bring us a few new customers." Her face softened for a moment. "You're too young and pretty to let yourself be used this way, child." Then, as if angry with herself for her brief lapse, she said tartly, "Of course, it makes no never mind to me! Come along with me to meet my husband—you'll be working for him tonight." As they left the kitchen behind and walked down a short hall, she asked suddenly, "Now then, what did you say your name was?"

Tess swallowed, her mouth dry. What *was* her name? Before she had time to think, she heard herself saying calmly, "Dolly. My name is Dolly." A half-hysterical bubble of laughter rose in her throat. She supposed that the name of an old farm horse was as good as any when you didn't know your own!

Henry Darley proved to be a congenial-looking man, but Tess immediately realized what the young girl in the kitchen had meant. He was a hard man, it was there in those small hazel eyes and in the selfish curve of his mouth. He wasn't a man to be crossed, and Tess's spirits, which had revived somewhat during the past several minutes, sank to the soles of her borrowed jean half-boots.

After introductions had been made, Harry looked her up and down and muttered, "Can't see as how that skinny little body of yours is going to do much to bring in the farm lads. But Tom says you know what you're doing and that he ain't had any dissatisfied customers yet, so we'll just have to see. In the meantime there is plenty of other work for you to do." He nodded to several rough oak tables that were scattered about the low-beamed room and cluttered with tankards, plates, and pitchers. "Start clearing those tables."

Filled with growing uneasiness, Tess set to work. Thank God she hadn't been confronted with some lusting, eager oaf! What in heaven's name was she to do when the time came, and there was no doubt that the time *would* come, that she was expected to take some strange man up the stairs and . . . uh . . . work her wiles on him? She shuddered, wondering if perhaps she hadn't gotten herself into a situation far worse than her previous one. Not knowing anything about herself, she realized, it was possible that she was just the sort of woman the Darleys thought she was. But she doubted it. It just didn't feel right.

Fortunately, Tess didn't intend to stay any longer than necessary, and she was hopeful that she'd be gone before she was faced with any more unpleasant situations. She was also fortunate in the stormy weather and lateness of the hour; business at the inn was slow, so the likelihood of one of the "farm lads" turning up and wanting to go upstairs with her tonight was extremely unlikely. And by tomorrow she'd be gone.

As she worked, she glanced about furtively, noting the long wooden bar against one wall, where Harry was conversing idly with two older men who were clearly farmers, and the big stone fireplace in the corner. The main room of the tavern was smoky and poorly lit, with only a few candles on the bar and the smoldering fire on the hearth giving any light, but it seemed a pleasant enough place. Listening to the rain lashing against the side of the building and the occasional distant boom of thunder, Tess was very glad to be inside.

Suddenly above the storm she heard shouts, the neigh of a horse, and realized that someone had arrived. A tray of dirty dishes in her small hands, she froze by a table, her gaze locked painfully on the low doorway that opened to the main passageway of the tavern. She heard the front doors slam open, the stamp of booted feet, and the sound of masculine voices. One of them riveted her attention, the rich, deep tones sending a curious shiver down her spine. The next instant the doorway was filled with the figure of a tall man, his many-caped greatcoat making his shoulders seem impossibly wide, his black boots gleaming with raindrops. Sweeping off his curly-brimmed beaver hat, he had to duck his dark head as he entered the room.

The innkeeper recognized "quality" when he saw it and hurried forward eagerly. "A wretched night, is it not, Your Lordship? Let me take your coat, and my wife will set as hot and filling a meal before you as you could find in the finest houses in London."

"Thank you," replied Nicolas Talmage, his black eyes carelessly sweeping the interior. "A room for myself and quarters for my servants for the night would be greatly appreciated." He smiled charmingly at the innkeeper. "It is indeed a wretched night—I had hoped to reach Sherbourne Court long before now, but the weather has made further travel impossible."

Tess could not tear her eyes away from the tall stranger, and at the name "Sherbourne Court" she nearly gasped aloud. She *knew* that name! But the recognition gave her no comfort; instead an icy trickle slid down her spine. Was this the man she feared? The nameless, dreaded nemesis?

Across the smoky room, she studied the lean, arrogantly handsome features of the gentleman as he spoke with Darley, questions flying wildly through her brain. Unexpectedly Nicolas looked up, and as her eyes met his black, probing gaze, Tess had the terrifying sensation of suddenly stepping off into a dark, fathomless abyss. . . .

Chapter Five

*T*here was a roaring in Tess's ears, and though she tried, she could not tear her gaze away from the commanding features of the dark stranger across the room. She had seen handsome men before—more handsome, she was positive, than this man—yet she felt utterly mesmerized by him. She could not look away, could not break the queer, powerful spell that seemed to wrap itself around her as the seconds passed.

It was as if they were the only two people in the room, and she had the sudden sensation that she *knew* him, recognized him from some long-ago time; yet she could have sworn she had never laid eyes on him before. Frightened and yet unaccountably drawn to him, she could not explain, nor did she understand, the conflicting emotions that raged through her. The fact that he seemed equally stunned to see her did not escape Tess and only added to the intensity of the moment.

It was the innkeeper who finally broke the spell, clapping his hands together as he said loudly, "You, girl, Dolly, don't just stand there! Haven't you ever seen a lord before? Go get Mrs. Darley—this very instant."

Tess started violently, finally breaking the hypnotic hold of the stranger's compelling black eyes. Breathlessly she turned on her heels and fled the room, hardly even aware of the rattle and clatter of the dishes on the tray that she still carried in her shaking hands.

It took but a moment to stammer out the innkeeper's demand, and after Mrs. Darley had bustled out of the kitchen, Tess sank onto a chair. Almost absently she noticed that her hands were still shaking, and more than any other time since she had first awakened with no memory, she wished desperately that she could remember who she was and what her past had been. Did she really know that gentleman in the caped greatcoat? Or had she just imagined the strange thrill of recognition that had gone through her when their eyes had met?

There was no time for further reflection—Mrs. Darley, her eyes sparkling, her cheeks pink with pleasure, came sailing back into the kitchen. "Quickly, quickly, everyone! We've the earl of Sherbourne staying with us tonight! It's only the weather that we have to thank for this unexpected boon, but if we can make a good impression, do *everything* necessary to see that he thoroughly enjoys himself tonight, I'm sure that we can expect Lord Sherbourne and his fancy friends to stop at the Black Pig regularly." She glanced archly at Tess. "My Harry noticed that His Lordship seemed quite taken with you, so perhaps you're going to prove yourself useful after all!"

Mrs. Darley's words didn't help Tess's state of mind at all, and she was suddenly conscious of feeling that pretending to be Tom Darley's fancy piece, even for one night, was possibly the worst thing that she could have done! She sprang to her feet and said urgently, "Mrs. Darley, there is something I *must* tell you. There has been a mistake. I'm not what you think I am!"

"Oh, now, don't get all in a flutter, my girl," Mrs. Darley returned lightly. "No one's asking you to do something you haven't done a dozen times already. And, oh my, ain't the earl a handsome fellow!" Feeling that she had settled the matter, Mrs. Darley turned to the two young servants who waited with excited expectancy and began to give out a long list of chores that had to be done immediately. Once she had both of them flying about the room intent upon their tasks, her attention returned to Tess. "Now come along, girl, and don't be shy—at the moment, all you need to do is help Mr. Darley serve His Lordship his dinner in our private parlor. *I'm* the one who will be upstairs working my fingers to the bone preparing his room!"

The innkeeper himself suddenly appeared on the threshold of the kitchen and said sharply, "Dolly, get yourself out here! His Lordship's port is ready."

When Tess hesitated, a protest forming on her lips, Mr. Darley stepped forward, his face darkening. Grasping her arm, he gave her a brutal shake. "I'll have none of your airs, my fine little madame! The earl's plainly taken with you, and by God, I'll not have you ruining this opportunity! Upset him in any way and you'll rue the day you ever crossed Henry Darley! If you doubt me—we'll just see how proud you act after I've taken a stout rod to you a few times! Now come along! And put a smile on that sour face of yours!"

He jerked Tess after him, not releasing the painful grip on her upper arm until they had returned to the main room. There was no sign of the earl, but as Darley tossed aside her arm, he said, "His Lordship is in the parlor, right across the hall there. Take this tray in and make damn sure you give good service or you'll have me to answer to!" His eyes narrowed. "I've ways of dealing with servants who upset the customers."

Tess swallowed with difficulty, her mouth suddenly dry as last year's straw. The urge to flee was strong, but self-preservation was equally strong. She was fairly positive that if she had to suffer at anyone's hands, she would much prefer the unknown earl to the savage punishment Darley would mete out . . . at least she *thought* she would. She wasn't so certain a few minutes later, when, carrying the heavy tray covered with all sorts of liquors to tempt an aristocratic palate, she tapped on the door to the private parlor and the earl's deep voice wrapped itself warmly about her as he bade her enter.

Her heart beating so frantically she thought it would leap

out of her chest, Tess pushed open the door and entered the parlor. It was a surprisingly pleasant little room; crisp muslin curtains hung over the double windows along one wall, a newly made fire leaped cheerily on the hearth, many candles in brass holders were scattered about, and there was a fine old carpet on the floor. Two worn overstuffed leather chairs were placed invitingly on either side of the fire; a carved oak sideboard and a small oak table with chairs to match constituted the remainder of the furnishings. But it was the man who stood with his back to the fire as he warmed himself who commanded Tess's entire attention.

He had removed his many-caped greatcoat, and she noted the intricate arrangement of his starched white cravat and the way his dark blue jacket fit his broad shoulders and powerful arms. His buff breeches boldly outlined every muscle and sinew of his thighs, but after one quick peek at his thoroughly masculine form, Tess kept her eyes firmly fixed on the tray in her hands. She crossed the room as quickly as she could and, her back to him, set the tray on the oak sideboard. Her voice brittle, she said, "If there is anything else you desire, Your Lordship, Mr. Darley says to let him know and he'll see that you have it right away."

Appreciatively regarding the stiff narrow back and slender hips presented to him, Nicolas decided there was a great deal that he *desired* and found it highly doubtful Mr. Darley could provide him with what he wanted. His black eyes narrowed. Then again, who knew—perhaps a word with Mr. Darley might insure that his bed was warmed this night by the unexpectedly bewitching little creature across the room from him. . . .

The Black Pig was not the sort of establishment that Nicolas frequented these days, although before inheriting the title he had spent quite a bit of time in places like it, not quite respectable yet not *un*respectable. If the nasty weather hadn't made it impossible to travel onward, he wouldn't have stopped tonight and might even now be standing comfortably before his own fire at Sherbourne Court. But the weather had been exceedingly treacherous, and he'd been inordinately grateful when he'd caught sight of the faint lights of the tavern winking dimly through the driving wind and rain. But if in the beginning it had only been shelter for which he'd been grateful, that was no longer the case—and hadn't been since he had first ducked through the archway into the main room of the tavern and caught sight of the girl. . . .

Even now, just staring at her as she fiddled nervously with the various bottles and glasses on the tray, he could feel the same sense of familiarity, of having known her before; could feel the same sudden hot passion that had flared deep in his belly when his eyes had met hers. But it was the strong, almost overpowering sense of possession, a certainty that she was *his,* that puzzled him greatly. He'd swear he'd never seen her before, and yet . . . Consideringly, his eyes traveled over the bright hair, the fiery tendrils that escaped the untidy braid and caressed her cheeks and neck. His gaze was caught by one particular wispy curl, right where her neck joined her shoulder, and he knew an urge to cross the room and place his lips right on that exact spot.

The urge was so powerful that Nicolas had taken an impetuous step forward before he realized what he was doing, and only the knowledge that he would not be able to stop with a mere kiss enabled him to remain in his position near the fire. He scowled blackly. What the devil was the matter with him? Had it been *that* long since he'd had a woman?

A trifle embarrassed by his own reactions to a complete stranger, Nicolas cleared his throat and said, "Uh, no, there's nothing else I need for the time being. Just something to eat when it is ready. You may go now."

Hardly daring to believe that she was going to escape so easily, Tess turned and sent him a blinding smile . . . which proved to be a bad mistake. Their eyes met across the room and time stood still, the world falling away until there was just the two of them staring at each other.

Tess could not have moved if her life had depended upon it. As if waking from a long and terrible dream to find herself safe and cherished, she stared at his face, taking in the high cheekbones and the bold jut of his nose. It was an arrogant face, a hard face, but it was those large, thickly lashed eyes, eyes of such a compelling blackness that she felt as if she were drowning in their unfathomable darkness every time she met them, that made him more than just a handsome man. Those eyes and that mouth . . .

Her gaze dropped to his lips, almost dreamily traveling over its chiseled shape. The upper lip was thin, with a hint of cruelty about it, but the lower lip was full and generous, a sensual curve inherent in its form. As she stared at it, the urge to touch it with her own became almost unbearable. She knew what those lips would feel like against her own, how warm they would be, how firm and knowing they would be as they moved on hers. . . . Hardly aware of what she was doing, the need to be in his arms suddenly overpowering, she began to drift slowly toward him.

As transfixed as she, Nicolas met her in the middle of the room, his arms sweeping her into a powerful embrace as his head lowered and his mouth met hers. Drowning in the sweetness he found, he pulled her closer, the soft brush of her body against his utter magic.

His kiss was everything Tess had known it would be, the warmth of his lips, their firm, expert movement upon her own pure heaven. Ardently she returned his caress, her body molding itself eagerly against his long length. They kissed for an endless time, neither aware of the raging storm outside or the extreme oddity of their sudden, overpowering attraction to each other.

It was only when his hand cupped one small breast, his fingers tugging urgently at the hard nipple beneath the worn pink gown, that sanity returned to Tess. Stunned at how effortlessly she had gone into his arms, appalled that she had gone into his arms at all, she jerked away violently, pushing frantically against his chest. "Oh, don't!" she exclaimed breathlessly, hardly able to believe that she was actually in his embrace and had been kissing him. "Please let me go—there is some mistake!"

Foggily, still gripped by the most powerful passion he had ever known in his life, Nicolas regarded her distressed features. A mistake? A mirthless laugh rose up inside of him. There was no mistake. The swift beating of his heart, the hungry yearning that twisted in his belly, and the hard, throbbing ache between his thighs were unmistakable. He had wanted other women before, but not like this. *Never* like this! Lightning had struck him when he'd kissed her—even now he felt as if he were consumed by fire. And she dared to call it a mistake?

But like Tess, as desire slowly faded, he became aware of the insanity of his actions and his hold on her loosened. Had he gone mad? She was a stranger—a mere tavern maid—and while he had tumbled his share of willing wenches in the past, he'd never been faced with quite this sort of situation. He couldn't deny that sometimes he had awakened in strange surroundings with an unfamiliar woman lying in bed with him. But that had always been after a night of deep drinking, when to escape the horrors of war or the pain of Maryanne's betrayal, he had deliberately gone in search of the sweet oblivion to be found in a pair of soft, welcoming arms. Lust he had no trouble identifying, nor the sudden urge to find out what her mouth and body would feel like mated to his—those emotions he understood. It was the queer feeling of possession, the odd sense of protectiveness intertwined with desire for this woman that disturbed him. . . .

His black eyes hard and unfathomable as Tess danced nimbly away from him, he growled, "Who the hell are you? What's your name?"

Her mouth still tingling from his kiss, her heart acting in a most peculiar manner, Tess replied breathlessly, "Dolly. They call me Dolly."

Nicolas frowned. Now why did that sound false to him? Why did he have the feeling that she was lying? Puzzled by his reactions, he asked slowly, "And your family? Who are they? *Where* are they?"

His belligerent stance before the fire and his questions filled her with an inexplicable fear. Improvising quickly, she stammered out, "T-they're not from a-a-around here— t-t-they're in London!"

"And how is it that you come to be working in the Black Pig? Isn't the pastoral serenity of Kent a great change from the bustle of London for you?"

"I like the country," she answered defensively, realizing suddenly that it was true. She *did* like the country. Was it possible that she had told the truth without knowing it? That her family *was* in London and that she had left London because she preferred the quiet of the countryside? She bit her lip, wishing desperately that there was someone to whom she could turn—someone who could help banish the thick gray fog that clouded her brain. She felt so helpless and alone, so frightened and uncertain.

Some of her emotions showed on her revealing face. Moved in a way he had not thought possible, Nicolas asked softly, "What is it, my dear? What makes you look so?"

The expression of warm concern on his face was nearly Tess's undoing, but with an effort she fought back the urge to fling herself into his arms and pour out her poor, wretched tale. There was so much that she did not understand—not the feeling of recognition she had for him, nor her sudden need to be kissed by him. She acknowledged that he had not recognized her, but her dread of a faceless nemesis would not go away. What if he were the man she had been running away from? What if he were playing some sort of cruel game with her? Pretending not to know her, to lure her farther into his trap?

She needed to get away from him, now. Smoothing her skirts nervously, she kept her eyes downcast as she said with suspicious airiness, "I don't know what you're talking about, Your Lordship. I hope you'll find everything here at the Black Pig to your satisfaction. Now if you'll excuse me, I must return to the kitchen to see if Mrs. Darley needs any help serving your dinner."

Not waiting for his dismissal, she shot out the door and, avoiding the main room of the tavern, scurried down a hall that led directly to the kitchen. Her return was timely—several huge trays, all heaped with meat and sauces and soups and vegetables, were spread out on every conceivable surface. The moment she stepped into the kitchen, Mrs. Darley exclaimed in harassed tones, "Oh, thank goodness, you're back! His Lordship's dinner is all ready to serve. If you'll take that tray on the table, I'll follow with this one."

The next several minutes were very busy, and though she was in and out of the parlor where the earl was eating, there were no private moments between them. Mr. or Mrs. Darley was always hovering about, fussing and fawning over His Lordship. Tess was grateful. She didn't trust the earl or herself, but as long as there were people about, she didn't fear a repeat of their earlier embrace.

As she hurried about her chores, that embrace stayed in her mind, even though she tried to erase the memory. She couldn't understand what had come over her, and again she wondered what sort of life she had led before she had woken with no memory. Had she been a promiscuous wench? The kind of woman who was eager to fall into the nearest pair of masculine arms? Her reaction to the earl of Sherbourne only added to the many unanswered questions that swirled in her brain, and she wished fiercely that she had never laid eyes on him. She had enough to worry about without mooning over a pair of knowing black eyes and a sensuous mouth that had the power to arouse the most indelicate sensations within her!

There were many trips to be made back and forth between the earl's parlor and the kitchen. By the time the earl had retired for the night to his room upstairs and Tess had carried the last tray out of the room where he had eaten his meal, she was bone weary and her feet ached. But her chores were not done until she had helped Jane and Willy, the two youngsters in the kitchen, finish the washing and scouring of the pots. By then the hour was late and she was longing for nothing more than her bed.

At that moment Mr. Darley appeared in the kitchen, carrying a tray of liquors. "You, Dolly, take this upstairs to His Lordship!" he said, a smirk on his lips. "After that, your time is your own. . . ."

Tess was too exhausted to catch the innuendo in his voice. Only the knowledge that, after this one last task was done, she could seek out her bed, caught her attention. Brushing back a stray curl from her now nearly nonexistent braid, she took the tray and made her way up the stairs to the room Darley had indicated. She was so fatigued from the events of the day that not even the sound of the earl's voice bidding her enter aroused much interest in her. Just a few minutes more and she would be in her own bed. . . .

Like the parlor, the bedchamber given the earl was an unexpectedly pleasant place. It was small, with open beams and a gray rock fireplace that took up nearly one wall. The floor was of heavy oak planks, worn pale gold with age, and the four-poster bed was piled high with colorful quilts of scarlet and yellow. There were other furnishings, but when she entered and spied the earl sprawled carelessly on a chair as he warmed his bare feet before the fire, his cravat discarded, his fine white linen shirt half undone, Tess saw nothing else.

As she watched the light from the leaping flames caress his chiseled features, the broad brow, the proud nose, and mesmerizing mouth, her weariness vanished as if by magic, and she was aware of feeling gloriously alive. An excited flush on her cheeks, she gripped the tray tighter and with a light step walked into the room. A small table was pushed under a pair of chintz-curtained windows. Crossing the room toward the table, she said, "Mr. Darley sent this up for you, sir."

Setting down the tray, she turned around to look in his direction. "Will that be all, Your Lordship?" Her words were meant to be respectful, but even she heard the teasing quality to her voice, and the flush on her cheeks deepened with embarrassment. How *could* she have said those words, in just *that* manner?

The earl's heavy lids lifted, and something in that black steady gaze made Tess's heart beat with thick, painful strokes. His eyes moved leisurely over her, from the top of her unruly red hair to her curling toes in her borrowed shoes.

She was lovely as she stood there before him, with violet eyes wide and startled as that of a newborn fawn, her soft mouth as pink and inviting as the first rose of spring. . . . With an effort he jerked his eyes from the beguiling curve of that sweet mouth and let them drift lazily down her slim form, to the small, tempting bosom, the narrow waist, and the teasing hint of her thighs beneath the faded pink gown.

Nicolas had been very contented a moment ago before she had knocked on the door. He had been well fed and warm, with the sound of the storm raging outside the inn soothing rather than disruptive. He had been looking forward to slipping into the comfortable-looking bed, but all that had vanished the moment she entered the room.

Suddenly he was ravenous, and his appetite had nothing to do with food. Desire, powerful and demanding, beat in his veins, the heaviness of his swelling manhood lay against his thigh, and he was conscious of a feeling of inevitability. He was going to make love to her . . . tonight . . . all this long, stormy night. Any second now he was going to get up, walk across the room, lift her up in his arms, and carry her to that bed to find out if the magic that seemed to flow between them was real or imagined. But in the meantime there was no hurry, no reason to rush; after all, they did have all night. . . .

To Tess's astonishment, he smiled at her, a whimsical smile

that pulled at her heartstrings. "Join me," he said huskily, indicating a chair on the other side of the fire. "Sit and talk with me awhile."

Tempted unbearably, Tess halfheartedly sought to retreat. "I'll just pour your b-b-brandy and leave, if you don't mind, Your Lordship. I'm very tired." That fascinating mouth quirked slightly, and those heavy-lidded eyes moved over her. Tess could feel her resistance, faint though it had been, melting away.

"Pour yourself some brandy, too, then come and rest here in front of the fire—I'm sure there won't be a fire in your room." He grinned. "And don't worry, I won't bite—at least not very hard—I swear it."

Every instinct Tess possessed told her to leave the room immediately. She knew there was great danger to her unpredictable heart with every second that she remained in this man's presence, yet she remained precisely where she was. Even worse, to her astonishment, she found herself smiling back at him and pouring *two* snifters of brandy.

Wondering if she had lost her mind, urged on by some force over which she had no control, she picked up the two snifters and walked across the room. After shyly handing one to the earl, she sat down primly on the chair he had indicated.

Rather amazed at her brazenness, but deciding that she had rather be hung as a lion than a lamb, Tess gradually relaxed back into the welcoming softness of the chair and took a hearty swallow of the brandy. The bite of it caught her by surprise and she choked.

Nicolas smiled at her and said, "Brandy is to be savored—swirl the liquor around your snifter like this and let the aroma drift up to you, let the scent enfold you—then and only then do you take a sip. You don't gulp it, you take your time, letting the flavor linger on your tongue, then you swallow."

Tess watched as he demonstrated, fascinated by the workings of his long brown throat when he finally swallowed the amber liquid. He took such carnal delight in the entire act of appreciating the brandy that she knew he would make love the same way. . . .

Startled at her thought, she glanced away, suddenly conscious of a tingling in her bosom, of a warmth spreading downward through her body to pool achingly between her thighs. What in heaven's name was the matter with her? She was certain she had never felt this way before in her life. A twisted smile curved her mouth. But then what did she really know about herself—her memories began only twelve or so hours ago when she had awakened under that oak tree—perhaps she felt this way all the time, with many different men.

It was an unpleasant thought, and Tess pushed it away. Sending the earl an uncertain smile, she followed his directions and tasted the brandy once more. He was right, she decided happily as the smoky flavor of the brandy coated her tongue and then flowed warmly down her throat. It was much better his way!

He grinned at her and lifted his snifter in a silent toast. She returned his gesture, and together they each took another swallow, smiling at each other idiotically over the rim of their snifters.

They sat together for some time, talking aimlessly about very little, a companionable silence falling between them now and then. The storm continued to make itself heard, with the rain lashing against the shutters, the wind tearing at the roof, and rolling booms of thunder. But as Tess and Nicolas sat cozily by the fire, the storm hardly impinged upon their senses at all.

Eventually Nicolas arose, picked up the brandy decanter, and refilled their glasses. After putting the decanter on the hearth, he seated himself once more. They drank another snifter or two. Tess didn't keep track, and she wasn't quite certain when or how it happened, but shortly after the third or fourth snifter, she found herself sitting on his lap, her head nestled snugly against his shoulder, her feet dangling carelessly over his strong thighs, her shoes on the floor next to his boots.

With the potent liquor spreading its numbing warmth all through her body, Tess suspected that she was drunk. She giggled. *Very* drunk.

Looking up at Nicolas owlishly, she asked, "Am I foxed, do you think?"

He smiled at her lazily, one hand caressing her fiery curls, and slowly nodded his dark head. "We both are, sweetheart—although I believe that you are perhaps a *bit* more foxed than I am. *I* still know what we are doing. . . ."

"Oh!" Tess returned, a slightly fuzzy expression on her lovely face. "What are we doing?"

Nicolas set down his brandy snifter carefully, then took her snifter away and set it next to his. Cupping her face between his hands, he brushed his mouth tantalizingly across hers. "We are," he said thickly against her lips, "going to do what I have wanted to do since the moment I first laid eyes on you. . . ." He bit gently at the corner of her mouth. "In just a few minutes I am going to pick you up and carry you over to that very large, very comfortable bed, and then . . . after I have stripped every scrap of clothing from this delectable body of yours, I am going to make love to you. Very *thorough* love."

Tess's heart began to thump madly in her breast, her nipples became suddenly hard and aching, and the heat between her legs flared hotter and more intensely than before. She looked up into his dark face, a thousand different emotions rioting through her. Tracing the outline of his sensually curved bottom lip, she asked breathlessly, "But suppose I don't want to make love with you? What happens then?"

Nicolas hadn't lied when he had said he was as foxed as she was. Somewhat foggily he regarded her, trying to form a coherent answer. What the devil *would* he do if she didn't want him to make love to her? he wondered dejectedly. He had never forced a woman in his life, and not even to possess this beguiling little siren was he going to start now—even if every instinct cried out to the contrary. "I suppose," he said heavily, his reluctance obvious, "that you would leave and we wouldn't make love."

The idea of *not* making love to him, of not knowing what it would be like to lie in his arms and feel his strong body move against hers, was suddenly so painful to Tess that she could not bear it. It was as if she had waited years for him, had hungered for his kiss and possession for such a long time, that to wait one moment longer was unthinkable.

Astonishing both of them, she flung her arms passionately around his neck. Raining soft, achingly sweet kisses across his face, she murmured, "Then I think that I had better stay, don't you?"

Chapter Six

With something between a groan and a laugh, Nicolas swept her into his arms and carried her across the room to the waiting bed. Together they sank into the welcoming softness of the quilts on the feather-filled mattress.

If Tess knew even a moment of uncertainty, it vanished the instant Nicolas's mouth closed on hers. His kisses were every bit as intoxicating and drugging as the brandy, and with a sigh of pleasure she offered her mouth and body and pushed aside all the doubts and fears of the day. Tomorrow would be soon enough to worry about who she was and the consequences of tonight. Right now, she needed this man, needed his warmth and power, needed the sweet sense of belonging, the sure feeling that *this* was meant to happen.

He kissed her hungrily, his tongue seeking entrance to the honey warmth behind her lips, and shyly, hesitantly, Tess opened her mouth to give him what he sought. Nicolas gave a small satisfied groan when his tongue surged into her mouth, and Tess's fingers unconsciously dug into his broad back at the explosion of feeling that erupted through her at that betraying sound. The warm intimacy of his tongue leisurely exploring her mouth was a revelation to her, the notion of something so simple giving so much pleasure, arousing so many new emotions within her, utterly overwhelming.

Her body felt as if it were on fire, her breasts swelling, yearning for his touch, her loins aching and demanding release from the increasingly voluptuous sensations that racked her.

It was an intoxicating madness to lie in his arms, to have his knowing mouth wreak its rapture on hers, to feel his hard body pushing hers deeper into the soft mattress. Her arms were wrapped tightly around his neck, her restless fingers tangling in his thick dark hair. Until this moment, Tess had never been so vitally aware of the elemental difference between men and women. His broad chest was crushed against her breasts, his lower body was half lying on hers, the rigid bar of flesh between his legs pressed insistently against her thigh, and she was both excited and frightened by the wanton certainty that whoever she may be, whatever her past, after tonight she would never be the same again.

But it didn't matter; none of it mattered, except that she be freed from these sweet demons that rode her, that she find her way with this man to the thrilling pinnacle she knew awaited them. How she knew what great pleasure she would find in his arms was a mystery, but she knew it, knew it with every fiber of her being.

Nicolas's lips slid from her mouth, down her throat, and Tess's clothes suddenly felt too tight, too restricting, the worn material pressing too tightly against her breasts, rubbing too persistently against her entire body. She twisted helplessly beneath him, and as if guessing her discomfort, he laughed low and brushed a teasing hand over her breast, lingering on her nipples.

Tess gasped, her eyes flying open at the sharp sensation that shot through her as his fingers toyed lightly with her peaked nipple. Astonished, she stared at his dark, lean face, hardly able to believe how desperately she wanted to be naked—to have him touch her again in just that manner, but with no barriers between them. To her mortification, she saw that her own questing hands had already half pushed off his shirt. The sight of his near naked chest, of that smooth, heavily muscled expanse of golden skin, made something clench deep within her body.

Nicolas smiled at the expression on her face and said with far more lightness than he felt, "I think it's time to dispense with these infernal bits of cloth, don't you?"

Dazedly Tess nodded, watching breathlessly as he rose from the bed and carelessly shrugged out of his garments. In naked splendor, one brow cocked quizzically, he stared back at her.

"Does, er, everything meet with m'lady's approval?" he asked mockingly, his black eyes full of sensual amusement.

Oh my! Tess thought giddily. Meet with her approval? Oh *yes*! He was beautiful! Undeniably the most beautiful creature, human or otherwise, she had ever seen in her life, she admitted, almost mesmerized by the way the wavering candlelight caressed his golden brown flesh. Despite the broadness of his shoulders, his powerful arms and height, there was nothing coarse about his body—he was elegantly made, his hips lean and narrow, his long legs well shaped and attractively muscled. Tess could not tear her gaze away from him, the feeling of familiarity once again very strong. Did she know him? Had they been lovers? Almost angrily she pushed aside the questions, unaware how hungrily her eyes were moving over him, unaware of how her unabashedly admiring stare was affecting him.

As the seconds passed, Nicolas could feel the rampant heat rising deep within him, could feel his already hard and aching member growing larger and stiffer, and he wondered if she knew how close he was to losing control. It was all he could do to just stand there and let her look her fill. Only the knowledge that shortly he intended to take his own thorough enjoyment of *her* charms kept him where he stood. But it was not easy, not when his hot blood was clamoring in his veins, not when his entire body was nearly trembling from the force of desire she aroused by a few mere kisses.

The sight of his naked form did odd things to Tess's breathing; her heart seemed to be acting even more erratically than it had since she had first laid eyes on him. He was so beautiful, she thought again, so handsome, from the top of his head to the soles of his feet. And in between . . . oh, in between, was simply *fascinating*. . . . Those straight shoulders and the sleekness of his broad chest had certainly earned her admiration, but it was the lower area, the area covered by a thick fleecy pelt of inky black curly hair, that held her rapt stare— that and the impressive shaft that thrust upright and unashamedly between his thighs. Oh my! she thought again, how *very* handsome!

A glint entered the violet eyes, and demurely she said, "I'm sure that very few females have ever found fault with anything that you possess!"

Nicolas grinned and crossed the small space that divided them. Dropping a brief kiss on her mouth, he said huskily, "If you have nothing more to say, sweetheart, I think that it is *my* turn to find out if, underneath that deplorable gown, you are as lovely as I have imagined these past few hours."

Tess's eyes got very big and round, and her breathing grew even more ragged. She'd known this moment would come, but it suddenly seemed an enormous step to take, and she didn't know whether she was thrilled or terrified at the idea of being naked before him. But as she lost herself in the depths of those hypnotic black eyes, she found herself dazedly pulling at her gown, needing to be rid of it, needing to have nothing between his warm gaze and her body.

Nicolas helped her, his big hands moving surely over the fastenings of the gown, lifting it over her head. The gown was disposed of in seconds, and it fell in a rumpled heap at the foot of the bed where Nicolas tossed it.

His own breathing was strained and uneven at the sight of her kneeling so sweetly in the middle of the quilt-strewn bed in nothing more than a frilly chemise of fine lawn, her fire red hair falling wildly about her soft, white shoulders. Above the chemise he could see the swell of the tops of her small breasts, and he was conscious of an aching tenderness. She was so delicate, so exquisitely made, that he almost feared to continue this tormenting little game, afraid that the treacherous hold he had on his passion would shatter and that he would fall on her like a ravening beast, unable to stop himself until he had satisfied the demons of desire that clawed through him.

His fingers tightened on the flimsy material of the chemise, the urge to rip it from her body very strong, and it was then that he actually noticed the chemise for the first time. A little frown appeared between his eyes. He was no expert on women's apparel, but this garment was vastly different in material and workmanship from the old gown he had thrown on the floor. It was very expensive, he decided, having clothed the occasional mistress in his day. It was finely made and definitely not the sort of clothing a tavern wench would be wearing.

His troubled gaze traveled to her face, the patrician cast to her features striking him anew. She didn't belong here, he mused uncomfortably, the conviction growing that she was no common tavern wench. Hell! She was no *common* anything! But who was she? And what the devil was she doing here? More important, why did he feel that he had met her before? His eyes narrowed as an unpleasant thought occurred to him. Was it a trap? Was some matchmaking mama so determined to marry off her daughter that she would sink to these depths?

Tess sensed the change in him, and her violet eyes lifted to his dark face. "What is it?" she asked softly. "Don't I please you?"

Not please him? Nicolas groaned at the ridiculousness of her question, suddenly not caring to pursue his own uneasy speculations further. He wanted her, he craved her, his body was on fire to have her, and by heaven, he would have her— and matchmaking mamas be damned!

Unable to help himself, in one violent motion he ripped the chemise down the middle, destroying it as much because of the questions the garment aroused as for the driving need to finally see the tempting flesh it covered. His breath caught in his throat at the incredible loveliness he had revealed.

She was everything he had imagined she would be and more, her skin as smooth and pale as the finest alabaster; her shape, the proud little bosom, slim waist and hips, and delicate, utterly feminine thighs undoubtedly fashioned by the gods. His own personal Venus, Nicolas thought hazily, his gaze dropping down the length of her. Her breasts were small and high, the pale apricot aureoles and nipples making his mouth ache to touch them. Impulsively he did just that, bending forward to flick his tongue against their sweetness, his hands closing around her hips, pulling her forward.

Tess arched up uncontrollably at the feel of his warm mouth and tongue against her naked flesh, and her fingers clenched in the thick black hair on his head. The sensations that seared through her as he suckled hungrily at her breast made her moan softly and sway helplessly in his hold, her pelvis rocking lightly against him. His low growl of approval when their flesh met drew her deeper and deeper into this powerful web of desire, until she was boneless with longing, eager to discover what further magic she might find in his arms.

The sweetness of her response to his caresses, the tantalizing brush of her lower body against his, were almost more than Nicolas could bear. His hands tightened fiercely around her hips and he jerked her hard against him. Buffeted by the elemental emotions that tore through him, he kissed her with urgency, his tongue surging boldly into her mouth as he mimicked the motions of his lower body, where his swollen, aching member slid smoothly back and forth between her thighs.

Tess returned his kisses with an ardor that matched his, trembling with the force of the desire that held her in its inescapable grip. She was mindless with wanting, her arms wrapped passionately around his neck as they kissed with increasing urgency, their hands moving wildly over each other's bodies. Tess delighted in the feel of his hard back and muscled arms, but it wasn't enough. Instinctively her thighs clamped tightly around his shaft and she ground her body down along its length, discovering a new source of pleasure. She did it again and again, the fire low in her belly making her insensible to everything but the primeval need that dominated her. When Nicolas's hands suddenly clamped tightly on her hips, stilling her blatantly carnal movements, she gave a soft cry of despair.

"Shh, sweetheart," he breathed against her mouth. "Delicious as this is, we're going to have to stop it—unless you want me to disgrace myself this very instant!"

Tess blinked at him, not having the faintest idea what he was talking about, her body trembling with unsatisfied hunger. She ached. She burned. She wanted. *Needed.*

What she was feeling was there on her expressive face, and Nicolas groaned at the sight of all that sweet passion—all that sweet passion just for him. She was no more in control of her emotions than he was. Pushing her back into the mattress, he slid onto the bed and then pulled her into his arms.

There was an intentness about him now that made Tess shiver with excitement. His hand barely brushed her breasts before it traveled downward across her flat belly to the tangle of fiery curls at the junction of her thighs. He lingered there but a second, pulling gently on the short soft hair, before his fingers found the sweet, plump flesh hidden beneath the tiny curls.

Tess stiffened in astonishment and pleasure when he parted that moist, silky flesh and slowly began to imitate the motions of his tongue in her mouth. With helpless abandon she writhed up against his tormenting caresses, engulfed by a sheet of fiery sensation. He explored her there for a long time as a slick warmth pooled between her thighs and her hunger for something more, her desire to reach some barely-guessed-at pinnacle, increased with every thrust of his fingers.

Nicolas needed to reach that same pinnacle just as desperately as Tess did, and finally, when he could bear it no longer, he shifted his body and slid between her thighs. Cupping her buttocks, he lifted her and with something between a growl and a groan began to sink slowly within her.

Drowning in pleasure, the feel of his smooth hard flesh pushing itself deeper and deeper within her welcoming body utter ecstasy, Tess was totally unprepared for any resistance. That she would suffer pain never occurred to her, but suddenly it was there, both resistance and pain. Instinctively she fought against it, her hands pushing against his chest, her body rigid against his invasion.

Lost in his own intoxicating ascent toward sweet gratification, Nicolas found the unexpected resistance and its implication an unpleasant shock. His eyes snapped open and he stared down into her face in dismay, his thoughts jumbled and disorganized.

It was pure hell to hold himself motionless, half buried within her, to feel the tight warmth of her silken flesh clasping him so seductively and not finish the act. Fighting against the urgent demands of his own body, trembling from the effort it took to control himself, he muttered, "Why didn't you . . . ? *Jesus!* A virgin! What the devil are you playing at? Who the hell are you?"

Her eyes still smoky with desire, Tess stared back into his dark, oddly familiar face, wondering if she dared tell him the truth—that she wasn't *playing* at anything. That she had no idea who she was, and that her virginity was as much of a shock to her as it was to him! The cruel knowledge that she had unknowingly given this man, this man she knew and yet did not know, the gift of her innocence filled her with humiliation, yet . . . yet despite everything, she didn't want this moment to end. To her great shame and despair, she discovered that she wanted him to continue, she wanted him to complete his utter possession of her, and she most ardently wanted to recapture the sensual glory that had been hers only seconds ago. That primitive need banished all other considerations from her mind, and her arms tightened around his neck, her fingers tangling in his hair. Brushing her lips across his, she asked huskily, "Does it matter? Must we solve those mysteries tonight?"

All of Nicolas's earlier suspicions came flooding back, and he was half prepared to have the door to his room fly open and to be confronted by a triumphant matchmaking mama. Had he let himself be blinded by a beautiful face and become a victim of one of the oldest traps of all time?

Tess wiggled experimentally beneath him, discovering to her delight that the worst of the pain had ebbed and that she liked the feel of his solid length embedded within her. Her body felt deliciously stretched, her senses were singing a song as old as time, and she wanted this magical moment to continue. She moved again, catching her breath as he slipped deeper within her.

At her unconsciously seductive movement, a spasm of pleasure racked through Nicolas, and he knew that he could not tear himself away from her. Who she was or what her motives were didn't matter to him at the moment—he'd been looking for a bride anyway, and if he had to marry the scheming little witch in order to partake of this incredibly sweet joining, then so be it. . . .

When Tess squirmed again beneath him, he let out a shuddering breath. Brushing his mouth against Tess's, he said thickly, "Nothing matters right now, sweetheart, but that I have you . . . *nothing* else. . . ."

He caught her mouth in a deep, demanding kiss and slowly rocked his hips forward, his swollen manhood sliding full length into her narrow passage. She was so tight, so hot, so damned *sweet*, that he feared to move, feared that even one stroke would send him over the edge. It was a delicious agony, the need to thrust himself repeatedly in and out of her addicting warmth fighting fiercely with the need just to savor the incredible pleasure that was flowing through him as they remained locked together.

Tess had gasped when Nicolas had penetrated her fully, one more brief flash of pain accompanying that final thrust, but as the seconds passed she was conscious of fascinating reactions in her body. Her breasts were just as tender—if anything, they were even more sensitized as they rubbed against his smooth, warm chest. She was amazed that her body so easily accommodated his great bulk; she ached slightly from his possession, but it was the urgent demand throbbing low in her loins that captured her attention. That demand had her arms clinging to his neck, her tongue sliding daringly into his mouth, and her hips moving with unconscious seduction as she arched up against him, inviting his eager participation in this erotic dance.

Nicolas could not resist her, and the stray bemused thought crossed his mind that he would *never* be able to resist her. Then he thought of nothing, nothing except the slick heat of her body, the exquisite softness of her flesh, and the sweetness of her kiss as he drove himself time after time deep within her. The low sounds that came from her every time he buried himself in her silky tightness increased his own excitement and fed his hungry desire to bring them both to that longed-for rapture.

Tess reached it first; a soft moan escaped her, and her body stiffened in delight as a wave of intense pleasure suddenly erupted up through her body. The sheer power of it, the utter sweetness of it, left her dazed and half delirious as she lay beneath his driving body.

Hearing her cry and feeling the tremors racing through her body, Nicolas felt something snap inside him. Groaning aloud his own exultance, he thrust more frantically into her welcoming warmth, reveling in the sensations that cascaded through him. It was dark magic they had created between them, a magic he had never felt before in any woman's arms. When the red mist of fulfillment exploded in his brain and he found ecstasy, at that precise moment, he knew that by pure blind chance he had discovered something very rare and precious, something he could never let go. . . .

It was a long time before he could bring himself to slide from her. It was too sweet, too intoxicating, to lie here and rock slowly back and forth against her body, to kiss her softly, warm, teasing kisses that brought him great satisfaction and, judging from the pleased little sighs he heard, were equally appreciated by her. Eventually, though, he did lever himself away and slip down to lie beside her, pulling her against him and cradling her head on his shoulder.

Boneless with pleasure, the brandy still working its fuzzy spell, and worn out from the excitement and terrors of the day, Tess made no attempt to escape from him. She wanted never to move again . . . it was simply wonderful to lie here, to feel safe and protected, to listen drowsily to the fall of the rain, and to know that whatever else the future might hold, at least she'd had tonight. . . . With a child's trust, she rested her head easily where he had placed it; with her body curved along his warm, hard length, it wasn't very many moments before her eyes drifted shut and she fell deeply asleep.

Attuned to her in a way he couldn't understand, Nicolas knew the instant she went to sleep. Shifting her slightly, he raised up and stared down into her guileless face.

The flickering candlelight danced across her dainty features, and he was aware of a thickness in his chest. Who the devil was she? And what the devil was he going to do with her?

A frown crossed his face. It was out of the question to leave her behind. And with every second that passed, his suspicions about matchmaking mamas lessened. But she'd been a virgin, he thought again, puzzled and slightly angry at that fact. Unlike many of his peers, he'd never made a vice of initiating young virgins into the pleasures of physical love, and to have discovered that she had never known a lover filled him with conflicting emotions.

He couldn't deny that he had been oddly touched and enormously gratified to discover that she had been a virgin, but he was also wary of the reasons why she had chosen him to initiate her into the pleasures of physical love. She would not be the first woman who had been more dazzled by the size of his pocket than the amount of his charm, and at that thought his frown became more pronounced. He found the idea distasteful that she might have fallen so easily into his arms because of his title, but he could not dismiss the possibility entirely, and it made him angry—with himself for perhaps being blinded by another pair of lovely eyes and with her for probably having her gaze set on the main chance. His mouth twisted. It was highly unlikely that the Black Pig saw many lords, and he supposed if he were a fair-minded man, he wouldn't fault her decision to give herself for the first time to a man of wealth and prestige. But, he admitted grimly to himself, he was *not* a fair-minded man—at least not where she was concerned!

It angered him deeply that there might have been anything mercenary behind her actions tonight. Forgetting that paying generously for his pleasures had never bothered him in the past, he grew even angrier at the notion that Tess had given herself to him simply for money. He was aware of a furious impulse to shake her awake and demand to know her reasons for giving herself to him so sweetly. What had she been thinking of? And why? Why had she chosen him? Because of his title? His money? Or because . . .

Nicolas smiled wryly. What the devil was the matter with him? Did he expect her to wake and confess undying love for him? That she had taken one look at him and been swept off her feet? He chuckled slightly at himself. How ridiculous he was being. He should be pleased that he had so unexpectedly found such a bewitching companion to share his bed, and that she had been a virgin should have aroused nothing more than satisfaction within him.

He *was* satisfied, but he was also aware of a feeling of possession, of a strange tenderness that he should not have felt. Irritated because he could not dismiss tonight's events as mere novelty, he lay awake for several more minutes, trying to figure out what made her different, what had made tonight different. He came to no conclusions, and eventually sleep overtook him.

Tess woke first, the pounding in her head driving all other considerations from her mind. Only when she sat up with a groan, her fingers pressing into her aching temples, and the room slowly swam into focus did the events of the previous evening come trickling back. The pain in her head forgotten, she stared in horror at the naked man sleeping by her side.

He was a very handsome man, she admitted, with his tousled black hair and attractively chiseled features, but he was an utter stranger to her. Her own naked state suddenly impinged upon her consciousness, and the memory of what had happened between them last night exploded in vivid detail in her throbbing brain. As the minutes passed, the wretchedness of her position hit her with the force of a tidal wave.

She had half hoped that with the dawn of a new day her memory would miraculously come back, but such was not the case—beyond the moment when she had awakened beneath the oak tree yesterday afternoon, she remembered nothing. Now, still not knowing her name or who she was, she had compounded her troubles by losing her virginity to a man she had never seen before in her life! And if her despicable memory served her correctly, she had eagerly participated in the act. Oh, dear God, she thought sickly, what have I done?

Tess's immediate instinct was to escape, as if by fleeing from him and this room, she could forget what had happened. She shot off the bed as if she had been fired from a cannon. Ignoring the wave of dizziness that swept over her when she stood up, she glanced frantically around for her clothing. Spying her torn chemise on the floor nearby, she retrieved it swiftly and scrambled into the ruined garment. She had just reached for her gown when the man in the bed woke and sat up.

Her eyes huge in her small face, charming tendrils of fire-colored hair tumbling down to her shoulders, the worn pink gown clutched to her chest, Tess stared at Nicolas. He stared back at her, a frown gathering on his face.

"What the devil do you think you're doing?" he demanded irritably. "Put that damn thing down and come back to bed."

Her mouth set resolutely, Tess clutched her gown more tightly to her chest and said, "No! I—I'm sure that Mrs. Darley needs me in the kitchen. I must go!"

"Don't be a little fool! As long as I am kept happy, Mrs. Darley won't care what you're doing." He smiled at her and said softly, "Dolly, come to me . . . please, I want you. . . ."

The feeling that she knew him, that she could trust him, came back again very strong, and the pull of attraction between them was nearly overpowering; but Tess grimly fought against it. She had made a mistake last night, a terrible one, and had let the brandy and his abundant charm blind her to reality. But this morning, in spite of her aching head, she was thinking clearly and knew that she dared not linger here. He was a stranger, despite those flashes of familiarity, and until she knew the truth about herself, it would be the height of folly to let herself fall into his arms.

Drawing herself up, she said stiffly, "I'm sure that you're right about Mrs. Darley, but that still doesn't change the fact that she is my employer and she doesn't employ me to loll about in the beds of the guests of the tavern!"

"Oh, really?" Nicolas drawled sarcastically, getting out of bed and reaching for his breeches. "That wasn't the impression I got from *Mr.* Darley last night. In fact, I was left with the distinct feeling that, er, lolling about in bed was *precisely* what you had been hired to do!"

A humiliating blush spread across Tess's face. Biting her lip, she looked away from him. How could she explain? About her own lack of identity and that she had let the Darleys think she was someone else—someone else who *had* been hired to provide the services he was alluding to?

She took a deep breath. She would just have to tell him the truth. Not telling the truth seemed to be getting her deeper and deeper in trouble; perhaps once he knew the real situation, he would help her and this nightmare would end.

Her shoulders squared, she was trying to find the right words to begin her tale when Nicolas said slowly, "Actually, I want to talk to you about those services. . . ."

Diverted, Tess stared at him. "Services," she said breathlessly. "What about them?"

Nicolas didn't answer right away. Despite the hour, he poured himself a small snifter of brandy; after tossing it off, he looked across at her and said bluntly, "I don't want your *services* being offered to all and sundry. . . . I intend to take you away from here and set you up in a tidy little place I own . . . as my mistress."

As Tess stared at him in dumbstruck horror, he walked over to her. Capturing her chin in his fingers, he brushed a brandy-scented kiss across her mouth. "I want," he said huskily, "all those sweet services of yours, for myself and myself alone. . . ."

Chapter Seven

*I*t was instinctual on her part, Tess didn't even think about her actions; the words had barely left his mouth before her hand shot out and she slapped him soundly across the face. Bosom heaving, her eyes flashing purple fire, she spat, "How *dare* you! Just who do you think you are to insult me in this fashion?"

To say which one of them was more astonished by her violent reaction would have been anybody's guess. There was a stunned silence as they stared at each other, the imprint of her hand burning scarlet on his lean cheek.

Tess recovered first. Smothering a gasp of horror, her gown still clutched to her chest, she bolted toward the door, her destination unclear even to herself. One thing was apparent, however—it was imperative that she put as much distance between herself and the very angry man she had just struck.

"Oh, no, you don't," Nicolas growled as he reached out and captured one of her arms. Effortlessly he jerked her around to face him. "And as for insulting you, my fine little madame, there are several women of far better breeding than yours who would be *honored* to become my mistress!" His eyes glittering with fury, he snapped, "More to the point—I would have thought having to please only one man would be preferable to being at the beck and call of any stranger who wandered in and felt the need to avail himself of all that sweet passion you possess—or perhaps, now that I have removed your virginity, you actually *want* to become a common whore!"

Tess struggled in his powerful grip, so enraged by his words that waves of crimson flashed before her eyes. Since it seemed obvious that she wasn't going to get another chance to hit him and also rather obvious that she wasn't going anywhere until he was good and ready to let her, she ceased her attempts after a few moments. The violence of her reaction to his suggestion that she become his mistress had shocked her, raising more questions within her, and the need to escape from his disturbing presence battled with an equal desire to explain her actions. She might have lost her identity, but she was aware that most women would have been flattered to become the object of his attention—certainly a little nobody working in a tavern like the Black Pig would not have thrown his offer back in his face the way she had! Which led her to wonder what her station in life had been before she had lost her memory. . . .

With sickening clarity, Tess suddenly realized that she had no one but herself to blame for this predicament. She should have spoken the truth the instant she had laid eyes on Mrs. Darley—if she had, she certainly wouldn't have lost her virginity to a man she had met less than twelve hours ago, and she wouldn't have been forced to listen to his offer to become his mistress. Whatever her instincts may have told her at the time, it was painfully apparent that they had failed her.

Drawing herself up, Tess said stiffly, "I apologize for slapping you, but I don't apologize for being insulted by your offer to make me your mistress. And before this situation goes any farther, there are a few things I think you should know about me—things I should have told you last night."

Nicolas growled something low in his throat that Tess was just as glad she didn't understand, but to her relief he released her and indicated that she sit on one of the chairs before the hearth. The fire had long since died down, but it took only an instant for him to stir up the coals and throw on a few pieces of wood that had been stacked neatly off to the side.

Once the fire was burning brightly again, he glanced at her and said coldly, "If you don't mind, I'd like to finish dressing, and I would suggest that you do the same."

Ignoring her, he walked over to the door to their room and opened it, bellowing, "Lovejoy, where the hell are you? Get me some hot water and some coffee—*now!*" Slamming the door, he stalked back to stand in front of the fire. His back to the fire, he eyed the torn chemise and crumpled gown she still clutched in her hands distastefully and with frigid politeness he said, "You'll probably want other clothes—I'll have my man bring you something else from your room."

Tess swallowed, wishing she had the nerve to say that she'd prefer to go to her room herself and get her own clothes. But something in his expression told her that she wasn't going to have that option. "That would be very nice," she replied weakly, "but I'm afraid I don't have anything else, except my riding habit and cloak. In fact, this gown is borrowed from Mrs. Darley—it was her daughter's."

His brows snapped together in a frown, but before he could utter the question hovering on his lips, the door opened and Lovejoy, his long face carefully blank, entered the room. After setting down the heavy tray he had brought in with him, he carried a china bowl and large pitcher to the small washstand in the corner of the room. "Ah, but it's a fine morning, m'lord!" he said lightly as he returned and began to unload the other items from the tray. "The sun is shining and no sign of last night's storm but a few clouds. Now that's some nice hot water over there for your use, and Mrs. Darley has sent up a pot of coffee, some sliced ham, and buns still warm from the oven. Butter and jam, too."

Nicolas muttered something and, walking over to his servant, said levelly, "A word with you, outside." Looking back at Tess, he added, "You may wash while I give Lovejoy his orders for the day."

Only when the door shut behind the pair of men did Tess get up and walk over to the washstand. She longed for a luxurious bath but resigned herself to a quick wash. The water was warm, and Mrs. Darley had included a small scrap of soap, which Tess used diligently. It was amazing how much better she felt afterward, even if it had been only a hasty flick of a wet rag here and there.

Despite the ruined state of her chemise, she kept it on and swiftly donned the pink gown. There were no mirrors in the room, and she knew that her hair was a mass of tangled curls, but beyond brushing it with her fingers and hands, there was nothing she could do about it.

She was just starting to get restless and was seriously thinking of trying to slip away when the door reopened and Nicolas came back inside. He glanced at her and said, "Help yourself to the food and coffee—I'll be dressed in a moment."

Tess didn't argue with him; she was hungry, and who knew when she'd have her next meal? The buns were wonderful, warm and meltingly tender, and the coffee was strong and hot. *Just what I need,* she told herself bracingly, not looking forward to the next several minutes. Eating her third bun slathered with strawberry jam, and sipping her coffee, she studiously ignored the sound of the earl's swift ablutions. She did such a good job of it that she wasn't aware he had finished until his voice just behind her caused her to jump and look around.

He was simply garbed as he stood there regarding her closely, arms akimbo, wearing a clean white linen shirt open at the throat, buff breeches, and gleaming high-topped black boots. It was obvious from the set of his hard jaw and the look in his eyes that the delay hadn't lessened his anger or distracted him. Just as if no time had elapsed between her earlier statement and now, he poured himself a cup of coffee, spread jam on a bun, and asked harshly, "What do you mean that you have no clothing other than your riding habit?"

Tess took a deep breath, praying that she wasn't making another terrible blunder. "Simply that this has all been a ghastly mistake. I am not a tavern wench—at least, I don't believe that I am. I have absolutely no idea *who* I am—I don't even know my own name, nor how I came to be in this vicinity." She grimaced. "Dolly is just the name of a farmer's nag that I passed on my way to the Black Pig. When a name was needed, it popped into my mind."

Nicolas scowled. "I don't like games," he said slowly, "and I particularly dislike games when the object is to make a fool of me. You would be wise to remember that."

He didn't believe her! Tess swallowed. She had feared that reaction in the beginning, but after what had occurred last night and this morning, facing ridicule had seemed the lesser of two evils. Cursing herself for not having spoken sooner, she said vehemently, "It's not a game—and it certainly wasn't a game last night when I lost my virginity! That, I can tell you, was as big a shock to me as it was to you!"

"Oh, I'm sure it was," he replied dryly. "But tell me, is this the moment that you suddenly remember who you are and your anxious relatives come banging on my door?"

Tess frowned. "What do you mean? I've just told you that *I don't know who I am!* And if any anxious relatives were to come banging on your door, I would be elated!"

"I'm sure you would," he answered, something in his tone and the expression on his face making Tess distinctly uneasy.

"But I'm telling you the truth!" she exclaimed desperately. "I woke up late yesterday afternoon some miles from here, lying under an oak tree. From the state of my clothes, I suspect that I may have lain out there all night. And that's all I know!"

"Hmm. Not quite all you know. You knew enough to come to the Black Pig, and you knew enough to insinuate yourself into my bed." Ignoring her look of outrage, he seated himself before the fire and sipped his coffee. Eyeing her over the cup, he said coolly, "Shall I tell you what I think?" At Tess's curt nod, he went on blandly, "I think that you're a clever little liar, and that you or your family saw an opportunity to snare a rich husband, and that, with a great deal of luck and some coincidence, you managed to put yourself in my path . . . and bed."

"Are you mad?" Tess burst out furiously. "Or so arrogant that you think every woman who lays eyes on you becomes so enamored that she is willing to go to ridiculous lengths to get your attention?"

Nicolas had the grace to blush, a spot of red burning high on his cheeks, but he wasn't backing down. The certainty that she was part of a plot to force an offer of marriage from him had returned and would not go away. Not after the most interesting conversation he'd had with Lovejoy in the hall. . . .

Grimly he said, "No. I'm not *that* arrogant, but I'd like you to explain to me precisely how you, an apparently gently born young woman showed up here, after dark, in the midst of a raging storm, with no companions, no sign of transportation, and proceeded to convince Mrs. Darley that you were her brother-in-law's whore from London!" Tess opened her mouth to speak, frantic, angry words boiling up in her throat, but Nicolas forestalled her by holding up a long-fingered hand and saying, "You'll have your turn, but hear me out . . . you might decide to tell the truth for a change."

Tess gasped with outrage, but he went on calmly, "My man, Lovejoy, has had a very illuminating conversation with the Darleys this morning—they both confirm the time and manner of your arrival, and they both confirm that you claimed to be the woman mentioned in a letter to them from Darley's brother, Tom. I think you'll understand their confusion when at first light a young woman more in the style they were expecting showed up and insisted rather vociferously that *she* was Tom's doxy, Lucy Jones, and that she has a tattoo on a rather, er, private part of her anatomy to prove it! She also knows a great deal about the family—some things only Tom's woman would know. According to Lovejoy, it's very clear she is who she says she is . . . and that you aren't! I must say, again according to Lovejoy, that the Darleys are not best pleased with you—they are, in fact, quite angry at the trick you played on them. Now, don't you think it's time you told me the truth?"

"I told you," Tess got out between gritted teeth, her eyes glittering dangerously, "I don't know *who* I am!"

"Perhaps . . . but it's rather convenient for you, don't you think? Especially considering what passed between us last night." His mouth twisted derisively. "Your family must be in desperate straits indeed to sink to this sort of tawdry strategy. . . ." His gaze raked up and down her body. "You really didn't have to go to such lengths to catch my attention, sweetheart—I assure you, had we met under more conventional means, I would have noticed you, and there is every probability that I would have pursued you—you're a very fetching little minx. Unfortunately, I don't like my hand being forced and dislike even more being made a fool of! Now, for the last time, who are you and when may I expect to meet the rest of your charming family?"

Tess was so furious that she could hardly think; the urge to slap and claw at the mocking face was uppermost in her mind. She took a deep breath. Holding on to her temper, barely, she managed to say quietly enough, "I told you—I don't know. My memory only begins with yesterday afternoon, when I awoke under that blasted oak tree!"

His expression didn't change, and Tess knew with a sinking heart that he didn't believe her. Fighting an urge to stamp her feet and throw a tantrum, she sought for some way to convince him of the truth. Something occurred to her, and her eyes narrowed. Almost triumphantly she demanded, "If this is all a plot, how did I know you would be here? How could my family have possibly known you were going to stop here for the night? Tell me that, you rabbit-brained jackass!"

Unfazed by her insult, he replied levelly, "I'll grant you that there was some luck and some coincidence, the storm being the luck and the expected arrival of Lucy Jones being the coincidence, but while my departure from London was not planned, it would have been simple enough to have been found out shortly before I left—I made no secret of it when I returned home from Lady Grover's ball. Servants gossip, and to anyone interested in my movements, my sudden departure wouldn't have been hard to discover." He took another sip of his coffee, then continued dryly, "Perhaps a footman in your employ has been seeing one of the maids in my employ. It's possible they saw each other before I left London and that it was mentioned that the master was leaving for Kent." He shot her a hard look. "Was that when this nasty little scenario was plotted?"

"I don't know," Tess said tightly, her hands clenched at her sides. "I wasn't there!"

"Oh, that's right, I forgot, you lost your memory," he drawled with obvious disdain. "As I said earlier, how convenient for you."

"Damn you! It's the truth! And even if everything you say could have happened, how could we have known you'd stop *here* or that there'd be a storm?"

He shrugged. "As I said, you've had some luck. What precisely the original plan was, I have no idea, but I'm quite certain that once the storm began in earnest, it wouldn't have taken a genius to figure out that it would be extremely difficult and uncomfortable for me to make it to Sherbourne Court and that I would be stopping for the night somewhere along the way. You just had to guess which tavern I would choose, and since there are not many along this stretch of road, the Black Pig would be the obvious choice." He flashed her a level glance. "As I said, luck paid an enormous part—someone guessed right, and you managed to be here and in place ahead of me." His voice hardened. "According to Mrs. Darley, you didn't arrive too much before I did." He gave a bitter laugh. "And I'll wager you felt quite smug when I walked in—after all, I could have decided not to stop and then all your efforts would have been for naught. But you gambled and the gamble paid off—in aces, I would say!"

"You're absolutely mad," Tess ground out, so furious she could hardly speak.

"And you're very stupid if you think I'm going to be taken in by that absurd tale of yours! I have been, over the months since I inherited my brother's title, the object of too many matchmaking schemes to fall for this one. Now then, are you going to tell me your name or not?"

Her chin lifted rebelliously, *"Not!"* she said, her eyes nearly black with anger.

Nicolas shrugged. "Very well, it makes little difference to me—keep your secrets! Now if you will excuse me, I must be on my way."

He rose to his feet, walked over to the table, and set down his empty cup. Seeming oblivious of Tess's presence, he found his jacket and, after putting it on, opened the door and shouted once more for Lovejoy. Upon Lovejoy's immediate entrance into the room, Nicolas asked him, "Are the horses and rig ready?" At Lovejoy's nod, he continued, "Good! If you'll pack up my belongings, we can be on the road in five minutes."

Tess had watched him in open perplexity, unable to believe that he was simply going to leave things as they were and calmly drive away from the tavern . . . and her. There was an uncomfortable feeling in the middle of her chest, and she was conscious of a sudden desire to burst into tears. She felt abandoned and betrayed, though she had no real reason to feel either. How can he leave me this way? she wondered sickly. Didn't last night, don't *I*, mean anything to him? Apparently not, she conceded miserably as Lovejoy quickly gathered up the earl's few things and placed them neatly in a black leather valise. Nicolas, his handsome face impassive, stood negligently by the door, his arms folded across his chest, utterly ignoring her.

If Tess had thought she had been frightened yesterday when she had awakened with no memory, it was nothing compared to the idea of the earl leaving the Black Pig and riding out of

her life without so much as a backward look. She was filled
with rage and not a little terror. The knowledge that Lucy
Jones had arrived and been accepted by the Darleys made it
obvious that they weren't going to look very kindly on *her*.
Glumly she reminded herself that the Black Pig had been
meant as a temporary refuge anyway, but things had happened
so swiftly that she wasn't ready to venture immediately out on
her own. The unpleasant notion that she was running away
from someone, that she was in some sort of danger, hadn't
lessened, and her spirit quailed at the prospect before her.

Tess bit her lip. Her situation was dreadful. She was wearing torn and borrowed clothing; she had just spent the night
with a man she didn't know and had lost her virginity; she still
didn't know who she was; she still had no money, and it
looked as though once the earl drove away, she would be
thrown out onto the road—if she was lucky, at least in her
own clothes! She was suddenly more frightened than she had
ever been since this whole horrible nightmare had begun.

Unaware of the terror lurking in her wide eyes, she glanced
at Nicolas, determined not to beg for his help. Somehow she
was going to find a way out of her appalling situation, and if
she had to do it alone . . . Her shoulders squared and her chin
lifted. She'd find a way, somehow!

Having finished his task, Lovejoy straightened and, clasping the valise, laid the earl's many-caped greatcoat across the
bed. "Will that be all, sir?"

Nicolas nodded curtly, saying as Lovejoy reached the door,
"I'll be down in just a few minutes. You've taken care of
everything?"

"Yes, just as you ordered."

The room was very quiet after Lovejoy departed, only the
occasional hiss and pop of the fire breaking the silence.
Moodily Nicolas stared across the room at Tess's slender figure in the worn pink gown. What the hell did he do now?

He cocked an eyebrow and murmured, "Well? What's your
answer?"

Tess gaped at him. "M-m-my answer? I'm afraid I don't understand."

Forcing himself not to respond to the desolate expression on her lovely face, he said crisply, "My offer. It still stands. Are you coming or not?"

Tess swallowed painfully. It was a terrible choice, but one she had to make. Her lips thinned as she said tightly, "If you mean am I willing to become your mistress, the answer is still no!"

His arms dropped, and he strolled over toward her, the expression on his face hard to define. Stopping just inches from her, he reached out and ran one finger lightly down her cheek. "Oh? And why not? What is it about my offer that you find offensive? I can be a very generous man—you'd have a house, servants, silks, and jewels, and if last night was anything to go by, you certainly found no fault with either my person or my lovemaking—so why do you hesitate now?" His black eyes hardened. "I would be the first to admit that a certain amount of reluctance is charming, but I wouldn't make me wait too long, sweetheart—and if you are thinking that an offer of another sort will be forthcoming if you withhold your favors—you delude yourself. I may be searching for a bride, but I will not be *forced* into taking one—especially one who has tricked me as you have!"

Tess knocked aside his hand and looked away. "I didn't 'trick' you, and I never expected you to marry me," she said softly. "I don't know what I expected. . . ." The memory of the certainty that she knew him, that she could trust him, rolled over her, and she blinked rapidly, but she still couldn't stop one tiny tear from sliding down the side of her face.

That tear was Nicolas's undoing. Cursing under his breath, he dragged her into his arms and kissed her angrily. "Damn you!" he swore when he finally lifted his punishing mouth from hers. "You're coming with me whether you like it or not! I'm not leaving you behind, and as for the other—we'll settle that question later and in surroundings far more comfortable than these!"

He gave her no chance to argue, merely wrapped his great-coat around her and swung her up in his arms. Tess still retained enough of her senses to struggle against the arms that held her, but one part of her was almost relieved to have the decision taken out of her hands. Heedless of anyone who might be watching, Nicolas bounded down the stairs and strode purposefully through the small hall and out of the tavern into the tepid October sunshine.

Tess's efforts to free herself had been futile. He was too strong for her, and her limbs had been tangled and trapped by the heavy folds of the greatcoat, hampering her ability to escape. All too soon she found herself tossed like a bag of oats onto the seat of a handsomely built curricle, a pair of equally handsome and perfectly matched black geldings harnessed to the vehicle. She bounced upright immediately and, brushing back a strand of her disheveled hair from her face, glared at him as he lithely entered the curricle and picked up the reins. "This is abduction," she said hotly. "You're taking me away from here against my will."

Nicolas sent her a cool smile. "Am I, my dear? Am I really? Last night certainly wasn't against your will. As a matter of fact, if memory serves me correctly, I distinctly remember that you were *very* willing! And I doubt that you are as unwilling now as you pretend."

Tess drew in a sharp, angry breath, but neither waiting for nor expecting an answer, Nicolas looked away from her and flicked the reins. Instantly the horses leaped forward, the powerful surge knocking her back against the seat. As the Black Pig disappeared behind them, she sat up and demanded, "Where are you taking me?"

"A place to put you did give me some pause," Nicolas returned pleasantly. "I hadn't planned on meeting you, you see, so I had not made any arrangements, but fortunately, I remembered the old gatekeeper's cottage on the far edge of my estate. It is in the middle of a large wood, and it hasn't been occupied in years. In fact, I doubt that many people even remember its existence. I had Lovejoy send my groom ahead to make certain all is in readiness for our arrival. It should do just fine for you."

Drawing herself up proudly, Tess said, "Not only do I not have a choice in being with you, but it seems that I am to be kept a prisoner in some shabby deserted old building! I must say, you *are* a generous protector!"

Nicolas's lips tightened and he shot her a dark look. "I think," he began stiffly, "that you will be very surprised when you see 'the shabby, deserted old building!' And I think that you have forgotten that I am Sherbourne and that the earls of Sherbourne are seldom mentioned in connection with anything *shabby*."

There was little speech between them after that, as Nicolas concentrated on controlling his high-spirited pair and Tess suddenly became aware that Lovejoy was riding in the groom's seat at the rear of the curricle. Filled with mortification that someone else should have overheard their acrimonious conversation, she kept her eyes resolutely on the road in front of them.

As the miles sped by, some of her anger and embarrassment lessened, although she still resented being abducted so high-handedly. But since Lovejoy's presence made further private speech impossible, she began to glance around, hoping that something in the passing scenery would wake her memory.

Nothing did. The tree-dotted, gently rolling green terrain brought nothing to mind. They went by the occasional farm, several orchards, and even an inn or two, but everything remained depressingly unfamiliar. It was still fairly early in the morning, and they passed only a few vehicles—mostly farmers hauling their produce to market.

It was, Tess admitted reluctantly, a lovely day. The sunshine was bright, and there was only a dark-skirted cloud now and then to mar the brilliant blue of the sky. The leather top of the curricle was still up after last night's storm; for a moment she toyed with the idea of asking him to lower it, then abandoned it. First of all, she wasn't asking him for anything, and second, while the discovery of her identity was imperative, she was still uneasy about who might recognize her. Suppose the person who aroused that powerful urge to flee were to see her? The feeling had lessened slightly for a while, but with every mile they traveled it came back stronger and stronger. She swallowed and unconsciously sank back farther under the concealing hood of the curricle.

As they came around a curve in the road, they met a dashing black highflier being driven at a reckless pace. The gentleman pushing his grays to a dangerous speed was fashionably dressed, with York tan gloves upon his hands and a curly-brimmed beaver hat sitting at a rakish angle on his blond locks. Tess took one glance at that hard, handsome face as his vehicle flashed by and was aware that she was suddenly afraid. Very afraid. She didn't recognize the man, but for some reason just the sight of him filled her with unspeakable terror.

She looked at Nicolas and, noting the grim expression on his face, she asked timidly, "What is it? Do you know that man?"

"Yes, I know him," he said tightly. "That was Avery Mandeville . . . or I should say *Baron* Mandeville—a more despicable fellow you are unlikely to meet! As for the rest of that wretched family, they are no improvement!" He scowled. "I should tell you that many years ago they were the cause of great pain and scandal in my family. The locals claim that because of those cursed Mandevilles, there is no love at Sherbourne Court—that it disappeared with my grandfather." He laughed mirthlessly. "Now that I am looking for a bride, everyone is waiting to see if love returns, but since I don't imagine mine will be a love-match, it appears that they shall have to continue to wait." He jerked his head in the direction in which the other man had driven. "That damned family has always been bad luck for mine—it was the previous baron who killed my brother, and that fellow who just passed us is probably the worst of the lot! Believe me, you'll not hear any of my family speaking kindly of a Mandeville!"

Chapter Eight

*T*here was such hatred and contempt in his voice when he hurled out those words that Tess was very glad that *she* wasn't a Mandeville! At least, she amended thoughtfully, she *hoped* she wasn't a Mandeville. The earl of Sherbourne would make a bad enemy, and the notion of being a Mandeville and totally within his power made her shiver.

Tess was even more subdued after the earl's outburst, and for several miles she stared out blindly at the passing countryside, her mind on her reaction to the sight of Baron Mandeville. She had been frightened, but she didn't know why—was it because he was the source of the instinctive need to run, or was there some other reason? The Mandeville name struck some chord deep within her, but she didn't know whether it was because the name was simply familiar to her or because it had some personal significance.

Tess let out a big sigh. It was difficult not knowing even your own name, and she wondered miserably if she'd ever remember who she was and where she had come from. Was there someone, somewhere, who loved her? Missed her? Was someone even now searching desperately for her?

Nicolas had heard her sigh. He slanted a covert glance at her, and the expression on her face caused a knife blade of pain in his chest and lacerated an already guilty conscience.

He was aware that he had forcibly abducted her—he was even appalled by his own actions—but he'd had no control over the insane impulse that had driven him to take her with him. Only by repeatedly reminding himself that he meant her no harm, that he *would* keep her safe and treat her far better than whoever had put her in this situation in the first place, was he able to soothe his guilt pangs. But the unhappy look on her face didn't help him come to grips with what he had done.

He'd never done anything so outrageous and incomprehensible in his life, and he shook his head at his own folly. I must have been mad, he decided sourly. There can be no other explanation for my actions. Yet he knew that wasn't true. Some other emotion had been goading him, and while he could admit that he had acted wrongly and even suffer a painful conscience over it, he was bitterly aware that it changed nothing—that he would do the same thing all over again if it meant keeping this beguiling little creature by his side.

Aloud he said quietly, "It won't be so very bad, you know. I *am* a generous man, and I swear that I shall not mistreat you." He smiled winningly at her. "I know it is not what you planned, but would it be so awful to be my mistress?" A husky note entered his deep voice. "To share a bed with me?"

Tess's eyes met his, and as their gazes locked she was conscious of a powerful yearning to throw caution to the winds and freely admit that sharing a bed with him wasn't such a terrible fate. In some strange way he was so familiar, so dear to her, as if she had seen that smile before, felt those lips on hers before, known the heady magic of his embrace previously. It would be so easy to agree with him, so easy just to let events happen, but something held her back, something deep inside her warned that it would be unwise, foolish in the extreme, to do so.

She broke away from the mesmerizing quality of his stare and said in a small voice, "I'm certain that you think you're being kind, but until I know who I am and what my situation is, I cannot commit myself to such an arrangement. It would be wrong and unfair to whatever family or friends I have—I could even have a fiancée . . . and if he exists, I have already wronged him enough."

Nicolas's lips thinned. "I see. We are still going to play that little game, are we?"

"It is *not* a game!"

"Isn't it, my dear, sweet Dolly? Isn't it a very clever little game to convince me of the truth of what you claim? A game in which to arouse my sympathy and concern for you?"

Her eyes flashed. "Don't call me Dolly! I told you that was the name of a farmer's nag!"

"You'll forgive me," he said dryly, "if I doubt your word. And if you don't wish to be called 'Dolly,' what other name would you prefer?"

"My own!"

"And that is?" he asked softly, one black brow cocked quizzically.

The palm of her hand itched to slap that mocking face, but suddenly she was tired of fighting with him, of knowing that he firmly believed she was a liar and that nothing she could say would convince him otherwise. She turned away and said wearily, "Never mind! Call me Dolly if you like—it doesn't matter."

Silence fell again, and for the remainder of the journey there was no more conversation between them. Tess curled up on her side of the curricle and stared unhappily out at the countryside as they bowled on down the road, her thoughts most unpleasant and mournful.

It was almost two hours later when Nicolas finally turned the curricle off the more heavily traveled road they had been following and guided his horses down a series of small country lanes. Eventually he turned them onto a narrow path that was clearly seldom used but still quite passable. There were ruts and grooves in the road, and the occasional overhanging tree limb scraped against the sides of the curricle, but their careful progress was not further impeded.

They came finally to an ornate pair of rusty old gates, and Lovejoy jumped down from his seat at the rear of the curricle and threw them open. Only after Nicolas had driven the horses through the gates did Tess notice a wagon pulled by a team of horses stopped in front of a charming half-timbered dwelling of comfortable size, set back from the road.

There were signs that the weeds and grass in front of the building had been newly scythed, and the windows were thrown wide, the freshly washed square-leaded panes gleaming in the sunshine. Off to the right and behind the main house could be seen a small barn and stables, and at the side of the house were the remnants of what once must have been a pleasant rose garden.

Although the dwelling was obviously very old, it was like no gatekeeper's cottage that Tess had ever seen. It was far too elegant, with its wide double oak front doors and second-story gables. She frowned as that thought crossed her mind. How did she know it was far too elegant?

Her curiosity evident, she asked, "If this is where I am to stay, it's rather grand for a mere gatekeeper's cottage, isn't it?"

Pulling his horses to a stop, Nicolas appeared uncomfortable. "It, um, wasn't originally built for the gatekeeper."

Tess sent him a long, thoughtful look. He fidgeted and muttered, "An ancestor built it for a, uh, favorite mistress in the late 1500s." One of Tess's slender brows arched, and Nicolas added, "A few years later it was decided to make this the main entrance to the estate, and a gatekeeper and his family were installed—until a new road was constructed in the early 1700s, this was the main entrance to Sherbourne Court. After the new road began being used, the gatekeeper was moved to a new residence near it, and no one has lived here. At least not, um, regularly. There are family stories that some later ancestors put it to the same use as the earl who had the place built originally." The expression on Tess's face made him add hastily, "However, those are just family stories . . . more gossip than anything, I'm sure."

"How interesting," Tess said dryly. "Your family obviously has the charming habit of housing their mistresses on their estates. Tell me, didn't their countesses object—having their husbands' mistresses practically on their doorstep?"

Nicolas's fine mouth tightened. "It's not a habit! I won't pretend that the men in my family haven't had their faults, especially where women were concerned, but we don't, as a rule, behave shabbily to our wives! And I'd like to remind you that I am *not* married, so my relationship with you isn't harming anyone."

Suddenly enjoying herself, Tess replied airily, "Oh, really? Didn't you mention at the tavern that you were searching for a bride? I wonder how she'll feel, when you find her, of course, to know that you kept a mistress here while you courted her?"

"You have a sassy mouth," Nicolas said silkily, the glint in his dark eyes giving Tess pause. "I think that I shall have to come up with a way to keep it occupied. A way that will be quite, quite pleasurable. . . ."

His intention clear, he leaned toward her, and Tess shrank back into the cushions of the curricle, her amethyst eyes wide and uncertain. "D-d-don't you touch me!" she said breathlessly. Spying Lovejoy and a man and woman who appeared in the doorway of the cottage, she added swiftly, "The servants are watching!"

Nicolas hesitated and then, with a wry twist of his lips, sat back. "You're right, this is not the place for what I want to do with you. But remember, sweetheart, that the servants are not going to be around all the time. . . ."

To her intense humiliation, Tess wasn't as frightened or repulsed by that threat as she should have been. She straightened up and, haughtily wrapping the folds of his greatcoat closer around her, said, "Since you insist on keeping me prisoner, I suppose that I might as well view my prison."

Laughing, Nicolas jumped down from the curricle. "Yes, I suppose you should—I just hope the, er, prison meets with m'lady's approval!"

Another couple had joined the original trio, and as she and Nicolas approached, Tess could discern a definite family resemblance among the three men and one of the women. The youngest gentleman turned out to be Nicolas's groom, John Laidlaw; the second man, standing by his side, was not very many years older and was his brother Thomas. Lovejoy, Tess wasn't surprised to learn, was their uncle, and the youngest of the two women, Jenny, with the same blue eyes as her brothers, was their youngest sister. The last woman, a shy, retiring creature with a gentle smile, was Tom's wife, Rose. Thomas, Rose, and Jenny, Nicolas informed her lightly, would constitute her staff, along with their mother, Sara, who was busy in the kitchen preparing some refreshments.

Tess was slightly overwhelmed, and she wondered nervously if she had ever supervised staff. Had she had servants of her own? Uncertainly she eyed the three younger Laidlaws, wondering how they would all manage together. The shy, reassuring smile that Rose sent her way and the twinkle in Tom's eyes suddenly made her feel more at ease with the situation. She only hoped that the mother, Sara, would be as kind and pleasant as her children and daughter-in-law appeared to be. But it didn't matter how nice these people were, she suddenly reminded herself, she wasn't staying here! Or was she?

It had been John whom Nicolas had sent ahead to make things ready for their arrival and who arranged for the others to be in residence. His young face earnest, John said nervously, "I didn't arrive too much before Your Lordship, so me and the others haven't gotten as much done as you may have wished. But we did get the place swept out, and Jen and Rose washed windows and helped Tom place some of the items you told me to get from the storeroom." Proudly he added, "I took care of the outside."

"And my grandmother, were you able to avoid her?"

"Oh, yes, my lord. Her Ladyship was still abed, but it was a near thing when we were loading up the wagon—Lady Athena almost discovered us."

Nicolas grimaced and muttered, "Better my grandmother than Athena!"

Laidlaw grinned, and an answering smile twitched at the corner of Nicolas's mouth. "From the looks of things, considering the shortness of your time, you and your family are to be commended. Well done!"

A great deal had been accomplished in the relatively short time that Laidlaw and his family had been busy. If the dwelling had sat empty and unused, as Nicolas had stated, there was certainly no sign of neglect as Tess was guided through the doorway, across a large entry hall, and into the spacious main room.

The scent of lemon and beeswax met her nostrils, and with dawning delight she glanced around her. A huge stone fireplace took up a large portion of one wall, windows lined another, a Brussels tapestry adorned a farther wall, and the lovely arches of the timber roof gave the room grandeur and charm. An Oriental carpet in jeweled tones of sapphire and burgundy, the colors softened with time, had been laid on the polished wooden floor, and several pieces of furniture, elegant in rich woods and satin and silks, were scattered haphazardly about the room.

Despite the sunny day, there was a faint chill in the air, and the fire had been lit and a pile of newly chopped wood laid nearby. Tess walked over to stand in front of the fire, grateful for its warmth. Her back to the leaping flames, she glanced across at Nicolas, who stood blocking the entrance to the room, one broad shoulder propped negligently against the wide doorjamb. He was watching her intently, the expression on his dark face hard to define. Satisfaction? Regret? Desire?

Desperate to break the sudden heavy silence that had fallen between them, she rushed into speech. "The Laidlaws seem like very nice people. How were you able to obtain them so quickly?"

Nicolas shrugged. Servants were the last thing on his mind—now that he actually had her where he wanted her, he discovered that his body had some definite plans of its own. But tamping down his baser instincts, he drawled, "The Laidlaws have served the Talmages for centuries. Sara's husband died unexpectedly when the children were all young, and work was found for her on the estate—you'll find that she is an excellent cook. As for the others, Jenny should make a fine housemaid, and Rose has been trained as a lady's maid—both should suit you." Impatiently he added, "Under the gimlet eye of Bellingham at the main house, Thomas has been learning all that he will need to eventually become as terrifyingly efficient a butler as Bellingham is himself." Nicolas sent her an enigmatic glance. "Bellingham is also Sara and Lovejoy's uncle . . . as you can see, we take care of our own."

There was a wealth of meaning—and promise—in those simple words, and Tess's eyes dropped from his. She wished that she wasn't so aware of him, of the power of that long, lean body beneath its civilized trappings; aware too of the way her own silly emotions seemed to spin out of control at his nearness.

She put a hand to her temple, trying to think sensibly, trying to make sense of all that had happened to her, wondering what she should do next, and trying not to think of all she had done so far. If only, she thought despairingly, she could remember who she was! As it was, she felt like a piece of flotsam caught in a flood, carried willy-nilly wherever whim took her. It was a terrible feeling, and his presence didn't help her. This was all his fault! Resentfully, she looked back at him, and the sight of that dark, intent face, the obstinate line of that hard jaw, sent another of those peculiar flashes of familiarity through her. His hair should be longer, and he should be wearing laces, she thought stupidly, laces and black velvet . . . a sword hanging at his side. . . .

Her heart suddenly began to race, and she had the crazy notion that this scene had been played out before—that she had been in the room before . . . with him! It was impossible and yet . . . the way his gaze moved over her, the hunger she glimpsed burning in those brilliant black eyes, was very familiar to her. With an effort she tore her eyes from his and glanced blindly around.

More for something to say than from any real wish to see the rest of the house, she asked tremulously, "May I see the other rooms, please?"

Nicolas shrugged and pushed away from the doorjamb. "Of course. I hope you will find everything to your satisfaction—but don't be surprised at the lack of furnishings—John was ordered to get just enough to make you comfortable for tonight. Tomorrow I'll raid the storerooms myself and have a few more things brought over for your use."

Despite the situation, Tess nearly smiled. They were being so formal, like polite strangers, and yet last night she had lain naked in his arms, had felt the power of his possession. . . . Looking at him, at that wide, mobile mouth of his, she was suddenly conscious of a thickening in her blood, of sweet fire gliding sensually through her body, of a tingle low in her belly, and she was filled with despair.

Last night, she repeated vehemently to herself, was *not* going to be repeated. There were reasons, excuses, for last night, she told herself stoutly as they began to walk up a broad, curving staircase. Last night she had been confused and exhausted—and he had deliberately plied her with brandy, until she hadn't been in control of her senses. . . . Tess had none of those excuses, frail though they were, to blame her behavior on now, and she fought to bring her unruly emotions under control.

Their bodies brushed tantalizingly against one another as they moved up the stairs, and Nicolas was as aware of her as she was of him. With every step they climbed, he could feel his body hardening, could feel the heat pooling between his thighs. He was conscious of the galling fact that it was as if last night had never happened—he wanted her just as desperately as he had then. The craving that her mere presence created within him was just as powerful, just as compelling, as it had been before he had made love to her. He told himself that his body's reactions were perfectly normal. He'd been a long time without a woman, and there was no denying that this conniving little baggage walking so calmly by his side was the most bewitching, infuriating creature he had ever met in his life—he doubted that a lifetime of taking her to bed would satisfy him. There was also, he admitted brazenly, an exciting awareness that he was the only man who had ever known all the sweet passion she possessed. . . . And it's damn well going to stay that way, he decided grimly as they reached the top of the stairs and found themselves in a long wide hallway.

Half a dozen doorways broke the length of the empty, uncarpeted hall, three on either side of the staircase. Placing a hand beneath Tess's arm, Nicolas guided her to the second doorway on the left of the staircase. After pushing open the door, he motioned her to enter.

It was a very large room in which Tess found herself. Much like the main room downstairs, a commanding stone fireplace, newly swept and laid with kindling, graced one wall, and a row of leaded square-paned windows, broken in the middle by a pair of French doors, took up nearly the entire length of the other—she suspected that the doors opened onto a small balcony that overlooked the rose garden she had spied earlier. The remaining two walls were of gleaming oak, and with the timbered ceiling, there was a rustic air about the room.

Stepping farther into the room, Tess noted another carpet on the floor, this one in shades of deep green and russet. A charming settee covered in pale yellow velvet and a small table had been set near the fireplace, a huge bed dominated the far wall, the feather mattress heaped untidily in the center of it, a pile of linens sitting on top of that. Heavy gold-and-green silk bed hangings spilled carelessly over the arm of a large, comfortable chair that had been placed near the bed; beyond it against the wall was a delicate marble-topped washstand, a layer of dust marring its smooth finish. Obviously the Laidlaws hadn't finished in this room.

Tess kept her eyes studiously averted from the bed, too conscious of their remoteness from the others, too conscious of the warmth of his body as he stood just behind her. Was he going to demand that she share that bed with him tonight? she wondered uneasily. Perhaps even right now? Most important, would she be able to resist him if he took her into his arms and kissed her? Suddenly as frightened of herself as of him, she took a step away from him and cleared her throat nervously.

"It's, uh, very nice," she finally managed to say when the silence became nearly unbearable. Noting a doorway in one of the walls, she asked, "Where does that lead?"

"A dressing room," Nicolas replied, his own eyes lingering on the unmade bed, the image of her lying there naked leaping into his mind. "I doubt the Laidlaw women have had a chance to clean it properly yet, but if you'd like to look at it . . ."

"Oh no. There is no need," Tess said hurriedly. She cleared her throat again. "And the other rooms?"

Nicolas shrugged. "More bedrooms and dressing rooms, I suppose. Since I only gave Laidlaw orders to get a bedchamber and the main room ready for tonight, I imagine that they are dusty and unappealing. If you wish to see them, however . . ."

"Uh, no, that's fine. I, uh, just wondered . . ." Her voice trailed off, and she glanced at him uncertainly.

Her nervousness was palpable, and it was obvious that she was scared to death he was going to pounce upon her the first moment she let down her guard. Smothering a curse, Nicolas closed the distance that separated them and grasped her shoulders, giving her a brief shake. "I am not," he said curtly, "an unfeeling monster! I know you are frightened and exhausted right now, and I have no intention of forcing you to submit to me this very instant." His features softened, and he touched her cheek with one lean finger. "I can't deny that the idea of tossing you onto that pile of linens hasn't occurred to me, but I have no intention of forcing myself upon you!"

Shaking off some of her fears, Tess said tartly, "How can I be certain of what you say—you forced me to come with you!"

"Would you rather I'd left you behind to the tender mercies of the Darleys?" he asked scathingly, his black brows meeting in a thunderous scowl.

It was on the tip of Tess's tongue to shout, "Yes!" but prudence held her back. She didn't really want to have remained behind at the Black Pig, but she didn't really want to be his mistress, either. Besides, he thought she was a liar and was convinced that she had tried to trap him into marriage! How could she possibly find him appealing? Or want to be with him?

A thought suddenly occurred to her. Cocking her head slightly to one side, she asked boldly, "Aren't you frightened of my family? How do you think they're going to act when they discover what you have done?"

His eyes narrowed, and the idea that he would make a dangerous enemy crossed Tess's mind once again. "I'm quite certain," he began levelly, "that they are going to be very disappointed that their little scheme didn't work—or at least, didn't work the way they had planned it. I think, however, that my patronage, or a generous gift of money, will probably soothe their disappointments, once they realize that I will not be coerced into marrying you—no matter how much scandal they threaten to bring down on my head." He smiled without amusement. "You're ruined, my dear. You can either take what I offer or leave empty-handed, it matters not to me. As for your family—I'm confident that whatever their situation, they won't be foolish enough to want this affair to become public knowledge, and it they do . . ." His jaw hardened. "As I said, you're ruined, one way or another."

Tess's eyes blazed, and a rosy flush covered her cheeks. "You're vile!" she spat angrily, her rage at his words driving away the last of her fears.

Suddenly angry himself, Nicolas did what he had longed to do all morning. "Vile am I?" he growled, dragging her into his arms. "No more vile than you, my dear—at least I was honest about what I wanted! I didn't offer one thing and then demand another!" His mouth found hers, and he kissed her with passionate intensity, his lips warm and hungry against hers, his arms pulling her even tighter to him.

The touch of his demanding mouth on hers, the sensation of being enveloped in that powerful embrace, sent a wave of wild emotion surging through Tess. Incredibly, despite everything, she discovered that this was where she longed to be, wrapped in his arms, her body crushed against his. His lips were magic, his embrace heaven. Desire like sun-warmed honey flowed in her veins, weakening her resolve. Drugged by his nearness, by the swift, unfurling needs of her own body, she melted against him, her hands unknowingly clutching the lapels of his jacket to hold him near. For a moment the world spun away and there was just the two of them. . . .

With a gasp, Tess suddenly realized what she was doing and frantically began to struggle to get away from him. Jerking her mouth from the seductive pull of his, her hands curled into fists, she beat against his chest. "Let me go!" she panted, twisting in his arms. "Let me go!"

Breathing heavily, his eyes glazed with passion, Nicolas reluctantly loosed his hold on her. It took a second longer for him to recover control of himself; desire thrummed in his blood, and his manhood strained indecently against the confines of his breeches, the primitive urge to finish what had been started almost overpowering. He shook his head as if to clear the last vestiges of the powerful forces that dominated him. Grimly he looked across at Tess, who had retreated to stand behind the settee.

She faced him defiantly, her chin lifted, her eyes dark with emotion. "I never," she began shakily, just as if the passionate interlude had never occurred, "*demanded* that you marry me! That was all your idea!"

For a moment Nicolas looked nonplused. It was true that she had never broached the subject . . . but if it wasn't marriage she had been after, why the devil had she gone to such great lengths to share a bed with him? For just a second his conviction that she was after a marriage proposal faltered. Suppose her tale of lost memory . . .

With cold deliberation he shoved aside his unfinished thought. It was preposterous! Of course she was after marriage. She had to be, because to think otherwise . . .

His face shuttered. Nicolas regarded her somberly as she stood behind the settee, his greatcoat still hanging from her slender shoulders. She looked so young, so defenseless, so in need of protection against the evils of the world . . . something tightened in his chest, and he was aware of an unwanted feeling of tenderness for her.

"I'll have to see that you have some new clothes," he said abruptly, changing the subject. "There is a seamstress in the village—I'm sure that she can come up with something suitable until I can make other arrangements for your wardrobe."

Tess gaped at him. He was ignoring her! Pretending that she had not spoken! He thought she was a liar and a conniver, and when she tried to defend herself, he simply closed his mind to her words. Frustration welled up inside of her. So angry she could barely speak, she snapped, "Fine! Buy me clothes! Give me jewels and servants!" Her small bosom heaving, she glared at him. "I only hope you find that I'm worth it, because I promise you—you're going to rue the day you ever set eyes on me!"

Nicolas smiled faintly, his black eyes moving possessively over her slender form. "As long as you're in my bed,

I don't give a damn what sort of mischief you get up to, sweetheart!"

Sheer rage billowed up through Tess. The unmitigated arrogance of the man! Recklessly she shot back, "Well! At least we understand each other!"

Chapter Nine

Sleep came hard to Tess that night. Alone in that big bed, she stared sightlessly at the leaping shadows created by the low fire burning on the hearth, her thoughts going round and round in her head.

How could she have spoken so rashly? The minute the words had left her mouth, she'd known that her unruly tongue had gotten her into trouble once more—the satisfied smile on Sherbourne's face had only confirmed it.

But rage had ruled her, and though she had longed to call the words back, had sought frantically in her mind for some way to undo the damage her hot temper had done, plain old stubbornness and pride would not let her. She was not going to humiliate herself further!

Perhaps if Nicolas had attempted to consummate their relationship then and there, she might have been compelled to retreat, but almost as if he knew what she was going through, he had ushered her gently from the room and had spent the next several hours being utterly charming to her. Damn him!

He had been the perfect host. Making cleverly soothing conversation, he had escorted her down the stairs and given her a tour of the remainder of the house and the grounds—such as they were. The meeting with Sara in the kitchen had gone smoothly, and any concerns Tess might have had about being faced with a disapproving martinet faded the moment she laid eyes on Sara Laidlaw's plump little figure and pleasant face.

As the afternoon progressed, one thing had been made very clear to Tess—the Laidlaws adored the earl of Sherbourne, and it was depressingly obvious that they considered his word law. Whatever he wanted they would obtain. Period. And she wasn't quite positive how he had done it, but the point was subtly made that if she tried to escape . . . the Laidlaws would swiftly put an end to that sort of nonsense!

More than once that afternoon, as he had shown her about, she had wished passionately that he would drop his polite mask and do something that she could take issue with. Unfortunately, he did not. Nicolas either blandly ignored or simply changed the subject whenever she made any leading comments, and he played the solicitous host and guide to perfection.

In spite of the turmoil within her, she found the tour of the house and grounds fascinating. Ever solicitous, he had walked her through the remainder of the building, showing her the empty dining room, with its rich mahogany wainscoting; a delightful morning room; and the small room at the rear of the house that had probably been used as an office. The kitchen, the pantry, and the surprisingly spacious rooms where Thomas and Rose and Sara would be living were viewed last, and Tess had to admit—privately, of course—that once the place had been thoroughly cleaned and appropriately furnished, it would be quite comfortable and charming. A perfect love-nest, she thought with a bitter twist to her mouth.

A few roses were still blooming in the garden behind the house. Tess had been pleased to discover the remains of a once extensive herb garden, straggly lavender and pungent thyme and rosemary spilling over the half-buried stone walkways. There were other outbuildings, but by then the day was growing chilly and neither she nor Nicolas had seen the point of her viewing them.

They had eaten a light repast together in the main room of the house, propping their plates on their knees as they were served by Thomas. Then, as daylight had begun to fade, Nicolas had risen from his seat by the fire and bade her good-bye. Puzzlement apparent in her lovely eyes, Tess had watched him as he had called for Lovejoy and driven away.

She didn't understand him, she finally decided. He had abducted her and had made no bones about her position in his life, and yet . . . and yet, in his own fashion, even believing that she was determined to wring a marriage proposal out of him by any means possible, he had been kind to her.

But what was she to do? she thought despairingly for the tenth time since she had come to bed. Snuggling deeper into the soft, lavender-scented covers, listening to the mournful hoot of an owl, she admitted wryly that all things considered, she would much rather be here than at the Black Pig! But that aside, she also knew that Nicolas wasn't going to allow her to sleep in solitary splendor every night, that soon, mayhap even tomorrow, he would appear and make demands upon her, demands she wasn't sure she could resist. . . .

Tess twisted restlessly in the bed, closing her mind to the vividly erotic images that suddenly danced before her eyes. If only she knew who she was! And why she was so fearful of the man identified as Baron Mandeville. . . . Perhaps if she had those answers, she might be able to come to some conclusions about her relationship with the infuriatingly attractive earl of Sherbourne. And so it went: one moment chafing at the situation between herself and the earl; the next, wondering about her lost memory; and then once again back to the relationship between herself and the man with flashing dark eyes who seemed to have so effortlessly mesmerized her.

Nicolas found sleep equally elusive, but not for the same reasons that bedeviled Tess. He at least knew who he was, but after the evening he had just spent with his eldest sister, Athena, he wasn't so positive that family was such a great thing. He and Athena had never gotten along well, and now that he'd had the temerity to outlive her adored Randal and dared to inherit the title, well, it didn't help matters.

The decade between Athena's birth and his created a natural chasm between them, but their personalities were so different that it was unlikely, even had they been closer in age, that there would have been anything more than simmering conflict between them. Randal, the middle child, had acted as a much needed buffer between the two combative siblings. These days, however, without Randal's leavening influence, there were constant clashes between Nicolas and Athena. She had always resented not having been born a male, thinking it unfair that first Randal and now Nick had inherited all the Sherbourne wealth. While she had been resigned to Randal's assumption of their father's estates, it galled her that Nick now stood in that same position. And she wasn't quiet about it.

Thinking of her arrogant manners, Nicolas shook his head, not at all surprised that Athena had never married. What man alive would want to listen to that shrewish tongue for the rest of his life? He sighed. Unless something drastic happened, it looked as though he'd be the one who would have to put up with her for the rest of *his* life!

It wasn't a pleasant thought. Having dismissed Lovejoy earlier, when he had retired to his suite of rooms for the night, Nicolas slowly stripped off his cravat and absently tossed his jacket onto a chair. Perhaps he could find a husband for her, he mused. She'd be forty-two in less than a month and had long been considered on the shelf, but if he settled enough money on her . . . ?

She was still an attractive woman, he conceded reluctantly at the memory of how she had looked earlier when she had come sweeping regally down the stairs to greet him upon his arrival at Sherbourne Court, her low-cut, high-waisted apple green gown billowing out behind her. As tall as the average man, Athena was built on queenly lines—and had, as Nicolas would be the first to admit, all the imperiousness to go with it. "Handsome" better described her than "beautiful," and she had the thick black hair and large lustrous black eyes of the Talmages, as well as a slightly softened version of Nicolas's own nose and chin.

Not for the first time, Nicolas wondered why she had never married—in youth she would have been stunning, and that sharp tongue of hers, he thought acidly, wouldn't have been so razor honed. Certainly if she had married, she wouldn't now be *his* problem and the clashes between them wouldn't occur so frequently—clashes not even the normally calming presence of their grandmother could avert.

Thinking of his grandmother Pallas, Nick's hard face softened. She was, he decided fondly, probably the only member of his family whom he really loved—which was probably because she was the only member of the family who had ever expressed any deep affection for him. Not that his parents hadn't loved him; it was just that they had been busy with their own lives, and as the youngest son and not the heir, Nicolas had been viewed almost as an afterthought—or insurance, should something happen to Randal. . . .

His mouth twisted. Well, something *had* happened to Randal, and he wished to hell that Athena would just accept that fact and stop acting as if he had somehow planned Randal's untimely death. He shook his head. Randal would soon be dead almost a year, yet she still hadn't been able to bring herself to acknowledge that *he* was the earl of Sherbourne.

And if she doesn't stop sniping at me in front of Pallas, I am going to insist that she remove herself to the Dower House! A mirthless smile crossed Nicolas's face. Oh, and wouldn't she berate me unmercifully if I dared. For just a moment he let himself dwell on Athena's probable rage, but eventually he pushed it from his mind. It was his grandmother he wanted to think about—and the fact that he had not progressed very far in his quest for a bride.

After pouring himself a snifter of brandy from a crystal decanter, he settled himself on an overstuffed chair of red Cordovan leather. His booted feet stretched out before him, he sipped the amber-colored liquor, his thoughts drifting irresistibly back to last night and the sharing of a different decanter of brandy with a certain flame-haired little witch. . . .

With a jerk, he stopped his erotic wanderings and brought himself back to the matter at hand: his grandmother Pallas and her urgent desire to see him married before much more time elapsed.

His grandmother, he admitted slowly, was a most admirable woman. An arranged marriage at fifteen. Motherhood at sixteen. And left alone to face the thundering scandal that her husband and his grandfather Benedict had created when he had disappeared, along with the Sherbourne diamonds and the wife of their nearest neighbor!

But if Pallas was an admirable woman, she was also eighty-three years old and to him, at least, looking very frail and fragile. A knot formed in his chest. He didn't want his grandmother to die, and he especially didn't want to disappoint her by not providing her with the one thing she had ever asked of him—a wife and, in due course, an heir. And if she wanted him married and busy fathering another generation of Talmages, then by God, he was going to do it!

A rueful expression crossed his handsome face. Just as soon as he found *precisely* the right bride. To his intense annoyance, a piquant face with great lavender eyes and glinting red curls flashed before him, but he deliberately pushed aside the errant thought. The Dollys of the world made excellent mistresses, not wives!

But his grandmother wanted him married, and while not enthusiastic about it, he was committed to obliging her. He understood the need for an heir. He was the last of his line—if something unforeseen were to happen to him, there would be no more earls of Sherbourne Court. His dark head resting against the fine leather of his chair, he sipped his brandy and considered the future.

Since inheriting the title, Nicolas couldn't deny that he looked at his home differently, took a deeper pride in it, and was very aware that the weight of responsibility for everyone within its environs rested upon his shoulders. Not only the court itself, but the farms and village also looked to him for their well-being, and he had discovered within himself a strong desire to see that his lands were prosperous and his people comfortable, and that they knew they had nothing to fear from him—that he had only their good at heart.

He grimaced. This was one of the reasons he concurred with his grandmother's desire for an heir. Everyone needed to know that the line would continue, that their futures were secure. Lord knew, he thought sardonically, if things were left in Athena's hands, which could happen if something untoward were to happen to him, she would depart gleefully for London and proceed to bleed the estate dry until the day she died. She and Randal both had had a decided penchant for the gaming tables and all manner of games of chance, and while the Sherbourne fortune was immense, it wasn't inexhaustible. If the pair of them had continued their costly ways, the next generation might have found themselves with little to inherit—beyond debts.

It was Athena's gambling debts that had precipitated an argument between them tonight. Dinner had just been finished, and not particularly inclined to drink his port in solitary pomp, Nicolas had immediately joined the two ladies in the blue salon—his grandmother's favorite room.

Pallas had been pleased by his actions. Seating himself upon a delicate Louis Quinze chair in pale blue-striped satin, he had settled back to enjoy the remainder of the evening. His grandmother had been presiding over the pouring of tea from her position on a matching settee, and as he had sat down, they had exchanged affectionate looks.

Her blue eyes gleaming with amusement, Pallas had said, "Not fond of your own company?"

Nicolas had smiled. "Not when I can be with you."

The countess of Sherbourne was a tiny woman, her once fair hair now silver, her soft pink-and-white complexion glowing; but the signs of her eighty-three years were obvious. Nicolas knew that she tired easily these days and that she no longer rose at first light as she had years ago. Staring at the thin, blue-veined hands as she offered him a cup of tea, he was suddenly conscious of how quickly she could be taken from him.

Concern in his eyes, he asked lightly, "All is well with you, sweetheart?"

"Oh, my, yes!" A limpid glance met his. "Especially since you are here."

Athena was seated on a chair across from them, near the flames that burned brightly in the gray marble-fronted fireplace, and at Pallas's words, an unladylike snort came from her. "Oh, Grandmother!" she said disgustedly. "Don't toady to him! He is full enough of himself as it is—he likes lording it over the rest of us that he is the *earl* of Sherbourne!"

Nicolas's eyes narrowed, and he glanced at her. "Really?" he drawled. "Considering I wasn't reared for the job, I thought I was handling myself rather circumspectly. Do you have some complaint?" It was the wrong thing to say.

"You know I do!" Athena returned hotly. "God! If only I'd been born a man, *I'd* be the earl! And then I wouldn't have to try to live on that paltry allowance you give me."

Nicolas sighed. "If you wouldn't gamble so recklessly, you'd find it ample. And it's not paltry, nor was I the one who decided upon the amount—it was Randal, if you remember. I merely continued his wishes—if you'll remember, when we discussed this some months ago, you told me that it was sufficient for your needs."

"But Randal," she said from between gritted teeth, "always gave me advances when I found myself in dun territory! He never would have told me to return to Sherbourne if I had found my pockets to let!"

"You were coming home within the month—and having seen how you spent your funds, I didn't see any reason to advance you more money so that you could throw it away on the gaming tables—or *another* pair of slippers with diamond-studded heels!"

Athena surged to her feet, her hands curled in fists at her sides. "I pity your poor wife—if you're fortunate enough to find some pathetic creature who is willing to put up with your despotic ways! I wish to God that it had been you who had died in that bloody duel and not Randal!"

"Oh, Athena, dear," began Pallas unhappily, "you don't really mean that!"

"Don't I?" she ground out, and swept furiously from the room.

Nicolas and his grandmother exchanged glances. Pallas's eyes were full of distress. "You'd think, after all these years, she'd have learned to control that temper of hers. And I'm sure she didn't really mean those awful things. You know Athena—she always speaks before she thinks. You mustn't let her words hurt you, Nicolas dear."

Nicolas smiled and gently held one of her hands in his. "I don't, Grandmother, and I know it's hard for her—she and Randal were very close, and he *did* indulge her shamelessly."

"You, ah, couldn't bring yourself to do the same?" Pallas asked hopefully.

"If it will make you happy, I'll talk to Robertson about increasing her quarterly allowances enough to keep peace in the family."

"Oh, you don't have to do it for me—but for Athena . . . and perhaps, for a better understanding between the two of you?"

Nicolas sighed. "For all of us."

Pallas smiled warmly at him. "You won't be sorry, and I hope that someday you come to appreciate your sister. She can be exasperating, but she really isn't as arrogant and sharp tongued as she appears—winter before last, when I was so ill with that terrible racking cough, it hung on for *months,* she hardly ever left my side and was so good and considerate of me—the two of you just seem to bring out the worst in the other."

"If you say so," Nicolas replied dryly.

"I do." Her blue eyes twinkled at him over the rim of her cup. After taking a sip of tea, she set down her cup and said forthrightly, "And now, please tell me why you have returned home so unexpectedly. I thought you were going to stay in London until the end of the 'little' season . . . or until you had found . . . ?"

Nicolas's mouth twisted wryly. Now what the hell was he to tell her? He could hardly say that it had been his growing uneasiness that he might weaken and find himself offering for the hand of Lady Maryanne Halliwell that had brought him home so precipitously. The whole purpose of going to London had been to find a bride. And as for the conversation he'd had with the duke of Roxbury . . . No, the fewer people who knew about that aspect of his return to Sherbourne Court, the better.

Her head cocked to one side, Pallas regarded him thoughtfully. "It wouldn't have anything to do with that dreadful Maryanne person, would it?"

Nicolas jumped as if stabbed. "How did you know about her?" he asked before he had time to think.

Pallas smiled. "Darling, you know there are no secrets in a household like ours—the servants know everything. When you first met her years ago, Lovejoy wrote to his uncle Bellingham about it, and Bellingham mentioned it in passing to my dresser, Simpson, who told me that there had been a young lady who had caught your eye. It was only later that we learned she'd had the very bad taste to choose someone older and richer. From several of my friends who go out in society more than I do, I know she's a widow now and very beautiful. . . . Is she throwing out lures to you?"

"You are," Nicolas said, half dismayed, half amused, "an absolute witch! Can I keep nothing secret from you?"

His grandmother chuckled and, after taking another sip of her tea, murmured, "Oh, I expect that if there was something that you especially didn't want me to know about, I would have a very difficult time discovering it." A gleam in her faded blue eyes, she added, "Of course, you'd have to be very clever about hiding it from me!"

Nicolas snorted. "Damned clever! But to answer your question, yes, I suppose it was because of Maryanne that I left London so unexpectedly." He shot her a keen look. "She'd be willing to marry me now, you know. . . ."

"Really, dear? But of course she won't do, will she? After all, she had her chance and she threw it away." Pallas's little nose wrinkled with distaste. "We Talmages do not settle for secondhand goods—unless your heart is set upon her. Then I would suppose that we would just have to make do!"

Putting down his cup and saucer, Nicolas said moodily, "My heart isn't set on her, but I'm afraid that finding a bride is not quite as easy as I thought it would be."

"Well, naturally not! You're not buying a brood mare for your stables, you know. You're looking for a wife. Someone who will be the mother of your children and someone with whom you will share the rest of your life." His grandmother leaned forward intently. "I know that you want to please me, and it is vital that you marry soon, but Nicolas," she said softly, "you must also please yourself. That is paramount. You will live with this woman, hopefully, for many years after I am moldering in my grave." Her face became pensive. "Don't be in such a rush that you make a dreadful mistake. . . ."

"As you did?" he asked quietly.

Pallas looked dismayed, and she knew exactly what he was referring to. "Oh, no, my dear!" she said passionately. "I never thought marrying your grandfather was a mistake!"

It was not a subject that had been discussed between them—his grandfather's name was seldom mentioned and then usually in scandalous tones—but it suddenly dawned on Nicolas that he had never heard Pallas ever speak ill of her husband. "You don't blame him for leaving you? For treating you in such a shameful manner?" he asked incredulously.

A soft light entered her eyes, and she glanced over at the huge painting that dominated one wall of the room. "No," she said huskily, "I've never blamed him. I loved him, respected him, and pitied him more than I can ever say. . . ."

His curiosity aroused, Nicolas stood and walked over to stand in front of the oil painting. "You made a handsome couple," he said neutrally as he stared at the picture.

The portrait of his grandparents had been painted when they had been married for only six months, and there was such a glow on Pallas's young face, such open love for her tall, commanding husband at her side, that it hurt Nicolas every time he looked at it. Pallas had been painted seated in this very room, grandly garbed in a ball gown of pale blue silk and fairly dripping with all of the famous Sherbourne diamonds—the tiara, the earrings, the necklace, the brooch, the bracelet, and the stunning ring that had comprised the largest diamond Nicolas had ever seen—diamonds that had disappeared along with her husband.

Wresting his gaze from that ring, Nicolas studied his grandfather's face—a face startlingly similar to his own. It was a proud face, arrogant even, the thick black hair brushed back from his noble brow, the Spanish black eyes gleaming with a hint of humor, the chin determined, and the long, mobile mouth curved with a faint cynicism. It wasn't, Nicolas admitted slowly, on the surface, the face of a man who would steal another man's wife, carelessly abandoning his own wife and newborn son in the process. In the portrait, Benedict's hand lay possessively along the back of the chair on which Pallas had sat, and his other hand rested suggestively on the sword that hung at his side. Nicolas had the curious conviction that those two simple gestures told a great deal about his grandfather, that they were not mere poses. Everything about him stated clearly that this was a man who took care of his own.

"I always thought that you must have hated him," he said slowly as he turned and walked back to his chair.

Pallas shook her white head. "Never. He was good to me,

Nicolas. Kind. Considerate." She looked off, her eyes seeing things that he could not. "I was so young. And so in love with him—I still am. I knew the whole, horrid tale of the broken betrothal and Gregory's dastardly abduction of Theresa, but I was so certain . . ." Her mouth twisted ruefully. "I was so certain that I could make Benedict love me, that I could drive out Theresa's image from his heart. . . ." She smiled faintly. "I couldn't, of course. The bond between them was too strong. It wasn't their fault that they loved each other so desperately, and I couldn't even hate him for marrying me while loving her—after all, he did need an heir. And though I know that she had all his love, in his manner with me, he never once let me know that his heart was elsewhere, never once gave the smallest sign that he had married me only because circumstances had decreed that the line must be carried on. He always treated me with respect and consideration—something few wives of my generation can claim about their husbands!"

His gaze thoughtful, Nicolas asked abruptly, "What do you think happened to them? From what I've heard, it was as if they vanished off the face of the earth."

Pallas shrugged, but there was a flicker of pain in her eyes, and Nicolas marveled that after all these years, an event that had taken place over sixty-five years ago could arouse such deep emotion. "I don't know. In my kinder moments, I like to think that they managed to make it to the Colonies and that they have had a long and fulfilling life together." She bent her head and admitted fiercely, "Other times, I hope that they had a long, *miserable* life together, that his beloved Theresa turned out to be a carroty-topped, purple-eyed shrew!"

Nicolas laughed, and they exchanged a glance of amusement. Thinking they had spoken long enough of the painful past, he said lightly, "Well, enough of ancient history for tonight. Now tell me what has been happening since I was last home."

They conversed idly for several moments as Pallas brought him up-to-date on local happenings and life at Sherbourne

Court. Leaning comfortably back on his chair, Nicolas let her gentle chatter wash over him. But then she said something that made him sit up and pay attention.

"Old Squire Frampton is dead? I thought the old devil was so stubborn and irascible that he wouldn't *let* himself die!"

"Hmm, yes, I know—I thought so, too," Pallas replied. "But he did finally die, oh, I guess about three years ago. His oldest son, John, is now the squire. Do you remember him?"

Nicolas shook his head. "Not very well. He's a few years older than I am, isn't he?"

"Yes, I think he's about thirty-nine. . . . He and your sister sometimes seem uncommonly friendly."

"Oh?"

"Well, it probably doesn't mean very much, and I really must say that I don't care much for his friends—raffish-looking fellows who are strangers to the area. There have been quite a few stories of some strange doings at the Hall these days." An expression of displeasure on her face, she added, "I understand that for a lark they like to join the 'owlers' upon occasion, helping them move their goods. Apparently tweaking the noses of the dragoons is considered great fun. The old squire would never have countenanced such goings-on!"

Nicolas sat up straighter on his chair. Frampton Hall was located at the edge of Romney Marsh, and the smugglers headquartered in that area had long been referred to as "owlers" by the local inhabitants. With Roxbury's request uppermost in his mind, he found it most interesting that the new squire, even if just for amusement, was helping the smugglers—especially those "raffish" friends of his. . . .

"Have the smugglers increased their activities these days?" Nicolas asked with deceptive idleness.

Pallas fluttered her lashes at him. "Now how would I know about such illegal goings-on?"

"Because," he returned with a laugh, "there is very little that occurs within fifty miles of here that you *don't* know about!"

She smiled. "Perhaps, but I don't want to talk about those nasty owlers! Let me tell you about some of the newcomers to the neighborhood." She looked very sly. "And their daughters. . . ."

Nicolas groaned. "Grandmother! I know I've promised to find a bride, but I had hoped for a brief respite from simpering damsels in clinging muslin!"

"Oh, pooh! Stop complaining—you'll like these young women, I'm certain. And while your happiness is uppermost in my mind, there is no need for you to be so fussy about your bride that no female alive will ever suit you!" When Nicolas merely grimaced, she smiled and went on, "First there is Lord Spencer—a most delightful man—do you remember his cousin?" As Nicolas shook his head, she continued, "Well, he inherited the title and estate from his cousin about four years ago, and he and his family, two daughters and a son, live there very quietly, nearly year round. They are not extremely wealthy, but they do own several farms in the marsh and they are very well connected. The daughters are both intrepid horsewomen and with the jolliest personalities." When Nicolas did not appear to be thrilled with this information, Pallas frowned at him.

"Nicolas, dear," she finally said, "I know this is hard for you, but you must *sincerely* try to find a wife. At least meet these girls and look them over. You might be agreeably surprised at what you will find right under your nose." Brightening, she said happily, "There is also Admiral Brownell's daughter—he retired a few years ago and they have settled in the old Caldwell house. You know, that odd place practically in the middle of the marsh—he's done some marvelous renovations with the house. Anyway, Jane is just turned eighteen, and she has the most charming manners—but of course, being the baby of her family, she *is* a little spoiled. There are a couple of older sons, too—you might enjoy their company." Pallas hesitated. "Although," she admitted reluctantly, "the oldest son, Robert, is considered somewhat wild, and, I be-

lieve, much to his father's dismay, sometimes joins John
Frampton and his friends in their smuggling escapades." She
smiled angelically at him. "Now that you're here, perhaps
you'll be a good influence on the men in the neighborhood."

Recalling that conversation and the look of hopeful expectancy upon his grandmother's face, as he sipped his
brandy in his rooms, Nicolas grimaced. Good God! If he had
known what awaited him at Sherbourne Court, he would have
certainly thought twice about leaving London. But then,
thinking of the slender charms of the flame-haired occupant
of the old gatekeeper's cottage, he smiled. Perhaps it wouldn't
be too bad fending off a trio of simpering damsels and playing nursemaid to a group of hell-born rapscallions, if it meant
he could have Dolly, or whatever she called herself, in his
arms. . . .

Chapter Ten

———◆◆———

*T*ess woke with a start, her heart thudding painfully. As the remnants of the disturbing dream faded from her mind, she stared around her blankly, the unfamiliar surroundings making her heart pound even faster; but then, as she recognized the room where she lay, her breathing evened and she grimaced. The dream had been confusing and frightening, but not nearly as terrifying as waking and discovering that her memory still had not returned.

She went to bed each night with the childlike hope that the next morning she would wake and find that she had regained her memory. So far that hope had not been fulfilled, and to her growing dismay, she could still recall nothing of herself beyond the moment she had awakened lying in a sodden riding habit beneath the oak tree. It was as if her life began in those first seconds of consciousness—and no dream could be any more frightening.

But it had been an odd dream, she thought as she lay there in the lavender-scented bedclothes. The dream had been fragmented and was even now fuzzy in her mind, yet she could recall clearly the common thread that had run through it—urgency, the sensation that she must escape, the certainty that she had been running away from something. Vaguely she remembered that there had been two women in the dream—

one had been white-haired, the other a sweet-faced woman well past her youth—but beyond that she could remember little about them, other than the fact that she had sensed they were extremely important to her, that they were, perhaps, the reason for her continued feeling of urgency.

Though the hour was early, Tess knew that she would sleep no more. Reluctantly she left the warmth of the bed. Remembering that a pitcher of water and a china bowl had been provided for her and left in the adjacent dressing room last night, she headed in that direction. After she had completed a hasty wash in the chilly water in the barren dressing room, she scuttled back into the main room to the fireplace and poked the dying embers into flames, throwing on a few pieces of wood to make a toasty fire. A brush and comb had also been provided, and seated on a small rug before the fire, she began to brush her hair in long, soothing strokes, her mind on the dream and what it might mean to her.

It was all jumbled and made no sense, but she was convinced that it held the answer to her memory loss—or at least the events leading up to her loss of memory. Her gaze far away, she tried to remember every detail about the dream that she could. There wasn't much. The two women; a long, dark gallery; spooky booms of thunder and great slashes of lightning against a black sky. A frantic ride through a storm; a looming, ominous figure and the Baron Mandeville. . . .

She frowned, her hand stilling its rhythmic motions. Why had just that brief sighting of Mandeville caused such a violent reaction within her yesterday? Did she know him? Or did he simply remind her of someone she feared? And why had he been in her dreams? Was he somehow mixed up in her past? She shuddered. She hoped not. There had been something about that coldly handsome face that even now caused a feeling of deep unease within her. He frightened her, yet . . . yet she was conscious of a great anger, a rage that burned in her breast whenever she thought of him.

The rattle of crockery caught her attention, and a moment

later the door was opened cautiously and Jenny peeked her head around its solid bulk. Her eyes widened when she spied Tess sitting on the floor, and she cried with dismay, "Oh, miss! I know it's very early, but I thought I'd just sneak in and leave you some nice hot tea and some fresh-baked buns to have when you woke—and here you are already up!" Worry on her face, she asked, "Wasn't the bed comfortable? The master won't be best pleased if you don't have everything you want. He made that very clear before he left last night." She beamed at her. "He's very taken with you!"

Under Jenny's interested stare, Tess could feel a hot blush staining her cheeks. Since awakening this morning, she had been caught up with thinking about her disjointed dream, but it was true that she had deliberately *not* thought about her invidious position and in particular the man who had placed her in it—the arrogant earl of Sherbourne! Deciding to ignore any reference to the earl, she muttered, "That's very nice of you, and some tea would be wonderful."

Jenny smiled at her. Setting the heavily laden tray on one of the tables near the fire, she said, "I'll go get your gown—Mum did her best with it, and it should do nicely until the master can see about getting you some nice things." Sympathy apparent in her eyes, she added, "It certainly was awful that your coach overturned and all your things were trampled and muddy. I think it's just terrible that you lost everything and had to borrow an old gown from an innkeeper's wife to have anything to wear!" At Tess's astonished expression, Jenny said kindly, "The earl explained everything to Mum yesterday. I thought it was just so exciting—I mean, your running away from a wicked stepfather and then your coach overturning and the earl rescuing you and all. And to think he was so struck by you that he immediately brought you here. So romantic!"

Tess nearly choked on the cup of tea she had helped herself to and wondered darkly if the earl had any more romantic tales with which to regale the servants. "Er, yes, it was, ah, quite adventuresome," she said weakly.

Jenny beamed at her once more and then, promising to return shortly with the refurbished gown, bustled from the room. Tess watched her go, her thoughts of the earl not kind. A wicked stepfather! An overturned coach! She supposed she should be grateful that he hadn't claimed she was an actress! But how, the unpleasant thought suddenly occurred to her, did she know she *wasn't* an actress?

I'm not an actress, she insisted stubbornly to herself. I'd feel differently, if I were, I know I would. Her lips tightened. And I certainly wouldn't have been a virgin!

While not wanting to give herself airs, Tess was becoming more and more convinced that she was one of those fortunate members of the upper class. It wasn't that she felt superior to anyone, it was just little things—her easy acceptance of servants: her instinctive knowledge of the proper knife and fork; even the ability to recognize fine things and her innate expectation of a degree of comfort. She was more and more convinced that she wasn't a farmer's or shopkeeper's daughter any more than she was an actress or a tavern maid. Or, she thought bitterly, a whore. Nor did she believe that her role in life was the one a certain black-eyed earl had selected for her. But *who* was she?

By the time Jenny had returned with the pink gown and Tess had shooed her away and dressed and braided her hair on her own, she still didn't have any answers. Sighing, she wandered about the room, stopping now and then to gaze out the lead-paned windows. The sunshine of yesterday was a thing of the past—it was raining again, and the day was not inviting. As a matter of fact, staring out at the damp view—the wet, fading rose garden, the dripping foliage, and the occasional glimpse of the great Romney Marsh through breaks in the trees—Tess decided that her mood fit the weather: bleak and not very inviting.

It was still very early in the day. Deciding to sample a second cup of tea and enjoy another one of the plump currant-filled buns, she settled herself once more before the fire. At least, she reminded herself gloomily, she was warm and dry and fed. She supposed she should be grateful, but the notion lingered that she was going to pay a high price, had *already* paid a high price for such common comforts.

How long Tess sat there, sipping her tea, eating her bun, and staring blankly at the fire, she didn't know. It was some time, she knew. Her unhappy thoughts had not brought her to any conclusions, but gradually, as the minutes passed, almost imperceptibly she became conscious of a disturbingly odd feeling. A prickling sensation was sliding down her spine, an awareness that she couldn't explain. She had the feeling that she was no longer alone, that someone else was in the room with her. She looked quickly around, but she was alone; no one had entered to disturb her solitude. . . . Yet the feeling persisted, growing stronger, and as she stared about her, she suddenly had the curious impression that she had been here before—frequently. That she *recognized* this room. Recognized the intricate arrangement of the timbered ceiling; the peculiar-shaped pane in the left-hand corner of one of the windows that overlooked the rose garden; the rough-edged stone just below the mantel in the middle of the fireplace. . . . It was the same sort of compelling recognition that she had felt when she had first laid eyes on the earl of Sherbourne at the Black Pig. The more she stared, the more familiar the room became, even the bed and its faded silk hangings—only in her mind's eye the fabric was newer, the colors were brighter, and the bed was placed in a different position from where it currently sat. With paralyzing certainty she knew that this was not the first time she had stayed here.

It was unsettling, and she sprang to her feet and then laughed nervously at herself. What was the matter with her? One would think that she was being haunted by ghosts or some such sort of nonsense! It was ridiculous!

She might be able to dismiss her thoughts as lively imagination, but overcome with the need for human company, she fairly bolted from the room. Only when she stepped into the wide hall downstairs was she able to stop her headlong rush and walk into the main room of the cottage with any amount of decorum.

A fire had been lit in anticipation of her arrival. Feeling the need for its warmth, Tess hurried over to stand in front of it. She could hear Rose and Jenny laughing in the next room as they went about cleaning the cottage, and in spite of the rain, it appeared that another wagonload of furniture had arrived from the earl's seemingly cavernous storerooms. The double doors of the house banged open, and she heard Tom and John muttering and swearing as they maneuvered a huge, blanket-covered table into the room in which she stood.

Catching sight of her, Tom flushed and muttered, "Miss! We do apologize—Mum would have our ears if she knew that we had used such language in front of you. We had no idea you had come downstairs."

Tess smiled at their anxious faces and said, "That's quite all right—if I had to struggle with the load you're carrying, I'm sure that I might forget myself and say something equally as, er, earthy!"

Rose and Jenny had been drawn by their conversation, and spying Tess standing by the fire, they both bobbed a quick curtsy. "Would you like some more tea or buns?" Jenny asked. "Or, if you'd like, Mum will cook you up a rasher or two of bacon and some fine country eggs."

"No, no, I'm fine," Tess replied with an easy smile. "Just continue what you were doing."

The quartet took her at her word. Rose and Jenny disappeared immediately, and the two men continued to haul the unwieldy table toward its destination. Tess found herself following in their wake, as much because she wanted to see what they were doing as from a need *not* to be alone and beset with silly notions! Hauntings and ghosts indeed!

During the morning impressive progress had been made in the dining room. Despite the weather, the windows glistened and the room was taking on an appealing appearance of which

Tess approved. A grand, old-fashioned crystal chandelier had been hung in the center of the room; heavy velvet drapes had also been hung, the color softened with age to a warm, rich, pale burgundy; and an Aubusson carpet in cream and burgundy lay on the polished oak floor. The table the men had been carrying was lowered gently into place beneath the chandelier, and when the blankets were removed, Tess gazed with admiration upon its fine mahogany finish and Baroque style.

With time on her hands and not wishing to dwell on her situation, she spent most of the remainder of the morning busily supervising the unloading and placement of the furniture throughout the cottage. By the time the last object had been brought inside, and there seemed an enormous amount of them, the place had begun to take on a charmingly comfortable air: deeply hued draperies hung at the windows; vibrant oil paintings were on the walls; and exquisite odds and ends were scattered about the cottage. Many of the pieces were old, but all were of excellent workmanship and in beautiful condition. Looking around her, Tess decided that *if* she really were the sort of woman to become the mistress of an earl, she would be very pleased with the setting that had been provided for her.

Around two o'clock in the afternoon she ate a light repast at a small table that had been placed near one of the large windows in the main salon—having decided that the dining room was far too grand and spacious for a simple meal—or a lone diner. When she'd finished, she pushed aside the remains of her meal and, sipping a cup of hot tea, stared out at the rainy day, her thoughts drifting irresistibly to the earl.

By keeping occupied, she had managed to keep at bay all the thorny dilemmas that beset her, but now, with the rain beating softly against the panes, the fire crackling pleasantly on the hearth, she knew that she could put it off no longer. When he arrived, as he was certain to do, how was she to greet him—politely? frigidly? angrily? indifferently? She grimaced, not liking any of the choices.

If only I knew who I was, she thought despondently. She was faced with decisions any decent woman would find difficult, but knowing nothing about herself made her task even more formidable. What if, she wondered, plainly horrified, it turned out that she was the daughter of some country vicar? Or the cosseted daughter of some powerful lord? Or a great heiress? Suppose she were betrothed? Or had been a novitiate in a nunnery? She giggled at that idea, then sobered—the problem was, she could be any of those things! And that stubborn, obstinate, *infuriating* gentleman who had brought her here, didn't believe her story of lost memory!

It would serve him right, she thought darkly, if I did turn out to be a great heiress from a powerful family. Tess amused herself for several minutes as she contemplated the thunderstruck expression on the earl's face if such should prove to be the case.

The sound of a vehicle and horses caught her attention, and as if she had conjured him up, Nicolas's equipage swung into view and a second later he had tossed his reins to John, who had run to greet him, and was quickly crossing to the house. Her mouth suddenly dry, her fingers trembling slightly, she stood and faced the entrance to the room.

Her hands clasped tightly in front of her to hide their tremors, she greeted him with outward calm. "Good afternoon, my lord. Rather a beastly day, isn't it?"

Tossing aside his dripping greatcoat and curly-brimmed beaver hat, Nicolas grinned at her, his teeth flashing whitely in his dark face. "I've been in far worse with far less comfort." He glanced around, noticing the additions. "Good! I see that the rest of the furnishings arrived—I had wondered if the rain wouldn't cause a delay. Is everything satisfactory?"

"It's very comfortable," Tess replied stiffly, wishing he didn't look so vital and handsome as he stood there in a form-fitting russet jacket and buckskin breeches, the fabric molding itself lovingly to his muscled thighs. She tried to remember all the reasons why she was supposed to view him with loathing, but her wretched brain seemed to have gone fuzzy. All she could do was stare at him and remember his mouth moving hungrily on hers and the feel of that warm, hard body pressed intimately against her own. . . .

Nicolas cocked an eyebrow at her tone and rigid stance and strolled over to her, tipping up her chin. His thumb rubbing rhythmically against her bottom lip, he asked lightly, "Miss me, sweetheart?"

With an effort, Tess kept herself from jerking her chin away from his disturbing touch. "Of course not! I had other more important things to do than think about you!"

"Hmm, is that so?" he murmured, bending closer. "Obviously I arrived not a moment too soon. . . ."

His hands shifted, and Tess suddenly found herself swept into an embrace, that fascinating mouth capturing hers, his arms cradling her next to him as he kissed her thoroughly. Despite her best intentions, she couldn't help responding to him, her fingers curling in his thick black hair, her slim body leaning into his as the surprisingly familiar ache flared into life low in her belly. Her mouth softened, and Nicolas muttered a thick sound as his hands slipped to her buttocks and tightened around the yielding flesh he found there, pulling her against the rapidly rising bulge in his breeches.

Giddy with the emotions flooding her body, Tess welcomed his liberties; no thought of resisting him crossed her mind as her lips parted and his tongue surged into the honeyed warmth of her mouth. She shuddered as stronger, more powerful sensations began to wreak havoc with whatever frail barriers she had managed to erect against him. To her despair, she realized she *had* missed him . . . immensely; that she had been only half alive since he had left her last evening; that she had been unconsciously longing for his return. Dimly she was also aware that she had already made her decisions about him—

had made them that first, almost mystical moment she had laid eyes on him. . . .

It was Nicolas who broke the kiss, pushing her away from him, his expression dark and stormy as he stared down into her face. "How do you do that?" he asked roughly, desire clearly evident in the glitter in his eyes. "I had no intention of kissing you, certainly no intention of tipping you over that damned table and easing myself between those soft white thighs of yours! Yet all I had to do was look at you and that's exactly what I want to do! What are you? A witch?"

Still shaken by the fierce emotions he had aroused so easily within her, Tess trembled violently, trying desperately to regain some semblance of normality. Nicolas mistook her reaction, and with a muttered curse, he swept her up in his arms and swiftly carried her to a long, low sofa. His lips brushing against her ear, he murmured, "Sweetheart! I didn't mean to frighten you—I know I haven't given you any choice about this, but I'm not a monster. You don't have to fear me—*never* be afraid of me." He smiled crookedly at her. "Not even when I'm in the devil's own temper—which I suspect will be often enough where you are concerned."

He laid her gently on the sofa, seated himself on the edge, and took one of her hands in his. Pressing a light kiss on her fingers, he said, "I know I've handled this badly. . . ." He grinned at her ruefully. "I've done some rash things before, but I've never abducted anyone in my life. And to my ever-lasting damnation, I find that I do not feel the least remorse about it! But I will not harm you, and while I seem unable to keep my hands off of you, rape is something that you do not have to fear from me."

Tess regarded him with wide violet eyes, a funny little ache in her chest. He was so handsome, so oddly dear, as he stared down at her, his features intent and concerned, a lock of black hair falling rakishly across his brow. It was so unfair, she thought miserably. She was supposed to hate him, yet he had only to touch her and, to her shame, she melted spinelessly into his arms. It would certainly make her task easier, she decided blackly, if he'd act the brute instead of treating her with kindness.

She took a deep, steadying breath and casually took her hand from his, deciding to test the strength of his words. "Does this mean that if I say I don't want to be your mistress, you'll let me go?"

Nicolas grimaced and looked uncomfortable. "Not exactly," he admitted reluctantly.

Her eyes sparkled warningly. "Then what exactly *do* you mean?"

Nicolas ran a caressing finger down her cheek. His eyes locked on hers, he said, "It means that I will not *force* myself upon you, but that I maintain the right to keep you safe and in my keeping."

"You're not going to make love to me anymore?" Tess blurted out incredulously, alarmed and ashamed at the feeling of disappointment that swept through her.

A sensual curve to his full lower lip, Nicolas replied huskily, "I didn't say that—I said I wouldn't force you, and I have enough confidence in my own ability to make you welcome—nay, eager—for my lovemaking."

"Do you really?" Tess asked icily, scooting away from him and sitting bolt upright on the sofa, an angry flush staining her cheeks.

A watchful expression in his black eyes, he slowly nodded. "Yes, I do—the night we spent together at the Black Pig, as well as the kiss we just shared, only proved my point—you might pretend not to want me, you *say* you don't want me, but you forget that I've tasted all that sweet passion of yours. I can remember quite vividly the way you *willingly* gave yourself to me not two nights ago."

"Only after you plied me with brandy!" she replied hotly. "I was exhausted and confused, and you took base advantage of me! You know you did!"

A muscle jumped along his jaw. "Shall I prove the lie of

your own words?" he demanded. "You're not exhausted now, and I doubt very much that you can claim to have been at the brandy decanter at this hour of the day."

"That has nothing to do with it!" she shot back desperately, gallingly aware that he had only to touch her to make her forget all her rational resolutions.

"Doesn't it?" he replied grimly, reaching for her, his hands closing firmly around her shoulders. Despite her efforts to avoid him, he pulled her across his lap, and with her clenched fists jammed between their bodies, he held her against his broad chest.

Tess guessed that he was *very* angry, that her words had pricked his pride, cast aspersions on his manhood, and she tensed. Expecting the harsh assault of his mouth on hers, she was prepared to resist with all her might, but to her astonishment and despair, his lips, when they found hers, were gentle, deliberately coaxing a response from her. She held herself stiffly, trying not to react, but at the touch of his mouth applying teasing pressure against her lips, her senses seemed to explode within her, her breasts tingling, her unruly body responding wildly to him.

He didn't rush things, just held her and took his time kissing her, his teeth nibbling seductively at her tightly held lips. The hands that had held her prisoner now caressed her neck and spine. Tess could feel herself weakening, could feel the tension draining from her body, could feel herself leaning into him, her lips half clinging to his. She was hardly aware of his hand traveling to her breast, and when he lightly cupped her there, she gave a muffled groan of hopelessness.

Nicolas's head lifted. "Will it help," he said thickly, "if I confess that I have no control where you are concerned—that I have only to touch you and I cannot think of anything but how sweet you taste, the pleasure it will give me to sink deep within you and hear your own joyful cries of release?"

Tess had no answer for him, but he must have read something revealing in her expression, for without another word he swung her up in his arms and carried her toward the stairs. As he ascended the staircase, her traitorous body made no effort to escape from him; her thoughts were foggy and unclear, desire thick and compelling eddying in her veins.

Never hesitating in his destination, he kicked open the door to her room and with his shoulder slammed it shut behind them. Then and only then did he release her, letting her soft form slide down his body, his hands guiding her gently. As her feet grazed the floor, he pulled her hard against him, his mouth finding hers.

There was nothing gentle about the kiss that he gave her—it was an aroused male kiss, his lips urgent and demanding, his tongue hot and bold as he took what he wanted. Tess denied him nothing; her mouth opened to allow him to plunder where he would, her arms clung to his neck, her body strained eagerly against the rigid flesh between his thighs.

When finally he lifted his head, they were both breathing hard, and Tess knew that her eyes glistened with the same dark passion she saw in his, that her cheeks were as flushed as his, and that they shared the same driving need. She wanted him—it was that simple and that complicated. . . .

His hands on her waist, he backed her into the center of the room, those mesmerizing black eyes never moving from her face. After releasing her, his gaze still locked on hers, he slowly, deliberately, tore apart the neat, intricate folds of his cravat and tossed the crumpled linen to the floor. His jacket went next and then his boots. With his shirt half undone, he pulled her unresisting form into his arms once more.

Hating him and herself as well, Tess went blindly into his embrace, her mouth lifting obediently for the hungry possession of his. He kissed her passionately, and as her lips parted easily for him, his arms tightened painfully around her and a shudder went through him.

He gave a muttered imprecation and swiftly lifted her into his arms. He carried her to the bed, his body following her slim form down into the soft feather-filled mattress to lie beside her. She was vaguely aware that she was allowing him to seduce her once more, but his touch, his kisses, his caresses, were far too potent for her to resist.

She ached everywhere—her lips for his kiss; her breasts for his touch; her body for his possession. Damning herself for a weak-willed little fool, she gave up any pretense of resistance. She wanted this, wanted him, wanted to feel him moving fiercely within her, and she could not deny it.

His hand at her breast surprised a soft moan of pleasure from her, and she arched up helplessly into his palm. The sweet ache of desire was burning stronger within her with every passing second; her blood flowed hot and thick in her veins, her nipples swelled, her lower body softened and throbbed. The elemental need to join with him overrode all other senses.

Hardly aware of what she was doing, almost impatiently, Tess shoved aside his shirt, her own questing fingers seeking his flat male nipple. He shuddered at her first uncertain caress; his mouth crushed hers even more hungrily, and she gloried in the half-savage, half-tender pressure. When his lips left hers to slide warmly down her throat to her breast, she felt oddly bereft, but the feel of his mouth closing around her nipple sent a surge of delight through her. Her hands closed around his dark head, holding him to her as he suckled her breasts, and an odd feeling of tenderness speared through her. It is not, she thought dizzily, just passion that binds me to him, not just his touch that I crave . . . but something more. Ah, God! *So* much more!

Nicolas's head suddenly lifted and he growled thickly, "I'm sorry, sweetheart, but I'm afraid that these infernal clothes of ours *really* must go!"

Rearing up from her, he tore off his shirt and quickly dispensed with his breeches. Tess's breath caught in her throat at the sheer magnificence of his naked body, her gaze riveted by his engorged, upstanding member. But then she had no time to think as he reached for her and impatiently, ruthlessly, stripped her clothes from her, ripping the old fabric.

When his long, muscled length was finally once more pressed intimately against hers, the warmth of his flesh nearly scorching her, Tess wondered how she could have imagined forbidding herself this intensely sensual pleasure. Their limbs entangled, and his mouth returned to her breast, a sigh coming from both of them as his tongue curled erotically around an aching nipple.

"Do you know," he said softly against her breast, "that I've thought of little else but making love to you this past twenty-four hours? I was a fool to leave you alone last night, but I swore to myself that I would not rush you, that I would give you time to get used to the idea." He looked at her, a twisted smile on his lips. "At least that's what I tried to do, but I find that when I am near you, the baser promptings of my body override all other considerations. I want you, sweetheart, and if you're truthful to yourself, you want me just as desperately."

Not waiting for a reply, he brushed her stiffened nipples with his warm lips, one hand gliding down to cup the curly mound between her legs. Tess's breath quickened, and to her embarrassment, her thighs parted automatically for his exploration. He glanced up at her, satisfaction flaring in the black eyes. Huskily he asked, "Are you going to tell me again that you don't want me? That you're not as hungry as I am to share again the pleasure we found in each other's arms?"

Tess almost hated him at that moment; he was making her admit, once and for all, how helpless she was against him, making her admit aloud how very much she wanted him. Oh, dear heaven, she did want him, she *ached* for him, burned for him, was nearly dying for him to continue his ravishing caresses. . . .

Impassively he watched the struggle within her, and then his head dipped, his mouth once again brushing against her nipples, a gently probing finger sinking deeply within her damp, welcoming flesh. Tess moaned with pleasure.

"Do you want me, sweetheart?" he asked again, nipping her breast lightly. "Do you?"

She gave a groan of defeat and arched up as a second finger joined the other, seductively stretching the clinging flesh. "Damn you!" she cried shakily, the lavender eyes dark with desire. *"Yes!"*

Chapter Eleven

*H*er capitulation should have filled him with satisfaction, but it didn't. He was all too aware of the hollowness of his victory—her *body* wanted him, but the part of her that made her unique, the heart and soul of her, did not. Beyond insuring that his partner achieved an equal measure of pleasure in his previous amatory experiences, Nicolas had never wondered what might be going on inside a woman's head. This time, however, he did—because it mattered, he admitted bitterly. It mattered a great deal.

It shouldn't have—she was, after all, just a scheming little minx, albeit an utterly adorable one, who had tried her wiles on the wrong man and was now paying the price. But, to his astonishment, he discovered that he didn't want *just* her physical cooperation, he wanted something more, something he had never expected from or shared with another woman—he wanted her to feel for him, some intangible emotion that he dared not identify, and *that* knowledge terrified him.

Tess moved with innocent wantonness beneath his caressing fingers, her thigh brushing against his swollen, aching member, and suddenly he lost the thread of his thoughts. She was so sweet, so hot, and he so ready to give them both the ecstasy they craved that he could think of nothing but how much he wanted her, how very badly he needed to feel himself glide slowly within her slick, silken depths.

Calling himself a besotted fool for even caring about anything other than the immediate physical gratification to be found between her thighs, Nick let his teeth close gently around her nipple. The shudder of pleasure her body gave was all the encouragement he needed to leave off his unsatisfactory musings. Driving his fingers deeper within her, he lost himself in the carnal delights that awaited both of them.

Snared by the elemental needs that were in command of her body, hungry for that moment when he would join their bodies together, Tess tossed restlessly on the bed, her hips moving in a primitive rhythm to the probing caresses of his fingers. She ached for him. Every part of her ached for him— her mouth for the thrust of his tongue, her breasts for the hot, tugging caress of his mouth, and between her thighs . . . oh, dear heaven! That ached most of all. The sweet sensations seemed more powerful this time, more intense; this time she knew what was going to happen, and she was eager for it, needing him, wanting him desperately. Every thrusting movement of his fingers within her, every pull at her breast, increased the hunger within her, and a sharp moan of half demand, half need burst from her throat. She could not wait. She wanted him now!

Her hands closed around his dark head at her breast, urging him upward, and when their lips met she surprised both of them by kissing him deeply, her tongue sliding between his lips to tangle with his. Drunk on the flavor of his mouth, her fingers tangled in his thick hair, Tess gave herself up to a sensual revelry, her senses on fire; nothing mattered except this wild, bittersweet emotion that held her in thrall. Helplessly she arched up against his moving fingers, the yearning he had aroused between her thighs driving her half mad.

"Please, please, *please,*" she moaned softly into his mouth, the increasingly frantic movements of her body revealing her need as clearly as her words.

Her actions shattered the last of his control; his fingers slipped from the warm dampness of her flesh and his hands tightened on her thighs, pushing them farther apart, making room for his big body between her legs. Nicolas was nearly shaking from the force of the desire that consumed him, as little in command of himself as the woman twisting on the bed, and he could think of nothing but the smooth warmth of her skin, the taste of her mouth, and the sweet burning heat in which he would bury himself.

Tess knew a moment of vulnerability as he pushed her thighs apart and slid between her legs, but as he settled his weight against her, as his chest brushed against her breasts, it vanished, leaving only breathless, eager anticipation in its wake. His warm hands left her thighs, one now gently stroking her mound, making her writhe with pleasure, the other swiftly guiding his hard shaft to the hot silken sheath hidden by the fiery red curls between her legs.

She was tight, but so moist and hot that with little impediment Nicolas slid full length within her, shuddering when at last he was buried to the hilt. His hands moved to her hips, pulling her even closer to him, and his lips crushed hers, his tongue delving deep, filling her mouth as fully as his rigid, broad member filled her body.

Tess welcomed both invasions, her arms closing around his shoulders, her legs wrapping around his hips, and her mouth opening to accept the urgent probe of his tongue. She was filled with him, her body stretched and deliciously broached by him, every nerve, every fiber of her being seeming to have been imbued by him. She ached, but it was a different ache now, harder, stronger, hungrier than before, more demanding, more insistent. She pushed up wildly against him, pleasure flooding through her when he groaned and half gently, half painfully, bit her lower lip, his lower body rocking violently against hers.

"You're burning me alive, sweetheart," he gasped, his hold

on her hips tightening. His mouth slid to her throat. "But it's a fire in which I gladly burn."

Tess couldn't think, couldn't speak; all she could do was feel, and when he began to move on her, his powerful body driving again and again into hers, when his plundering mouth traveled from her throat to her breasts and then back up to her waiting lips, she wondered if a person could die of pleasure. The intensity of sensation grew until she thought she could not bear it a second longer, and she twisted and strained to meet his every thrust, her body humming with wanton eagerness, wanting, *needing* to reach that most passionately longed-for pinnacle. Suddenly her body clenched, and splintering into a thousand pieces, she cried out, her hips bucking frantically upward as ecstasy exploded through her.

Her cry was captured hungrily in Nicolas's mouth, his own body pumping madly into hers as his seed erupted from him and he drowned in the sweet, *sweet* delirium of utter pleasure. Buried deep within her, his movements slowed, but his hands held her hips hard against him, and he savored every moment, every tremor that came from either of them.

Tess was floating, her entire body feeling sensitized, almost as if she had embraced lightning. She tingled and burned, but the urgency was gone; now there was just lazy contentment spreading slowly through her.

Nicolas's kisses softened, the hard edge of passion momentarily satiated, but it was with great reluctance that he finally slid from her body and lay beside her. He pulled her next to him, putting her head on his shoulder, his arm around her, his hand lightly caressing her hip. They lay there for a long time, neither saying a word, busy with their own thoughts.

Tess didn't want to think about what had just happened between them, but she couldn't help doing so. A battle had been fought, and she had the lowering feeling that she had lost—badly. Whatever unfair means he had used, the fact still remained that he had forced her to admit that no matter what she might say or do, she wanted him. She was painfully aware that there was no going back—why keep fighting the same battle, a battle one knows will be lost? Whether she liked it or not, she had become the mistress of the earl of Sherbourne, and she could not pretend otherwise.

Nicolas moved just then, interrupting her unhappy thoughts. His mouth brushing her hair, he said simply, "I want you. Again. Now."

She didn't even offer a token protest; she had come too far for that. He had taught her traitorous body well, and just his very words sent a delicious thrill through her—to her resentment, her nipples tightened into hard little peaks. When he leaned over her and his mouth settled warmly on hers, her mind shut down and she let the dictates of her flesh rule her.

There were few preliminaries this time once he had made certain that her body was ready for him. His mouth crushed against hers, he sank slowly and deeply into her tight little sheath, and effortlessly he took them both to the edge and over into an abyss of carnal pleasure.

It was with some reluctance that Nicolas left the bed several minutes later. To his great astonishment, and despite the near blinding ecstasy he had found *twice* in her arms in a remarkably short period of time this afternoon, he discovered that with very little exertion on his part he could do so again quite willingly. He gave a rueful smile. He hadn't been this randy since his youth—nor possessed of the stamina!

His back to her, he dressed swiftly, his thoughts troubled. This afternoon hadn't gone as he had planned; he had planned merely to visit and present her with the much needed additions to her wardrobe—additions he had discreetly spent the morning procuring, raiding the stock of every modiste and seamstress within a twenty-mile radius. His chaise was currently half full of all manner of feminine fripperies that he'd had Lovejoy buy from the few dressmakers in the area. There weren't many, and they seldom kept finished garments on hand; but Lovejoy hadn't fared too badly, and at the earl's direction, several more elaborate gowns were already being sewn up. He'd arranged for fittings in two weeks' time. Unfortunately, while he had never considered himself a particularly sensitive man, even he could realize that after what had just happened between them, his little Dolly wasn't going to be overjoyed with his generosity. Even he could see that it would smack too much of payment for services rendered. *I should have kept my hands off her—as I had planned to do, dammit!* he thought with a scowl, attempting to make some order of his crumpled cravat.

But he hadn't, and glancing at the worn pink gown on the floor where he'd thrown it, he saw that he'd also ripped it badly in his haste to get her out of it. He sighed. He wasn't, it appeared, even going to be able to wait until tomorrow to give her the new clothes.

Angry at the situation, especially at his own lack of control, Nicolas turned to look at her. His face softened. She looked well loved as she lay there among the tumbled bedclothes, her lips still red and slightly swollen from his passion, her fiery hair cascading wildly across the white linen pillow, and one coral-tipped nipple peeking from beneath the sheets that enticingly outlined her slender body. She looked vastly appealing, and it was all he could do to prevent himself from tearing off his clothes and rejoining her in the bed.

Becoming a little annoyed at his body's blatant response just to the sight of her, he said flatly, "I'm sorry about your gown—I'm afraid that I ruined it."

Tess was almost grateful to have something as mundane as the state of her clothes to think about. Clutching the sheet modestly to her body, she sat up and looked around for her gown. Spying the crumpled pink fabric, she held the sheet even more protectively against her and scrambled from the bed, reaching for the garment. She hadn't wanted to believe him, but it was obvious that the gown was beyond repair.

With an accusatory expression on her face, she looked at him. "And what," she asked tartly, "am I to do now? Or is it your intention that I am to be kept naked—ever ready for your use?"

Nicolas winced at her choice of words. He didn't want her to view their relationship in that ugly manner, and her words angered him. Why couldn't she just accept the situation? None of his other mistresses had ever given him this sort of trouble, and even as that thought crossed his mind, he realized that she wasn't *just* another mistress, that inexplicably, in the startlingly brief time they had known each other, she had come to mean much more to him. Yet she *was* his mistress—there was no denying it. So what the hell do you want from her? he asked himself savagely. He had no answers. Deciding to get the unpleasantness over with at once, he said, "While that is an excellent idea, it won't be necessary. They may not fit you exactly or be the style and color that you prefer, but I have several new garments for you in my chaise. I hope that they prove satisfactory until other clothing more to your liking can be procured."

He sounded pompous. Feeling out of sorts and confused by the entire situation, he turned away from her and mumbled, "I'll have Rose and Jenny bring the things up to you—and some, er, other things for your use."

Tess wanted very much to fling his words back into his arrogant face. But since she had no enthusiasm for parading around naked, it seemed best to swallow her rage and pride and wear the damned clothing. She didn't have to like it, but she had to accept it, and she found *that* most galling of all. She stared bitterly at the door as it closed behind his tall form. Why was it, she wondered gloomily, that he always won? Why did she seem always to be in a position that forced her to bow to the situations of his making?

Muttering vile fates for him, she kept the sheet wrapped around her body and waited impatiently for the arrival of the servants. Deliberately she kept her thoughts focused on his imperious ways, cataloged all his sins—it was either that or remember how she had come apart in his arms, remember the feel of his big body pressed intimately against hers, the taste

of his mouth, and the easy way she had allowed him to ma-
nipulate her. . . .

Suddenly she heard a great ruckus in the dressing room.
Peeking her head around the door, she watched with wide
eyes as Tom and John struggled to place a huge brass tub into
the center of the empty room. They caught sight of her and
grinned. "The earl thought that you might like a tub set up
permanently in this room," Tom said. "There's water heating
on the stove, and we'll have it filled for you in no time. Is that
all right?"

Embarrassed and oddly tongue-tied, Tess nodded her curly
head. Mindful of her state of undress, she ducked back behind
the door. Her thoughts went irresistibly to the notion of how
wonderful it would feel to actually have a bath. A real bath,
not just a hasty scrub. Tess told herself not to be so happy
about such a commonplace event, but she couldn't help it—
the earl might be an overbearing, arrogant, obstinate, *infuriating* man, but he was also thoughtful—damn him!

Forty-five minutes later a fire burned merrily on the hearth
of the small fireplace in the dressing room and half-opened
boxes and packages overflowing with laces and muslins were
scattered willy-nilly about the room. From her vantage point
in the middle of the huge brass tub, Tess let out a sigh of sheer
bliss. The water was oh, so warm and silky, and the sweet
scent of roses and carnations hung in the air. To her delight,
despite telling herself not to be distracted by such frivolous
things, there had been wonderfully scented soaps and bath
oils in one of the packages the earl had sent up, and she had
not hesitated to use them.

Tess soaked a long time, washing her hair, humming
lightly, and generally enjoying herself. Fate, with perhaps a
few mistakes on her part, had brought her this far, and for the
moment she was willing to drift. If only, she thought for the
hundredth time, I knew who I was. *Then* I could make decisions. Was she hiding from the truth? she wondered uneasily.

Mayhap, in her heart of hearts, she wanted to be precisely where she was. . . .

She wrinkled her little nose in distaste and quickly stepped from the tub, wrapping a large towel around herself. Torn between appreciation of the many expensive items of apparel the earl had lavishly provided for her and revulsion for what they represented, Tess gingerly rummaged through several of the boxes and packages.

Finally selecting from the vast array before her a cambric chemise trimmed in delicate lace and an apple green gown of fine muslin, as well as some dark green satin ribbons and slippers and silk stockings, Tess dressed quickly. The clothing fit surprisingly well. The high-waisted gown was just a little loose through the shoulders and bosom, but otherwise she had no complaints. With nimble fingers she braided the dark green ribbon through her damp hair and fastened the colorful plaits on top of her head.

Taking a last look at herself in the cheval glass that had been among the furnishings added to the room that morning, Tess took a deep breath. It would be easy, she admitted unhappily, to remain up here, away from the earl's disturbing presence, but that would be the coward's way. Her mouth twisted. If she'd been a little more *cowardly* in the beginning, she probably wouldn't be here right now! Straightening her shoulders, her chin held at a pugnacious angle, she marched from the room.

When she entered the main room of the house, it was to find the earl warming himself before the fire, his hands clasped behind his back as he stood facing the doorway through which she came. He had managed to erase most of the signs of their recent romp in the bed upstairs. Except for the less-than-perfect condition of his cravat, he looked as elegant as always.

Halfway into the room, Tess hesitated, feeling oddly shy. Which was ridiculous, she thought crossly, remembering that hardly an hour ago they had been lying naked in each other's arms, his body buried in hers. She swallowed, grimly pushing aside the erotic images that leaped to mind.

Seating herself primly on the settee near the fire, she asked stiffly, "Would you like something to drink or eat?"

Nicolas was hardly able to take his eyes off her. In the old, unfashionable pink gown, her hair hastily tied back with a faded ribbon, she had been eye-catching, but now . . . With all that bright hair caught up in a queenly coronet, she was incredibly lovely, the heavily lashed amethyst eyes and the high cheekbones clearly defined. As far as he was concerned, the gown fit admirably, the green hue intensifying her coloring and discreetly revealing the slim body it clothed before falling in graceful folds to the floor. She looked . . . His gaze hardened. She looked every inch the daughter of aristocrats, from the elegant bright hair to the silk slippers on her feet. He should know—he had just spent the last several months courting the type of creature she appeared: well-bred, eligible, pampered darlings offered by their parents or guardians in marriage to the highest bidder at Almack's, London's greatest marriage mart! Any doubts he might have had about her story of lost memory were banished. It was obvious from the way she looked now that his first wild surmise had been correct: she had been after a marriage proposal and had been willing to stop at nothing to obtain it.

But why, the question irritatingly persisted, with her beauty and obvious well-bred background had she gone to such lengths? No dowry? Some unforgivable scandal in the background? Not quite *so* well connected? Or simply ambitious? It could have been all or any of those reasons, and he refused to speculate on it further. Whatever she and her cohorts had so rashly planned, it hadn't worked. She was his mistress, not his wife!

There was an uncomfortable silence between them. The fire cracked and popped on the hearth, and an ormolu clock on the mantel quietly ticked off the minutes.

Nicolas cleared his throat. "Did you, uh, find the items satisfactory?"

"Yes."

He scowled. He wasn't used to having his generosity dismissed so curtly, and while he didn't really want her to fawn over him, her short answer rankled. None of his other— He bit off that thought impatiently. He'd already decided that she was nothing like his other mistresses. Feeling at a loss, he growled, "Do you want me to leave?"

Tess looked up at him, her brow furrowing. She wanted him to leave, didn't she? No, she admitted unhappily to herself, she didn't want him to leave, and that decision had nothing to do with the long, lonely hours that would stretch out once he had departed. Even if the house were filled with the most witty and entertaining people to be found, her world would be considerably duller without his dynamic presence to give it light and life.

It was a damning admission, and Tess's breath caught in her throat. She couldn't be falling in love with him, could she? It was a terrifying notion, one she didn't like at all. To escape thinking about it, her eyes fixed painfully on her slippers, she blurted out, "No, m'lord, I don't want you to leave."

Nicolas cut off a sharp comment and snapped, "Nicolas, my name is Nicolas, or Nick, and after all we've shared, I think that we can safely dispense with formality!"

"Very well, then, *Nicolas,*" she repeated obediently, "I don't want you to leave." Mindful of her duties as hostess, she added politely, "Will you be staying for dinner?"

"No, not tonight, thank you." This was a ridiculous conversation, he decided impatiently. Both of them as stiff and punctilious as if they were meeting under the stern gaze of one of the patronesses of Almack's. Feeling clumsy and stupid, Nicolas stared at her, wanting to say more but oddly ill at ease. Dammit, he thought angrily, why does she tie me up in knots this way?

Before the silence became too awkward, there was a welcome interruption in the form of Jenny. With a worried look on her lively face, she entered the room and, after dropping a quick curtsy, said hurriedly, "Forgive me for intruding on you, m'lord, but Mum said it was important. Thank heavens you're still here! It's the owlers, sir! They're using the cellars of the cottage to store their contraband! Tom discovered it when he went to put up the liquor you had sent over from the court."

A few minutes later, with Tess peering over his shoulder, Nicolas could see for himself the truth of Jenny's words. The owlers *were* using the abandoned cellars of the onetime gate-keeper's cottage as a storage place for their smuggled goods.

It hadn't been his idea for Tess to accompany him, but after a brief argument, which Nicolas had lost, the two of them had quickly followed Jenny to the kitchen. Armed with some candles that Sara had thrust into their hands, they had stepped into the pantry and discovered the narrow winding staircase that led to the cellars.

Guided by the flickering yellow light of their candles, they had cautiously descended the stone steps to find themselves in a vast room, with what looked like several tunnels branching off from the main area. It was a dark and gloomy place, with dusty cobwebs hanging in great curtains from the low wooden ceiling and a musty smell permeating the air. Tom and John were there ahead of them. Their lanterns were a welcoming beacon, as sinister black shadows jumped beyond the small, comforting circle of light.

"M'lord! Look what we've found!" Tom cried. "The owlers are hiding their goods right under your very nose!"

At their feet were the opened boxes containing the brandy and wines that Tom and John had brought down to the cellar to put into the wine rack. But it was the other crates and barrels a little behind them that commanded everyone's attention. The objects were heaped carelessly in the middle of the room. It was obvious from the many tracks on the floor and the absence of any cobwebs in that vicinity that this was not the first time the gatekeeper's cottage had been used for this purpose.

Nicolas said nothing for several minutes as he took in the scene. "Is the way through the pantry," he finally asked, "the only entrance into the cellars?"

"No, m'lord," Tom said quickly. "If you'll come over here, I can show you the outside entrance. John and I discovered it while we were waiting for you—and we haven't explored the areas branching off from this room." He looked worried. "There could be another entrance that we don't know about."

Nicolas made no comment but decided to have the cellar thoroughly examined tomorrow and to have any other way in blocked off.

The ease and silence with which Tom and John were able to throw open the horizontal double doors to reveal the gray, rainy sky above made it apparent that this was the entrance used regularly by the smugglers. The owlers were, Nicolas thought grimly, so confident that no one would dare disturb their contraband that they hadn't even bothered to lock the doors. He examined the hinges carefully and saw that they had been well oiled.

Looking back at the two young men, he inquired, "Were you down here yesterday?"

"Yesterday afternoon," Tom answered. "We came down to dust the wine racks—and there was nothing here then."

"You mean they hid all these things here last night? When we were asleep in our beds?" Jenny asked in a high voice.

Nicolas shot Tess a look, but beyond paling a trifle, she didn't look overly disturbed to discover that while she had slept last night, a band of murderous cutthroats had been boldly making use of the cellars of the house. He was far less sanguine about it—a cold rage swept through him at the knowledge that she might have been harmed if she had awakened and stumbled across them while the smugglers had been brazenly going about their activities.

Deciding that he didn't need the obviously nervous Jenny

infecting Dolly with hysterics, Nicolas sent the young woman upstairs to join her mother. With a frown on his face, he spoke quietly with Tom and John for several moments, the three men discussing what was to be done. Nicolas wasn't particularly enthusiastic about informing the magistrate of their find, mainly because he didn't want Dolly's presence at the gatekeeper's cottage to become common knowledge. He had enough reservations about setting her up this close to the court—and his grandmother and sister—as it was. And the opportunity to spy on the owlers couldn't be ignored, he reflected as his conversation with Roxbury flashed through his mind. Telling Tom and John to leave the matter in his hands, he dismissed them after ordering them to remove all signs of their activity in the cellars.

While Nicolas had been talking to the servants, Tess had wandered off, doing a little exploring of her own. She was so intent upon her task that when Nicolas came up behind her, she gave a little gasp and whirled around.

With her eyes very big, she grumbled, "Don't sneak up on me that way! You startled me!"

He grinned faintly. "I apologize. It is," he added, glancing around, "a rather uninviting place, isn't it?"

"Hmm, yes, I suppose so," she replied absently as she picked her way over the uneven floor. "But I'd love to go rummaging about down here—all those mysterious hallways or whatever leading out of this main area. I wouldn't be surprised at all to learn that the owlers have been using this place for years." Her eyes sparkled with excitement. "It's even possible that those tunnels lead to other rooms."

Nicolas grimaced as the thought of her merrily tripping down dark, cavernous hallways that led God knew where made his blood run cold. "I don't think that it would be a good idea for you to go exploring on your own." The mutinous expression on her face warned him he was on treacherous ground. Knowing that if he forbade her presence in the cellars, it would make them that much more alluring, he added hastily, "Um, perhaps very soon we can do some exploring down here together."

"Perhaps," Tess said airily, already planning a foray for to-morrow morning.

His eyes narrowed. "Dolly, this is not some sort of amuse-ment I arranged for your benefit. The owlers are dangerous men. And audaciously brazen in the bargain—if concealing this contraband here last night with the house occupied is any indication of their nature."

Tess looked thoughtful. "They probably didn't realize that the house was occupied. If they followed their normal prac-tice, it would have been well after midnight before the ships were unloaded and the goods hidden. The house would have been dark, and there would have been no one about to alert them that it was now being used." She glanced up at him. "Don't forget it is only yesterday that we arrived—and unless they checked on the cottage periodically, they would have as-sumed, no doubt, that the house was still abandoned and empty. In daylight, of course, the changes would be obvious, but not at night. . . ." She paused. "But I doubt that even our presence would have stopped them—the owlers are notorious for doing what they please, and they certainly wouldn't have expected us to object. *That* wouldn't be very wise."

"And just how, my love, do you know so very much about our Kentish smugglers?" Nicolas asked dryly. "Memory con-veniently returning, hmm?"

Chapter Twelve

———— ◆ ————

*T*ess stared at him, his words going round in her brain. It was true—not that her memory had returned, but that she did know a great deal about the Kentish smugglers. A bolt of excitement shot through her. She *had* to be from around this area! Or, she thought with a little less enthusiasm, she had lived in this area at some time in the past. But that didn't feel right—the information about the owlers had come forth as naturally as breathing; that must count for something. Her excitement ebbed as she realized that there could be other reasons for her knowledge, such as the gloomy possibility that she had merely been close to someone else who was familiar with smuggler ways and had told her about them. The fact that she knew about the owlers wasn't necessarily the momentous revelation she had first thought it.

She met Nicolas's cynical gaze squarely. "The fact that I seem to know about smugglers shouldn't come as any great surprise to you. Anyone who lives in the vicinity of the Romney Marsh would know about them—the Kentish owlers are infamous. I imagine that there are lots of people who have never been within fifty miles of the marsh and still know about them. And as for their ways, nearly everyone knows how the smugglers operate. It's not," she finished tartly, "a great secret!"

"You've a very agile tongue," Nicolas replied grimly. "But you'll forgive me if I don't take your word as gospel. Your memory appears to be very selective, and I wait in breathless anticipation for the moment that you will conveniently remember everything!"

Tess's eyes darkened with anger. "If you weren't such a despicable, philandering, obnoxious, overbearing man, you'd realize that I'm telling the truth! And just because I happen to have flashes of memory doesn't mean that I'm lying!"

She was beautiful in a temper, her eyes bright, her cheeks flushed rosily, that stubborn little chin carried at a fighting angle. Nicolas was very aware that instead of arguing with her, he would much rather carry her back to the bedroom and proceed to make love to her again. . . .

Cursing under his breath, he jerked his wayward thoughts away from the pleasures to be found between her thighs. Grasping her arm, he urged her toward the narrow steps that led up to the pantry. In offended silence Tess allowed him to guide her upstairs and into the kitchen, where Rose, having joined the other two women, awaited them.

They were met with a barrage of questions, but Nicolas quickly soothed their fears, telling them that events were well in hand and they were not to worry about anything. Having reassured them, he whisked Tess back into the main salon.

Tess had barely seated herself once more on the settee before she guessed shrewdly, "You're going to try to trap them when they come for the goods tonight, aren't you?"

"Not only an agile tongue, but a clever little brain, too. Tell me, my dear, have you also decided how I plan to, er, trap them, I believe you said?"

She eyed him uncertainly. "You don't mean you're going to simply turn things over to Sir Charles, do you?"

Nicolas cocked his thick black brow. "Sir Charles?"

She suddenly looked very confused. Almost inaudibly she said, "Sir Charles Wetherby—the local magistrate."

"Ah, is this *another* convenient scrap of memory?" he asked sardonically.

Absently she nodded her head. "His name just popped into my mind." She regarded him earnestly. "Do you think that my memory is gradually coming back to me?"

There was such pitiful longing in her eyes that Nicolas bit back the unkind comment that hovered on his tongue. She was a very good little actress. Shrugging his broad shoulders, he said, "Perhaps. Who knows—tomorrow you may awaken and remember precisely who you are. . . ." He smiled coolly. "Besides being my mistress, of course."

"Of course," she replied in a colorless tone. Unable to hold his derisive gaze any longer, she looked away and asked, "What *are* you going to do about the smugglers?"

Nick sighed. "I don't know," he admitted, surprising both of them. "Turning the information over to Sir Charles is the most logical thing to do, but I find myself wishing to meet these bold gentlemen. Or at least observe them."

"You mean *spy* on them?" she asked breathlessly, her violet eyes glittering with excitement. Obviously enamored of this idea, she went on in lively tones, "We could conceal ourselves in the cellars and await their return and follow them! We might even discover who their leader is—the head smuggler!"

Since that was precisely what Nicolas had planned to do, *alone,* he almost groaned aloud at her nearly palpable delight at the idea of confronting the mastermind behind the smugglers. Feeling distinctly harassed, he muttered, "Hiding in the cellars and spying on smugglers is no pastime for you! These men are quite capable of killing anyone who gets in their way. They are desperate, savage cutthroats, and I shudder to think what your fate might be if you fell into their hands. I want you safely away from any trouble, and no matter what I eventually decide to do about the situation, I don't want you peering over my shoulder while I do it!"

A heated argument ensued and ended only when Nicolas

said in crushing tones, "You will *not,* under any circum-stances, have anything to do with these blasted owlers." His black eyes hard and uncompromising, he added grimly, "If the only way I can be assured that you will not continue to meddle in something that could be *very* dangerous is to gag you and tie you to your bed upstairs, believe me, sweetheart, I'll do it. Now do I have your promise not to interfere?"

Her mouth set in stubborn lines, Tess glared up at him. "How do you know that I'll keep my word?" she asked in scornful accents. "You already think I'm a liar."

"But not about this," he said slowly, knowing he spoke the truth. He couldn't explain it, but there was an instinctive knowledge that if she gave her promise, she would keep it. How the hell do I know that? he asked himself, bewildered. How can I be so certain that I can trust her to keep her word? It was unanswerable. Sending her a hard look, he demanded, "Well, do I have your word?"

Tess sighed, aware that he wasn't going to budge on this issue and that further argument would prove fruitless. He could be so stubborn! "Oh, very well," she snapped, "you have my word on it."

He smiled crookedly. "A little plainer than that, my dear— I may trust your word, but I don't trust you!"

She made a face. "You have my word that I will not try to observe the smugglers, or find out anything else about them."

"And?"

"And I won't go exploring in the cellars without your per-mission."

"Thank you," Nicolas said softly, a warm gleam in his dark eyes. "I know that it cost you to give me that promise, but it *is* for your own safety."

Tess merely looked disgusted. "I don't know why men get to have all the adventures! You *are* going to try to trap them, aren't you?"

Nicolas nodded slowly. "The thought had crossed my mind."

"I *knew* it," Tess muttered, and bounded up from the settee. After taking several agitated steps around the room, she looked back at him with a scowl.

"And what am I going to be doing while you're off merrily chasing smugglers?"

He crossed to where she stood, drew her into his arms, and kissed her on the nose. "You, my sweet, are going to be upstairs, tucked safely in your bed, breathlessly awaiting my triumphant return!"

Tess snorted and slipped out of his arms. "How utterly boring! If the last two days are anything to go by, being a mistress seems a rather dull profession to me," she said caustically.

A sensual smile curved his long mouth, and Nicolas pulled her slowly back into his arms. Brushing his mouth tantalizingly across hers, he murmured, "I have been rather remiss with you, haven't I?" His lips settled a little more fully on hers, and Tess's heart began to race. "I promise that my next visit will not be so brief and that I shall show you then just how unboring being my mistress can be."

He kissed her then. Hungrily. Hotly. And with great and obvious relish.

The subject of the smugglers and the boring fate of mistresses vanished from her mind. Desire, sweet and demanding, surged up through her, and she gave a soft moan as her arms, completely against her wishes, crept up around his neck. At least she *told* herself it was against her wishes, but as he kissed her even more deeply and as her fingers caressed his dark hair, as his wickedly knowing mouth and mesmerizing nearness wreaked their dark magic on her, it didn't really matter anymore. . . .

With something between a curse and a plea, Nicolas finally tore himself from her. His black eyes glittered with passion, and his breathing was labored. He said thickly, "You are undoubtedly the most tempting little baggage it has ever been my fortune—or misfortune—to find! I touch you and I go up in flames, and if I'm not touching you, kissing you, holding you, all I can think about is how much I want to. You *are* a sorceress!" He pressed a hard, swift kiss on her stinging mouth. "I cannot stay—other plans were made for me this evening—but I will be back just as soon as I can." He smiled regretfully at her. "It will probably be after midnight, and as much as I would like nothing better than to join you in your warm bed—it will be the smugglers who hold my attention then."

Still half dizzy from his kisses, Tess stared at him as the knowledge that he might be doing something exceedingly foolhardy and dangerous suddenly occurred to her. If, as he said—and she didn't doubt him—these bold smugglers were desperate, savage cutthroats, wasn't *his* life in jeopardy? What would be his fate if they were to discover him spying on them? Would they murder him?

Fear seized her. Her eyes dark with the powerful emotions churning in her breast, she said huskily, "You will be careful? You won't take any foolish risks? You won't . . ." She swallowed painfully. "Let them hurt you?"

Her words and her obvious concern touched something deep inside of him. No one, except perhaps his grandmother, had ever expressed any worry about him. His handsome face was full of tenderness as he cradled her against him. "No, sweetheart, I won't let them hurt me." He dropped a kiss on her fiery hair and in an odd tone muttered, "There was a time when I felt no risk was too great. . . ." His mouth twisted. "Believe me, minx, I have no intention of allowing any simple smuggler to keep me from your bed!" He kissed her again and, after shrugging into his many-caped greatcoat, was gone.

Tess stared at the empty doorway through which he had disappeared. What was happening to her? How was it that this man, this infuriating, beguiling man, could have made such a difference in her life in just forty-eight hours? How was it that his mere presence made her happy? That his absence left her feeling hollow and bereft? And how was it that while she railed against him and sometimes thought she hated him, the very idea of him going into danger filled her with terror? Surely she didn't *care* for the beast?

Driving swiftly through the falling rain, Nicolas frowned, his thoughts surprisingly similar to hers as he wondered what it was about Dolly that sent his blood racing and his heart thudding. He'd never felt this way before about a woman! His frown grew blacker. Except for those mad, halcyon days when he had believed himself in love with Maryanne. . . .

Biting back a curse, he jerked his thoughts away from the puzzling little chit he had just left and began to think about the evening ahead. He wasn't looking forward to it, but he could hardly have refused his grandmother this morning, when she had especially asked that he dine at home this evening. She was inviting a few *dear* friends over for an impromptu dinner party to welcome him back to the neighborhood. Nicolas grimaced. He doubted that there would be very many of his grandmother's friends in to dine this evening, but he would have wagered a small fortune that some, if not all, of the young ladies mentioned by his grandmother last night would be there!

Sometime later, standing tall and urbane at his grandmother's side, a coolly polite smile pasted on his mouth, he greeted her guests, his handsome features never giving a clue as to what was going on behind his polite facade. They were all there—Lord and Lady Spencer, their son, and his sisters; Admiral Brownell, his wife, their two older sons, and their daughter, Jane; and John Frampton, the squire, and his friend from London, Edward Dickerson. Athena was there, too, an almost pitying look in her fine dark eyes whenever she glanced his way. It was going to be, Nicolas thought dismally, a *long* evening.

The evening was every bit as long and bad as Nicolas had feared. When he wasn't being treated to simpering smiles and giggles from the young ladies and arch looks from the parents, he found himself surrounded by a bevy of eager young

men who bombarded him with questions about Sir Arthur
Wellesley and the war with Boney on the peninsula. It had
been nearly a year since he had resigned his commission and
returned to England, and while his information was months
old and long out of date, it didn't seem to matter to the gentlemen—even Lord Spencer and Admiral Brownell appeared
to hang on his every word. It was pleasant at first, but it soon
grew wearying, and Nicolas began to wish he had followed
his first instincts and told his grandmother that he'd made
other plans.

He had to confess, though, that there had been an ulterior
motive for his being so amenable to Pallas's blatant matchmaking: tonight would give him a chance to observe John
Frampton and young Robert Brownell in a neutral setting and
allow him to decide how to use the information Pallas had
given him about their possible connection to the smugglers . . . and whoever might be passing along vital secrets to
the French!

It was apparent that Robert, a dark, brooding-faced young
man of twenty-four, should have been allowed to join the cavalry unit as he passionately longed to do. Nicolas watched
him closely after the ladies had departed from the dining
room and the gentlemen were enjoying their cigars and port.
He could well imagine that Robert, bored and restless, full of
youthful high spirits, and stuck in the country with nothing to
do, might very well join in John Frampton's wilder activities.
The second Brownell son, Jeremy, was a mild-mannered
youth two years younger than Robert. From the intricate folds
of his starched cravat and the daringly embroidered white
waistcoat he wore, it seemed that this particular sprout's highest ambition was to take the London dandy set by storm.
Robert appeared to hold Jeremy in great scorn; his lip curled
constantly at his younger brother's conversation, which focused mainly on the cut and style of clothing.

Nicolas's eyes drifted around the table, skipping over the
rotund, bald-pated Admiral Brownell and the slim, elegant,

gray-haired Lord Spencer before resting for a moment on the
bold, hawkish features of the squire. John Frampton more resembled his late, unlamented father than his amiable mother;
his hair was dark brown, his mouth was full to the point of
sulkiness, and his eyes were a restless deep blue. A raffish air
hung about him, despite his fashionable attire, and Nicolas
had no trouble picturing him skulking about the neighborhood
in the wee hours of the morning, in the company of lowborn
smugglers, or outriding dragoons.

His friend, Dickerson, was much of the same mold. Idly
observing the two of them, Dickerson and Frampton, as they
talked animatedly with the younger men, Nicolas wondered
why they were wasting their time in the bucolic hills of Kent.
From their form-fitting jackets by Weston, the neat but unre-
markable folds of their white cravats, it appeared they both
followed the sporting set—their conversation was sprinkled
with comments about Tattersall's, nights at Limmer's Hotel,
and boxing matches held at Fives Court. Why, Nicolas wondered, had Frampton and his friend buried themselves in the
country?

"I say, Sherbourne, it's a good thing that you decided to
spend the winter at home," said Admiral Brownell, breaking
into Nicolas's thoughts. "Perhaps with you in residence these
damn owlers won't be quite so bold! Do you know," he added
in outraged accents, "they actually had the nerve to take three
of my best hunters the other night to transport their goods?
Brazen fellows!"

The admiral's comment caused a moment of silence. It
was Lindsey, Lord Spencer's son, whose blue eyes held the
expression of a startled fawn, who said hastily, "Well, you
know, sir, Caldwell House is near one of the paths used frequently by the owlers. In this area it's to be expected that
occasionally they might, um, borrow some of your stock.
They never really do any harm, and it's common practice
for them to leave behind a cask of brandy or two to com-
pensate for the use of the animals."

Ignoring his son's words, Lord Spencer, sitting to the left of Nicolas, said, "It's true that something should be done about them—decent people cannot sleep easy in their beds while they're about!"

Nicolas regarded his brandy snifter, not certain how to respond. He wanted to reassure the two older men that he did indeed intend to do something about the smugglers, but it would be foolhardy to bluntly admit that he had more than a cursory interest in the smugglers. Certainly he had no intention of mentioning the hidden goods in the cellars of the old gatekeeper's cottage. Idly twisting the stem of his snifter, he said evenly, "I daresay you're right, but I don't really see what you expect me to do about it. It's my understanding that there is a company of dragoons stationed in the area—surely they can do something!"

A sly snicker came from Frampton, bringing an angry flush to the admiral's face. Making no attempt to hide his displeasure, he said angrily, "Oh, yes! I'm sure that you young bucks think it is amusing—I've heard tales of your outrageous high jinks, but you mark my words—you won't be able to outfox His Majesty's hardworking servants forever! You think it's a great lark now, but one of these nights, you'll come a cropper—mark my words!"

"Oh, come now, sir," said John Frampton. "It *is* a lark! What harm is there in tweaking the noses of some stiff-rumped dragoons?"

"Yes, Father, what harm does it do?" demanded Robert, his dark face intent. "It's not as if one is actually *smuggling* anything. Surely there is nothing wrong in just baiting the revenuers or riding with the smugglers. God knows there is nothing else here to do for excitement!"

Nicolas thought for one moment that the admiral was going to suffer an apoplectic fit. His eyes bulged, his heavy jowls turned an alarming red, and he stared at his eldest son as if he had sired a monster. "Nothing wrong?" he finally choked out.

"I'll tell you what's wrong, you young rapscallion—it's a crime! A damned bloody crime! Smugglers are hanged!"

"Better hanged than rotting away in this tedious backwater!" Robert grumbled.

The admiral's color deepened. Seeking to avert a full-blown argument, Nicolas rose and said hastily, "I think that we have lingered here long enough. Shall we join the ladies?"

In the general exodus from the dining room, the disagreement between the Brownells was smoothed over and the topic of the smugglers was gratefully left behind. Steeling himself as if for battle, Nicolas led the way into the blue sitting room, where the ladies were scattered decoratively about, sipping their tea.

Upon the appearance of the gentlemen, particularly Nicolas, there was a flurry of movement, and the younger ladies suddenly became quite animated. Gowns were twitched into place, demure glances were flashed his way, and there was much head tossing and many soft giggles. Nicolas sighed. Yes, it was definitely a long evening.

The gentlemen spread out around the room, and Nicolas took his usual place standing before the fire. After those wishing tea were served, the conversation became general. Nicolas noted that Lindsey gravitated in Jane Brownell's direction near the blue sofa, followed closely by Dickerson. To his astonishment, Frampton walked directly over to where Athena was sitting and began a light flirtation with her. Frampton and Athena? Well, well, well! Perhaps his grandmother had the correct reading of the situation after all.

Athena glanced his way, and Nicolas arched a quizzical eyebrow. She smiled sweetly and coolly turned back to her companion.

Pallas caught his attention just then as she said, "Nicolas, dear, Athena and I have been talking with the other ladies and we all think that it would be an excellent idea if we held a ball in the near future to celebrate your return to the neighborhood. Would you like that?" She glanced fondly around the room. "The young ladies have already indicated that they think it a capital notion!" There was an unholy gleam of amusement in her eyes that made him distinctly uneasy. "I've told them that it is entirely up to you, dear."

Nicolas was instantly engulfed by a cloud of giggling, pleading-eyed young ladies, their pastel-hued muslin skirts fluttering as they descended upon him. Over the heads of his fair besiegers, he shot his grandmother a look of wry amusement. She had outflanked him and trapped him neatly.

Looking down at the young ladies who crowded around him, he smiled teasingly. "And what is your pleasure, mademoiselles—shall we have a ball?"

"Oh, please, Lord Sherbourne, *do* say yes!" begged Jane Brownell prettily as she stood in front of him, her fair hair gleaming in the light from the chandeliers.

"It would be most exciting," exclaimed Frances Spencer, Lord Spencer's eldest daughter. A tall girl, Frances was built on strapping lines, but she had a kind face and her big brown eyes sparkled attractively.

Her sister, Rosemary, chimed in with, "A ball at Sherbourne Court! Oh, it would be just divine!"

With amusement in his eyes, Nicolas glanced down at the eager upturned faces and said, "With such lovely supplicants, how can I refuse? Of course we shall have a ball at the court."

Amid much squealing and clapping of hands, Nicolas escaped and sat beside his grandmother. Under his breath, he said, "Happy now?"

She flashed him a demure glance. "You know that you always make me happy, dear."

Choking back a laugh, Nicolas brushed aside her offer to fix him tea and helped himself from the silver tray in front of him. Drinking his tea, he glanced around the room, listening idly to the conversation that swirled around him. To his left, the young ladies were busily discussing the promised delights of the ball; Lindsey and Jeremy joined their group, seeming to be caught up in the unexpected treat that lay before them, although they did try to act as if a ball at Sherbourne Court were nothing out of the ordinary.

Athena, Lady Edwina Spencer, an attractive woman of some fifty years, and the admiral's wife, Sophie, a formidable matron in puce satin and diamonds, were seated in a semi-circle in front of the settee where Nicolas sat with his grandmother. After some polite chitchat with him, all the older ladies were soon deep in conversation about the ball. The remaining gentlemen were gathered at one end of the room, and from the snippets that drifted his way, Nicolas surmised they were enjoying a lively discussion about a cockfight that had recently been held in the area.

For the moment everyone seemed occupied, and with deceptive idleness, Nicolas gazed slowly about the room. The conversation about the smugglers had been most interesting. It was obvious from the reactions around the table that John Frampton, no doubt aided by Dickerson, was definitely chasing excitement by joining with the owlers—and, perhaps less regularly, so was young Robert. Nicolas's eyes rested thoughtfully on that young man's dark, intense features. Yes, a cavalry regiment was just what Robert needed to funnel all that youthful daredevil energy into something worthwhile. He wondered why the admiral hadn't made the arrangements long before this. Not enough money to buy a pair of colors? Which led him to wonder in general about the finances of both the Brownells and the Spencers.

If pressed, Nicolas would have guessed that both families were comfortable rather than wealthy—comfortable, that was, if one didn't have a quiver full of offspring to establish respectably. . . . The price of a military career could be costly, and a London season to launch a daughter—in the case of the Spencers *two* daughters—could be ruinous to a man of even considerable means.

Speculatively his gaze traveled from Admiral Brownell's hearty features to the more ascetic face of Lord Spencer. Both men were relatively new to the neighborhood, and the argument could be made that the pressures of providing for their families *might* drive them to take a course that would normally be abhorrent to them. They both might have spoken out about the smugglers, but that didn't prove anything. Nicolas admitted it was highly unlikely that either man was his spy, but he wasn't going to overlook anyone. At the moment, however, his favorite choice for Roxbury's spy was Frampton—who knew the ways of the owlers better than someone born and raised in the area?

Nicolas frowned slightly, wishing he knew more about the new squire and the Frampton fortune. Had the old squire been as warm as everyone had surmised? Or were his famous clutch-fisted ways born of necessity? And would lack of a fortune entice his son into dangerous and infamous activities in order to present a dashing facade to the world?

The evening hadn't proven as useless as he had first assumed. He'd had a chance to meet with some very good, ah, suspects. Brownell. Spencer. Frampton. And last but certainly not least, Dickerson. For the time being it was those four who would hold his attention. As for Robert, Jeremy, and Lindsey . . . it was possible that one of them was an inordinately clever youth and had begun dark dabblings at an early age—Alexander the Great had conquered the known world by age thirty—but Nicolas doubted that any one of these three possessed such spectacular abilities.

At a chiding remark from Sophie Brownell, the gentlemen broke off their sporting talk and joined the circle around Nicolas and Pallas, as did Jeremy and Lindsey. Teacups were being refilled, and there was a momentary lull in the conversation. It was at that precise moment that his grandmother laid her hand on his arm and asked, "Oh, while I'm thinking of it, Nicolas, what is this ridiculous tale I'm hearing that you have raided half my staff and are refurbishing the old gatekeeper's cottage on the north part of the estate?"

Even as he fumbled for an answer and cursed the arrogance that had led him to believe that his use of the cottage would go without comment, he was aware of a hastily smothered gasp from someone in the group near him. In that same instant, the cup that Athena had been passing to one of the men—Frampton? Dickerson? or had it been Spencer?—went tumbling to the floor. Hot tea splashed everywhere. In the commotion that followed, Pallas's question was completely forgotten. But long after everyone had left, Nicolas couldn't get that scene out of his mind.

Alone in his office, he had quickly written a note to Roxbury, informing him of all that he had discovered, including his plans for the evening. After dropping sealing wax on the missive, he rang for Lovejoy. Upon Lovejoy's arrival, he handed him the letter and said, "I want Roxbury to have this information as soon as possible—little though it is. See to it, please."

Lovejoy nodded and departed, the letter held firmly in his capable hand.

Slipping out of the house a few minutes later for, he hoped, a rendezvous with the smugglers, Nicolas thought back once more to that scene in his grandmother's parlor. The information about the gatekeeper's cottage had upset someone. But who? And why? The contraband goods? Or something else entirely?

Chapter Thirteen

*N*icolas still had no answers by the time the gatekeeper's cottage came into view. The rain, which had fallen steadily throughout the day and evening, had lessened to a foggy mist; the sky was starless, and there was no moonlight. A perfect night for any self-respecting smuggler to be out and about, he thought with a grin as he tied his horse in the end stall of the stable.

He had debated the wisdom of placing the animal there—the very presence of a saddled horse in a place it shouldn't be, would, if discovered, alert the smugglers that someone was in the area. But an earlier examination of the stables had shown that, at least so far, here was one place the smugglers had not ventured. A feed bag full of grain tied around the horse's head should also insure that the animal would stand quietly, even if there were the sounds of other horses nearby.

His horse taken care of, Nicolas crossed to the house and slipped silently into the back of the darkened building. He had left orders that all the fires be put out early in the evening and the curtains drawn so that no sign of light shone to the outside. There had been no discernible smell of smoke in the air, nor had he seen any hint of light as he had approached the house, and he was confident the smugglers would still think the cottage deserted. Unless, of course, the news that the cottage was now occupied had been spread to the smugglers by one of his grandmother's guests. . . .

Shutting the back door quietly behind him, Nicolas was surprised to see a faint glow coming from the kitchen area. Could the smugglers be here already? He checked his pistol, making certain it was loaded and primed, and then with a stealthy tread, he made his way forward to where the light became stronger.

He halted in the doorway to the kitchen. Spying Tess seated at the scrubbed oak table, eating an apple, he relaxed. It was the light from her small candle that he had seen.

Pocketing his pistol, he strode forward, torn between pleasure at seeing her and annoyance that she was not tucked safely into her bed upstairs. She had not heard him enter. When he suddenly loomed up out of the darkness, she gave a faint scream and leaped to her feet.

She regarded him unkindly. "You frightened me!" she said sharply.

"Far better that *I* frighten you than one of our owlers," he returned dryly. "I thought you were supposed to be in bed."

Clutching the new bright blue wool wrapper closer to her, she looked adorably guilty. "I was," she admitted. "But I got hungry, and I only came down for something to eat—all the curtains and shutters were closed, so I didn't think any light would show through."

"It didn't, but you still took a chance of being discovered." His face grave, he said softly, "Don't let it happen again—I'd hate for you to come to harm."

She made a face. "I just didn't think that it would matter. Besides, it's too early for the owlers to be out and about, isn't it?"

Nicolas shrugged. "Perhaps, but it is well past midnight, and I expect that they don't have a set hour to begin their activities. I just hope that I am not too late."

"Why?" She suddenly looked alarmed. "You don't think that they've come and gone, do you?"

"No, but there was an incident tonight. . . ."

Looking even more alarmed, she drew nearer to him. "What? What happened?"

Nicolas shrugged again. "Oh, nothing that dramatic, but my grandmother asked me—with regrettable clarity in a room full of people, I might add—about all the goings-on here at the cottage. Everyone heard her remarks, and the news that the place was now occupied seemed to provoke a noticeable reaction from some of her guests." Making light of it, he quickly told her what had happened.

He was surprised to find himself telling her about the incident at all—he was not normally one to go babbling his business to all and sundry, preferring to play his cards close to his chest—but it seemed the most natural thing in the world to discuss the curious episode in the drawing room with her. With even more surprise, he discovered that he wanted to know what she thought about it and if she had come to the same conclusions he had.

He had barely finished speaking when she exclaimed with equal parts of elation and apprehension, "Someone there tonight knows about the hidden contraband!" Her eyes got even bigger. "And if they do, they'll be desperate to move the goods before you discover them—assuming they believe that you haven't *already* discovered them!"

"My sentiments precisely. Which is why you are going upstairs this very moment and I am going down to the cellars to await their arrival."

"Oh, you can't," she cried out in agitated tones. "Not now! It could be a trap!" When he appeared unmoved by her words, she grabbed the front of his greatcoat and shook him, saying urgently, "Don't you realize—they could be waiting for you!"

Placing his hands over hers, he said quietly, "Hush! I was careful not to give any indication that there was anything untoward in the cottage. I'm sure they believe that the goods have not yet been discovered, and I'm equally certain that you're right—they *will* be desperate to remove the contraband, immediately! Don't you see, sweetheart, this is a stroke of luck! Who knows when they would have come for the hidden goods? It might have been a week or two before they felt safe to move them. A week or two, I might add, that I'd have had to spend lurking about that cold, damp cellar waiting for their appearance. But now they can't wait—it *has* to be tonight." His voice hardened. "Now that the cottage is occupied, every moment they delay is dangerous. They dare not wait to move the goods."

"But Nick, don't you see?" she said passionately. "Now that they know someone is living here, you've lost the element of surprise. They'll be twice as wary as they would be normally. What you planned to do before was dangerous, but now it is foolhardy! You *must* give it up!"

"I can't," he said simply. "I have to do it. There is more involved here than just mere smuggling." As soon as the words left his mouth, he cursed his runaway tongue. Good God! This woman had indeed bewitched him. In her presence he began to chatter like an old village gossip and seemed to forget everything he'd ever learned in the military about secrets and the need to keep them *secret*.

Disgusted with himself, he pushed her away and said, "Enough of this! I've got to get in the cellar and positioned before they arrive." Bluntly he added, "Every second I remain here arguing with you increases the danger of my being discovered. Now, are you going up to bed?"

Anger darkened her eyes, and with her mouth set in grim lines, she increased the distance between them. "Very well— damn you! Go get yourself killed! See if I care!"

With a flash of blue wool she was gone, taking her candle with her. As he stood there in the blackness of the kitchen, Nicolas snorted. Women, he thought irascibly, were the *very* devil!

But he didn't have time to dwell on such subjects and carefully made his way to the pantry. It was even blacker inside the smaller room, and after knocking his shins several times on various items scattered about, he decided to risk a small light. He lit the tiny candle he had brought with him for exactly that purpose, and seconds later, with no more stumbling and fumbling, he was near enough to the cellar doorway to blow out his candle.

He stood there silently for several moments, listening intently, but no sound came to his ears, nor did any gleam of light show between the bottom of the door and the sill. He didn't like the idea of going down those steep cellar steps in the impenetrable darkness, but he had no choice, not unless he wanted to run the risk of alerting the smugglers, if they were anywhere nearby, to his presence. Of course, if he fell down and broke his neck, he thought wryly, that would certainly put an end to any scheme of his *not* to alert them!

Taking a deep breath, he opened the door carefully. Utter and complete blackness met his gaze. Since there was no sign of light, it would appear that he had arrived in time. Groping through the darkness, he found the railing, and as quickly and silently as he could in the smothering blackness, he hurried downward.

At the base of the stairs he hesitated, his ears cocked for the slightest sound, his eyes straining to pierce the darkness. Once again he decided to risk the tiny light of his candle and relit it. A hasty inspection revealed everything as the smugglers had left it. While the signs of his and the others' presence had been greatly obliterated, a searching eye would see that someone had recently been in the cellar. Nicolas sighed. He hoped the smugglers would simply come for their goods and leave and not decide to look about.

He hadn't been certain where the best spot would be to hide and yet have a fairly clear view of what was going on, and he suddenly wished that he had taken more time this afternoon to explore the area. One of the many narrow corridors branching off from the main part of the cellar seemed his most likely choice, and he swiftly crossed to the one he had selected. It was nearly opposite from the outside doors, which was the way he assumed that the smugglers would enter, and from it he still had a decent view of the contraband goods. Satisfied with his position, he blew out his candle. Darkness descended like a black cloak over his head, and as he leaned gingerly back against the wall, he wondered how long he would have to wait—or if he had sent himself on a sleeveless errand.

Time passed with paralyzing slowness; the darkness was oppressive, the silence heavy and unnerving. Fifteen minutes crept by; a half hour—at least Nicolas thought it was a half hour—seemed an eternity. An hour dragged by and then another, and just when he was beginning to think that he had misjudged the situation, there was a whisper of sound.

In his hiding place he stiffened, his heart beginning to race. There it was again, coming from the direction of the outside cellar doors. He gripped his pistol and waited.

It was difficult to tell when the outside doors were thrown wide; it was a moonless night, and the hinges were well oiled. But as he stared tensely in that direction, Nicolas thought he could discern the cellar opening and he definitely could hear a variety of faint, furtive little noises that drifted through the darkness to him.

Suddenly there was a flash, and a second later, as his eyes adjusted, he realized that whoever had entered the cellar had lit a lantern. In the soft yellow glow that permeated the area, he could clearly see the four rough-garbed men as they approached the pile of contraband goods. A low murmur of voices came to him as he edged closer to get a better view.

Nicolas watched closely during the next several minutes as the men moved about and began to cart boxes out of the cellar. It was apparent that they were common laborers—not only their clothing, but their speech and manner gave them away, and he was aware of a little stab of disappointment. *His* quarry, the master spy, was obviously not going to make an appearance here tonight. He was going to have to follow these men and hope that they eventually did meet with their leader.

His mouth twisted. Their leader, the man he was counting on to be his spy . . .

There was no denying that there were several smuggler bands in this area, and for the first time it occurred to him that these particular ruffians might not necessarily be involved in the smuggling of state secrets or have a spy in their ranks. If that was true, he was wasting his time, and his spirits sank. It had seemed so opportune: the smuggled goods right here under his nose and the unexpected opportunity presenting itself to observe the smugglers almost immediately upon his arrival in Kent. He hadn't had to waste time asking discreet questions and nosing around. It had seemed a gift from the gods. And then there was the incident tonight in his grandmother's drawing room. Was he placing too much importance upon it? Had it been just coincidence?

He didn't think so. He and Roxbury had agreed that whoever the spy might eventually turn out to be would be a man of rank and substance. Someone who could move freely through the salons of the ton, the offices at Whitehall, and the rooms at the Horse Guards. Someone who could pick up information here and there and never be questioned. . . .

Nicolas was convinced that the man he wanted had been at his grandmother's tonight. He was also convinced that *these* men would lead him to that person and that for whatever reasons—coincidence? or fate?—he'd had a miraculous stroke of luck to have stumbled across this cache of contraband goods in his own damned cellar!

Though moving quietly, the men were making fast work of lugging the casks and boxes up out of the cellar. Just when Nicolas was certain that their leader was not going to show himself, a tall, greatcoated figure suddenly appeared in the outside doorway.

In the dim light of the lantern, Nicolas surveyed the man who stepped coolly into the room, his bearing as well as his clothing bespeaking a man of taste and wealth. In addition to the many-caped greatcoat, the newcomer was wearing a stylish curly-brimmed hat pulled low across his forehead, obscuring his features, but Nicolas had no doubt that he was looking at his quarry. His heartbeat quickened. If only the man would move farther into the light. Step out of the shadows. Let me see your face, damn you!

The first four men greeted the arrival of the fifth man with little enthusiasm.

"Time you showed up," growled one burly individual. "After dragging us out at a minute's notice, I'd have thought you'd come and help move the blasted stuff yourself, if it was so damn-fire urgent that we get it out of here."

"What's the rush, guvnor?" asked another fellow, a small man with a grizzled beard. "We've been safely hiding things here for years. Never tell me that the revenuers have discovered us!"

The newcomer made some comment; Nicolas couldn't hear what it was, but from the other's reactions he could guess what it was.

"Blimey! What'd he want to go and do that for! This place has been deserted ever since I can remember."

"Living 'ere! Bloody earl's got a grand 'ouse, why'd 'e need this place?"

There was another murmur from the man in the greatcoat. Suddenly his head shot up, and Nicolas could have sworn he looked directly at him. Instinctively he shrank against the wall, forcing himself deeper into the shadows, and it was only then that he realized that not only was there light from the lantern in the main room of the cellar, but that there was light coming from *behind* him!

Cursing himself for not having explored the area more thoroughly, Nicolas was in the act of spinning around when the blow caught him. He had barely a glimpse of another man garbed much as the newcomer before the pain exploded along the side of his head and the blackness rushed up to greet him.

Standing over Nicolas's fallen body, the sixth man stared dispassionately down at him. Holding his lantern higher, a short billy club held in the other, he called out to the men, "Come over here, you fools, and see how close we came to ruin tonight."

The five crowded into the narrow passageway, one of them saying dumbly, "Gor! Blimey, Mr. Brown! It's the earl! Wot's he doing 'ere?"

"It doesn't matter," retorted the gentleman called Mr. Brown. "All that matters is that we get these goods to a new hiding place. Now get busy, but next time I tell you to watch yourselves, make certain you do! If I hadn't have decided to use the back way into the cellars tonight, there is a very good chance we'd all be riding the three-legged mare in a very short time!"

The original four men hurried back to their task, leaving the two gentlemen in their caped greatcoats with Nicolas's unconscious body. The other man looked at Mr. Brown. "Now what? This does complicate matters, doesn't it?"

Mr. Brown grimaced. "It complicates them far more than you know. It wasn't a whim that brought me through the back entrance—I did a little snooping before I came and discovered that our *friend* here is using the cottage as a love-nest for his latest ladybird! I suspected he might be about, but I'll admit I didn't really expect to find him down here."

The other man looked worried. "Obviously he knows that we were using the cottage as a place to hide the goods until it was safer to transport them to London. Wonder why he didn't inform Sir Charles?"

Mr. Brown smiled tightly. "Oh, I imagine our grand earl was in need of a bit of excitement after his great adventures on the peninsula. Probably thought to be a hero."

"That may be, but what if he *does* inform Sir Charles of what he's found? What then? This has been perfect for our uses. Now that we've been discovered, I cannot think of any other place that would suit even half as well."

"You worry too much! By the time the earl awakes, all trace of our recent activities will be gone. He'll look a fool if he goes running to Sir Charles complaining about smugglers." A sneer curved Mr. Brown's mouth. "And I doubt he'd want it known that he had been struck down by a mere owler! But enough of him—we'll just have to move our operation for a few months, and once the earl's soiled dove is no longer in residence, we shall be able to make use of the cottage again—albeit with much more stealth and caution."

"But what if the affair with his lightskirt goes on for any length of time?" demanded the taller one. "It's possible that he might be thoroughly infatuated with her and their affair might last for months. What then?"

Mr. Brown stared thoughtfully at Nicolas's body. "I doubt such is the case, but I think to insure that the cottage is soon deserted, the, uh, lady is going to have to suffer an accident. A fatal one."

"You mean murder a *woman*?"

Their eyes met. "Why not? You weren't so squeamish about the others. What difference does it make if this time it's a woman? The stakes are certainly high enough . . . or would you rather run the risk of our *very* profitable little sideline being discovered? It was the *money* that overcame your scruples, wasn't it?"

The taller man's mouth tightened. "You know damn well it was—I never meant to become a traitor, nor a murderer, and if it weren't for that bastard—"

"This isn't getting us anywhere. We're in too deep, and we're certainly not letting anything stand in our way at this late stage, even the murder of a little tart!" Mr. Brown glanced over into the main part of the cellar. "The men are done. Let us be off—we can discuss what we plan to do later."

"What about him?"

A contemptuous smile curved the chiseled lips of Mr. Brown. "Leave him. The worst our fine earl will probably suffer is a blazing headache."

The words were prophetic. Sometime later, as Nicolas slowly swam up into consciousness, the first thing he became aware of was a blinding pain in his head. The next was the hard, cold, damp surface of the cellar floor. Then he realized that he was not alone, that Dolly was kneeling by his side, shaking him urgently and calling his name.

He opened his eyes, only to close them immediately as the light from her lantern sent a knife blade of pain ricocheting through his head. "Move the damned light before you blind me," he growled ungratefully, struggling into a sitting position. "And what the hell are you doing down here?"

"I was trying to see if you were alive or dead!" Tess retorted from between clenched teeth. Standing up, she lifted the lantern from the floor where she had set it and said, "Since it would appear that you *are* alive and not dead as I first feared, I shall be only too happy to leave you here. Good night!"

Nicolas grimaced. "Wait!" he said in more normal tones. "I'm sorry I snapped at you, but I'm not best pleased with myself at the moment, and I've got a devil of a headache."

"Oh, Nick," Tess cried, all her anger evaporating in an instant as she reached out a hand to help him to his feet. "I was so worried about you! I know you told me to stay upstairs, and I *did*! But when positively *hours* had passed and you hadn't returned, I grew frightened and I knew I had to come in search of you." Her gaze traveled anxiously over him. "I was certain the owlers either hadn't come tonight, or if they had . . ." She swallowed. "I *knew* something was wrong, and when I found you lying there so cold and still . . ." Speech was suspended as she fought with her emotions. In a small voice she finally said, "I thought you were dead!"

"It takes more than a knock on the head to kill me, sweetheart," he said lightly, and pulled her gently against him. Dropping a kiss on her head, he murmured, "Thank you for coming to find me. Now, shall we go upstairs and see if we can get a warm fire going—it's bloody cold down here!"

Tess gave a watery chuckle, and together they left the cellar and made their way to the kitchen. It took a few minutes, but soon enough there was a fire blazing on the kitchen hearth and Tess had hung a kettle of water over it to heat. By the time the water was hot and she had discovered where Sara kept the tea, Nicolas had found the brandy. In a short while, they were sitting near the fire, sipping some piping hot tea liberally laced with brandy.

Nicolas's headache was abating slightly, and there was now just a faint throb in his temple. Looking far more robust than he had any right to, he found himself telling Tess what had happened.

When the tale was done, her eyes were very big in her small face. "A secret entrance! The master smuggler hit you from *behind*! Oh, how thrilling!"

Nicolas cocked a brow at her. "You could spare a bit of sympathy for me, you know," he said with a teasing gleam in his eyes, "before you get all excited about master smugglers and secret entrances."

She made a face at him. "You are perfectly recovered and you know it. And it *is* exciting to think that there is a secret entrance to the cellar. Admit it! Oh, Nick, just think—an entrance that no one except the master smuggler knows about." Her eyes gleamed. "There is no telling what we might find."

A reluctant laugh was dragged from him. "You're incorrigible! But I'll grant you one thing—I'm mightily interested in finding that unknown entrance." They smiled at each other, wrapped in an inexplicable feeling of comradeship.

"And you're going to let me help look for it, aren't you?" she asked confidently, leaning forward, her amethyst eyes sparkling.

A rueful expression crossed Nick's face. "Yes, I believe I am—much against my will and much to my astonishment. But first you must swear to me that you won't go looking for it without waiting for me."

Tess nodded eagerly. "You have it. I swear. When do we start?"

A sudden yawn took Nicolas by surprise. Setting down his

cup, he said, "Not immediately, I'm afraid. After the night we've spent I suspect it will be midday before either of us arises. So for now I'll bid you good night, and I'll see you early afternoon." He shot her a warning glance. "And no exploring until I get here."

"No exploring," Tess answered sunnily, too happy that he had agreed to let her help to argue with him.

He pressed a warm, lingering kiss on her mouth, and a moment later he was gone. Sitting in the kitchen by herself, Tess didn't know whether to be relieved or annoyed that he'd made no mention of spending the remainder of the night with her.

A little morosely, she left the kitchen and wandered through the dark house upstairs to her rooms. Since the smugglers had come and gone *and* discovered Nicolas, there was no reason to be careful anymore, and conscious of the chill, she quickly started a fire. Wide awake, she eyed her bed with distaste. It had to be nearing five o'clock in the morning, and despite having been up most of the night, she doubted that she'd be able to sleep a wink.

She lit a couple of candles and moved restlessly about the room. The news that there was a hidden entrance to the cellars entranced her, and the knowledge that Nicolas wasn't going to be an utter beast about her accompanying him when he went looking for it pleased her inordinately.

She finally sat down, staring at the fire, too excited and impatient for the adventure to begin to sleep. And as she sat there, almost imperceptibly she became aware of a feeling of déjà vu . . . as if she had once before sat in this room, eager for the dawning of the next day. . . .

She shivered, not certain she liked these peculiar snippets of memory that came over her. Were these queer moments glimpses into her past? Or something else? She had the curious and unnerving impression that it wasn't *her* past she was experiencing, but the past of someone else. . . . Someone she had known?

The feeling of familiarity was so strong, so powerful, that

it seemed to press against her, cajoling, begging, *demanding* that she remember. Helplessly her eyes moved around the room as she tried to find some clue to her strange feelings. For a second she stared at the bed where she and Nicolas had made love yesterday afternoon, the brilliant colors of the silk hangings delicately muted with age. . . . Like one in a trance, she sat there looking at the rumpled bed, and then, before her stunned gaze, the faint smoky shape of another man and woman, a man and woman who bore startling similarity to her and Nicolas, seemed to form before her eyes. They knelt facing each other on the bed, and with great tenderness the naked shadowy forms embraced, kissing each other with frank passion. Mesmerized, Tess was unable to tear her gaze away, yet she had no sensation of prying—it was like watching a mirror image of herself and Nicolas. . . .

The ghostly figures faded, and a loud pop from the fireplace brought her out of the strange mood. She blinked, and when she looked at the bed again there was nothing there. It was just an empty bed with scattered blankets.

Glancing back at the fire, she shook her head as if to clear it. Was she going mad? Seeing visions and things that weren't really there? Again her eyes wandered around the room, a frown forming on her forehead. What was it about this room? This cottage? It felt so familiar, and yet she was certain she had never been here before.

Inexplicably, the fire on the hearth suddenly flared up, cracking and snapping noisily, the flames soaring upward as if blown by a wind, jerking her gaze to the fireplace. As she stared, the flames slowly died down to the cheerful little blaze that had been there only a moment ago, but she did not look away again. Instead her gaze traveled slowly over the rock face of the fireplace itself.

Drawn by something stronger than herself, she stood and walked nearer the fireplace. Without volition, her hand reached out and her fingers unknowingly caressed the rough surface of the stone, lingering, moving irresistibly toward the jagged-shapped stone she had noticed earlier. As if guided by some inner knowledge, her fingers curved around the uneven edges, tugging and pulling, twisting, and her heart leaped when, without warning, the stone moved imperceptibly and gave way.

The queer trancelike state that had been over her the past several minutes vanished, and all her attention was focused on freeing the stone. With growing excitement Tess struggled to break the stone loose from its moorings. When it finally came loose, she gave a soft crow of triumph.

Eyes shining, she stared at the dark recess revealed behind the stone. Then, after carefully putting down the heavy stone, she reached for a candle and brought it closer.

The flickering light revealed an old-fashioned, small steel box resting in the hidden recess. Her heartbeat quickening, she touched it gingerly. Her fingers tingled, and almost reverently, she brought out the small box from the place it had lain concealed for who knew how long—perhaps decades, centuries. . . .

She put down the candle on a nearby table, the box clutched tightly in her grasp, and sank onto a chair next to the fire. Heart pounding, she stared for a long time at the box she held in her lap.

She was excited, scared; eager and reluctant at the same time to open the seemingly innocent box. There was no telling what lay inside.

Tess took a deep breath and, in one quick motion, opened the box. To her disappointment, it was empty except for a small leather-bound volume. As her initial disappointment faded, she became curious about the contents of that small volume. Someone had gone to a great deal of trouble to keep it concealed from prying eyes. What was so vital that its owner would feel impelled to place it in such a secret hiding place?

Her interest renewed, Tess picked it up and began to examine the old volume. Strong black strokes crossing the pages, it

appeared to be a diary. Her eye fell to the date of the page she
had opened to—October 5, 1742:

> *She came to me again last night—*
> *despite all our vows not to meet*
> *anymore. These furtive, hasty*
> *couplings are destroying both of*
> *us and yet, dear God! I cannot,*
> *even if I condemn my very soul to*
> *hellfire, give her up! I love her*
> *beyond reason—she is the other*
> *half of me—to never see her again,*
> *her smile, her sweet face, to never hold*
> *her, to never again kiss her*
> *or feel her body moving beneath mine*
> *would be like ripping the still beating*
> *heart from my body! And yet it becomes too*
> *dangerous—her husband, damn his soul,*
> *suspects. . . .*

Chapter Fourteen

With trembling fingers, Tess slowly closed the small leather-bound volume. She could read no farther. There was something so intensely personal about the words, the emotions that came across so vividly, that she felt embarrassed—as if she were spying on a stranger's most intimate, most private feelings. Yet . . . there was something . . . something nagged at her. . . . She glanced at the date, October 5, 1742.

Now what significance could that year have for her? A date of nearly seventy years ago? She could guess the writer's identity—the script and content were that of an educated man, certainly not a gatekeeper. And hadn't Nicolas mentioned that one of his relatives had built the cottage to house a mistress? The writer had to be one of Nicolas's ancestors. But which one? His grandfather? A great-grandfather? Or even farther back? And the woman? Who was she?

A huge yawn escaped her, and Tess suddenly became aware that her eyes were scratchy and ached from lack of sleep. Another yawn took her. She blinked. She really was very tired.

For a few seconds longer she stared at the diary in her hands, wanting to read farther, wanting to know more about the writer. Yet she was oddly unwilling to pry. She yawned again. Sleep. That's what she needed now.

She returned the small volume to the steel box and carefully slid it back into the hiding place. The stone was a little harder to position, but after some shoving and tilting she managed to lock it into place.

It was amazing, she thought as she stepped back from the fireplace, but if one didn't know that there was a secret compartment, it wouldn't be found. The pivotal stone blended in magically with its neighbors, and there was nothing to indicate a hidden niche at all. Which made it even more peculiar that she'd noticed it. . . .

Yawning widely, she walked to the bed. Laying aside her wrapper, she crawled gratefully between the covers. She lay there a minute, thinking about the diary. She'd have to tell Nicolas about it when she saw him . . . and that was her last coherent thought. Despite the faint hint of dawn's light at her shuttered window and the excitement of the night, not two minutes after her head hit the pillow, she was sound asleep.

Sleep had not been tardy coming to Nicolas, either. He had hurried back to Sherbourne Court and managed to enter his rooms without incident. After hastily shedding his damp, filthy clothing, he wrapped himself in a wildly embroidered robe of deep ruby silk and helped himself to a generous snifter of brandy. Sipping his brandy, he sat before the crackling fire in his room and contemplated the events of the night.

It had certainly not been boring, he thought with a faint smile. Even his grandmother's dinner party had proven to be most interesting. Gingerly he touched the aching spot on his temple. And he supposed that getting knocked in the head by a smuggler would certainly not be characterized as boring! Although, he decided with a grimace, it was a bit of excitement that he could have done very well without.

The fact that there was another entrance into the cellars of the gatekeeper's cottage was a serious matter—as was the unfortunate fact that the smugglers had found him spying on them. He frowned. They were going to be twice as wary, and it was unlikely that they'd be bold enough to continue to use the cellars now that they knew the place was occupied and that he had been snooping around.

He sighed for the lost opportunity and, after finishing his brandy, sought out his bed.

Nicolas had planned to rise at midmorning, but it was nearly noon before he awakened. Guessing that Dolly had slept in as well, he saw no reason to hurry to her side. There would be time enough this afternoon to start their explorations.

Along with his coffee, Lovejoy brought him some welcome news: his missive to Roxbury had left hours ago, and his grandmother and Athena had gone shopping and to visit friends in Romney and wouldn't be back until early evening.

Reminded of his letter to Roxbury, Nicolas made a face. Another was certainly in order. He wrote it immediately, bringing Roxbury up-to-date. Handing it to Lovejoy a few minutes later, Nick grinned. "I'm afraid that I have need of another one of my grandmother's staff for a speedy journey to London. Her own trip couldn't have come at a more opportune time—otherwise, she would badger me with all sorts of questions about her disappearing servants!"

The propitious trip had been prompted by his grandmother's wish for a particular shade of thread she needed to finish some embroidery work she had started and a long-standing invitation to visit with her dearest friend, Lady Throckmorton. If the weather turned bad, Lovejoy had reported, there was the possibility they might stay the night, so they had packed accordingly. The information that for perhaps the next twenty-four hours he need satisfy only his own wants pleased Nicolas—at least for a while it put off some embarrassing questions.

When he had chosen the gatekeeper's cottage as a perfect place to set up a household for his mistress, he hadn't realized the amount of subterfuge that would be entailed for him to slip away to see her. Pallas already knew he had opened the gatekeeper's cottage, and he was resigned to her eventually discovering the reason. He winced. Call him cowardly, but he would have preferred that his grandmother *not* learn he had brazenly installed his mistress on the family estate. I should have thought out the situation a bit more thoroughly, he admitted wryly. Now, when it was too late, he knew that he should have put Dolly in a snug little house either in Hythe or Romney—certainly not at his grandmother's very back door. But the damage was done, and he was cynically aware that it wasn't the fact that he had a mistress that would displease Pallas, but *where* he had placed her. Women, he thought again as he lowered himself into a big brass tub, were indeed the very devil!

It was just a few minutes after one o'clock in the afternoon when he seated himself in the morning room and began to eat with relish the tasty breakfast Cook had freshly prepared for him. His stomach rumbling in anticipation, he had piled his plate high with crisp bacon, fresh kidneys, rare roast beef, piping hot scrambled eggs, and sweet buns still warm from the oven.

When his meal was finished, Nicolas poured himself another cup of coffee and pushed back his chair, stretching his long legs out in front of him. Refreshed, his belly full, he was feeling very satisfied with himself at the moment, and the only thing that would have made the day more perfect would have been the sight of Dolly's lovely little face at the other end of his table.

It occurred to him that, unlike his other mistresses, Dolly would fit in very well at Sherbourne Court. There was an air about her. . . . He frowned. God knew what her people had been thinking when they had placed her at the Black Pig.

As he sat there staring out the window at the fine fall afternoon unfolding before his gaze, he wondered, not for the first time, when her family was going to make their presence felt. They must have realized by now that he had no intention of marrying her. It was strange that they had not come forth and demanded some sort of recompense—after all, it had been money that had prompted their actions. He was more than willing to give them a sizable sum for their efforts, and of course, when he was through with Dolly, he would see to it that she was well taken care of. He moved restlessly, not liking to think, even idly, about the day she would depart from his life. It would be, he admitted testily, a damn long time from now!

Bellingham's entrance into the morning room disturbed his thoughts, and Nicolas glanced at his butler.

Bellingham bowed majestically, his outward bearing as stiff and unbending as usual. As if displaying a fine ruby before Nicolas, he placed on the table a silver salver upon which rested two cards. "Sir," he began in his deep, melodious voice, "you have visitors."

"Well, of course he has visitors!" came an irascible voice from the doorway. Without further ado, two tall, impeccably dressed gentlemen surged into the room. "And we'd have been here sooner if you hadn't been so stiff rumped, Belly! You know Nick's going to see us, so you needn't have tried to fob us off with that nonsense about inquiring if he was receiving visitors. Besides, we ain't *exactly* visitors."

Bellingham closed his eyes as if in anguish. "Sir, as you can see, Baron Rockwell and his brother have come to call."

Nicolas grinned. "Yes, I can see. Thank you, Bellingham. Oh, and ask Cook if she would mind sending in some more food. My friends will no doubt be hungry."

"Indeed we are," replied Alexander Rockwell, the baron's brother, as he carelessly tossed his greatcoat and gloves at Bellingham and seated himself confidently at the table near Nicolas. "It's been a damn long time since that meager breakfast we ate on the road this morning. I swear, I could eat a horse! Oh, and Nick, we'll be staying awhile—got a problem. Tom can tell you all about it."

Nicolas sent his butler a smiling look. "Would you see to it that rooms are readied for the baron and his brother? Oh, and any servants they may have brought with them?"

"Of course," Bellingham replied in spectral tones. His arms

laden with the outer garments from both the Rockwell brothers, he marched sedately from the room.

His black eyes twinkling, Nicolas regarded his two friends as they settled themselves more comfortably. Both were garbed stylishly in dark blue jackets, buff pantaloons, and gleaming black boots, their cravats as white and starched and tastefully arranged as even that demanding arbiter of taste, Brummell, could have wished.

Lord Rockwell was a strikingly handsome man with corn fair hair and brilliant blue eyes, and with his great fortune and estates, it was amazing that he had reached the advanced age of forty and had not yet married. While not quite the catch his brother was, Alexander Rockwell was not to be overlooked. He didn't have a title, but his fortune was nearly as large and he had the same tall, slender physique. Though his curly locks were merely an attractive brown and his eyes didn't possess the startling clarity of the baron's, he had caused many a maiden to wish longingly for his attentions. To the dismay of several matchmaking mamas, Alexander had turned thirty-six in March and, like his brother, still showed no signs of abandoning his rakish ways and finding a wife.

Nicolas had known both men for almost as long as he could remember. Baron Rockwell had actually been Randal's friend, but being of a far warmer nature than the previous earl, Tom Rockwell had always had a kind word or a quick wink for young Nick. In fact, much to Randal's irritation, it had been Tom who had seen to it that Nicolas had gone to his first prizefight and had even guided Nicolas's and Alexander's eager, uncertain steps into less respectable pastimes. . . .

Nicolas and Alexander had been boon companions practically from the first moment they had met at the Cornwall estate of the Rockwell family; their parents had been friends, and for a while Nick had known there had been great hopes between the families that Tom's fancy would alight upon Athena. Fortunately, Nicolas thought with a grin, that terrible fate hadn't befallen the baron.

The two younger boys had gone to school together and served briefly together in the army. Alexander had eventually grown bored with a military career, and since there was no need for him to earn a living, unlike Nick in those days, he had sold out his captaincy some years previously. The Rockwell brothers had been among the first to exuberantly welcome Nick back to England.

Despite not being known for their discretion, for the next several moments the Rockwells contented themselves with polite conversation as food and drink were placed before them. It was only after the servants had finally departed that Alexander said, "Didn't think those fellows were ever going to leave us alone!" Glancing at the vast array of mouthwatering offerings scattered up and down the long table, he added hastily, "Not that I ain't glad your staff is so well trained—thing is, we've got a problem and can't talk in front of servants!"

Nicolas, sipping another cup of coffee, raised a quizzical brow. "A problem? What sort?"

"Not the sort that can be bandied about," Lord Rockwell said testily. "It's that damned Avery! I wish to hell that Boney's troops had blown him to the very devil!"

"My sentiments precisely," Nicolas returned dryly. "But how is Avery a problem for you?"

"M'niece," Lord Rockwell said gloomily, a worried expression crossing his normally sunny countenance.

Nicolas's brow rose higher. "The heiress? Thea? Theda? Something like that?"

"Tess. Short for 'Theresa.' Named after her great-grandmother. The one who ran away with your grandfather," Alexander offered helpfully.

Nicolas rolled his eyes. "I know which one. But why is she a problem? Has she run away with her dancing master or something equally scandalous?"

Taking a bite of rare roast beef slathered with spicy mustard, Tom said, "Wish it was that simple. Thing is, believe

Avery means to marry her. Came down here to see for ourselves." Tom's expression became even more gloomy. "Can't abide Avery. Like Tess. Wouldn't want to see her leg-shackled to a bounder like Avery!"

"Well, yes, I do see your problem, but if the chit's your niece, why don't you just whisk her way to Cornwall?"

"Can't," Alexander answered morosely. "Aunts."

Looking thoroughly confused, Nicolas repeated, "Ants? . . . Oh, you mean aunts? What do they have to do with the situation?"

"There is two of 'em, and Tess won't leave 'em. That clutch-fisted bastard Gregory left them damn near penniless. Dependent upon Avery. Tess insists that Avery would mistreat them if she weren't around to keep an eye on things."

"Well then, you're warm enough—set them up in their own household—Thea, er, *Tess* will be away from Avery and she'll have her two aunts with her. What could be more simple?"

"Got principles, the aunts, especially Hetty," Alexander answered bitterly. "Won't even let Tess use *her* money, let alone ours to rescue them from Avery's pinch-penny ways."

"Well then, you're just going to have to explain everything to, er, Tess and, for her own good, *make* her go with you to Cornwell. If the aunts' situation becomes desperate enough, I think," Nicolas finished coolly, "that you'll be able to overcome their principles."

Baron Rockwell looked keenly at Nicolas. "You ever met Tess?"

"Tom, she's a Mandeville! Now what do you think? I wouldn't know the chit if she came riding up to my front door."

"Thing is," Tom said grimly, "if you knew Tess, you'd know what a damn fool idea that notion of yours is. You can't *make* Tess go anywhere that she don't want to go. And she ain't leaving her aunts. Got a mind of her own, does Tess."

Nicolas sent him a look. "How old is this niece of yours, anyway?"

"Turned twenty-one this past April."

"Good God!" Nicolas muttered irritably. "Why didn't you take her in hand long before this? Or at least have married her off as soon as she came out of the schoolroom? If you're so worried about her marrying Avery, find a suitor you *do* like and get her married. Then you can let her husband teach her respect for male authority and he can handle the problem with the aunts."

Rockwell and Alexander exchanged glances. Silence fell. Rockwell leaned forward confidingly. "We've already thought of that," he said finally. He paused, looked at his brother again, and then said in a rush, "Thought you'd make a good match for Tess!"

Nicolas stared at his two friends as if they had suddenly sprouted daffodils from their ears. "You thought *what*? Knowing the estrangement between the Talmages and the Mandevilles, you thought I just might"—despite his best efforts, his voice rose—"want to *marry* Tess Mandeville! Good God! Have the pair of you lost your senses?"

"Told you he wasn't going to like it," Alexander said to his brother.

"Well then, *you* come up with a better idea," the baron retorted in harried accents.

"Didn't say it wasn't a good idea," Alexander replied thoughtfully. "Said I told you he wasn't going to like it."

"It's a ridiculous idea," Nicolas said scathingly. "And only a pair of maggot-brained fellows like yourselves would have thought of it!"

Both brothers looked at him innocently. "Think about it, Nick," Alexander persisted manfully. "Except for that bastard Gregory ..." He stopped and added scrupulously, "And Avery, all the Mandevilles got good blood in their veins. Well connected, too. Respectable family. Tess is a pretty little thing." Gloomily he admitted, "Not biddable, though. Got a temper." Then he brightened. "But she has a fortune. You need a wife. She needs a husband. Good idea if you married her."

Nicolas ground his teeth together. "I am *not* going to marry your bloody niece!"

Alexander sighed. Looked at his brother. "Told you he wouldn't like it."

The baron, normally as amiable and convivial a fellow as one could meet, sent his beloved brother a glance of acute dislike. "Stop staying that! I know he doesn't like it. If he won't marry her, what the devil are we going to do?"

His own temper cooling, and reminding himself that he'd been friends with the Rockwells for a long time and should have been used to their harum-scarum fits and starts, Nicolas said in calmer tones, "Why don't you just go talk to Tess? Explain your fears to her. If she's a reasonable young woman, she'll realize her own danger . . . unless, of course, she *wants* to marry Avery?"

Both Rockwells shook their head.

"Can't abide him," said the baron.

"Would like to skewer his liver," added Alexander.

"Well then, simply tell her," Nicolas said reasonably, "that if she doesn't want to find herself compromised, she would do well to follow your advice and remove herself, and her aunts, to Cornwell."

"Intended to, but can't. Told you we had a problem," Rockwell said indignantly. "Avery won't let us see her! Been there today already. Place is locked up tighter than a virgin's thighs. No one around but that hatchet-faced fellow of his, Lowell. Wouldn't even let us in the place! Said the master had gone to London, which I think is all hum, and that the ladies weren't receiving visitors!" His brilliant blue eyes kindled. "Visitors! I'm her damned uncle! She knew we were coming. Wrote her. Told her we'd be here today. Long visit. Mentioned going to Cornwell for Christmas."

Despite telling himself that it was none of his business, that he wasn't going to get involved, particularly with the affairs of anyone named Mandeville, Nicolas felt the first stirrings of unease for Tess Mandeville. From past experience he knew that Avery Mandeville was an unscrupulous bastard—in Portugal an entire loving little family had been destroyed because of him—and now he felt all the remembered fury and horror surge up through him. If the new baron had decided to marry the Rockwells' niece, she could very well be in a great deal of trouble. "Do you think Avery read your letter?" he asked abruptly.

Both men looked at him dumbfounded. "Could have," the baron said slowly. "If it arrived and Tess wasn't there. God knows Avery's scoundrel enough to read other people's letters."

Nick stared at his steepled fingers. "*If* Avery knew you were coming, and *if* he really does have plans to marry Tess, willingly or not, then the news of your impending arrival must have sent the wind up him. It wouldn't take a genius to realize that you must have heard talk of some sort in London that had you worried and that you were coming to Kent to discover how the land lay for yourselves. From what you've told me about the contents of your letter, its pretty obvious that once you arrived here, your niece wasn't going to be out of your company . . . or protection. Avery would also know that you were planning on spiriting her away to Cornwell for a visit that would last until after the first of the year—or longer. By which time you might have convinced her *not* to return to Mandeville Manor. That wouldn't," he ended quietly, "have pleased our dear Avery very much."

"Goddamn him!" Alexander burst out furiously, his blue eyes blazing. "If that bastard has harmed her or Hetty . . . laid a hand on them, I'll . . ." Words failed him.

Nick was frowning. "You know," he said, "it's possible that Lowell was telling the truth—that Avery is in London." When both men glanced at him, he added, "I passed him on my way down here a few days ago. He was alone and he was driving rapidly in the direction of the City." His frown grew.

"But if Avery is in London . . . why didn't the ladies welcome you?"

There was a horrified silence. Alexander blanched and swallowed painfully. "You don't think," he began in an appalled voice, "that he *murdered* Het—them, do you?"

"While Avery is very capable of murder," Nicolas said grimly, "I don't believe that it would be in his best interests to murder the young lady he plans to marry! Nor, I might add, her aunts—at least not until he had secured her fortune." Nick looked at the two men. "I think you need to see Tess, and as soon as possible."

"We know that," Alexander muttered. "That's why we have a plan."

"A plan?" Nick asked warily, reminding himself that while the Rockwell family were noted for their stunning looks, it was equally well known that none of them could be said to possess a high intellect. "What sort of plan?"

The brothers exchanged pleased glances. "We wait until after midnight and then we break into the house. Find the ladies and take them away. Simple!"

"Assuming that Avery is away and that you won't have to confront him, what do you suppose Lowell and the other servants at the manor are going to be doing while you two are busily breaking into the home of a lord of the realm, hmm?"

"Uh, sleeping?" Alexander offered hopefully.

The baron leaned forward. "Thing is, Nick, we need your help. After your exploits on the continent, you know all about getting in and out of tight spots undetected. We thought you'd help us."

Nicolas closed his eyes. Yes, only the Rockwells would think nothing of embroiling their friends in such a wild scheme, nor would they hesitate a moment to join in, if the situation were reversed. The problem for Nick was that, for all the reasons to refuse—and there were several—he knew he was going to help them.

Sighing, he said, "I will help you on one condition." He

sent them a hard look. "You do *exactly* what I say, when I say it. No improvising. No deciding halfway through that you have a better idea. Swear it!"

With alacrity both men gave him the vow he wanted, and the next several minutes were passed in laying out a plan for the storming of Mandeville Manor that night. Getting inside the manor, Nicolas told them acidly, was the easiest problem to solve. It was once they were inside that things would get complicated. Fortunately, the Rockwells had been guests at the manor several times and were quite intimate with its layout and design, which eliminated their fumbling around in unfamiliar territory. The greatest problem was the ladies: if they *were* being held against their will, it would be up to Nicolas and the Rockwells not only to free them, but to find a place for them to stay.

For obvious reasons Sherbourne Court was *not* one of the places to offer them sanctuary. In selecting a place for the women to stay, their rescuers had also to consider the possibility of scandal. Despite being notoriously indiscreet themselves, the Rockwells wanted as little gossip as possible about their niece and tonight's escapade. So taking the women just anywhere wasn't an option.

Inwardly Nick sighed, knowing the solution was right before his eyes—if Dolly wouldn't mind passing herself off as a servant for a day or two. His lips hardened. It shouldn't prove too arduous—hadn't she been playing the part of a servant the night he had found her? His mind was made up; Tess Mandeville and her aunts could be comfortably hidden away in the gatekeeper's cottage until another, more permanent solution could be found. He smiled suddenly. His grandmother might not be overly fond of the Mandeville women, but he suspected she would be more inclined to tolerate their presence at the gatekeeper's cottage than that of his mistress! He shook his head. Who would have believed there would come a time that he'd actually be grateful to the Mandevilles? At least for the moment, their presence gave him the excuse he needed to explain opening the old cottage.

Their scheme decided upon, conversation drifted onto other topics, and it was then that Nicolas realized his own plans for the afternoon and evening had been changed drastically. Explaining the need for Dolly to temporarily give up her rooms and move downstairs to the servants' quarters was not going to be pleasant and was not something he could simply put in a note. He'd have to tell her in person, and he glanced consideringly at the two men sprawled comfortably around his table.

It was unlikely he'd be able to escape any time soon, for any length of time, so he excused himself for a few moments. In his rooms he hastily wrote a short note to Dolly, telling her only that he was delayed but would see her later in the day. She was *not* to go exploring on her own, and he swore that just as soon as possible they would begin looking for the secret entrance to the cellars.

Handing the missive to Lovejoy, he said, "See that this is delivered to the young lady. Oh, and Lovejoy, do it discreetly, hmm? I thought it went without saying that I didn't want my grandmother or sister to be privy to my private life."

Lovejoy flushed and looked indignant. "Sorry, sir! It weren't me that done the tongue flapping! It was that bacon-brained Jenny—she came to get a few things for the cottage, and before you could say 'jack-be-quick' she was sitting at the servants' table, telling everyone who would listen about the goings-on at the old place. I spoke sharply to her when we had a private moment, and I don't think it'll happen again. I wasn't best happy about it."

"Neither was I," Nicolas replied dryly.

Tess wasn't happy with the contents of Nicolas's note, either. Like Nick, she had arisen later than planned. Considering the lateness of the hour, she had expected him at any moment, so she had hurried through her morning ablutions and then gulped down a light breakfast. As the hours had passed and he still had not appeared, she'd grown impatient. The contents of the note had been a great disappointment. And with it had come the realization of how very much she had been looking forward to his arrival—and not just because they'd be looking for a secret entrance! It had also occurred to her that if she were going to remain his mistress, she had better start learning to accept the fact that there were going to be many times when his plans with her were abruptly changed. The knowledge didn't sit well, and with a discontented expression on her face, she wandered about the main room of the cottage. She wasn't going to sit around and brood over his deflection. She also, she admitted with a twist of her lips, wasn't going to go looking for the secret entrance— she'd given her word. So what was she going to do all afternoon?

A glance out the window at the sunny afternoon decided her. There was a hint of darkening clouds on the horizon, which probably meant more rain by nightfall, but at the moment the day was most delightful. Draping a soft, brightly colored cashmere shawl about her shoulders, she explained to Rose that she was going for a short walk, and she stepped out into the warm fall sunshine.

Tess had no idea where she was going, she just wanted some exercise and fresh air. She was restless and eager to escape for a while from the confines of the cottage, and, she admitted a little guiltily, she wanted to see if she recognized anything.

She walked briskly down the road, looking about her interestedly. While she didn't expect to suddenly recognize a particular spot, she hoped that she might see something that would remind her of home—wherever that was!

She had walked about a half mile from the cottage when, some distance through the trees and brush, she spied the remnants of an old apple orchard. Curious, she left the road and, lifting her skirts to keep them from snagging on limbs and branches, made her way to the small clearing in which grew several ancient apple trees.

The orchard didn't spark any memory, but it was a pleasant place, and she wandered about idly, not looking at anything in particular. She was there for several moments before a feeling of unease swept over her. For no discernible reason, the orchard and forest suddenly seemed to press in on her, and she was seized by an inexplicable need to seek out the company of other people.

Without a backward glance, she began to hurry into the woods that separated her from the road, heedless of the racket she made. As she hastily made her way toward the road, she realized with horror that the crashing noises she heard were not hers alone: someone was chasing her!

With her heart slamming against her ribs, she broke into a dead run, not risking even a glance over her shoulder. The road was only yards away from her when a silk ribbon dropped over her head and almost instantly began to tighten around her neck.

She was nearly jerked off her feet by the suddenness of the brutal attack, and she fought madly, twisting and kicking, her hands clawing at the ribbon that bit mercilessly into her neck, choking her, cutting off her breath.

Several seconds passed as Tess and her attacker fought in grim, deadly silence, but her efforts to escape from the painful pressure around her neck proved futile. The ribbon was cutting cruelly into the soft skin of her throat, her lungs felt as if they were bursting, and there were terrifying black spots dancing in front of her eyes. A bolt of utter rage shot through her—she wasn't going to end her life this way! Like a wild thing she redoubled her efforts and fought for air, for life itself—all to no avail. It occurred to her then that she really was going to die . . . die without knowing who she was, by the hand of an unknown assailant, for an unknown reason, in a place she didn't recognize. . . .

Then blackness seized her and all went dark.

Chapter Fifteen

"Oh, *miss*! Dear God! Don't be dead! Thomas? Oh, Tom, *do* hurry!" cried Rose Laidlaw with great urgency. The limp body of her mistress was cradled in her arms as she sat on the ground. Rose looked around nervously, but nothing menacing met her gaze. Yet only moments before, incredibly, someone had tried to strangle the earl's mistress!

The sound of running feet and her husband's worried shout broke into Rose's agitated thoughts. With relief, she saw her husband and his brother pushing their way through the short distance of trees and brush that separated her from them. When they reached her and spied the still form in her arms, they both gasped.

"What happened?" demanded Tom. "Did she faint?"

Wordlessly Rose showed them the crimson ribbon that bit deep into Tess's neck.

"Never say someone tried to *murder* her!" John burst out incredulously.

"I don't know what happened," Rose replied almost tearfully. "Miss had said that she wanted to go for a walk, and it was only after she had been gone for several moments that I thought, with her being a stranger and all, that I should have gone with her. I told your mother where I was going and set out after her." Tenderly she brushed aside one of Tess's fiery curls from the pale face and said in trembling accents, "I was worried straightaway when I didn't see her on the road, and then I remembered the old orchard and thought she might have decided to explore. . . ." Her eyes widened with remembered terror. "Oh, Tom! It was horrible. I looked over here and there they were—miss fighting for all she was worth, and a gentleman, a tall gentleman in a greatcoat like the master's, standing behind her, *strangling* her with this ribbon." She gulped back tears. "I just stood there for a second staring, for I couldn't hardly believe my eyes, and then miss sort of went limp and slumped. I must have made a sound, for the man suddenly looked over at me. Oh, I was so frightened that he was going to come after me, but he just threw her to the ground and ran away into the woods."

Both men knelt beside the women, and while Tom comforted his sobbing wife, John quickly ascertained that the young lady, while unconscious and with a pitifully bruised and swollen neck, was alive. As Tom helped Rose to her feet, John swept Tess's small body up into his arms, and together they hurried down the road toward the cottage.

Pandemonium reigned for several moments when they finally reached their destination. There were frightened exclamations by Sara and Jenny and a babble of explanations from the others. The only thing that gave comfort to any of them was the faint but steady rise and fall of Tess's bosom.

Not wishing to leave her alone for a moment, and feeling the instinctive need to stick together, they all decided to set up a small bed in the kitchen. It made excellent sense. The kitchen was the heartbeat of the house, and everything needed for an invalid was readily at hand.

Only after a bed had been brought in and positioned near the hearth and Tess had been gently laid upon it did anyone think to notify the earl of this near tragic event. John, his face grim, a razor-sharp knife handy in his jacket pocket, set out a few minutes later for Sherbourne Court. Someone might have attacked miss, but they weren't going to get away unscathed if they tried for *him*!

At the court precious moments were lost while John argued with his uncle Bellingham that he had to see the earl immediately and that it was private! With ill grace and much muttering about "ungrateful upstart young whelps," Bellingham eventually went in search of Nicolas.

If Nicolas was surprised by his butler's whispered request that he see a visitor in his study this very instant, he gave no sign. He made some excuse to the Rockwells and left them merrily playing billiards in the game room, where they had been whiling away the hours until it was time for their foray upon the manor that evening. He swiftly followed Bellingham to the study.

Seeing John's face as he entered the room, Nicolas felt a knot of icy fear form in his belly. Something terrible had happened to Dolly! He knew it in every fiber of his being, and the idea that she might have been harmed filled him with a stark, helpless terror. It was like nothing he had ever experienced before in his life—not even when he had been in situations that he had known might cost him his own life.

The second the door shut behind the butler, barely taking time to dismiss a much interested Bellingham, he demanded roughly, "Dolly? Is she hurt?"

Quickly John told him what had happened. The news that Dolly was unconscious but alive lessened his fear only marginally, and he clung desperately to the only thing that gave any comfort at all—she was *alive!*

John's tale seemed incredible, and for a few seconds Nicolas simply stared at him in stunned disbelief. Good God! This was the bucolic Kentish countryside—not some vice-ridden London parish! Why in hell would someone want to murder his mistress? There was no reason. . . . Suddenly his eyes narrowed. The smugglers! Had they struck at Dolly to drive him away from the gatekeeper's cottage? Had the attack been a warning to him? Angrily he shook away those particular ideas. The reasons didn't matter right now—what *did* matter was the fact that someone had dared to strike out at the woman he considered his own. A renewed surge of rage went through him at that ugly knowledge. His hands clenched into fists, and for one moment he thought of the pleasure it would give him to face the coward who had struck down a defenseless woman.

The urgent need to see Dolly, to see for himself that she was indeed alive, suddenly overrode all other considerations—even those of vengeance. Motioning abruptly for John to follow him, he strode impatiently from the room. Not five minutes later, after a lightning raid on the stables for a pair of horses, which were saddled in a blink of the eye, they were riding swiftly toward the gatekeeper's cottage.

Nicolas tried to keep his roiling emotions in check as their horses thundered down the road. He fought against letting himself dwell on what had happened to Dolly, nor did he want even to examine how he would have felt if John's news had been more soul destroying—if her attacker had succeeded and she lay dead. . . . A shudder went through him, and he wrenched his thoughts away from the path they had so rebelliously taken. He couldn't even take solace in considering the improbability of it all. The who . . . the why. All that mattered was that she was alive and that he must reach her side in the shortest possible time.

The cottage came into view, and Nicolas brought his horse to a rearing halt. Flinging the reins in John's direction, he was dismounted and racing toward the door before his horse's hooves even hit the ground.

Like a wild man, he burst into the cottage through the kitchen entrance, only to skid to a halt in the doorway at the sight of Dolly, held half upright by Sara, painfully sipping a cup of warm milk. His heart, for the first time since he'd seen John's face, slowed its frantic pounding, and a huge wash of relief swept over him, leaving him weak and trembling.

She *was* alive and apparently now conscious. Fighting for control of his disordered emotions, Nicolas stood there a moment longer. Then, feeling as if he were once more in command of himself, he walked into the room.

On the surface it was a pleasant scene that greeted him. A small bed with a mahogany headboard, piled high with pillows and quilts, had been set up on one side of the kitchen, not far from the cheerfully burning fire. Jenny and Rose were busily stirring various pots and pans on the big black stove, the scent of baking bread and simmering sauces hung in the air, and Sara, her face soft with concern, hovered over Dolly. Nicolas was barely aware of the other women, his gaze locked on the slender woman in the bed. Seeing her sitting upright, those bright red curls tumbling in charming disarray around her pale features, he felt the last of his terror vanish. She was safe!

He tried for a casual note as he approached her bed, but the smile on his mouth was twisted and there was a husky tone to his voice as he said with forced lightness, "I understand that you had an adventure this afternoon—I suppose this will teach me not to leave you to your own devices very often."

"Nick!" Tess croaked out, tears springing to her eyes at the sight of his tall, broad-shouldered form. She hadn't known how desperately she wanted to see him until he had suddenly appeared.

He was at her side in an instant, kneeling on the floor and gently catching and enfolding her against him as Sara stepped aside and Tess flung herself into his arms. Oblivious of anything but the small woman in his arms, he held her a long time, her face nestled into his warm neck, her curls tickling his mouth and nose. If anything had happened to her . . . His arms tightened and he swallowed painfully, aware of the sting of tears at his own eyes.

Gruffly he asked, "How do you feel? Are you really all right?"

She gave him a misty smile. "My throat hurts awfully, and I can't seem to stop my teeth from chattering, nor my limbs from shaking, but other than that, I am fine."

Reluctantly Nick settled her into the bank of pillows Sara had thoughtfully arranged at her back. His eyes searched her lovely face, looking for the truth of her words. She did look fine, except, he thought with a thinning of his lips, for that angry red line around her slender throat. It looked hideous, an ugly scar against her soft white flesh, the black and purple of deep bruising already showing along the edges.

It wasn't until that moment that the enormity of what she had escaped hit him. *Someone had deliberately tried to murder her!* Again he felt rage well up inside of him, but he pushed it aside. Rage would not help now. No, now he needed a cool head. Logical thinking. Measured emotions. A plan. He had to find her attacker. Then, and only then, would he allow the great beast of rage within him free reign. . . .

He pulled up a chair beside her bed and held her hand. "Do you want to talk about it?" he asked softly.

Tess grimaced. "I don't *want* to talk about it, but I know I must. Oh, Nicolas, it was so incredible! One moment I was walking along, and the next . . ." Her eyes widened with remembered terror, and her breath caught painfully.

He brought her hand to his lips and kissed lightly. "Hush," he said. "You don't have to tell me about it right now. We'll talk about it in a few hours, hmm? When you're more yourself?"

She nodded, sending him a watery smile. "My head does ache so awfully," she admitted. "I think I hit it on something when I blacked out and fell to the ground." A shiver went through her.

"Now then, that's enough of that," scolded Sara. Giving the earl a stern glance, she bustled over to Tess's side with a fresh cup of warm milk, this time liberally laced with brandy. "The poor dear just only opened her eyes a few minutes before you came bursting through the door. You don't be pestering her with a lot of questions."

Not the least offended by Sara's familiar manner, Nicolas flashed her a charming smile. "I shall be guided by your superior knowledge, madame," he said, a teasing gleam dancing in his black eyes. "And shall only speak with the young lady when you deem it appropriate."

"Oh, go on with you!" Sara replied with a gratified smile. Shaking a finger at him, she added lightly, "You'll do exactly as you've always done since you were a small boy, Master Nick—precisely as you please!"

Nicolas laughed. "Guilty, madame, but in this case, I *shall* follow your wishes."

He glanced around as John entered the room and asked, "Robert? Where is he?"

It was Rose who answered. With anxious features she said, "He went back to the place where it happened. I asked him to wait for you and John, but he wanted to examine the area right away."

Nicolas nodded approvingly. "Since you ladies appear to have matters well in hand, we shall join him and see what we can discover before it gets any later." He pressed a swift, gentle kiss on Tess's lips, and then he was gone, with John following swiftly at his heels.

They found Robert a few minutes later, trudging down the road toward them. As soon as the other two men approached, he said, "I found where he tied his horse—there is a pile of droppings there, and you can see where the animal cropped the nearby vegetation—but other than that . . ."

Nicolas still wanted to see for himself where it had happened, so together the three men walked back through the falling dusk. There wasn't much to see; even the exact area where Dolly had fought for her life showed very little disturbance. After following Robert to a spot just beyond the old orchard and looking around, Nicolas was frowning. There was nothing, nothing except a pile of dung, where it was obvious

a horse had been recently tethered, to give him any clue as to
why and who had so brutally attacked Dolly. Nicolas sighed.
It would have been bloody convenient, he admitted wryly, if
the attacker had dropped a signet ring or an embroidered scarf
with his initials on it. Such wasn't likely to have occurred, but
he still wished there had been something. . . .

Walking back toward the cottage, he asked, "Did Dolly see
who it was? Perhaps Rose got a good look at him?"

Robert shook his head regretfully. "Neither one of them.
Once we knew that miss was all right and had made her comfortable, that was the first thing I asked her. Miss said she
never got even a glance at him. He attacked her from behind,
and she never saw him. She just knows he was a big, strong
man. Rose, now, had a better view, but she didn't see very
much. She said that he wore a gentleman's hat and that it was
pulled low over his face. When she first sighted him, his head
was bent over Dolly, so she saw nothing but the hat. She got
barely a glimpse of him when he looked up and saw her, but
there was too much brush in the way for her to see him
clearly. She didn't recognize him." His voice grim, Robert
added, "But she feels certain that he was a 'gentleman.' She
said not only was his hat like the ones you wear, but that he
was also wearing a greatcoat like yours. She said that her impression was that of a man of quality—not just some poacher
or farm worker."

Nicolas would have felt better if Rose had seen a poacher
or even one of the local smugglers—it would certainly have
made more sense. At least they might have been able to assign
a motive for the attack. If Dolly had stumbled across someone
with something to hide, it might explain what had happened.
But a "gentleman" put an entirely different light on the incident. . . .

The "gentleman" aspect of the attack nagged at him considerably and cast a great deal of doubt on his theory that the
owlers might have struck at Dolly as a warning to him—until
he remembered the "gentleman" that he himself had seen with

the smugglers just last night when he had been knocked unconscious. . . .

A grim smile crossed his face. He couldn't be certain, but he'd wager half his fortune that his attacker and Dolly's were the same man. The "gentleman" might even possibly be the mysterious "Mr. Brown" mentioned by Roxbury.

Thinking of the danger that Dolly had faced banished all other thoughts from his mind, and he was stricken with guilt. Had he not let the Rockwells' unexpected arrival deter him, Dolly would never have been harmed. It was *his* fault that she had nearly died.

Feeling angry and guilty at the same time, Nicolas entered the cottage and strode impatiently to the kitchen. His gaze went instantly to Dolly, and his spirits lifted like magic.

It was obvious that she was feeling better, although her features were still strained and pale and there was an expression in the depths of her eyes that made his heart clench painfully. The tamped-down rage within him struggled to break free. She was sitting up straighter against the pillows, and in the intervening time, she had changed into her nightgown and was modestly enveloped in the bright blue wool wrapper.

Her eyes met his, and she asked anxiously, "Did you find anything?"

Nicolas shook his dark head. Seating himself on the wooden chair near her bed, he sat down beside her once more. Taking her hand in his, he asked quietly, "Do you think you can talk about it now?"

Her mouth twisted ruefully. "There isn't much to tell. I had decided to go for a walk, and I spied the apple orchard. I walked over to it, and then . . ." She hesitated, her eyes growing dark. "I don't know, it was odd, but all of a sudden I felt frightened. Something inside told me that I should get away from there immediately."

Nick's mouth thinned. "Thank God you listened to your inner senses. If you had remained there, Rose might not have gotten to you in time. A few seconds longer with that damned ribbon around your throat and you wouldn't be sitting here telling me about it."

Tess smiled softly at him. "I know. You're saying what I've thought a hundred times since it happened. Anyway," she went on briskly, "I left the orchard and was some yards from the road when he attacked me." She stopped, unable to go on, and her body trembled uncontrollably.

Dropping a kiss on her hand, Nicolas said urgently, "You don't have to tell me anymore. Answer me two questions and we can leave this painful subject: Do you have any idea why someone would want to kill you? And would you recognize your attacker?"

Tess slowly shook her head. "Have you forgotten?" she asked quietly. "I don't know who I am, and because of that I can't tell you why someone might wish me dead. And as for recognizing him . . ." She gave a bitter little laugh. "I was too busy fighting for my life to see who was trying to strangle me!"

Tess wasn't telling exactly the entire truth. It *was* true that she hadn't recognized her attacker, and while she still didn't know who she was, ever since she had awakened there had been odd flashes, frustratingly brief, of what she was certain were memories of her past. She had been given a lightning glimpse of a long, portrait-hung gallery, where one portrait in particular seemed to leap out at her—a young woman with features strikingly similar to her own, and yet she knew it was not a portrait of herself. She had barely grasped what she was seeing before it was gone and her mind was as blank as ever. Several minutes later another flash had occurred; she had glimpsed a grand manor, and the same gentleman she had seen driving so recklessly down the road the morning she had left the Black Pig with Nicolas was walking down the steps. But even as she strained to remember, to put a name to those arrogantly handsome features, the memory had vanished. Just before Nick had arrived, a woman's face, a lovely face with violet eyes much like her own, had streaked through her thoughts. Tess was positive that if she could only concentrate, think hard enough, she would know the woman's name . . . and the man's. . . .

Tess sighed, looking regretfully at Nick. Since he didn't believe that she had lost her memory in the first place, there was no use telling him about what was happening to her.

Nicolas stared at her a long time. Even in the face of a brutal attempt on her life, she was still clinging tenaciously to that ridiculous story of hers. . . . The uneasy suspicion that she might be telling the truth took firmer root in his mind. If she really didn't know who she was . . . if there was no greedy, shadowy family in the background, waiting to reap the reward of her position in his life . . . if that were true, then God help him, he had taken base advantage of her loss of memory, and he had ravished and abducted an innocent maid!

Stubbornly he pushed away that decidedly unwelcome conclusion. He was overwrought, shaken by the attack on her— so ensnared by her charms that he was willing to believe anything she said. That was it—he was letting his fascination with her override all his common sense. Of course she knew who she was. And sooner or later her family *was* going to show up with its collective hand outstretched for his gold! But none of that answered the two questions uppermost in his mind: Who had tried to kill her, and why?

None of his thoughts showed on his face as he said bracingly, "Well, you did the most important thing, sweetheart— you survived, and that's all that counts!"

She sent him a faint smile. "Oh, Nick," she admitted honestly, "I was *so* frightened!"

He gathered her close to him once more and dropped soft kisses on her curly head, muttering inane words of comfort. He didn't know what he said, but they had the desired effect. A few minutes later she was sitting up in bed, looking less anxious.

Plucking nervously at the quilt, she said, "I'm going to sleep down here tonight. Jenny has said that she will bring in a mattress for herself, and Sara has said that she will leave the door to her room open. And Rose and Tom are just down the hall." Her eyes very big, she added, "I know I have a perfectly good bed upstairs, but for tonight, at least, I think I'd feel better if I was down here."

With an arrested expression on his face, Nicolas hesitated a moment before saying slowly, "I think that's a very good idea." He cleared his throat and looked oddly ill at ease. "As a matter of fact, before all this happened, I was going to, um, talk to you about some, er, *guests* who might be staying here for a few days. . . ."

"Guests?" she asked incredulously. "You're putting up your guests in the household of your mistress?"

Nicolas moved uncomfortably on his chair. He threw a harassed look at the servants, relieved that they were all on the other side of the room, busy with various tasks. Like the well-trained staff that they were, they were giving Nick and Tess a bit of privacy. In a low voice he said, "Well, they're not guests, exactly, they're simply some older maiden ladies who need temporary refuge."

Tess stared at him. "You are," she said finally, "the most *arrogant,* unfeeling *monster* I have ever known! You abduct me willy-nilly and give me no choice but to become your mistress, almost making a prisoner of me. I have just barely escaped with my life from a vicious attack, and you want to move me out of my own bedroom to provide refuge for some *maiden* ladies?"

Nicolas winced at the note in her voice. He didn't blame her in the least—he *was* being an unfeeling monster, but he didn't really have any choice. Not, he thought darkly, if he was to keep his reluctant promise to those harum-scarum Rockwell brothers. "I know it sounds improbable," he admitted, "but I swear to you that I will explain everything more fully to you later. In the meantime . . ." He flashed her a wry glance and, deciding that he had nothing to lose, asked bluntly, "Would you mind very much having your things removed from upstairs and just for a few days using the room at the rear of the house?" The expression on her face made him say hastily, "I *know* it's not the best time, and I promise they'll only be here until I can find a more suitable place for them."

Tess could hardly believe her ears. Her throat hurt, her head was aching unbearably, she felt dizzy, her life had nearly been taken from her, and he wanted to bring *guests* into the house? He was right about one thing—it wasn't the best time. But she was too shaken at the moment to argue with him. Her voice colorless, she said, "Whatever you wish. After all, I am merely your mistress. It is *your* house to do with as you please."

Nicolas sighed, guilt knifing through him. Damn the Rockwells! And Avery! And that blasted Tess Mandeville for being so foolishly stubborn in the first place! Taking Dolly's stiff little hand in his, he said quietly, "Sweetheart, I am the wickedest wretch alive! I shouldn't have mentioned it—especially now." He gave her a crooked smile. "It wasn't a very good idea in the first place. Don't worry, I'll think of somewhere else to put the ladies—you just concentrate on recovering—that's all that really matters. And of course you can sleep down here if you wish. Since I won't be able to stay the night with you for the next few days, you'll probably feel safer with Jenny and the other servants near at hand."

Tess looked at him with exasperation. He was being far too reasonable and meek. "Oh, bring your maiden ladies here," she said crossly, wishing she wasn't so spineless where he was concerned and that she didn't find him so appealing. He *was* a monster, but she seemed unable to resist him—even when he was at his most outrageous. "I wouldn't be using my rooms for the next few days anyway," she added dryly.

He sent her a keen look. "Are you certain? Your comfort *is* my first concern." With a rueful expression on his dark, handsome face, he said, "I really don't want you upset—despite what you might think. I shouldn't have brought the subject up, especially now."

"Then why did you?" Tess muttered, feeling with some justification that she was being sorely put upon.

"Stupidity? Unmitigated crassness?" he offered, a twinkle dancing in the depths of his black eyes that coaxed her to join in his debasement.

Despite her aches and pains, Tess grinned at him. "My feelings precisely!"

Staring at her, at the sweet curve of her rosy mouth, Nick was struck by the sudden unsettling knowledge that he would gladly vilify himself, act the fool, do just about anything, to keep her safe and happy. She was also, he admitted, letting him off the hook lightly. Bringing up the subject of the arrival of the Mandeville women within mere moments of her escaping near death had not been the most intelligent thing he'd ever done. The most thoughtless, certainly!

A husky note in his voice, he leaned nearer and asked, "Am I forgiven, sweetheart?"

"Yes—but you don't deserve it!" Her tone grew serious. "Nick, I meant what I said—bring your maiden ladies here. I won't mind."

He sent her a searching glance. What he saw must have reassured him, for he nodded slowly. "Very well. I will."

Rising to his feet, he said, "I must be off now—after I have a word with the servants about tonight's arrivals. I don't know what time I'll be back with them—it will be very late, that much I do know. I'll talk to you then." He hesitated. He had almost lost her, and that thought terrified him. Reluctant to leave her, but knowing he must, he bent over and kissed her soundly. "Don't ever let anything like this happen to you again!" he said fiercely. "And I swear I will find and kill the bastard who dared lay a hand on you."

Through dreamy eyes Tess watched him walk over to where Robert and the others were working. In a low voice he spoke with them for several moments, and then with one last, long, bone-melting glance in her direction, he was gone. His very presence had kept her feelings of terror and despair at bay, and the warm sensation of protection and tenderness that had enveloped her upon his arrival went with him. . . .

Tess swallowed, and the pain in her throat made her moan softly. Sara was at her side instantly and, after pressing some more warm milk on her, told her briskly, "Now then, miss, you rest. The master has everything in hand, and you needn't fret your pretty head over anything."

Too worn out by her ordeal to resist, Tess weakly sank back against the pillows. She didn't want to think about what had nearly happened to her. Nor did she want to speculate on why someone had tried to kill her. Or who. Her throat hurt unbearably, and the pounding in her head had risen to a savage crescendo. Her eyes closed as she sought to escape the pain. As the minutes passed, the warmth of the fire, the comforting sound of friendly voices nearby, and the brandy all did their work. In the morning, she thought drowsily, in the morning this will all seem a dream. . . .

It wasn't morning when Tess woke, nor did she discover that she had been dreaming. She woke up with a start shortly after midnight and found herself right in the middle of the worst nightmare she could ever have envisioned. The instant her eyes opened, like an avalanche her memory came crashing back.

Oh, God! She remembered! *Everything!* Avery. Her uncle's letter. The aunts. Her flight. The smugglers. Oh, God! The *aunts!* What had happened to them? She didn't dare think what might have been their fate.

Her eyes closed in anguish as the horrible knowledge about her own fate washed over her. She had left Mandeville Manor an innocent maid, fleeing from certain dishonor at the hands of a man she despised . . . and now she woke some five days later to discover that she was maid no longer and that she had, albeit reluctantly, become the mistress of one of the despised earls of Sherbourne. She was disgraced, dishonored, and debased! To her greater horror, she realized something else, too, something that had lurked uncomfortably at the edges of her consciousness for the last few days—she was, she feared, deeply in love with the very man who had brought her to such sordid depths! A man who had sworn that he would never marry her—no matter who she turned out to be. At least, she thought bitterly as she lay there in the darkness of the gate-keeper's cottage, Avery had offered marriage!

Chapter Sixteen

*W*ith the return of her memory, and the shameful realization of what she had become in the brief time since she had fled from her home, Tess's first instinct was to run. Run as far and as fast as she could. But even as she sat up in bed, it occurred to her that she had no place to run to.

She could not go back to Mandeville Manor. Nor could she go to her uncles. She was, she realized painfully, a ruined woman, and she would not bring scandal upon them.

But there was still the fate of the aunts to be considered, and even if her life, as she knew it, was over, she was determined to see that Hetty and Meg were safely settled somewhere away from Avery's machinations.

A bitter smile curved her mouth. How ironic! Her great-grandfather had stolen the bride-to-be of the heir to the earldom of Sherbourne, and now the present earl had dishonored the woman the current Baron Mandeville had wanted for a bride. Ironic, too, that like Theresa, she had fallen madly in love with the earl of Sherbourne . . . and a marriage between them was definitely not in the cards.

Dispiritedly she lay back. In the dim glow from the low-burning fire on the hearth, she stared blankly at the ceiling above. Oh, God! What was she going to do?

Telling Nicolas was out of the question. She could just

imagine his look of disbelief, and a shudder went through her when she considered his likely reaction if he *did* believe her. He would be furious! The confession of her real identity, while putting to rest his conviction that she had been angling for a wealthy husband, would not still all his suspicions about her. Stubbornly determined to believe the worst of her, he would no doubt decide that if money had not been the motive, the notion of becoming a countess had! And while, despite his protestations to the contrary, he might have brought himself to marry another woman in these circumstances, she was positive that he would *not* be willing to do the same for a Mandeville! Not that she wanted him to, she averred hastily. Who wanted to be married to a man who despised the very name of one's family? A man, furthermore, who had been *compelled* to marry one? She certainly didn't!

Tess sighed wearily. So what was she going to do? Keep her mouth shut and continue the pretense until she thought of some other way out of her terrible dilemma? No. She couldn't do that. Not now, knowing who she was and who he was. And as for loving him . . .

A small tear slipped down her cheek. She could almost wish that her memory had not returned, or that when it had, she had discovered that she was just a simple maid and that remaining the mistress of a charming, by-far-too-handsome aristocrat was not such a horrid fate after all.

It couldn't be; she accepted that knowledge, painful though it was. Sooner or later someone was going to recognize her. Only luck, good or bad, she couldn't decide which, had prevented that from happening before now.

The sound of the rain beating on the roof caught her attention, and it was fitting weather for her doleful mood. Lying there, listening to the steady fall of raindrops, Tess made several difficult decisions.

Despite her first inclination not to, she was going to have to tell Nicolas the truth. He *had* to be told—not tonight, but first thing in the morning. And while dreading it, she was going to have to return to Mandeville Manor. She had tried to run away from her problems once, and look where that had gotten her!

Avery's unwelcome suit was the least of her troubles at this point, and he certainly wasn't going to be interested in continuing his pursuit of her once he knew the truth. At least, she thought wryly, I'll have the satisfaction of watching his face when he learns how thoroughly I have put myself beyond the pale. Not even for my fortune would he be willing to marry me now! As for the aunts . . . Surely now they would agree to her plan for the three of them to set up their own household. Her mouth twisted. Avery definitely wasn't going to let her live at Mandeville Manor again!

For a little while she comforted herself with the picture of the life she and her aunts would live. On the surface nothing would change, except they would have their own residence and servants and there would be no male to gainsay their wishes. She doubted that beyond the few people who *had* to know, no one else would ever learn of the scandal that had brought about her near reclusive state. Oh, there was bound to be some speculation and gossip when she retired from society and lived the life of a hermit with her aunts, but it would soon pass. Nicolas certainly wasn't going to tell anyone. And Avery, while he might have liked to see her humbled, would not want any hint of scandal near him—it would ruin his chances with the *next* heiress he went scrambling after. Embarrassing questions as to why Tess had fled his home and protection might be raised. He definitely wouldn't like that!

Thunder rumbled suddenly overhead, and Tess jumped. The beat of the rain increased, and she realized that she had been wise to abandon any idea of leaving immediately. Somehow she would get though this night, and in the morning, after she had told him the truth, Nicolas no doubt would be *delighted* to send her swiftly on her way!

The ache in her heart was more powerful than any pain she had ever felt before in her life. Tess lay on her side, watching the slowly dying coals of the fire. *She loved Nicolas Talmage!*

That fact was irrefutable, and it explained so much, especially
the ease with which she had allowed herself to be seduced by
his dark charm. Even that first night . . . had she fallen in love
with him that quickly?

It was frightening to think that she had taken one look at his
chiseled features, stared only once into those wicked black
eyes, and fallen headlong in love with him. But that's what
happened, she thought painfully. She *had* taken just one look
and she had been instantly drawn to him, instantly aware of
him in a way she had been with no other man. The knowledge
was bitter and fraught with anguish.

With any other man, despite the deplorable circumstances
of their first meeting and its aftermath, there would have been
a chance that she could find a happy ending, but not with the
earl of Sherbourne. Not a Mandeville with a Talmage. Even if
they had met under more conventional terms, any hope of a
future between them would have been slight and highly unlikely. There was too wide a rift between the families, a rift
that had been going on since his grandfather had run away
with her great-grandmother. . . .

The diary! It had to have been Benedict Talmage's. And the
woman he wrote of so passionately had to have been her
great-grandmother Theresa. She sighed. It didn't change anything. Nothing could, not even her love for Benedict's grandson.

She squeezed her eyes shut, fighting against the tears. She
swallowed with difficulty, and the pain in her throat recalled
unpleasantly the attack on her life. Tess was almost grateful
for the reminder. It gave her miserable thoughts a different
subject to worry about. Woefully she admitted to herself that
she found it far easier to think about her near murder than to
dwell on the dreary, endless days without Nicholas that
stretched before her.

Why *had* someone tried to kill her? She frowned. The fact
that someone had tried to murder her was nearly incomprehensible. She had no enemies. Except, perhaps . . . Could her

attacker have been Avery? It didn't seem likely. He wanted to *marry* her, not murder her! Besides, she and Nicolas had seen him driving toward London on Thursday. . . . Had he caught a glimpse of her and followed them surreptitiously? Her heart beat very fast. Having snooped around and discovered how thoroughly she had ruined herself, had Avery decided simply to murder her in a mad attempt to hide her shame? She snorted. Her shame wouldn't have bothered Avery; it was her fortune he wanted! Had he concocted some wild scheme to get his hands on her money if she were dead? Her nose wrinkled. That didn't seem very plausible. The money came from her mother's side of the family. If she died, the documents were already in place for the bulk of it to go to her Mandeville aunts and her Rockwell uncles. Marriage to her was the only way Avery would ever get his hands on even one penny.

She frowned again. It couldn't have been Avery. But if not Avery . . . then who? And why? She bolted upright in her bed as an answer flashed across her mind. The *smugglers!* Of course! Why hadn't she considered them earlier? It made perfect sense. They had used the gatekeeper's cottage probably for years, and to discover that it was now occupied would have displeased them immensely. It was logical to believe that they would have taken steps to make life extremely unhealthy for the current occupants!

Convinced that she was on the right track, she lay back down and considered her premise from all angles, glad that she had something to take her mind off the ache in her heart and to help pass the time as she waited for Nicolas's reappearance. He had said that he would return late tonight, with his guests. . . .

An awful suspicion suddenly occurred to her. *His older, maiden-lady guests.* No. It couldn't be! It was impossible. He wouldn't have lifted a finger to help her aunts. How could he even have learned of their plight? A horrible connection was made instantly in her mind. Her uncles, she recalled uneasily, in spite of the coolness between the Mandevilles and Talmages, were very good friends with the Talmage family. One might even say *close* friends. . . .

Tess jerked upright in bed. Her uncles had planned to arrive today! Yesterday, now. Suppose something had happened that had alarmed them? News of her disappearance?

Oh, dear! Tess thought remorsefully. She hadn't even considered how her aunts must have felt when no word of her safe arrival in London had reached them. Her conscience pricked her. By now, she realized, they must be frantic!

Still, that didn't mean they would be Nicolas's mysterious guests, she reminded herself. But suppose her uncles had arrived at Mandeville Manor and found a situation that greatly disturbed them. Would they, knowing of the hostility between the two families, have gone to Nick for help? She couldn't imagine it. Even less could she imagine any situation that would cause the earl of Sherbourne to assist her aunts or, more important, bring them here. The entire premise was ridiculous! His guests couldn't possibly be her aunts! Yet the appalling suspicion would not go away. She would, she realized with a sinking feeling, simply have to wait and see what unfolded. It wasn't a comforting prospect.

Time passed. Sleep was unthinkable, and Tess tossed and turned. The hour was very late. Nicolas should have been here by now. Where was he?

At that precise moment, Nicolas was standing in the pouring rain, helping two frightened and distraught women into the small closed carriage that he had driven over and hidden in the thick woods near Mandeville Manor. In spite of the wretched weather, the Rockwell brothers had ridden their own horses to give the rescuers more maneuverability if it had been necessary. It hadn't been.

The lightning raid on Mandeville Manor had gone swiftly and smoothly. They had breached the outer perimeter of the estate without incident. A quick, efficient reconnoiter of the house had revealed an unlocked pair of French doors at the rear of the house. The rain and rumblings of the storm had covered any sounds they had made as they had stealthily entered the manor.

The three men had swiftly ascertained that the only occupants awake and likely to cause them trouble were Avery's two servants, the ubiquitous Lowell and the valet, Coleman. Seeing the two of them snoring drunk in the kitchen at Mandeville Manor, Nick recognized them immediately, and their presence made him all the more convinced that even if they were hated Mandevilles, the ladies definitely needed rescuing. Lowell and Coleman had been with Avery on the peninsula, and a pair more prone to rape and cruel violence would have been hard to find. They certainly weren't the type of men he would have introduced into *his* household! Convinced by their condition that Avery's henchmen would cause them no trouble, the trio had departed from the nether regions of the house and had quickly ascended to the upper rooms. It was only when they had reached the floor occupied by the bedchambers of the family that Rockwell had hesitated.

"What is it?" Nick had demanded in a low tone.

They had carried a small candelabra with them to pierce the complete darkness, and in the soft flickering light, Nicolas saw the indecision on the baron's face. "What is it?" he asked again.

Tom grimaced. "Thing is, I don't know exactly which room is Tess's or where the aunts sleep." He brightened. "Know I'm on the right floor."

Nick groaned, not liking the idea of searching through a dozen bedrooms. "I thought," he growled, "that you were familiar with the damned place!"

The baron looked shocked. "Not the ladies' bedchambers!"

Suppressing an urge to throttle his friend, Nicolas said grimly, "Very well, then, we'll have to split up and check every room on this floor."

A quick glance revealed several wall sconces. Nick grabbed the candles from a pair of them, lit them, and thrust them into the hands of his cohorts. "Be quiet, for God's sake, and if you find them, don't alarm the ladies—particularly, don't let them scream!"

As luck would have it, they didn't have to search far. The second door Nick tried he found locked. Certain the storm would cover him, with one powerful movement, he kicked open the door. Entering the room, he found two very frightened ladies huddled together in a large, silk-hung bed. Placing his fingers to his lips, he said softly, "Please, not a sound. I mean you no harm. Lord Rockwell and his brother are with me, and they are greatly concerned for your safety."

The younger of the two, her big violet eyes fixed painfully on his face, let out a shaky breath. "Oh, thank God! Thank God! Tess reached London. We have been worried sick."

A frown darkened Nicolas's brow. The niece, Tess, had reached London? It was the first he'd heard of it. Motioning the ladies to remain where they were, he hurriedly found the two men.

Hustling them down the hallway toward the room where he had discovered the women, Nicolas said, "I think, gentlemen, that we have another problem. Come along and see for yourselves."

The ladies had left the bed and had put on their wrappers by the time the three men returned. At the sight of the younger of the two women, Alexander, his handsome face full of relief, thrust his candle into the baron's hand and then strode swiftly toward her. Heedless of the others, he swept her into his arms and crushed her to him. His mouth buried in her tousled fair hair, he had exclaimed, "Oh, Hetty, my little love! Don't *ever* terrify me like this again! I have been most anxious about you! When we were denied entrance to the house today, I just knew that something was dangerously amiss. You're not hurt?"

Even in the faint candlelight, the blush on Hetty's pretty face was obvious. "Alexander! I knew you would come! And you were right to be worried—Avery has made us virtual prisoners in our own home. He has gone to London and left that monstrous Lowell and that unspeakably nasty valet of his in charge of the entire household. It has been utterly ghastly! We have been confined to this room since Wednesday. Not even our maids have been allowed to serve us. I have never been so furious or frightened in my life!"

Nicolas had watched the scene between the pair of them with interest. Sits the wind that direction, hmm? he mused. Then, jerking his thoughts away from further speculation about the state of Alexander's heart, he asked quietly, "You said earlier that 'Tess had reached London.' What did you mean?"

Alarm shone in Hetty's eyes. She gazed up at Alexander. "Tess didn't find you? She didn't send you?"

Alexander's chiseled jaw dropped. "She isn't with you? Tess ain't here at Mandeville?"

It was the older of the two ladies who spoke. "Oh, dear! I knew it was dangerous for her to try to reach you in London by herself, but we had no choice. Avery would have dishonored her without compunction. She *had* to leave." Her gentle blue eyes filled with tears. "We were so certain she would make it to you. She is such a valiant child." A look of horror crossed her face. "You don't suppose that she has fallen into Avery's clutches? That he has her hidden away somewhere and is even now forcing her to submit to his beastly demands?"

"What the devil are you talking about? We never saw Tess in London! We thought she was with *you!*" Baron Rockwell blurted out, anxiety sharpening his handsome face.

There was a shattering silence, and then Nicolas spoke, his features grim. "I think it's obvious that Tess did not reach London. Something must have happened to her on her journey, but we dare not tarry here discussing it. We must be off before we are discovered." He sent the two women a reassuring smile. "Don't worry. We'll find her. Safe and sound. There is no doubt a simple explanation for her delay in reaching London, but for now, getting the pair of you out of here is our first priority. Gather up a minimum of your clothing and let us be off before Lowell or Coleman come looking for us."

The two women obeyed hastily, and in a scant few minutes the five of them were creeping down the wide hallways of Mandeville Manor. Huddled in their hastily donned cloaks, pillowcases of haphazardly selected clothing clutched to their bosoms, Hetty and Meg were ushered swiftly from the house and to the carriage. Seconds later they were safely inside the coach, and with Nicolas driving and Thomas and Alexander acting as outriders, the ladies were borne away. The rescue was complete.

Nicolas should have felt a degree of satisfaction, but he was aware of a feeling of deep, *deep* unease. The fact that the blasted niece was missing disturbed him immensely, but even more than the disappearance of a young lady he had never met before was the unsettling feeling that he had stepped off into a dark, fathomless chasm. . . . Something was nagging at the back of his mind, some fact that he had overlooked. Frowning, he drove his horses as fast as he dared in the slashing rain, their way through the enveloping blackness lit only by the lanterns held by the Rockwells, who rode just ahead of the coach.

It was an unpleasant journey. The rain showed no sign of letting up, and by the time they finally reached the gatekeeper's cottage, Nicolas could only sigh with relief. He had left arrangements for his late arrival, and as he pulled the horses of the coach to a stop in front of the cottage, soft, welcoming light spilled out from one of the windows of the main salon.

Moments later the five of them were inside the cottage. The warmth of the main room was greeted with pleasure. The large silver candelabra that had been left lit near the window increased the feeling of welcome, as its golden light chased out the shadows. A banked fire glowed on the hearth; additional firewood was stacked within easy reach; and nearby on a table was a tray filled with refreshments—brandy and spicy mulled wine kept warm by a heated brick and sandwiches thick with ham and cheese.

Decorum had been left behind long ago, and almost as one, the entire party tossed aside their cloaks and coats. The fire was stirred into full blaze as Nicolas threw on some of the extra wood. More candles were lit about the room, and the ladies were guided into the chairs nearest the flames, goblets of the warm, mulled wine pressed into their hands. Brandy was poured for the gentlemen. Silence reigned as everyone took a deep, fortifying sip of their various libations.

As the brandy burned down his throat, Nicolas looked at the two guests, women who until this night had been despised unknowns to him. They were still in their nightgowns and wrappers, their hair in disarray, shock and strain obvious in their faces, but he found nothing incongruous about the sight of them sitting in his gatekeeper's cottage.

Feeling his brooding gaze upon her, Hetty looked across to where he stood near the fire, one arm resting on the carved wooden mantel. With a tremulous smile on her lovely mouth, she said softly, "I don't know who you are, but from the bottom of our hearts we thank you for helping the baron and his brother rescue us."

Nick smiled wryly. "You might not, once you know my name."

Meg gave a soft gasp. "I *thought* that I recognized you! I knew your father, but I could not believe a Talmage would ever help a Mandeville."

"Not to disillusion you, madame, but I think," Nick commented lightly, "that it can be said more correctly that I merely assisted the Baron Rockwell and his brother with *their* rescue of two charming ladies desperately in need of succor."

"Oh, I say! It wasn't like that at all, old fellow," Lord Rockwell expostulated. "Couldn't have done it without you. Your plan. Your coach. Your house. Everyone knows the Rockwells ain't got any brains! And that the man to have on your side in any tricky spot is Nick Talmage." He beamed at the two ladies. "Nick's got brains!"

Her eyes fixed intently on Nicolas's dark face, Hetty asked slowly, "Is he right? Are you Nicolas Talmage . . ." She faltered and then ended in a rush, "The earl of Sherbourne?"

Nicolas bowed in her direction. "At your service, madame."

"Oh, my," Hetty said weakly. "Isn't Avery going to be absolutely furious!"

Nick's mouth thinned. "For that reason alone, it gives me great pleasure to have taken part in your rescue, Madame . . . ?"

"Miss," Hetty said quickly. "Miss Hester Mandeville, but all my friends call me 'Hetty.'" Gallantly dropping a kiss on her outstretched hand, he asked in a teasing tone, "And am I to be considered a 'friend'?"

"After tonight?" Meg asked tartly. "I think that goes without saying. Now come over here, young man, and do the pretty with me!"

Smiling, Nick crossed to stand in front of her. Taking her hand in his, he murmured, "And you, madame? May I have your name?"

"My *friends* call me Meg," she said gruffly, a little blush of pleasure staining her cheeks.

Nick's smile faded. "It is a long time," he said quietly, "since there has been anything but enmity between our families. Do you really think that the events of this evening have obliterated the old feud?"

Alexander, who had been lounging nearby, spoke up. "Well, you sure as the devil can't wreak any vengeance on Meg and Hetty. They're your guests! Besides—*they* didn't do anything!" He paused, looked thoughtful. "Come to think of it, *you* ain't done anything, either! No reason why you shouldn't be friends."

"Sometimes, Alexander," Nick drawled, "you astonish me with your brilliance—unexpected though it may be." He glanced back at the ladies, his expression serious. "Now that the niceties have been dispensed with, I think it is time for you to tell us what has transpired at Mandeville Manor that placed you in such an invidious position. And we must discover what has happened to your niece. . . ."

The relaxed air that had permeated the comfortable room vanished. Remorse on her face, Hetty cried, "Oh, what a wicked wretch I am, sitting here warm and safe when who knows what may be happening to my poor Tess!"

"She didn't want to leave us," Meg said in a low tone. "But we convinced her that our only hope was for her to reach Rockwell in London." Her eyes filled with tears. "It is all our fault that she has disappeared!"

"If it is anyone's fault, I think that the blame can safely be laid at Avery Mandeville's door," Nick said in a hard voice. "But before we attempt to convict anyone of anything, I think it would be best if you told us everything, starting with *why* it became imperative for your niece to flee her home."

The two women exchanged glances. Then, sighing heavily, Meg said softly, "It all began with the arrival of Rockwell's letter. . . ."

It didn't take long for the sordid tale to unfold, and in a matter of moments the three men were aware of everything that had transpired. "It has been utterly ghastly these past few days," Hetty said toward the end of the ugly story. "When Avery discovered Wednesday morning that Tess had escaped him, he flew into a rage. And despite our protestations of innocence, he wasn't fooled. He knew that we had drugged his wine and had helped Tess to escape. He locked us in the room in which you found us and left almost immediately for London, hoping, I presume, to find Tess before she reached her uncles." Her eyes darkened with remembered distress. "We have no idea what happened after that, not to Tess or even to the rest of the staff—Lowell and Coleman have been the only servants, the only *people*, we have seen since Avery imprisoned us." Hetty took a deep breath. "Our plight grew more precarious with every passing day, but we never doubted that Tess would reach her uncles. We were certain that help was on the way, but I feared it would arrive too late to save us from a terrible fate." She shuddered. "Both Lowell and Coleman became more threatening and abusive to us. Several times when they brought us food or water, they were drunk, and I knew that if someone didn't arrive—either Avery back from London, or"—she glanced at Alexander—"that they were going to dishonor us, I just *knew* it! Thank God you arrived when you did!"

"Your niece escaped on Tuesday night?" Nicolas asked with a frown. His eyes were on Hetty's anxious features, his mind grappling with the unsettling knowledge that there was something familiar about her. . . . Again the sinking feeling that he had stepped off an abyss swept over him, but all he said was, "When she left Mandeville Manor that night on her way to London, that was the last time you saw her?"

Fear obvious in both pairs of eyes, the women nodded. "Yes," Hetty said painfully. "After we had drugged Avery we hurried to her rooms. We argued briefly about her leaving— she didn't like abandoning us, but we insisted. We watched her run down the hallway toward the gallery, and that was the last we saw of her. Oh, *where* can she be?"

In the kitchen, the object of the conversation gave up all pretense of trying to sleep. Tess had heard the arrival of Nicolas and the others, and with a combination of anticipation and dread, she had acknowledged the possibility that her aunts might very well be warming themselves by the fire just a few rooms away. Several minutes had passed as she had tossed and turned, envisioning the appalling scene that was likely to take place if she was correct about the identity of Nicolas's guests. Frazzled by the battle within herself, she finally decided that before much more time passed, she was going to have to find out for herself if her worst fears had been realized.

After getting quietly out of bed, she slipped on the blue

wool wrapper and silently left the kitchen. With great reluctance she approached the sound of the voices, and as their words and tones became clearer, her heart sank. In the darkness, just beyond the doorway of the room where the others were discussing her fate, Tess stood rooted to the floor, unable to deny the terrible knowledge: it *was* her aunts in the other room! Worse, while she hadn't heard them speak, she was positive that her uncles were also present. She closed her eyes in anguish.

Dear God in heaven, what was she going to do? Run away again? In the midst of a storm, in her nightclothes? Hardly! Wait and try to tell Nick the truth privately? She shuddered. Dared she wait? What if her identity were discovered before she had a chance to explain everything to him? It would make things so much worse—if that were possible, she thought with a wry twist of her lips.

So what was she going to do? She couldn't seem to bring herself to go forward or backward, yet she couldn't simply stand here like some poor dumb animal waiting for the final blow. . . .

Something, someone, brushed against her in the darkness, and with her nerves already stretched unbearably by the events of the day, she screamed. As did the other poor, equally startled soul, young Jenny.

"Oh, miss!" Jenny exclaimed in relieved tones. "What a fright you gave me! I saw you leave the kitchen and didn't think you should be wandering about by yourself, so I followed you, but I didn't realize that you had stopped and were standing here."

Nicolas had heard the screams, and under the astonished gazes of the others, he had snatched up a nearby candle and rushed away. His first thought had been that Dolly's attacker had returned, but seeing her and Jenny standing there together unharmed in the adjoining room, he realized immediately that nothing so serious as another attempt on Dolly's life was in the offing. A faint smile lifted one corner of his mouth. "What is it?" he asked teasingly. "Ghosts? Or mice?"

Tess heard the startled exclamations of her aunts and uncles in the main salon and knew with paralyzing certainty that in seconds they would no doubt be following close on Nick's heels. Her heart wept; time had run out for her. . . . She opened her mouth, frantic, hasty explanations hovering on her lips, but no sound came forth. She could only stare beseechingly at his beloved face, painfully aware of the coming denouement but unable to avert or stop it.

Nicolas sensed her distress and stepped nearer, asking softly, "What is it, sweetheart? What's wrong?"

The candlelight fell full on Tess's tense features, and as he stared into those unforgettable violet-hued eyes, the truth, the truth that he had been avoiding all evening, the truth he had been eluding and denying since he had first noticed the color of Hetty Mandeville's eyes, exploded through his brain. He sucked in his breath, the concerned expression in his black eyes cooling and freezing into icy implacability.

"It's not what you think," Tess said desperately. "My memory just returned a few hours ago."

"I believe I've said before," Nicolas snarled softly, "that you seem to have a *very* convenient memory."

"Who's got a convenient memory?" asked Rockwell as he came from the other room. Catching sight of the slim figure in the blue wrapper, the candlelight turning her hair to flame, he stopped. And confirming Nick's worst fears, he said in tones of greatest astonishment, "Good God! *Tess!* What in blazes are you doing here?"

Chapter Seventeen

As her uncle stood staring at her in open astonishment, Tess considered and rejected a dozen wild fabrications to explain her presence, garbed as she was, in Nicolas's house at this hour of the night. In the end she realized there was only one answer to her uncle's question: the truth.

With a wan smile on her face, she brushed back a lock of hair that had persisted in falling across her brow and said, "It is a long story."

"One," Nicolas said with silky menace, "which I await to hear with bated breath."

Rockwell glanced at him, a frown marring his handsome features. "Seems to me," he said slowly, "that you've got some explaining of your own to do."

Nicolas smiled sourly. "Indeed I do. But I believe," he added with a sardonic glance in Tess's direction, "in all politeness, that we should allow the lady to tell her tale first, don't you?"

Alexander, followed closely by the aunts, came through the doorway just then. At the sight of Tess, they all stopped abruptly to stare at her in disbelief. After that, chaos ruled for several seconds as, amid cries and exclamations of surprise and relief, Tess was kissed and hugged and swept from one thankful embrace to another.

It was only when the hubbub began to die down that Nicolas took charge. Recalling the presence of Jenny, who had watched the entire affair with wide eyes, he looked at her and said, "I think that will be all for now."

Reminded of her position, Jenny dropped a quick curtsy and vanished into the kitchen. Smoothly Nicolas herded everyone else back into the main salon.

The first amazement and deep relief at Tess's presence in Nicolas's house had faded, and uncomfortable questions were beginning to raise themselves in the minds of her aunts and uncles. No one looked very happy.

Tess was curled on a chair by the fire, her feet tucked demurely under the blue wool wrapper, her expression hard to define—a curious mixture of regret, wariness, despair, and relief. Nicolas stood a short distance beyond her, one arm resting along the top of the mantel, his face hard and set. The others were spread out around them, and a silence fell, broken only by the crackle of the fire.

The silence seemed deafening to Tess, and just when she thought she would scream if someone didn't say something, Rockwell cleared his throat and asked bluntly, "Well, Nick, what is going on here? How comes it that I find my niece, unchaperoned, garbed in her nightclothes in your house?"

"Why don't you ask the young lady?" Nicolas replied grimly. "She's the one with all the answers."

Tess suddenly found herself the cynosure of all eyes. Despite her best efforts not to, she found herself wiggling nervously on the chair, her mind scrabbling around, trying to find the right words with which to begin her story. Beseechingly her gaze met Hetty's.

An encouraging little smile on her lips, Hetty leaned forward and patted Tess's cold hand, saying softly, "Tell us, Tess. What happened after you left Mandeville Manor Tuesday night?"

"Yes, brat, we'd all like to know," chimed in Alexander, his eyes kind despite his tense expression.

Tess took a shaky breath, and keeping her eyes on her fingers as she unceasingly creased and folded and smoothed the hem of her wrapper, she began her story.

Flatly she told the events of that night: her escape from the manor itself, the fury of the storm, the frantic race along the narrow lanes and hedgerows in the menacing darkness, and the unexpected meeting with the smugglers. Her gaze lifted then, and looking directly at Nicolas, she said clearly, "When I woke that next afternoon, I had no memory. I didn't know my name, nor where I had come from, nor where I was going. Nothing."

Nicolas remained silent, merely shrugging his broad shoulders and taking a sip of his brandy, almost, but not quite, ignoring her. Tess could have slapped him.

"Oh, my poor Tess!" exclaimed Hetty. "You must have been terrified!"

Tess brought her gaze back to her aunt and smiled faintly. "Very," she admitted. "But I had to go on—I couldn't just lie there. I wanted to be recognized, and yet I was aware that I was frightened that someone, I realize now it was Avery, *would* recognize me." Quietly she continued the story, telling of her convoluted journey, of passing the farmer with the nag named Dolly, of finding the Black Pig and passing herself off as the expected wench of the owner's brother. She spared herself nothing, and it was only when she got to the part where Nicolas arrived at the tavern that she stumbled and floundered to a halt.

A flush stained her cheeks, and in spite of the fact that she could feel her family's warm reassurance flowing toward her, she couldn't bring herself to tell what had happened next. It was too embarrassing. Too humiliating. And too dangerous. During the telling of her story, an ugly thought had taken shape in her mind: What if her uncles felt compelled to defend her honor by challenging Nicolas to a duel? Her eyes closed. Could she bear it if Nick were killed by Rockwell? Or equally tragic, what if Nicolas killed either of her uncles? She'd already lost one beloved uncle to a duel . . . how could she live with herself, knowing that because of her, another one had died? She bit her lip, trying to think of a way to safely cross the treacherous ground that lay before her. A way, slim and chancy though it was, suddenly occurred to her.

Throwing truth to the winds, she said in a rush, "T-t-there was a moment when the e-e-earl and I were alone, and he seemed so k-k-kind that I took a risk and told him my story. He b-b-believed me and took pity on me." She swallowed with difficulty. "He could tell from my speech and m-m-mannerisms that working at the Black Pig wasn't my usual pastime, and since we had no idea of my real identity and I was deathly afraid of being discovered by the *wrong* person, he brought me here on Thursday morning. He has been discreetly trying to discover who I am ever since."

Hetty and Meg threw the hero of this tale glowing looks of gratitude. "We are indeed indebted to you, Lord Sherbourne," breathed Hetty, her eyes full of admiration.

"You have proven to be a savior to all of us," agreed Meg, her face warm with approval. "Who knows what awful fate might have befallen our dear niece except for your gallant and timely intervention."

The aunts may have swallowed the story, but while the Rockwells were not considered men of high intellect, they *were* men of the world, and Tess's tale didn't quite satisfy them. Besides, they knew Nick. . . .

His brows beetling, Rockwell demanded, "Is that the truth? Is that what happened, Sherbourne?"

"It sounds like a damned Banbury story to me!" growled Alexander, his eyes fixed intently on Nick's dark face.

An enigmatic expression in his gaze, Nicolas stared at Tess's downbent head. "You heard the young lady," he said slowly. "Do you doubt the veracity of her tale?"

"It ain't *that*!" burst out Rockwell. He threw an agonized glance at Hetty and Meg and mumbled, "Need to talk privately."

"No. We don't," Nicolas said firmly. "If you have anything to say, say it now."

A bit less constrained than his brother by the presence of the ladies, Alexander said, "Thing is, Nick, we *know* you— I've been wenching with you, and after finding a tempting little morsel like Tess at the Black Pig, you ain't likely to have passed up, uh, a sample."

The room fell deathly silent, everyone aware instantly of where this could lead. Her heart beating in thick, painful strokes, Tess stared miserably at the increasingly taut faces of the three men. She had known it was a gamble when she had concocted her silly little tale, but she had so hoped that fate might finally be kind to her. Apparently not! But she had to say something, do something, to intervene before the fatal words were spoken, words that would place her uncles at one end of the dueling field and Nicolas at the other.

Nicolas's black, brooding gaze pinned Alexander to the spot. "Are you, by any chance," he asked softly, "accusing me of having *seduced* your niece?"

Alexander blanched. Recalling Nicolas's expertise with the pistol *and* the sword, he cast an uneasy, harassed glance at his brother. Rockwell took a long swallow of his brandy and put it down carefully on a nearby table. He straightened his shoulders and, boldly meeting Nicolas's stare, asked coolly, "Did you?"

Tess dared not wait. Jumping to her feet, her hands curled into fists at her sides, she glared at her uncles. "Stop it! Stop it at once!" she cried fiercely. "I told you the truth! You have no right to badger him this way! He *saved* me, can't you understand that? He found me at the Black Pig and he brought me here, and that's *all* that happened! And to think that all the thanks he gets for acting a perfect gentleman is to be accused of seducing me!" Her voice rose. "It's ridiculous, absolutely ridiculous!"

Her uncles seemed taken aback by her vehement attack and glanced at each other uncertainly. They were in an untenable situation. They had known Nick since they were all boys together, and neither looked forward to meeting him on the dueling field—his expertise aside, dash it, they were fond of Nick! But their niece's reputation was at stake here. They were honor-bound to defend it. Even if what the earl said was true, there was no denying that Tess *had* been alone with him for several days. Whether he had taken advantage of her or not, she was effectively ruined.

Tess's passionate defense of Nicolas had given them all a few minutes' respite—and time for tempers to cool. Since a duel wouldn't accomplish anything, a different solution would have to be found.

Looking thoughtful, Rockwell finally said, "Rum situation, Nick. What are we going to do?"

Nick had known it would come to this the instant Tess's identity had been revealed. And while he'd had to admire her valiant attempt to avert just this sort of thing from happening, he had known all along that her efforts would prove futile. Anger at the trick fate had played him and resignation about the final outcome had been warring in his breast since the truth had come out. Anger and resignation aside, he had also been torn between a strong desire to strangle Dol—*Tess* and an equally strong, but definitely odd, sensation of satisfaction. He couldn't explain it, nor could he understand it, but marriage to Tess just felt *right*—as if it had been meant to be. . . . He'd been looking for a damned bride, hadn't he? So why the hell shouldn't he marry the little witch? Except for the family enmity, and that was a large hurdle, she was eminently suitable. He could attest to the fact that she had been a virgin when she had first lain in his arms, and there was no denying that she aroused him and pleased him in a way that he had never experienced with any woman before in his life. Nor could he pretend that he didn't want her in his bed. He did, desperately. It was unfortunate that she had turned out to be a young lady of quality, well born and well connected, but it didn't change anything. He had a strong aversion to being

backed into a corner, however, and his baiting of the Rockwells had been a halfhearted attempt to escape his fate. That
it *had* been halfhearted surprised him. There was no way in
hell that he would have allowed himself, no matter how scandalous the circumstances, to be coerced into marriage with a
woman he didn't want. Which raised an unsettling question
within him—he didn't *really* want to marry the Mandeville
minx, did he?"

Aware of the waiting silence, Nicolas tossed off the remainder of his brandy. Staring at the empty snifter, he said
quietly, "What we are going to do is very simple. At first light,
I shall leave for London to obtain a special license. You and
the ladies shall remain here. When I return, I shall marry your
niece with all due speed, with all of you as witnesses to the
ceremony, including my grandmother and sister. An announcement that our nuptials have taken place will be placed
in the *Times* immediately afterward." Nick rubbed a hand
wearily across his forehead. "The unexpectedness of it all,"
he admitted candidly, "will cause a nine days' wonder of gossip, but that will be the end of it." He slanted a crooked smile
at Rockwell. "It seems that you will have your wish and have
me married to your niece after all."

Tess swung round to face him. "I don't," she said from between clenched teeth, "want to marry *you!*"

"Doesn't matter," Nicolas said softly, "you don't have any
choice—it has all been decided. Hasn't it, Rockwell?"

"Afraid he's right, Tess," replied Rockwell. "You ain't got
any other choice but to marry him. Face ruin otherwise. Just
be glad that you'll be marrying a wealthy member of the peer-
age."

"A handsome, charming devil, too," said Alexander, a
coaxing glint in his eyes. "Couldn't find a better man, brat.
Think you should know that Rockwell and I had already approached him about a match between the pair of you. This
ain't the way we would have wished for it to come about, but
thing is, we approve."

Despair knifing through her, Tess glanced beseechingly at her two aunts. Meg shook her head slowly. "No, darling," she replied, answering Tess's unspoken plea. "There is nothing that we can do. Marriage to Sherbourne is the only way out of this unfortunate affair."

Hetty rose up to pull Tess against her. "It won't be so very bad, pet," she murmured into Tess's fiery curls. "You already know that he is a kind and noble man—didn't he rescue you from the Black Pig? You were alone and defenseless, and he could have taken base advantage of you. By your own words you have admitted that he did not. Doesn't that speak highly of the sort of man he is?"

Tess nearly choked on the bitter laughter that surged up through her. Oh, God, if Hetty only knew the truth! But it wouldn't change anything, she admitted grimly, even if she told them that he had, indeed, seduced her—that information would only make their demands for marriage all the more vociferous. But it rankled to have them think that he was such a *noble* man, and it didn't help to know that she had only herself to blame for everyone's distorted view of Nicolas. She should never have tried to shield him! Feeling rather put upon, Tess flung him a look of utter loathing, her temper fraying even more when she caught the glimmer of amusement flickering in his eyes.

"Believe me," she said tightly, "I know *exactly* what sort of man he is."

"Well, then," said Rockwell, beaming. "You know what a fortunate young lady you are! Just think—you'll soon be the countess of Sherbourne."

At that precise moment Tess didn't feel very fortunate, but she realized there was nothing she could do but put a good face on it. For better or worse, it seemed that she was destined to marry Nicolas Talmage, a man who was marrying her only because of a cruel twist of fate. . . . Heartsore and weary, she let the warm, teasing congratulations of her relatives wash over her.

If anyone noticed that Tess was singularly quiet while plans for her hasty wedding to Nicolas were discussed, no one commented on it. Probably too grateful that I gave in without more of a fight, she thought sourly as she curled up on her chair and stared moodily at the fire.

Eventually, when all had been settled to everyone's satisfaction, the three ladies disappeared upstairs, while the Rockwells remained in the main room of the cottage, planning on dozing in chairs by the fire for what remained of the night. Nick was leaving for Sherbourne Court and from there, almost immediately, for London.

Tess had thought she would be subjected to a great many pointed questions when she was finally alone with her aunts, but such was not the case. They were all exhausted after the night's events and, with very little conversation between them, retired to bed. There was some argument about sleeping arrangements, but it was finally agreed that Hetty and Meg would sleep in Tess's far more comfortable bed and Tess would take the small, narrow bed that had been set up earlier, in anticipation of the arrival of the two ladies.

For Nicolas there was to be no sleep that night. Leaving the Rockwells in command of the cottage, having quietly told them of the attack on Tess and his suspicions that the owlers had been behind it, and after warning them to be on the alert, he departed. At Sherbourne Court he roused Lovejoy and made his wishes known. After a hasty bath, a change of clothes, and a swiftly consumed meal, he was on the road to London.

Nick was extremely busy while in London, but he managed to make time for an exceedingly brief meeting with Roxbury. His face giving no clue to his thoughts, Roxbury listened in silence to Nick's convoluted tale. With a twinkle in his gray eyes, he finally said, "Then congratulations are in order? You are to be married?"

Nick grinned ruefully. "It would seem so, sir, and while the circumstances are scandalous, I find I cannot regret them."

Roxbury nodded, then said quietly, "You are to be commended for what you have discovered about our smugglers in such a short time. I had thought it would be weeks before you managed to make contact with them. Your information about a 'gentleman' and the attack on your lady is most interesting. I tend to agree with your opinion that he might very well be our 'Mr. Brown.'" The twinkle in the gray eyes returned, growing even more pronounced as he said, "In view of your excellent work, I think that for the time being . . . at least for a few days, you can forget about the owlers and concentrate on your bride."

Nick smiled and nodded. "I intend to!"

At that moment, Nick may have been smiling, but Avery, returning home to Mandeville Manor, was definitely *not*. He arrived home late Sunday afternoon—just about the time Nick was meeting with Roxbury. Tossing his reins to a grim-faced Lowell, who had hurried out to meet him, he snapped, "Has she returned? Has there been any sign of her? *Any* word?"

Lowell shook his head, deciding cravenly to let Coleman be the one to inform his master that the aunts, too, had disappeared. Seeing the expression of angry frustration that crossed Avery's face, Lowell was quite content to lead the horses to the stables and spend several minutes slowly unharnessing and rubbing down the sweaty animals—a task he would normally have felt was far beneath him.

Striding into the silent house, Avery headed for his study, where he shrugged off his greatcoat and tossed his York tan gloves onto a cherrywood desk. After ringing impatiently for Coleman, he stalked the room, his thoughts on precisely what he was going to do to Tess once he got his hands on her. There was no doubt in his mind that he *would* find her.

Somewhat warily, Coleman entered the room a few minutes later. "You rang, sir?" he asked nervously.

Avery, who had been staring blindly out the window, cursing fate in general and Tess Mandeville in particular, spun around and glared at him. "Of course I rang, you bloody fool! Now go get that pair of conniving bitches from upstairs and bring them here." His eyes hardened. "I want to have a talk with them—and this time I won't be gentle about it."

Coleman paled. "Uh, L-L-Lowell didn't tell you?"

Avery's eyes narrowed, and his mouth thinned to an angry line. "Tell me what?" he demanded with lethal menace.

Coleman swallowed, his thoughts bitter against the missing butler. "The ladies aren't here—they're gone."

Avery moved with the speed of a striking snake and grasped the lapels of Coleman's jacket, shaking him violently. "What the hell do you mean, *they're gone*?"

Coleman gulped, memories of his master's other rages flashing across his mind. "They disappeared sometime last night. We fed them about eight o'clock in the evening, and Lowell collected the trays about an hour later, locking the door behind him." Unable to bear the fury in Avery's eyes, he glanced away and muttered, "This morning, when I took up their breakfast, the door was ajar and the room was empty. During the night someone had kicked open the door and taken them away."

Avery's hands tightened on the lapels. His voice silky with sarcasm, he asked, "And I suppose you and Lowell never heard a thing?" At Coleman's unhappy nod, he shook him again and snarled, "The pair of you were probably too drunk to notice if an entire regiment had come marching through the house! Why the bloody hell I keep you—! I set you a simple task—to keep an eye on a pair of helpless females—and you let them escape! I ought to—!"

Coleman cringed, certain a beating was coming, but Avery merely threw him away, saying furiously, "If you and that oaf Lowell don't want to find yourselves looking for new positions, in the future you damn well better carry out my orders better than you have lately! Now get out of here and get me something to eat and drink—and send Lowell to me. I want a word with him."

Not envying Lowell his audience with Avery, Coleman bolted from the room.

Alone in his study, Avery paced the floor like an enraged beast, frustration eating away at him. It was obvious that until he found Tess he was going to need more funds. Mr. Brown was just going to have to be a bit more generous—whether it was part of their agreement or not. He smiled grimly. Considering the disaster Mr. Brown faced if just one little word were slipped to the right people, Avery didn't doubt for a moment that his demands would be met. A scowl replaced his smile, and his hands clenched into fists. When he got hold of that little red-haired bitch again . . . Lovingly he pictured several inventive ways of giving pain, but upon Lowell's appearance, he tore himself from that pleasant pastime to the present.

Avery was as menacing to Lowell as he had been to Coleman, even going so far as to strike his butler before demanding to be shown the broken door. With a frown on his face, he stared at the shattered wood, his mind racing.

Ignoring his two hovering servants, he returned to his study to consider all the implications of this latest disaster. Tess had to have been behind the escape of the aunts. He doubted she had been the one to kick in the door, but he was certain she had been involved. Which meant, he thought with an ugly smile, that she had to be somewhere nearby. . . .

In the morning he would set his less-than-satisfactory pair of servants to reconnoiter. His eyes narrowed. After the tongue-lashing they had received today, they wouldn't dare fail again. He would find Tess, and when he did . . .

Oblivious of Avery's sinister plans for Tess, Nick left London just before dusk that same evening, the special license tucked securely in the pocket of his greatcoat. There was no chance that he would arrive home before darkness fell, but he wanted to put several miles behind him before he stopped for the night.

The black sky was brilliant with stars when he finally pulled his horse to a halt before a prosperous coaching inn. A short while later, his stomach full of rich kidney pie and warm mulled punch, he sank exhaustedly into bed. Sleep descended instantly.

Waking the next morning, he looked around groggily, hardly aware of where he was. It was an unnerving sensation; nothing looked familiar, and for a terrifying second he couldn't even remember how he came to be sleeping in this particular bed. It was only when his eyes fell upon his greatcoat flung over a nearby chair that it all came back to him. Somewhat thoughtfully, he got out of bed. If Tess had been telling the truth about her memory loss . . .

His mouth tightened. He had no reason to doubt her word now, and he cursed himself again. He should have realized within minutes of seeing Tess that she wasn't one of the usual wenches to be found in places like the Black Pig. And perhaps he had. The problem was, he admitted disgustedly, that he had wanted her in a way he couldn't remember ever wanting another woman, and he hadn't been willing to let anything stand in his way—not even the fact that she clearly didn't belong where he had found her. If he'd been half the gentleman he'd always considered himself to be, he would have come to her aid instead of deflowering her and forcing her to become his mistress.

The plain and simple truth of the matter, Nick thought grimly as he got out of bed and pulled on his clothes, was that like a green boy, he had allowed his body to dictate to his brain—he'd taken one look at Tess, at those huge violet eyes and soft, rosy lips, and nothing else had mattered, except that she be in his bed. He smiled acidly. Unfortunately, that particular fact was still true. Hell. He was even willing to put aside who she was in order to marry her, so that she'd *always* be in his bed! It was a damning admission for him to make, and his mood darkened even more.

What he found most annoying about the situation wasn't that he was going to be marrying Tess Mandeville, but that the fury and resentment he was certain he would feel if he'd found himself trapped into marriage with any other woman wasn't within him. He *had* been furious when the truth had exploded in his face, but again, there had been that curious feeling of satisfaction. . . .

It wasn't until the inn had been left far behind him and he was on the final leg of his journey that Nicolas allowed himself to think about all the problems waiting for him at Sherbourne Court—not the least of these being his recalcitrant bride! He grinned. Tess was going to be a handful, he was well aware of that, and he rather thought that he was going to find being married to her more than tolerable—she'd never bore him, and there was no denying that he was definitely going to enjoy having her in his arms anywhere or anytime he chose.

The fact that she was a Mandeville would present some immediate difficulties, though. . . . His grandmother was not going to be pleased with his choice of bride. When the circumstances surrounding the hasty wedding were explained, she would no doubt agree that marriage was the only solution, but Nick found himself shying away from the prospect of telling her the unvarnished truth. Pallas was going to have trouble enough dealing with the fact that he was going to marry the great-granddaughter of the woman who had run off with her husband and the niece of the man who had killed her grandson, and she was going to lay the blame for the current situation solely at Tess's door—even if it more rightly should rest upon his shoulders.

He sighed. He couldn't think of any way to soften the blow, and he knew with a sinking heart that the truth must be told— he owed it to Pallas and to Tess, and to do otherwise would only sink him in a worse quagmire. With all the years of coldness between the two families, Pallas was certain to hate Tess even if the match had come about under more normal circumstances, and having the normal male's aversion to a household of warring women, he was uneasily aware that there were going to be some decidedly chancy days ahead.

It was afternoon before Nicolas arrived at Sherbourne Court, and the news that his grandmother was home, but that Athena had elected to remain a few more days visiting with friends, didn't displease him. He would have liked Athena to be present when he married Tess—it would have helped to still wagging tongues if the families presented a united front—but it couldn't be helped. He wasn't about to endanger the wary truce that presently existed between them by demanding that Athena return home immediately, nor was he willing to postpone the wedding. By this time tomorrow he had every intention of facing the world with his bride at his side—whether she wanted to be his bride or not!

Despite his firm conviction that marriage to Tess was the only answer to several pressing problems, her vehement rejection of marriage to him did weigh irritatingly on his mind. He couldn't pretend that his pride hadn't taken a battering. Any other woman, he thought resentfully as he went in search of his grandmother, would have been relieved and, yes, dammit, grateful that he was willing to do the honorable thing by her. A rueful smile curved his mouth. And if she had been, she wouldn't have been the fascinating little baggage he greatly feared had come to mean more than anything else in the world to him. . . .

Telling Pallas was every bit as hard as Nick had feared it would be. Though he spared himself nothing in the telling of the tale, it was clear from Pallas's stunned, angry white face that she was convinced it was all a plot on the part of the horrid Mandevilles. Not even mention of the Rockwells' approval of the match swayed her. He couldn't blame her—hadn't he thought, with far less evidence, that Tess had been trying to trap him into marriage? He could smile now at his own folly, but he understood his grandmother's reaction. More than anyone else she had borne the brunt of the painful scandal nearly seventy years ago. More recently, her eldest grandson had died at the hands of another Mandeville—her wounds went deeper than anyone's.

"I know I wanted you to marry," she admitted miserably after the first storm of anger and disbelief had passed. "And it's true that I have never met the young lady and that she might be utterly charming. I'm quite positive also that to any other family but ours, it might be considered an excellent match, but it isn't to *me!*"

She sent him a deeply reproachful glance that made Nicolas's heart twist. He had never wanted to hurt his grandmother. But dammit, he *was* going to marry Tess. Even in the midst of the painful discussion with Pallas, the astonishing knowledge suddenly occurred to him that he really did want to marry Tess Mandeville and that he was going to let nothing stand in his way. Not even Pallas.

In a gentle voice he asked, "Grandmother, can't you put aside the past? What happened long ago wasn't Tess's fault. And it is through no fault of her own that she has found herself compromised. More rightly you should be railing at me for acting the part of a cad."

"I know," Pallas said tiredly, her face worn and drawn, the blue eyes full of despair. "You've explained what happened in great detail, but even if it isn't her fault, you can't possibly expect me to welcome *that woman's* offspring into my home." She almost wailed, "And as your *bride!*"

"What would you have me do?" Nicolas asked. "Prove myself totally without honor and walk away from the situation? Or perhaps," he inquired grimly, knowing it was probably the only argument that would sway her, "you'd like me to face her uncles on the dueling field?"

Pallas's already pale features paled even more. Terror in her eyes, she breathed, "Oh, God! No! I couldn't go through that again!"

Her pain tore at his heart. Kneeling impetuously beside her where she sat on the sofa, he took one of her hands in his and pressed a kiss into the scented palm. "I'm sorry to have caused you such terrible anguish," he said gruffly. "God knows I never meant to! And if I could have spared you this ordeal, I would have, but there is nothing that can be done." His eyes met hers. "You must understand that as much as you dislike it, *hate* it, there is no alternative." Suddenly thinking of one last line of reasoning that might make his choice of a bride more acceptable, he asked softly, "Have you considered that Tess might even now be pregnant? That your first grandchild, your *only* grandchild, might even now be growing in her womb?"

Pallas's face crumpled. "Marry her if you will," she said in broken tones. "Oh, but, Nicolas, I cannot be happy about this. Don't ask it of me."

In the silence broken only by Pallas's muffled sobs as she looked away from him and sought to compose herself, Nicolas's face twisted. He had obtained a victory of sorts, but he wondered why it tasted like defeat.

Rising slowly to his feet a few minutes later, when the worst of his grandmother's tears had dried, he stared at her ravaged features and said dully, "Tess and her aunts shall remain at the cottage until the wedding. I will not inflict her or them upon you any sooner than I must."

Dabbing at her eyes with a lacy handkerchief, Pallas gave a watery chuckle. "Oh, Nick, life was so serene and predictable before you came home! One day following uneventfully after the other—our only suspense being in whether it would rain or not, or what Cook was fixing for dinner. Now look at us: we have a young lady fleeing from a wicked blackguard; smugglers lurking about everywhere, it seems; a lost memory; an attempted murder; a midnight rescue; and a sudden marriage!"

His eyes fixed intently upon her wan face, he asked quietly, "Are you really able to accept my marriage to Tess so easily?"

She looked thoughtful. "It isn't what I wanted, but I suppose one could say that things have worked out for the best—I *do* get to see you married before much more time elapses, and there is the possibility that before I die, I shall hold a grandchild or two in my arms. And of course, there is one other thing that makes the marriage more acceptable to me. . . ."

At Nicolas's puzzled expression, she said cheerfully, an impish twinkle in her blue eyes, "Just think how furious the current Baron Mandeville is going to be when he discovers who married the heiress this time!"

Chapter Eighteen

*W*hile Avery Mandeville hadn't yet learned the full extent of his defeat, he strongly suspected the earl's fine hand in at least *some* of his recent reversals.

The past several days had not been pleasant for the newest Baron Mandeville. The arrival of Rockwell's letter with the unwelcome news of the impending visit had been only the start of his troubles. In the beginning, Avery had seen his automatic interception of the letter as a stroke of luck and had immediately set into motion his plans for a forced marriage. And that, he thought sourly as he sat alone in the great hall of the manor that Monday evening, drinking glass after glass of excellent French burgundy, had been the last positive thing that had happened to him.

Upon reaching London, he had swiftly changed his clothes and refreshed himself at the Mandeville town house on Grosvenor Square—coincidentally just down and across the square from the Sherbourne town house. On the point of stepping into his carriage for the ride to Hanover Square, he'd chanced upon an acquaintance, and the subsequent conversation had given him pause. The loquacious gentleman had been full of the usual town gossip, but the information that he had breakfasted that very morning with Lord Rockwell had arrested Avery's attention.

A few discreet questions on Avery's part elicited the extremely interesting information that there had been no sign of, nor any mention of, Tess. In fact, according to this amiable soul, Rockwell had been full of plans to leave on Saturday for a visit with his niece and from there on to Cornwall for the remainder of the year. The knocker was being taken down from the town house door, dust covers were already being placed over furniture, and it was clear that the house was being closed up for the season.

Looking thoughtful, Avery canceled his carriage and returned to the house. Was it possible that Tess hadn't arrived in London? Could he have reached the City before her? It seemed unlikely—she'd had a head start of many hours—but there had been a storm last night. . . .

Deciding not to rush over to the Rockwell town house, he looked up an unsavory acquaintance of his. Avery wasn't one of Jack Denning's intimates, but they'd had a few dealings in the past. And Jack, with his connections within London's dark underbelly, was just the fellow Avery needed.

By Friday morning Avery was assured by Jack that Tess was not at her uncle's house. So where was she? Just a little worried now, he had Denning put someone to watch over the Hanover Square house and a few other cohorts to check the roads leading from Kent to London, and he forced himself to wait patiently. Tess was certain to show up at any time. And if she managed to slip through the watchers on the roads leading into the City—that red hair of hers was hard to miss— then the spy situated near the house was bound to see her. He also sent a message to his servants at the manor, inquiring if, by some wild chance, Tess had returned home.

While he waited for Tess's appearance or an answer to his message, Avery considered calling upon the Rockwells anyway, but caution held him back. He was very aware that Rockwell and his brother held a general dislike of him and would be suspicious of his unexpected arrival in Town. He saw no reason to tip his hand if it wasn't imperative. By the next day there was still no sign of Tess. He received the return message from Lowell informing him that all was well at the manor, but that the young lady was not there, either. It began to dawn on him that something had gone seriously wrong. His spies swore there had been no sign of her, either on the roads or at the Rockwell mansion.

There was nothing further to be gained by staying in London, and deciding that his next step would be a pertinent conversation with the aunts, he prepared to return home on Sunday. It was possible that Tess had taken refuge somewhere else . . . that he had been totally wrong in believing that she had fled to the protection of her uncles. He wasn't certain how to view this change of events. It could prove most fortunate if Tess were some place from which he could easily abduct her, but it could also create a host of new problems. Not in the best of moods, he ordered his carriage and horses and left for Mandeville, missing Nick's arrival in London to obtain the special license by mere minutes.

The news that greeted Avery upon his return home was almost as unsettling as Tess's disappearance. With the aunts' escape, for the first time he began to suspect that Nicolas Talmage had to be involved in some of his troubles. He knew all about the longtime friendship between the Rockwells and the Talmage family, and it would have taken someone a lot less suspicious than he not to have realized that once the Rockwells had been denied entrance to the manor, they would instantly have retired to the home of a friend who resided in the neighborhood. From there it was an easy leap to place Nick right in the middle of the aunts' escape from Mandeville Manor. But where was Tess?

His icy blue eyes narrowed. Was it possible that somehow Nick and Tess had met? He brooded over that for some time but eventually dismissed it. If Nick were behind Tess's nonarrival in London, the noble earl, Avery thought with a sneer on his face, wouldn't have waited until Saturday night to rescue the aunts. No. The rescue of the aunts had come about only because the Rockwells had gotten the wind up. He was positive of that.

Feeling a little better about that aspect of the various puzzles before him, Avery speculated on what would happen next. He knew he was in a dangerous corner. His finances were tight these days, and not even the profits from an uneasy liaison with the mysterious Mr. Brown could keep him afloat much longer. The aunts wouldn't remain silent either about his virtual incarceration of them or Tess's disappearance. . . . If ruin was to be averted, he had to act quickly.

Finding Tess seemed to be the key to his problem. Once he had her in his possession all his other problems would disappear. To that end, he had sent Lowell that very morning to make discreet inquiries about her along the probable route she would have taken to London. Perhaps they would discover some word of her; there could have been some sort of accident and she was lying hurt in some farmer's house, afraid to admit her identity in case he came looking for her. . . . Avery smiled without humor. And Tess knew that he *would* come looking for her.

Not only had Avery sent Lowell to look for Tess, but he'd had Coleman make a careful reconnoiter of Sherbourne Court. Coleman had nothing to report from his limited surveillance of the area, and a conversation that same evening with a footman from the court, after Coleman had plied him with liquor, had not elicited anything new. Considering the hostility between the two families, Avery hadn't expected the aunts to be there, but, dammit, they had to be somewhere nearby! Where? And why hadn't he heard from either the Rockwells or Nick himself? Presumably the aunts had told their pitiful tale by now, so why wasn't his home being assaulted by some outraged men?

His mouth twitched. Could it be that the greatly feared specter of disgrace and social ruin was going to save him? If Tess hadn't been with the aunts, and he knew she hadn't been . . . And if she also hadn't been with her uncles, of which he was fairly certain, then where was she? By now her relatives had no doubt discovered those unpleasant facts themselves and were, even as he sat here drinking, scrambling around frantically trying to discover Tess's whereabouts or trying to come up with a way to avert a full-blown scandal. Smiling nastily, he raised a silent toast to the rigid social strictures of the day and shortly thereafter went to bed, feeling certain that fate was going to throw him a lucky card after all.

It wasn't often that Nick thought about luck or fate, but that Tuesday evening in October of 1811 when Tess Mandeville became his bride, he could only marvel at the luck or fate that had brought him to the Black Pig a scant week ago. If Maryanne Halliwell hadn't murmured her agreeability to a closer alliance with him that night at Lady Grover's ball, he wouldn't have been riding pell-mell in a driving rainstorm toward Sherbourne Court and wouldn't have given the shabby little inn a second glance. Staring down into the face of his bride of less than a half hour, Nick was suddenly very thankful to Lady Halliwell—and whatever other forces may have brought him to the Black Pig that night.

He cast a glance over at his grandmother where she was talking quietly with Meg and Hetty. She seemed to be bearing up well, he decided. She had been gracious, if a bit stiff, when Tess and the aunts had been presented to her earlier, but her innate kindness had shone through. Watching her as she struggled to suppress the painful emotions he knew were churning within her, Nick had been aware of a great rush of deep affection. She was a grand lady.

The wedding had gone off splendidly. A small salon at the rear of the house had been filled with late-blooming flowers, and under the bemused gaze of their assembled relatives, Nick and Tess had been married by the local vicar. If the bride seemed a bit pale and reluctant in her responses, no one paid it any heed; and if the vicar privately thought that there was more an air of relief when the vows were finally said than of delight, he wisely kept the observation to himself.

Light refreshments were served following the wedding in his grandmother's favorite blue salon, the portrait of his grandfather dominating the room. The uncles beamed proudly, and Hetty and Meg smiled approvingly at the newly married pair. Lady Sherbourne still held herself slightly aloof, but there was an expression in the blue eyes that brooded well for the future.

There had not been time for much conversation between Pallas and Tess before the wedding, but as they stood together by one of the tables, Nick observed them carefully. They made polite conversation, each one picking her words with care. From the moment of their first meeting, Pallas had hardly been able to tear her gaze away from Tess's lovely young face. Feeling more relaxed now that she had met her grandson's bride and had seen for herself that Tess was not the scheming, manipulative termagant she had feared, Pallas was finally able to say what had been uppermost in her mind since she had first caught sight of the girl. Squarely meeting Tess's deeply hued violet eyes, she said abruptly, "You look very much like your great-grandmother, don't you?"

Tess nodded gravely, aware of the pain this frail, gentle-looking woman had suffered because of Theresa. "Yes. I've been told that there is a striking resemblance between us— there is a portrait of her in the gallery at Mandeville that leaves little doubt." She gave a small grimace. "We could almost be twins."

Pallas nodded her silvery head. "Yes, you could." She stared very hard at Tess for a minute longer, assessing the honesty and character she saw in Tess's face. Then, as if making up her mind about something, she patted Tess's hand and murmured almost to herself, "But you'll do. You'll do very nicely indeed, I think." She turned away and set about making her guests at ease.

Tess hadn't known what to think about her comments, but she was conscious of a little knot of apprehension easing in her chest. Meeting Lady Sherbourne had been just one of many dreaded hurdles she'd had to clear these past few days, and she was surprised at how much the acceptance of Nicolas's grandmother had meant to her. She bit her lip. None of it should have mattered, but she was grateful for Lady Sherbourne's easy manner with her.

She glanced up at Nick's dark face, and at the look of possessive desire glittering in his black eyes, her heart leaped. It was insane to feel even a flicker of happiness about their marriage, but, God help her, she did. Her lips curved ruefully. She *was* happy in an odd sort of way, and she couldn't explain the feeling of rightness, the powerful sensation of being where she belonged . . . of having come safely home after a long, perilous journey. It was a queer feeling—especially since she had been telling herself stoutly that she was adamantly opposed to the idea of being married to Nicolas Talmage from the moment it had first been brought forth.

Tess sighed, realizing that she shouldn't be surprised at her changeable emotions—in spite of everything, she *did* love Nicolas, and while he might not love her, he had proven to be an honorable and considerate man. He was also, she admitted candidly, inordinately handsome and, according to her uncles, extremely wealthy and generous—the settlements Nicolas had proposed had gratified Rockwell immensely. Nick was also kind; she could see that in the way he treated his grandmother. Few women would have found fault with a man like her very new husband.

Feeling Nick unobtrusively slip an arm around her waist and pull her slightly to him, she became tinglingly aware of the feel of him, of the warmth of his big body against her own. Her breathing quickened suddenly when she thought of the coming night. He was her husband now, their lives inalterably linked, and even more than a man with a mistress, he now had the right to her body. . . .

"Are you thinking about tonight?" Nick asked huskily against her ear. "I am. In fact, I can hardly wait until these festivities are over and I can have you all to myself." He brushed a discreet kiss against her temple. "I've missed you these past days, sweetheart—and while your aunts are very nice women and the Rockwells are good friends of mine, I have wished them in Hades a dozen times lately—it seems that one of them has always been under foot—I've not had a moment alone with you since Saturday night."

Nick's complaint was valid. Her relatives had watched the pair of them like hungry hawks—there had been no chance of a private tête-à-tête between them, and Tess didn't know whether she was pleased or unhappy about it. If she had been able to see him alone, would she have pleaded with him not to go through with the marriage? Was it so important to her that he love her that she was willing to face social ruin rather than marry him? She grimaced. She was a fool!

Forcing a smile to her lips, she said tartly, "If I remember correctly, you were the one who invited the aunts to stay at Sherbourne until the business with Avery was settled."

"Hmm, so I did," he replied idly. "And I suppose I did it for strictly altruistic reasons—I mean, it's not possible, is it, that I might have done so in order to please you? Or to make your first days here a little less strange?"

Startled, Tess gaped at him. "Did you?" she asked, incredulous. That thought had not occurred to her.

He smiled. "I'm afraid that particular puzzle you're going to have to work out all by yourself, sweetheart."

Pallas returned to their vicinity. Bestowing a brief kiss upon her tall grandson's cheek, she said, "I'm afraid that the events of the past few days have utterly worn me out. I've already pleaded my case to the others, and they have sent me on my way. So I'll wish you both a long and happy life together one more time, and then I shall retire."

Nick agreed that his grandmother was looking tired, and he knew very well that despite the gracious front she had put on, today had been a strain for her. A quizzical expression in his eyes, he asked softly, "And do you, Grandmother? Wish us a long and happy life together?"

She smiled with genuine warmth at both of them, one frail hand brushing a caress across Tess's cheek. "I do indeed." An imp of mischief suddenly lit her blue eyes. "And don't waste any time presenting me with grandbabies!"

Tess blushed delightfully, and with a little smile that was both pleased and sad, Pallas sailed regally from the room.

The vicar and his wife departed shortly thereafter, and the others did not linger long, either—they'd all been under tension the past week, and having accomplished their most immediate objective, everyone was feeling relaxed and relieved. After more hugs and misty-eyed smiles, the aunts retired upstairs to the splendid suite of rooms that Nicolas had provided for them. The uncles lingered for a few minutes longer, but soon enough they, too, took their leave.

Dropping a kiss on her cheek, Alexander said gruffly, "Be happy, brat. Nick's a fine man." He threw his friend a teasing glance. "Inclined to be a bit high-handed and arrogant upon occasion, but he'll be good to you."

Rockwell beamed down at her. "It's true. Nick's the man for you, Tess. You'll see. You might not have wanted to marry him, but you'll thank us for insisting upon it one day. You mark my words if you don't."

It had been decided that the Rockwells and the staff Nicolas had installed for Tess would continue to stay at the gatekeeper's cottage for the time being. With the smuggling question still to be resolved, and his mind on other things at the moment, Nick hadn't wanted to leave the cottage deserted. The baron and his brother, their fine eyes flashing with excitement, had insisted that they would be on the watch for any nefarious activities. Truth be told, both were looking forward to the prospect of midnight clashes with a band of murderous rogues, should the smugglers dare to return.

It was very quiet in the blue salon after they had departed. Somewhat uneasily, Tess looked at Nicolas. From the warmth of his glance and the sensual twist to his mouth, it was obvious that he wanted to make love to her.

"Don't worry," he murmured as if reading her thoughts, "while it's true that all I've thought about for the past few hours is the evening ahead and making love to you, I don't intend to ravish you on my grandmother's favorite sofa."

Tess blushed. "I didn't think you did," she replied breathlessly. The gleam in his eyes made her heart beat so fast, she was certain it would leap out of her chest. She stammered, "I-if you don't m-m-mind, I think I'll r-r-retire."

The sensual gleam in the black eyes deepened and made shivers of anticipation slide down her spine. "Yes," he said thickly, "that's a very good idea. I shall join you shortly." He brushed a teasing kiss across her lips. "Very shortly."

Tess fled from the room. To her shame, her body already hummed, eager for his touch. It seemed like months since she had last lain in his arms, and while scolding herself for being such a wanton baggage, she simply couldn't pretend that she wasn't looking forward to her wedding night. . . .

Nicolas remained alone in the blue salon for several more minutes, sipping a final snifter of brandy, thinking about the extraordinary turn his life had taken. He'd spent ten months single-mindedly searching for a suitable bride in the most select homes in all of England, and he had found her where he'd least expected—in a low tavern on a stormy night. He shook his head, smiling softly in memory.

What would have happened, he wondered idly, if he had met Tess under more normal circumstances? Would he have still felt that inexplicable rush of desire and recognition? Would he have realized at his first sight of her—say, at Almack's—that this was the woman for whom he had been looking? Even now he couldn't explain the powerful feeling that she was his, that they were *meant* to be together, that had come over him that night at the Black Pig. He'd taken one look at her, and he'd *known*.

His lips twisted. Well, he hadn't known that he was going to marry her, but certainly that he wanted her and that he'd waited a lifetime, perhaps several, to find her again. . . . What a strange thought! To find her *again*.

Shaking off his odd musings, he took another sip of brandy, wandering aimlessly through the silent room, the remains of the marriage feast still scattered atop the various tables. Though the deed was now done, Nick found it astonishing that he was married to Tess Mandeville. A week ago, if anyone had told him that he would take as his bride a daughter of the house of his family's sworn enemy, he would have laughed and thought the person mad. But he, Nicolas Talmage, tenth earl of Sherbourne, had married the heiress Tess Mandeville. Incredible!

Drawn to the portrait of his grandfather, Nick stood beneath it, staring up at the features so like his own. If Benedict had not disappeared with Theresa Mandeville and had remained at Sherbourne Court, what would his grandfather have said about such an unlikely outcome? he wondered. Would he have been satisfied? Pleased that *this* time it was his family who had snatched the heiress right out from underneath the nose of the Mandevilles?

Nicolas studied the chiseled, unsmiling face of his grandfather. None of it mattered now. It had all happened a long time ago. His grandfather was no doubt dead and moldering in his grave somewhere across the sea. Certainly beyond caring about what happened these days. It was he, Nick Talmage, who had a young, enchanting bride waiting for him upstairs, and it was time, he thought pleasurably, that he joined her.

Leaving his half-empty snifter on one of the tables, he walked eagerly to the door, a heavy, pulsating ache already building low in his body. But for some reason he stopped in the middle of the doorway, compelled to look back at the portrait of his grandfather. He blinked. Then he looked again and even took a startled step in that direction—then caught himself. No. It couldn't be. It was just a trick of the light, he told himself roundly as he left the blue salon in search of his bride. Just a trick of the light that for one second had seemed to make his grandfather's hard mouth curve in a faint, triumphant smile. . . .

Despite his eagerness to find her, it was several minutes before Nick stepped into Tess's rooms, which adjoined his. He had taken the time for a swift bath, and it was with his thick hair still damp and his body half dried that he had slid into a gray-and-maroon-striped dressing robe of heavy silk with wide dark gray lapels.

He paused at the door that separated her suite from his, aware of the sudden pounding of his heart and the instant hardening of his body. In a matter of minutes he was going to make love to Tess in the bed where generations of Talmages had been conceived, and he wondered if tonight he and his bride would begin a babe between them. The idea of Tess growing full and round with his baby inside her pleased him. But a baby really didn't matter, he realized with a start; all that really mattered, he admitted baldly, was that she was his!

He pushed open the door and walked into Tess's room. Candlelight bathed the handsome chamber in a golden glow, the flickering light dancing over the sumptuous furnishings and the magnificent bed directly across from him. The bed dominated the room, its silken canopy arched and flaring, four tall, ornately carved spindles draped in hangings of royal purple silk shot with silver. The silver threads gleamed and sparkled bewitchingly in the candlelight, but Nicolas had eyes only for the slim figure with a mass of fiery hair tumbling down her back who stood motionless near the pair of leaded-paned doors that opened to a spacious balcony.

The exultation he felt at the sight of her nearly overwhelmed him. The pulsating ache between his thighs made him aware of just how badly he wanted her and how very glad he was that she was his bride, no matter what the reasons for their marriage.

He stood there admiring the picture she made. She was wearing a gown and peignoir that he had purchased for her while he was in London—the instant he had laid eyes on it, in the shop of a well-known modiste, he had known that it would look breathtakingly enchanting on her, and he was right. It did.

Made of the finest silk, in a hue of such a deep purple that it looked almost black, the gown had long, full sleeves of some sheer, gauzy material in a color just a few shades lighter than the gown itself. The same gauzy material fashioned the peignoir's full, swinging skirt with its soft flounces. The image of Tess's white skin gleaming seductively through the sheer peignoir had provided him with several erotic daydreams recently, but tonight it was the way the gown looked on Tess that made his breath catch in his throat.

Her red-gold hair flashed like fire against the purple silk. The low-cut, scalloped neckline framed her shoulders and gave a provocative hint of her bosom, just as he had known it would. The narrowly cut garment clearly delineated her slender body, but it was the row of tiny silver buttons that ran from neckline to hem that had his gaze riveted—Nick had spent quite a few restless, sleepless hours of late, thinking of undoing those buttons one by one with his hot, seeking mouth. . . .

He nearly groaned aloud at the surge of desire that swept through him as he imagined how very sweet she was going to taste. She was still unaware of his presence. Tamping down the urge simply to scoop her up in his arms and make love to her, he said lightly, "I hope it is not anything I have done that has put that wistful expression on your sweet face."

Tess jumped and swung round to face him. "*Nick!* You startled me," she cried, startled from whatever unproductive musings had held her attention. "I didn't hear you enter."

He searched her pale features keenly, noting the shadows in the depths of her amethyst eyes. "What is it?" he asked huskily as he reached for her and pulled her against his hard body. "What makes you look like you are awaiting your jailor, instead of a husband who wants only happiness for you?"

Her eyes clung to his. "You can't pretend that you really wanted to marry me, that if circumstances had been different, you wouldn't have walked—no, run from marriage to *me.*"

"Hmm, is that so?" he asked mildly, dropping a warm kiss on her collarbone. "It seems to me," he murmured, "that I've gotten *precisely* the bride I wanted." At her expression of openmouthed astonishment, he laughed and swung her up in his arms. "Come to bed, sweetheart, and let me show you just how very much I want you. . . ."

Chapter Nineteen

—◆—

*T*ess knew that once he started making love to her, any opportunity to discuss their marriage calmly would be lost. The instant he laid her on the bed, she scrambled away from him. One hand held out, her eyes huge, she said breathlessly, "Wait! I know you want me—*that* has been plain from the beginning. But are you really as accepting of this marriage to me as you seem to be? Are you *really* able to dismiss the long-standing enmity between our two families so easily?"

The last thing Nick wanted to discuss was his own confused state of emotions, but it was apparent that his bride wasn't going to prove very cooperative of his plans for the remainder of the evening unless he answered her. He eyed her for a long moment, wondering if, with a few judiciously placed kisses he could avoid the subject she so obviously wanted to discuss. The determined look on her face told him not even to try.

Sighing, Nick threw himself onto the bed. Lying on his back, he put his hands behind his head. Staring at the purple-and-silver canopy above him, he admitted bluntly, "You're not the bride I thought I would find, and I won't pretend otherwise. On the other hand . . ." He sent her a long, slow look, the unfathomable black eyes moving over her like a warm ca-

ress. "On the other hand, you are *exactly* the bride I was looking for."

Tess looked confused and pleased at the same time. "What
do you mean?"

Nick held up one shapely hand and said, ticking off each
fact on his fingers, "You're well born. You're well connected.
And if Rockwell is to be believed"—he grinned at her—
"you're also an heiress. The first two were qualities I wanted
in my bride; the third, considering my own circumstances, is
merely a pleasant benefit."

"I see," Tess said slowly, not liking his words. "And those
reasons were sufficient to tie yourself to me for the rest of
your life?"

Turning onto his side, he reached out a caressing hand toward her face. "They would do," he said softly. "They have
been reasons enough for many couples of our ilk. But they
weren't the only reasons I was willing to marry you." His
voice deepening, the expression in his black eyes making Tess
feel decidedly weak, he murmured huskily, "You've lain in
my arms and I've tasted the fire in you and I find that I have
developed a certain addiction to that fire. . . ." He observed
the flush on her cheeks with interest for several seconds before adding, "You're also incredibly lovely, gallant, loyal, and
honest. A man could do worse than to marry a woman with
those qualities."

Tess's eyes dropped from the intensity of his gaze. She
couldn't help but be pleased and flattered by what he had said,
even if he hadn't said the words she most wanted to
hear. . . . Was she being silly to want to hear him say that he
had fallen madly in love with her . . . as she had with him?
Was she foolishly yearning for the moon? Sadly, she admitted
that she probably was and that for the time being, at least, she
should consider herself lucky that her husband thought she
was lovely and loyal. That knowledge warmed her, pushing
aside some of the foreboding that had plagued her. He didn't
love her yet, but perhaps in time . . .

His hand was warm against her cheek, and she was conscious of his long body lying on the bed and the fact that, underneath his robe, he was naked. And that he wanted her. . . . Increasingly aware of the erotic hum within herself, she wanted nothing more than to leave off questioning his motives and give herself up to the magic of his lovemaking. But there was one more question that she had to have answered.

Her eyes met his, and in a low voice she demanded, "And the feud between our families? You're able to put that aside?"

Nick hesitated, and Tess's heart sank. He hated her! He would *never* love her! And all because she was a Mandeville!

Correctly interpreting her expression, he shook his head. "No, I don't hate you—or your aunts." His expression thoughtful, he added quietly, "Alexander was perfectly correct, you know, when he said that the feud was none of our making and that there was no reason for us to continue it." His gaze met hers steadily. "I could have wished that you were *not* a Mandeville, but that fact isn't pertinent any longer—you're a Talmage, now." He brushed her mouth with his. "Have you forgotten," he said softly, "that as of this evening you became my very beautiful wife, the countess of Sherbourne?"

With an unexpected lump in her throat, Tess shook her head. "I haven't forgotten—I just didn't want the past to shadow our future." Her lips twisted. "We started out badly enough as it is."

"But *was* it so bad?" he asked intently, his hands framing her face, his mouth inches from hers. "I know that I shall always remember and look back with great fondness on that first night at the Black Pig. . . ."

Her eyes a misty hue of purple, Tess slowly shook her head. "No," she said huskily, "it wasn't so very bad."

Nick groaned, and unable to restrain himself a moment longer, he kissed her as he had been longing to do for days, his tongue taking blatant possession of her mouth. She was fine wine and sweet ambrosia all in one. The mere taste of her sent his head spinning, and the passion he had barely been able to hold in check these past days exploded through him.

He kissed her hungrily, his mouth hard against hers, his hands seeking her soft curves as he pushed her down into the waiting pillows of the bed. She was so soft, so sweet, and he wanted her so desperately that it was all he could do not to rip that lovely gown off her slender body and find relief from his aching manhood between her thighs. With an effort, he tore his mouth from hers. His lips buried against her throat, he muttered, "I've had all sorts of ideas about how I was going to take this slowly, woo you, but I find that one taste of you and all my plans have gone flying into the air—all I can think of is what dear heaven it will be to feel myself sinking into your silken warmth. . . ."

He was half lying on her, the weight of his body exciting and arousing, his rigid shaft pressing boldly against her thigh. At his evocative words, a shiver of anticipation went down her spine. Her body was already pliant and eager for him, her eyes dreamy, as she caressed his thick black hair. "What sort of ideas?" she asked hazily.

He raised up and looked into her face. A wicked grin slashed across his mouth. "Oh, ideas," he drawled, "*such* ideas, sweetheart, ideas that will give us both a great deal of pleasure. . . ."

His mouth came down warmly on hers, and he kissed her thoroughly, his hands holding her face still for his plundering. Her hands tightened in his hair, her body racked by burgeoning, hungry demands for more. He barely had to touch her and she came violently alive, the ache between her legs deepening and intensifying, her nipples filling and hardening, her breasts becoming heavy and sensitive to the slightest caress. Tess gave a soft moan when his lips finally left hers and traveled with tantalizing slowness down her throat and across her chest to the first button at the top of her low-cut gown.

Nick's mouth was busy with that first button, and his hands slid from her face to gently cup and fondle her small breasts.

The second button and then a third, a fourth, a fifth . . . a sixth gave way to his teeth, and Tess was aware of a burning impatience within herself. These gentle, half-teasing caresses were not enough; her body was on fire for him, and she was aware of a shocking desire simply to rip away the confining garment, to rend asunder anything that kept her body from his. . . . She twisted restlessly under his teasing caresses, her legs thrashing against the silky coverlet, as the fire low in her belly grew stronger and more fierce.

Eagerly she reached for him, her hands gliding across his shoulders, pushing aside the robe he wore. His flesh was warm and smooth, and she almost purred aloud at the pleasure it gave her to touch him, his broad shoulders, the smooth back, and the crisp, curly hair of his muscled chest.

The feel of his mouth against her naked breast, the flick of his tongue, the gentle rasp of his teeth, made her gasp. Unconsciously her fingers clenched against his chest, and he gave a low, muffled sound of encouragement. As fascinated by his body as he seemed to be with hers, she circled one flat nipple, exploring its pebbly hardness with her fingers, and he groaned again. Pleased with her efforts, she moved to the other nipple and played with it for a moment or two before her hand slid slowly downward, across his flat stomach to the loose knot in the sash of his robe.

Nick sucked in his breath when her fingers lingered there. Muttering incoherently, he reared up for a second, impatiently undid the sash, and shrugged out of the robe. He turned back to her, and with a crooked smile on his mouth, he murmured, "Now where was I?"

The look on his face made Tess suddenly breathless. Her gown was still only partially open, veeing down to a point almost to her stomach, the edges of her unbuttoned bodice lying on either side of her body. A warm glow lit his eyes as they fell upon her exposed breasts, her skin appearing almost as pale and smooth as fine alabaster against the deep purple gown, her nipples boldly upstanding and rosy from his ministrations. His smile slipped slightly, and in a thickened voice he said, "I think, I remember . . . I was right. . . ." He bent his head, and as his tongue curled hungrily around one nipple, he muttered, *"Here. . . ."*

A streak of sweet fire arrowed directly from the wicked teasing of his mouth to the pooling warmth between her legs, and Tess arched up against the tug of his teeth on her breast. A dozen emotions knifed through her as his hand swept lower, caressing her hip, then her buttocks, his strong fingers kneading the soft flesh he found there as his lips and teeth feasted on her. She burned for him. Wanted him. Ached for him. *Loved* him. . . .

Letting him work his dark wizardry on her eager flesh, she splayed her hands against his broad chest, her fingers clenching and unclenching contentedly like cat's claws in the springy hair. She could feel his rigid shaft, pushing warm and heavy between her thighs. Only the silken fabric of her gown prevented their joining as he half lay over her. Teasingly she moved against its thick, impressive length, reveling in her own powers when Nick groaned and cupped her buttocks and pulled her even closer.

"If you don't stop that," he said breathlessly, looking up at her, "I won't be able to show you the rest of my ideas. . . ."

With half-closed eyes, drowsy with desire, Tess stared at him, her fingers lovingly tracing the intelligent brow, the bold angle of his nose, and the chiseled outline of those wicked lips. "Oh?" she murmured. "You mean I can distract you from your goal?"

His eyes grew even blacker with the powerful emotions that went through him. "Yes," he said in a strange tone, "I'm very much afraid that you can. . . ."

She smiled dreamily, not really believing him but too aroused to care. "Then I suppose I should let you continue, shouldn't I?"

"Yes," he muttered, his hand tightening on her hips, crushing her for one provocative moment against his aching, swollen member, "you very definitely should—I think you'll find it quite, quite . . . *illuminating.* . . ."

His hands loosened and he shifted slightly away from her, his teeth instantly busy with more buttons, the heat of his mouth as he slowly, inexorably moved downward making Tess shiver. The urge to arch up and rub against him was overpowering, but she consoled herself by caressing his lean hips and long back.

Lost in her own erotic exploration, she hadn't really thought about what Nick was doing until his mouth began to work at the button low on her abdomen. Her breath caught, and dazedly she felt the scrape of his teeth at the top of the patch of tightly curled hair at the junction of her thighs. The next button was lower, just above where she was most yearning for his touch, and a shudder went through her when she felt his lips begin to toy maddeningly with that strategically placed button.

Her breath suspended, her heart racing, Tess waited impatiently for what would come next. She was already fully aroused, already wet and ready for him. Her breasts were unbearably sensitive, the nipples stinging pleasurably from his previous tastings, and she arched up helplessly against his marauding lips. When he buried his face deeper against her flesh, his warm breath and probing tongue pressing against the material that kept him from directly touching the soft, aching flesh between her legs, she stiffened and tried to move away. Sensations she had never dreamed of rose up within her, frightening her as much as they pleasured.

His hands caught her hips and held her still, as with tantalizing delay he continued to mouth and tease that one button that separated her naked, vulnerable flesh from his seeking lips. He breathed in her scent, sucked at the fabric, and then, unable to stand it any longer, undid the button. . . .

Besotted and drunk by his own handiwork, Nick was hardly even aware of Tess's low, excited moan when he was finally able to touch that intoxicating, secret flesh he had exposed. She was so sweet, so damn sweet, he thought dizzily as his mouth opened against her, his tongue flicking hotly against her slick warmth. Deliberately his hands slid lower on her hips, holding her thrashing body still as he explored and tasted deeply of the hidden delicate folds between her thighs. The fabric of the gown rubbed against his chin, preventing him from exploring as thoroughly as he wanted. Reluctantly abandoning part of his plans, he hurriedly undid several more buttons with one hand, opening the gown to her knees.

Her breathing suspended, all sensation centered between her legs, Tess hardly dared to move, afraid she would shatter into a thousand pieces. She had never dreamed . . . never imagined . . . The exquisite ache and frantic hunger he created with each carnal movement of his mouth and tongue were intense. Her head twisted from side to side, her hands reaching helplessly for him. She wanted to touch him, to caress him, to kiss him, but her restlessly moving hands could only touch his dark head. She had never felt such pleasure, never experienced such wanton emotions as were coursing through her this very minute.

His mouth buried in the thicket of curls at the top of her thighs, his tongue exploring and provoking the tiny bud he found there, Nick's hand slid up one thigh, and Tess stiffened and bucked up against him as one, then two long fingers sank deeply within her.

Oh, dear God! she thought wildly. What is he doing to me? The sensations were so incredible, so intense, that she couldn't control her body, and her hands tightened in his hair, her hips rising up eagerly to welcome his questing fingers.

He stroked her deeply time and again, his fingers moving slickly within her heat as he feasted hungrily on the succulent warmth between her thighs and his mouth and tongue brought her closer to the brink. His own body felt as if it would explode; just the brush of his throbbing shaft against the coverlet made him certain that he was going to disgrace himself. She was such fire. Such sweet, *sweet* fire. . . .

Tess was certain she couldn't stand another moment of this exquisitely carnal torture. She was already trembling, shaking from the power of the primitive feelings he was creating, and she was certain that *nothing* else could ever feel like this. In utter astonishment she suddenly felt her body coil, felt the hot pressure build, felt the first tiny quiver of pleasure come sweeping upward, and then, like a tidal wave, ecstasy exploded through her. "Oh, heavens . . . my dear God! *Nick!*"

Against his tongue, he felt her flesh jump and quiver, and he groaned, the sweet sounds of her climax nearly sending him over the edge. He fought to control himself, concentrating on giving her that last little bit of pleasure, his fingers and tongue moving ever so gently now. As the storm gradually ebbed, he lifted his head and stared up into her stunned face. "Did you," he asked thickly, "find it *illuminating*?"

Her body still throbbing from the most spectacular sensations she had ever felt in her life, Tess blushed delightfully. With her eyes clearly dilated, in a shaken voice she mumbled, *"Very!"*

He smiled. "And that, sweetheart, was just the beginning. . . ."

She was dimly aware that Nicolas had not reached the same blinding pinnacle that she had, that his body was still aching for fulfillment, but at the moment she was boneless and too satiated to do anything about it. Positive that she had misheard him, she asked dazedly, "Beginning?"

"Hmm, yes. Beginning," he said against her thigh, his lips just brushing the soft flesh.

She had not thought that passion could renew itself so swiftly, but not quite fifteen minutes later, as her gown lay completely open on either side of her naked body and Nick's hands and lips had once more worked their magic over every inch of her tingling flesh, she discovered how very mistaken she had been. He had completed his self-imposed task of unbuttoning the remainder of the gown, his teeth and lips traveling in a burning trail down to that very last silk button. From there he had gradually dallied upward, kissing her slim ankles, lingering along the way, his mouth teasing the spot behind her knee, brushing the length of her thigh, his hands seeking and finding every vulnerable spot, his lips and tongue following swiftly behind. By the time his mouth settled once more against her tight nipples, she was aflame, the demanding pull of her body drawing her deeper into his arms, her own seeking hands caressing and exploring him.

But Nick was too close, too needy, to endure very much of her gentle caresses, and when her hand closed around him, her fingers warmly stroking the swollen length of his manhood, he could bear it no longer. He caught her hands in his, and bringing them above her head, he slid onto her body, settling between her thighs. She twisted to escape his grasp, but he muttered against her mouth, "No, sweetheart. Another night I shall let you do as you will, but not tonight—I cannot wait any longer. I must have you *now*!" And he drove himself deep within her welcoming flesh, his mouth crushing hers.

She was so tight, so warm, so silky slick, that Nick trembled from the blatantly carnal pleasure that flooded through him as he thrust deeper into her. He groaned aloud at the feel of her hot little sheath closing snugly around his swollen shaft, his hands tightening involuntarily around her wrists, holding her a willing prisoner to his invasion. His tongue plunged into the wine depths of her mouth. Like a banquet before a starving man, her body was laid out beneath him, her soft curves meeting his hard planes, the silken caress of her warm bare skin teasing and arousing him, driving him closer to finding that precious release his body craved.

As aroused and eager for the same elemental sensation that consumed Nick, Tess arched up to meet him in near supplication. She was full of him, stretched near to bursting, and it brought her immense satisfaction. The sounds he made expressing his delight each time he sank deeply within her made her flesh tighten and tingle, made his possession all the sweeter.

Feeling that first sweet ripple of fulfillment sweep upward, she longed to touch him, to communicate her great pleasure. But all she could do as wave after wave of rapture burst through her body was to kiss him as fiercely as he was kissing her and to tangle her legs around his, pulling, drawing him even deeper within her.

Nick shuddered as her thighs tightened around him. Feeling the soft shocks that went through her body as she found that place they both sought so urgently, he finally loosed the iron hold he had placed on himself and let all the passion that was within him flow free. Releasing her hands, he let his own hands slide down to her hips. Holding her tightly to him, he drove fiercely within her, finding at last that sweet ecstacy he yearned for. A low, triumphant growl burst from him as he emptied himself into her.

Certain she would never move again, Tess lay limply beneath him, stunned by the intensity of the sensations that she had experienced in his arms. For the first time she realized how powerful a force, how fiercely demanding, passion could be . . . why some women risked everything for it and why some men killed for it.

She sighed with pleasure when Nick pulled her next to him and dropped a lazy kiss on her temple. His body was warm against hers, and she was content just to lie there, wrapped gently in his strong arms, her head resting on the hard plane of his shoulder.

There was silence for several moments, and then Nick said, "I much prefer you as my wife than my mistress. . . ."

"Oh? And why is that?" she asked drowsily.

"Because," he said huskily, dropping another kiss on her temple, "I don't have to leave your bed and seek out my own lonely one anymore—now I can make love to you whenever and wherever I wish."

Tess stiffened slightly, some of her soft glow fading. His words were not what she wanted to hear, but they didn't surprise her. That Nick wanted her had never been in doubt. . . .

Unwilling to dwell on the circumstances of their marriage, she wrested her wandering mind away from painful musings and smothered a sudden yawn. She was his wife and she loved him, and she would cling to that knowledge and hope that bearing his name and—a funny little thrill went through her—eventually his children would be enough to satisfy her in the long years ahead.

Nick was thinking of their children, too, and Tess would have been astonished to learn that he'd just realized he didn't want her to get pregnant right away. It was an incomprehensible turnabout for him. After all, he admitted reluctantly, the whole reason he had been looking so urgently for a bride had been to sire an heir. But *I don't*, he realized with a shock, want to share her with anyone just yet—not even my own flesh and blood!

For the first time, it occurred to Nick that what bound him to Tess might be something more substantial and lasting than mere passion for her body. He might, he decided uneasily, have committed that fatal act and fallen in love with her. . . . It was an incredible thought and terrifying, too. Love made one weak and vulnerable; made one totally helpless to the whims of another. And if it was not returned . . . He swallowed. He never again wanted to go through the agony that had been his when Maryanne had married another man. And while there was no danger of Tess becoming another man's wife, was he strong enough to endure unrequited love for the rest of his life? He didn't think so. His face hardened. He would *make* Tess love him. And what, he wondered sickly, had he done to make her love him? Nothing. He had ravished her. Declared her a liar. Abducted her and kept her prisoner for his own carnal needs.

But *I love her*, he thought savagely, knowing that it was true. He *did* love her. Had loved her from almost the moment his eyes had met hers across the room at the Black Pig. How else to explain his determined, single-minded acts since then?

Only a man in the grip of powerful emotions would have done as he had done.

He shifted slightly so that he was able to look down into her sleeping face. His own features softened, and he was conscious of a fierce pleasure in just looking at her, in knowing that she was his, his bride, his wife. After brushing an almost reverent kiss across her brow, he eased back down beside her and drifted off to sleep.

He woke just before dawn, his body hard and hungry for her. He reached for Tess and brought her slowly awake with gentle, persuasive caresses that soon had her fully alert and eager to continue down the path he was leading them. When he finally took her, their bodies merging together, there was such passion, such demanding tenderness in his possession, that Tess could only marvel at the utter sweetness of this joining. He must, she thought hazily as sleep claimed her once more, feel something more than lust for me. He must!

When she finally woke again some hours later, she was disappointed to find herself alone in the lovely silk-hung bed. A dreamy smile on her lips, she stretched like a cat and was startled to discover that she ached pleasantly in certain parts of her anatomy and that she was still wearing the purple gown and gauzy peignoir. Remembering explicitly the manner in which Nick had undone each button, and what had followed, she blushed and giggled and hugged the garments tightly to her, imagining his lips moving over her again.

Shaking off her decidedly erotic thoughts, she used the velvet bell rope hanging by the bed to ring for a servant. Her ring was answered almost immediately, and for quite some time afterward Tess was preoccupied with the morning rituals of bathing and dressing.

The morning was half gone by the time she descended the wide, sweeping staircase in half-shy, half-eager search of her new husband. Her red gold curls were expertly caught up in a silk ribbon the exact shade of her lavender muslin gown, and with a warm glow fairly radiating from her, roses blooming in her cheeks, and her eyes sparkling like jewels, she was a vision to behold.

Nick certainly thought so when she poked her head around the door to his study a moment later. His heart leaping, he wanted nothing more than to capture her in his arms and kiss that sweet mouth of hers, but he cursed her untimely arrival. The last thing he wanted her to see right now was Alexander's bruised and battered face! Nor was he particularly enthusiastic about giving her the explanation she was sure to demand. Hoping to forestall her, he hurried forward to greet her, but he was too late.

Already three steps into the room, Tess stopped abruptly as she spied her two uncles seated on comfortable black leather chairs before Nicolas's large desk. It wasn't the sight of her uncles that brought her to a dead halt so much as the sight of Alexander's face. He had obviously been in a fight—and gotten the worst of it, if the cuts and scrapes and the black-and-blue purpling that marred his handsome features were anything to go by!

Her eyes huge, she rushed over to Alexander. "What happened to you? Who did this?" she asked breathlessly.

Alexander looked uncomfortable, almost squirming on his chair as he fumbled for an answer. He threw Nick an apologetic glance and then muttered, "Someone broke into the gatekeeper's cottage last night and, er, attacked me."

"*Attacked* you!" Tess exclaimed, the roses in her cheeks fading. Her eyes traveled among the three men and, a frown forming on her forehead, finally locked on Nicolas's face. "Who even knew that they were staying there? And why attack Alexander?"

Nick met her gaze squarely. Bluntly he said, "It would appear that the man who tried to kill you on Saturday came back to try again. . . ."

Chapter Twenty

*T*ess stared at Nick's dark face, her eyes dilating with fear as his words sank in. "But why?" she demanded in a shaky tone. Slowly she sat on the black leather chair Rockwell had vacated upon her entrance into the room. "Why?"

Even as she asked the question, Nick realized the answer and cursed his thick head. "Jesus! What a fool I've been!" As the others looked at him in astonishment, he said grimly, "There's only one answer to these attacks—the smugglers! The owlers who have been using the cottage—"

"Of course!" Tess broke in eagerly. "It could be no one else."

Nick nodded and sent her a rueful glance. "I know you'll find it hard to believe, sweetheart, but I *did* consider that possibility the day you were attacked—I even discussed it briefly with your uncles, but I'm afraid that of late"—he gave her a crooked smile—"my mind has been on a certain saucy red-haired miss!"

Tess smiled faintly, pleased by his words and grateful for the light note. But, her eyes fixed intently on Nicolas's face, she said quietly, "Tell me what happened this morning."

Nick sighed and rose. Leaning against his desk and staring pensively at his glossy black boots, he said, "According to Alexander, something, he doesn't know what, woke him just before dawn. He lay there in your bed, listening, wondering at first if the noise he'd heard had been the smugglers moving about the cellars. He heard nothing else for several more minutes. Then, deciding that he must have been wrong, he was on the point of drifting back to sleep when he suddenly realized that the door to his room had been opened and that someone was creeping toward him. He waited, not wanting to frighten them off, and the next thing he knew, he sensed rather than actually saw a figure near the bed."

"It was the knife," Alexander blurted out, "that made me realize I was in mortal danger. It came slashing down near my shoulder—it nicked me, but didn't cause any real damage. I think the fellow was aiming for my heart, but in the darkness he miscalculated his mark." Alexander swallowed. "If I'd been asleep, he no doubt would have managed the task. As it was, I immediately sprang up and we grappled and fought." A little lopsided smile crossed Alexander's battered features. "You wouldn't know it by looking at me, but I gave a very good account of myself. Managed to get in several telling blows, but the fellow fought like a madman. We knocked over tables and sent chairs flying. I managed to get the knife away from him early on, and in the darkness neither one of us could find it, so it turned into a brawl. By this time, Rockwell had awakened from the noise we were making. Upon hearing his approach, the fellow managed to strike a tremendous blow to my head and kicked my legs out from underneath me. By that time we were in the hallway, and as Rockwell came up, I caught barely a glimpse of the man as he bolted down the stairs and disappeared."

Disgust evident in his tones, Rockwell took up the story. "We immediately woke the entire house and did a thorough search, but we found nothing, except for a side door standing open. . . ."

Almost shamefacedly Alexander said, "I'm sorry, Tess, but I couldn't hang on to the slippery devil—he twisted and squirmed and always managed to break my hold—and I'm not a weakling!"

"Oh, no, you're certainly not!" Tess exclaimed with a warm glow in her eyes. "You're strong and brave, and I'm sure that you did everything within your power to capture him."

There was silence in the room for a few minutes. Then, looking at Alexander, Tess asked hopefully, "Was there anything about him that you recognized? I know it was dark, but during your fight, did you gain any impressions? Something that might help us identify him?"

Alexander shrugged. "He didn't announce his name, if that's what you're hoping. He was strong and fairly tall and broad. In the fleeting look I got in the light from Rockwell's candle, as the scoundrel leaped down the stairs, I'd say that he was garbed as a gentleman."

Tess caught her breath. Looking at Nick, she said tightly, "The description sounds very like the one Rose gave of my attacker on Saturday."

Nick nodded. "If we're right that the gang of owlers using the cottage are behind these attacks, then I think we can safely assume it's the same man."

Tess swallowed painfully. "He does seem rather . . . *tenacious,* doesn't he?"

Nick nodded again, wishing savagely that there was some way to keep her from this ugly knowledge.

At his nod, Tess smiled lamely. "And to think that there was a time I thought I lived a very boring, conventional life— and chafed against its very ordinariness. . . ." She sighed. "An ordinariness that I'd give anything to know again."

With a twinkle in his eyes, Nick caught her hand in his. Dropping a kiss on it, he said, "Knowing your wishes, madame, I shall try to be a very *ordinary* husband!"

Alexander and Rockwell guffawed, and even Tess chuckled.

"I don't believe," she said tartly, "that you could be ordinary if you tried."

"Thank you—I think." His features growing serious, Nick returned to the subject at hand. Sitting around Nick's desk, the four of them discussed the situation at length, the certainty that the smugglers were behind the attack becoming firmer with every passing moment.

Their speculations were soon interrupted by a gentle rap on the door. Nick quickly crossed the room and opened the door.

Hetty's voice came clearly to the others as she said to Nick, "I'm sorry to disturb you, my lord, but my dresser—a friendly and voluble young woman—mentioned that the baron and his brother had arrived here early this morning—before you had arisen. . . . We apologize, after all you have done for us, for appearing to pry into your private affairs, but in view of the unusual situation that presently exists, Meg and I were wondering if there was some pressing reason for their arrival at the, er, 'crack of dawn,' I believe the young woman said."

While Nick sought for a way to deflect the two ladies, Tess said quietly from behind him, "They should know. They're as much involved as anyone"

Nick sighed and stepped aside, ushering the ladies into the room. He had barely shut the door behind them when Hetty cried out in great distress, "Oh, *Alexander*! Dear heart, what has happened to you! Your poor face!"

Oblivious of anything else, Alexander rose and met Hetty halfway across the room. He took her hands in his and pressed an urgent kiss against her soft palms. "Now don't get in a snit," he muttered. "It ain't anything serious. Just a little dust-up with a prowler."

Her trembling fingers touched his bruised face, the depth of her emotions plain to see on her lovely face. "Never tell me that a *common* prowler," she said, her eyes searching his, "did this to you?"

Tess's mouth nearly fell open at the blatant tenderness between them, the way their bodies were nearly touching as they stood there together. Almost idly she noted the pleased expression on Rockwell's face and the satisfied smile on Meg's lips. When had this happened? she wondered. Alexander and *Hetty*?

As if becoming aware of the fascinated stares of the other occupants, Hetty blushed and stepped quickly away from Alexander. With a spot of color burning high on his cheekbones, Alexander said gruffly, "Yes. A prowler." Grabbing a nearby chair, he offered it to Meg. "Miss Mandeville, won't you please sit down?"

While Rockwell saw to a chair for Hetty, Meg took the seat offered by Alexander. More chairs for the two gentlemen were drawn up, and in a few minutes it was as if the scene between Hetty and Alexander had never taken place.

The conversation began immediately with the recital of the facts surrounding the first attack on Tess and finished with the latest events at the cottage. There were expressions and exclamations of horror, but overcoming their natural trepidation, the aunts were determined to help in any way that they could. When the use of the cottage by the owlers and the strong suspicion that the smugglers were behind all the attacks were explained, Hetty and Meg readily agreed.

Bellingham arrived just then in answer to Nick's summons on the bell rope, and soon they were all refreshing themselves from the tray of hot coffee and small cakes and biscuits that were served.

When Bellingham had departed, the topic of the attacks and the smugglers raged once more. With a thoughtful look on his face, Nick set down his cup and said, "It would seem that Tess was never the real object of the owlers—*anyone* staying at the cottage would have elicited the same reaction. I suspect that our attacker didn't even realize Tess was no longer staying there, and I imagine he was as stunned as Alexander by what transpired. I'm sure that he had a nasty shock when he discovered a brawny male in that bed instead of a slim, defenseless woman."

There was more discussion, a lighter air having entered the room with the collective feeling that they had hit upon not only the reasons for the attacks, but also the perpetrators.

"But what are we going to do about the cottage? And the smugglers?" Tess asked eventually.

"I think," Nick began slowly, "that we'll do precisely what they want us to—abandon the cottage."

"You're going to let them win?" Alexander asked incredulously, his eyes blazing.

Nick smiled. "No. Not win. But allow them to *think* that they have won. . . ."

Alexander stared hard at Nick for several moments, and then, as enlightenment dawned, he grinned. "What a jolly good idea! They'll think they've beaten us and start using the cottage again, and when they least expect it, we'll snaffle them!"

"Precisely! In the meantime, I'll have the staff remove themselves and their belongings from the cottage and close up the place, as if it were no longer going to be used—dust covers on the furniture, shutters latched, and so forth. You two will, of course, stay here at the court." Nick paused and, looking at the two men, added softly, "But before we totally retreat from the field, I want to take a better look at those cellars. It may be highly dangerous, and I have no idea what we may find or run into—are you with me?"

"Absolutely," vowed Alexander, his face flushed with enthusiasm. "It'll be like the old army days, won't it?"

"Count me in," the baron averred. "I'd like to teach these bloody basta—" Remembering the ladies, he coughed and muttered, "Er, rascals a lesson!"

"And what about us?" Tess asked with asperity. "Are we to sit calmly here at the court, drinking tea, while you gentlemen go riding off to risk life and limb? Having *all* the adventures?"

"Well, I had hoped," Nick began warily, not liking the militant sparkle in her violet eyes, "that you would agree to do just that."

Tess opened her mouth to disabuse him of that notion, but before she could speak, Aunt Meg said gently, "You know, my dear, I believe that your husband's idea, while unpalatable to a spirited young lady like yourself, is really very sound." And as Tess's mouth shut with an audible snap, she added, "If there was to be danger, perhaps a surprise attack by the smugglers, his first instinct would be to keep you safe—and that might put him in grave jeopardy. Just think how you would feel if he came to harm simply because you insisted upon accompanying him this afternoon." Not meeting Tess's fulminating glare, she folded her hands primly in her lap and said, "A much better solution would be to see the cellars once the gentlemen have ascertained that they are safe...." She paused, smiled kindly at her great-niece, and murmured, "I know that I shall certainly look forward to being shown this smuggler's haunt in the very near future."

Nick could have kissed Meg's wrinkled cheek, but he wisely withheld his enthusiasm for her suggestion. Cocking an eyebrow, he glanced at his wife. "Well?" he asked.

Tess threw him a dark look, her reluctance to abandon her earlier stance clear. Then she sighed and grimaced, admitting reluctantly, "Aunt Meg is right. I wouldn't want you getting hurt because of me." She shook a finger at his grinning features. "But don't think that you've heard the end of this—you *will* take us exploring in those cellars! And not six months from now, either!"

Nick laughed and swept her up in his arms, swinging her around. "I swear it, Madame Wife! Your wish shall be my command." He set her on her feet. Then, looking at the two men, he said, "Well, shall we set events into motion?"

A few minutes later the room was empty except for the three ladies. Her face anxious, Tess said uneasily, "Oh, Aunt Meg, I hope I've done the right thing. I'll never forgive myself if something happens to him."

"And what do you think you could do to prevent it, if you were with him?" she asked dryly. "Throw yourself in front of him and take the bullet, knife, or blow meant for him? That would certainly accomplish a lot, wouldn't it? Instead of just one of you being hurt, you both might come to grief."

There was no arguing with Aunt Meg's logic, but Tess couldn't help saying stubbornly, "I wouldn't have been totally useless—I might have been able to warn him of danger, and if we were attacked, I could help him fight off the smugglers."

Aunt Meg snorted. "Distract him from what needs to be done, more likely!"

"Oh, stop it, you two," Hetty said sharply. "Don't we have enough on our minds without discussing all that can go wrong? Isn't it enough that Alexander . . . and the others, too, of course, are risking their lives chasing after those wretched smugglers?"

"*Who* is chasing after wretched smugglers?" Pallas asked lightly as she entered the room. She glanced around in puzzlement. "My goodness, didn't Bellingham show you to the front salon? I can't imagine what he was thinking, bringing you in here to Nicolas's study."

There was a tense moment as the three other ladies exchanged glances. How much to tell Lady Sherbourne?

"Er, Nicolas and my uncles were here earlier and, um, we had joined them," Tess said hastily.

Pallas studied Tess's young face for a long moment. "And?"

Tess threw a troubled look to her aunts and then, taking a deep breath, said, "Won't you please sit down and have some tea? There was an, um, incident last night at the cottage where my uncles were staying, and the gentlemen have gone to investigate."

Pallas's considering stare moved slowly from one face to the other. After seating herself on one of the black leather chairs near the desk and carefully arranging the folds of her pale blue gown to her satisfaction, she said in a tone that brooked no opposition, "Tell me."

Tess swallowed and glanced to her aunts for guidance. They looked as uncertain and uncomfortable as she felt. Deciding that Nicolas's grandmother had as much a right to know what was going on as anybody else, she plunged into the story, beginning with the discovery of the cellars and Nick's brush with the smugglers. She told the tale hurriedly, but she left out none of the pertinent facts.

When Tess finished speaking, it was clear that Pallas was horrified and appalled by what she had heard . . . and very worried about Nick. Keeping a rigid command of her emotions, though, she said calmly enough, "And Nick has gone now to explore these cellars?"

Tess nodded, hoping she had done the right thing by telling her everything and wishing there was some way she could wipe off that taut, stricken expression from Pallas's face.

Pallas took a deep breath, fighting for composure. Finally gaining some mastery over the anxious emotions that churned in her breast, she muttered, "I knew I should have had those blasted passages destroyed years ago! And to think that a nest of vipers has been nurturing itself right here at my very door!"

"You know about the cellars?" Tess asked in astonishment.

Pallas smiled thinly. "Oh, yes, my dear, I know about those cellars. . . ." The words hung in the air, and then she seemed to shake off some of her fears for Nick. Sitting up straighter on her chair, she said briskly, "Well, there doesn't seem to be anything that we can do about the situation at the moment— Nick knows how to take care of himself. And since the gentlemen seem to have abandoned us for the time being, I propose that you ladies allow me to give you a tour of the house—it will, I hope," she added with a faint, unhappy smile at Tess, "help keep our minds off what the gentlemen are doing."

Rising regally to her feet, Pallas said bluntly, "I must say that this is certainly an odd way to spend one's honeymoon! But since nothing else about your marriage has been exactly conventional, I'm not at all surprised that your husband has gone off to chase after smugglers instead of doting on his charming bride." Her smile faded, and she sighed. "I had so hoped that Nick had outgrown these fits and starts, that once his army days were behind him, my worries about him would be over. But it seems I was mistaken. Well, there is no use pining over it—he has always gone his own way." Tucking Tess's hand beneath her arm, she said kindly, "Come along, my dear—now that Sherbourne Court is going to be your home, I think you'll find the place very much to your liking. I know that I have."

Pallas kept up a stream of pleasant conversation as they moved out of the room, and Tess knew that she was trying to keep her mind off Nick and the danger he might be facing. For that same reason, she tried hard to concentrate on what Pallas was saying. But as they walked down the wide hallways of the palatial house, Hetty and Meg following in their wake, her thoughts kept straying to her husband. . . . What was he doing? Had the smugglers returned? Was Nick safe?

As it happened, at that moment Nick had events well in hand. The servants at the cottage were busily packing and preparing to close up the house as he had ordered. Adding John Laidlaw to their party, armed with pistols and lanterns, the four men had cautiously descended into the cellars to begin their exploration.

The cellars proved far more extensive and convoluted than Nicolas had ever imagined. Deciding at the onset that the wisest course would be to keep together in case of an unexpected meeting with the smugglers, they spent several fruitless hours wandering down first one passage and then another. Some of the corridors ended abruptly in a blank wall; others were much smaller tunnels, more roughly hewn, which angled off in all different directions. Several times, after traversing endlessly this way and that, they found themselves led back to where they'd begun. The place, Nicolas thought disgustedly, was a damned maze!

They lost all track of time down there in the bowels of the earth, their only light the flickering blaze of the lanterns they carried, and it wasn't until Nick's stomach gave a loud, forceful growl that he realized the hour must have grown quite late. A check of the baron's pocket watch revealed that it was well after nine o'clock—they had been wandering in the cellars for over six hours.

Nick called a halt to their explorations, and somewhat dispiritedly they made the long, circuitous walk back to the main room. The hours had not been a complete loss, though— they now knew and had marked clearly which corridors terminated in dead ends. They had also found ample evidence that the passages were well used. The floors were worn smooth over the years by the passing of many feet, and the smugglers had left behind an occasional empty wine bottle and several half-burnt candles and ropes and canvasses.

Exploring the cellars was not going to be the simple task he had first envisioned, and as they rode slowly back through the star-studded darkness toward the court, Nick decided that on the morrow he would concentrate his efforts on discovering the passage his attacker must have taken the night he had been struck down. The place had been like a rat warren, and it was possible that the smugglers had provided themselves with many different escape routes in case they were ever tracked to their lair.

It was after ten o'clock that evening when, filthy, tired, and hungry, they finally reached the court. Telling Bellingham to let his grandmother and wife know immediately that they had all returned safely, Nicolas dismissed John Laidlaw for the night and saw to it that the Rockwells were amply provided with food and drink and were comfortably settled in their rooms before considering his own needs.

His duties as host taken care of, Nick retreated eagerly to his own bedchamber to bathe and change clothes. The hot, steaming bath kept in readiness in his dressing room by Lovejoy revived him somewhat—as did the huge tray of bite-size sandwiches filled with fresh country cheese and thinly sliced smoked ham. The glass or two of port that he drank as he ate, as well as the pleasing knowledge that he would see his bride in a few minutes, had helped enormously to restore his spirits, and by the time he had dismissed Lovejoy and left his rooms, he was feeling much refreshed.

Meeting Rockwell and Alexander on the stairs, the three men descended together and went in search of the ladies. Despite the lateness of the hour and the fact that his grandmother usually went to bed early, Nick wasn't surprised to find all four ladies waiting impatiently for them in the blue salon. Nor was he surprised that they were bombarded with questions the moment they stepped into the room.

Laughing slightly, Nicolas held up a hand. "Please! One question at a time."

"That's all very well for you to say," snapped his grandmother, her face showing the strain she had been under. "You haven't been the one sitting here patiently all day wondering if you were still alive!"

Tess was standing behind his grandmother, her hands resting on the top of the chair in which Pallas sat. "You have been gone a dreadfully long time," she said softly, her eyes betraying her delight at seeing him. "Your grandmother was nearly sick with worry."

Nick smiled slightly and crossed to stand in front of Tess. He took one of her hands in his and brushed a kiss across her wrist. "And you, sweetheart?" he murmured. "Did you worry?"

Tess blushed and would not look at him. "Of course not," she muttered. "Everyone knows that the devil always looks after his own!"

Pallas choked back a laugh. "Good for you, child! And now enough of this—tell us what you have discovered."

Nick looked rueful. "Precious little, I'm afraid. The only useful thing we found out is that it's going to take several days to explore all the various corridors that radiate out in all directions from the main room of the cellar. It's like a rabbit warren down there! The smugglers must have been using the place for decades."

"Never seen anything like it," added Rockwell. "Must be dozens of tunnels. Some connect, some don't. Some go on almost endlessly, others are less than a hundred feet long, then end abruptly. Some are taller than a man, others we had to crouch down in order to traverse."

"I'm not surprised," Pallas said, looking at Nicolas. "Some of the original tunnels were built, I believe, to provide escape routes for priests and Catholics during Cromwell's time. Benedict's father explained to me once that they were devised to confuse and throw off any pursuit. And if, as you say, the smugglers are now using them, they have no doubt added and expanded the area."

Nick frowned. "You *know* about the tunnels?"

Pallas shrugged. "Of course. But I'm afraid I didn't know that they had been discovered by the smugglers and were being used by them! As a matter of fact, I'd deliberately forgotten all about those wretched tunnels, until I learned where you had gone today."

"Deliberately?" Nick asked curiously.

Pallas suddenly looked all of her eighty-three years. Glancing around at the others, she gave a bitter little laugh. "I forget all of you, except for Margaret, and she was only a child, were not even born when the great scandal took place and my husband ran off with Theresa."

There was a sudden, shocked silence, and all eyes riveted on Pallas's worn features. She smiled painfully. "Haven't you guessed yet?" she inquired wearily. When no one replied, she sighed deeply and asked Nick, "Did you know that the cottage where Tess had been staying is situated not far from the line between the Mandeville and Talmage properties?" Nick shook his head, staring at her intently. Her voice thick with remembered pain, she said, "I understand that a short distance in on Mandeville land, there once was a hidden entrance . . . there is supposed to be another one somewhere not very far from this house." As comprehension leaped into Nick's face, Pallas nodded and said heavily,

"Yes. It was some of those very same tunnels which you explored today that your grandfather and Theresa would use to avoid prying eyes when they wanted to meet each other at their favorite trysting place . . . the gatekeeper's cottage. . . ."

Chapter Twenty-one

———❖———

*T*here was a short, painful silence. Everyone in the room was aware of how much it had cost this proud, frail old lady to talk so openly of the terrible scandal that had torn her life apart so many years ago. Pallas gave a twisted smile. "And now you know why I *deliberately* forgot about those blasted tunnels."

His heart feeling as if it were being ripped in two, Nick knelt impetuously beside her chair. "Grandmother!" he cried. "Forgive me. I never guessed that . . . if I'd had any inkling, I *never* would have—"

"I know, my dear," Pallas said gently, her blue eyes full of love for him. "Perhaps it's for the best, though—with your marriage to Tess, there is a new beginning between the Mandevilles and the Talmages. Perhaps it's time for the old scandal to be laid out in the light of day." She smiled whimsically. "Who knows, perhaps you will discover some clue within those cellars that will reveal to us where Benedict and Theresa were going when they disappeared."

Tess swallowed a gasp, her eyes widening, as the talk of Benedict and Theresa suddenly reminded her of the hidden diary. How could she have forgotten about it? Her only excuse, she decided, was that in all the confusion and activity surrounding the return of her memory, the aunts' arrival at the cottage, and her hasty wedding to Nick, the momentous dis-

covery had slipped her mind. It was on the tip of her tongue
to blurt out about the diary, but something held her back. It
occurred to her that the contents of Benedict's diary—especially when he wrote of his fierce love for Theresa and, no
doubt, their plans to run away together—would more than
likely cause Lady Sherbourne more pain—something Tess,
with her innate soft heart, didn't want to do. She toyed briefly
with the notion of keeping her discovery a secret, of letting
that little black book remain undisturbed where it had lain for
nearly seventy years, but she realized that the diary might also
answer the very question Lady Sherbourne had just mentioned—the destination of Nicolas's grandfather and her own
great-grandmother.

No one had noticed her startled reaction, and Tess was
grateful. The conversation had become more general, her darling aunt Meg quickly smoothing over the painful moment
with a gentle stream of idle chatter. The others, giving Pallas
time to compose herself, had quickly joined in, and the tragic
subject was left behind—for the present.

There was more talk and speculation about the cellars and
the owlers and what Nick and the men intended to do the next
day. But while it was all very exciting, it was also quite late,
and very soon, after several discreet yawns, the group broke
up. They all ascended the broad staircase together.

Being Nick's bride was a new sensation for Tess, and when
he bade the others good night and opened the door to her
rooms, coolly following behind her, she couldn't control the
blush that stained her cheeks. With her heart beating faster,
she watched as he shut the door and then turned, leaning his
broad shoulders back against it and just looking at her.

"And now," he said softly, a glitter in his eyes that made her
heart nearly race out of control, "for the moment I have been
waiting for since I left your bed this morning." He pulled her
effortlessly into his arms and kissed her as if he were starving
for her. "God!" he said against her lips several moments later,

"I've missed you, sweetheart—and I've begun to see the wisdom of a honeymoon."

"Oh," Tess murmured dreamily, her thoughts fuzzy, her lips stinging from his hungry kiss. "Why is that?"

"Because," he said thickly, his hands settling on her hips, moving her erotically against the hard bulge in his breeches, "we could lie abed the entire time, and I could make love to you endlessly. No grandmother. No aunts. No uncles. Just you and me. . . ." He sent her a bone-melting smile. "And a bed, a very *big* bed, with the softest feather mattress to be found in the kingdom." He bent his head and kissed her again, his tongue surging warmly into her eager mouth. For a while the diary and the question of what to do about it disappeared utterly from her thoughts.

It was some time later, after Nick had stripped her naked and had shown her precisely how much he had missed her, that the diary came floating back into her brain. They were lying in the middle of her bed, and she had no clear memory of how they had gotten there. Her body was gradually returning to normal after Nick's passionate lovemaking when she suddenly remembered the diary. She shot upright in bed and stared at him, an appalled expression on her face as she blurted out, "Oh, my heavens! I forgot *again*."

"Hmm, and what have you forgotten again?" he asked idly, too sated and content to take a great deal of interest in what she was saying.

"The *diary*!" she exclaimed. "I forgot to tell you about the diary I found hidden behind one of the stones in the fireplace in my bedroom at the gatekeeper's cottage. Your grandfather's diary!"

It took her a few minutes to tell the tale, as Nick's impatient interruptions slowed her recital. By the time she was finished, all signs of his earlier contentment had vanished. In fact, he was fairly scowling at her.

"Why the devil didn't you say something earlier?" he demanded with an edge to his voice. Sitting upright beside her, he ran an agitated hand through his hair. "I can understand you not saying anything downstairs tonight," he added in a less accusatory tone. "In fact, that was very wise of you. But dash it! You should have said something *days* ago." He threw her a dark look and growled, "Do you know how important that little book might be? *If* it is indeed my grandfather's diary. Dammit, Tess! You should have told me about it much sooner."

"Well, I'm afraid I had other things on my mind," she said tartly. "Nearly getting murdered, getting my memory back . . . getting married, making love to you, things like that."

His mood changed in an instant, the irritation dying out of his face as he laughed. Catching hold of her he lay back, pulling her down into the pillows with him. Sprawled across his chest, her fiery hair tumbling in charming disarray around her lovely face, she regarded him uncertainly. He smiled lazily up at her. Brushing back a strand of her hair, his hand lingering against her cheek, he murmured, "Hmm, yes. I think I understand how those sort of things could, ah, distract a person."

"Yes, I thought perhaps you would understand, when you'd thought about it for a minute," Tess returned breathlessly, her skin beginning to tingle when his wandering hand traveled down her spine to fondle and explore her buttocks. To her unashamed delight, she could feel him stirring once more, his staff lengthening and hardening against her thighs even as they spoke.

"And since," he muttered, his mouth just barely touching hers, "it is too late to do anything about the diary tonight . . . I guess we'll just have to find something to do to amuse ourselves until the morning. . . ." His lips caught hers, and Tess didn't give the diary another thought that night. Nor, it might be added, did her extremely virile and nearly insatiable husband.

At first light, however, Nick gently woke Tess. She blinked

at him sleepily, surprised to find that he was already dressed for the day.

"Tell me again about the diary, sweetheart," he said softly. "Exactly where that stone is situated."

"I'll go with you," she declared eagerly, pushing her hair from her eyes and preparing to get out of bed. "It'll only take me a moment to find something to wear."

"No. I don't want you stepping foot in that place until I know it's safe. Now tell me what I want to know. I can be there and back before anyone knows I've gone."

Her lips set in a mutinous line. Ignoring him, Tess shrugged into a silk wrapper that was lying across the foot of the mattress and crossed to her dressing room. Heedless of him following in her wake with a frown beginning to form on his handsome face, she poured some water from the china pitcher and washed her face. Cleaning her teeth came next and, after that, brushing her hair, while Nick stood and watched with growing impatience.

"You're not going to go with me!" he said grimly when she began to pull on her clothing, a full-skirted jonquil-striped muslin gown.

"Yes, I am," his wife returned confidently. "Because I'm *not* telling which stone! However," she added kindly as she tied her hair back with a ribbon, "if you want to spend several fruitless hours attempting to dismantle the fireplace, that's fine with me."

"Did no one ever beat you when you were a child?" he asked dangerously.

Tess smiled sunnily at him and rose on her toes to press a brief kiss on his chin. "Of course not. They all thought that it might damage my tender spirits." Ignoring his scowl, she flung a fine wool cloak around her shoulders and said, "Now let's go!"

With her husband following closely behind her, muttering about the dire consequences of *not* applying the rod to a certain backside, Tess hurried down the stairs. She stopped suddenly when she reached the grand black-and-white-tiled marble entry hall. Flashing Nick a demure glance, she offered sweetly, "Perhaps you would care to lead the way to the stables? I'm afraid that I don't know where they are."

Nick choked back a laugh, unable to remain at odds with her for very long. With a twinkle in his black eyes, he murmured, "Well, I'm pleased that you'll allow that I have *some* uses."

Tess blushed, memory of some of his decidedly erotic uses suddenly flitting across her mind. He watched the blush climbing higher in her cheeks with interest. Correctly guessing the cause, he said softly, "Other uses besides those."

Tess looked away, unable to bear the teasing scrutiny of those wickedly knowing eyes a moment longer. Clearing her throat, she muttered, "Shouldn't we be going?"

Nick laughed under his breath and resisted the urge to tease her further. Taking her arm, he said, "Of course. Whatever madame wishes."

The stables consisted of a long, steep-roofed building some distance from the main house. From its size it appeared obvious that the earl kept a large stable, and this fact was confirmed when they entered the building and Tess glimpsed the lengthy row of spacious box stalls. A confirmed horse lover, she found the odor of sweet hay and horses and leather intoxicating. They were greeted by a chorus of soft nickers, and silken heads in a variety of colors—chestnuts, bays, and blacks—appeared over the top half of several of the stall doors. Tess was enchanted.

"Oh, they're lovely, aren't they?" she crooned, walking over to stroke the lowered head of a fine bay mare.

"I like to think so," Nicolas replied, looking around to see if any of the stable servants were about. It was barely daylight, but he wasn't surprised to see a lone, sleepy-eyed stable boy walking quickly toward them.

"My lord!" cried the startled young man. "We weren't expecting you. Shall I call the stable master?"

Nick shook his head and explained their needs. Curiosity evident in his face, the boy hurried to saddle a pair of horses.

Left to her own devices, Tess wandered happily down the long aisle, stopping to pet and murmur first to this horse and then to that. She was about halfway down the row when she stopped abruptly, staring in shocked disbelief at the small horse in one particular stall. The animal looked very familiar, too familiar. She stepped closer to the stall and took a longer, more thorough look. The horse was obviously of good breeding, but it was the small white star in the middle of its forehead and the white hind foot that made her heart catch in her throat. The fact that the small chestnut gelding seemed inordinately glad to see her, nuzzling her hand and whickering in that low tone reserved only for her, confirmed her suspicions. It was Fireball—the horse she had been riding the night she had met the smugglers!

Her thoughts racing, she stared at the gelding. How had he gotten here? The last she'd seen of Fireball, he'd been in the hands of the smugglers. . . .

Nick's sudden appearance at her shoulder made her jump, and she let out a small squeak of surprise. "Sorry," he said, smiling down at her when she spun around to face him. "I didn't mean to frighten you, but our horses are ready."

He took a closer look at her and realized that something was seriously amiss. He asked urgently, "What is it? Why are you looking at me that way?"

"Where did you get this horse?" she demanded, half-formed suspicions rioting through her brain. Her face clearly revealed that she considered him suspect of something very dire.

His features reflected surprise as he shrugged his broad shoulders. "I have no idea. He's not one of mine—perhaps he belongs to my sister or my grandmother—although she doesn't ride very often anymore. Why do you ask?"

Tess took a deep, steadying breath, realizing that she was being silly—of course Nick could have had nothing to do with what had happened to her the night she'd met the smugglers—he'd been in London! There was bound to be a simple answer to explain Fireball's presence here in his stables.

"Well?" he asked impatiently. "What's so interesting about this particular animal?"

"Nothing . . . only that I recognize him—in fact, he belongs to me. His name is Fireball, and I was riding him the night I escaped from Avery—the night I met the smugglers."

Nick's brows snapped together, the reason for the suspicion he'd seen in her face obvious. "And you think that I—" He bit back an oath and fought to gain control of the sudden surge of fury that erupted through him. Grimly he asked, "Are you certain it is the same horse? He is not in any way remarkable."

"I can recognize my own horse, thank you!" she said tightly, and as if to prove her words, Fireball began what was clearly a familiar action, gently nibbling the ribbon that held back her hair.

His jaw tight, Nick looked from her to the small gelding. "Very well. When we get back from our errand, I'll make some inquiries."

In stiff silence they rode toward their destination, Tess's unspoken suspicions lying like an iron bar between them. Avoiding the longer, winding lane, Nick had chosen a short cut through the formally planted woods that had been laid out over two centuries ago when, to celebrate his ascension to an earldom, the first earl of Sherbourne had overseen their planting.

It was a lovely morning, cool and crisp, the leaves of the oaks and beech beginning to turn, the sun rising round and yellow above the tops of the trees. Under other circumstances Tess would have enjoyed it enormously. But Fireball's presence in Nicolas's stables had unsettled her, even though she was confident *he* could have had nothing to do with it. She risked a glance at Nick's face. Seeing the hard line of his jaw, she knew that he was still offended that she had considered, even fleetingly, that he could have had something to do with her brush with the smugglers.

Tess made a face. "My lord," she finally said softly, "I'm sorry. I didn't really believe that you were in league with the owlers—I was just startled to see Fireball there in your stables—that was all."

Some of the hardness left his face, and Nick grimaced. "Apology accepted—I don't exactly blame you for being suspicious—we haven't been given much of a chance to learn to trust each other, have we?"

A lump rose in her throat. Perhaps not, but she knew that she would trust him with her life. Sending him a misty smile, she said, "No, we haven't, but we'll just have to try harder in the future. . . ."

He smiled, and in restored harmony they finished their ride.

Even after one day with no habitation, the cottage looked deserted and abandoned, no sign of smoke coming from the chimneys, the windows barred and shuttered. Nick halted his horse at the front of the building, dismounted quickly and lifted Tess down.

"I don't expect to find any smugglers lurking about this time of day," he began quietly, "but stay close and do exactly as I say. Is that understood?"

Tess nodded, and a few minutes later they were inside the cottage. After Nick found one of the candles that had been left behind by the servants and lit it, they hurried up the stairs that led to the upper floor. The shuttered windows made the interior dark and shadowy, and the cottage now seemed to Tess oddly spooky and forbidding. She could hardly wait to get back outside in the sunlight.

They entered her former bedroom. The room looked lonely and forlorn, dust covers hiding the elegant charm of the furnishings. It took her but a moment to reach the fireplace, and a few minutes after that, she was smiling shyly and handing the small black book to Nick.

Nick was astonished to see that his fingers were trembling slightly as he took the small book from her. He stood there staring down at the worn black leather cover, aware that this little book was very like a Pandora's box—the knowledge within it, once released, could never be returned.

Despite the need for haste, he couldn't help opening the book. In the faint, flickering light of his candle, he read:

> *December 12, 1742:*
>
> *My worst fears are realized—my father and the King have put their heads together and decided upon a bride for me. Giving in to the constant pressures and demands of my family, during the past few weeks, I have met with her twice. Her name is Pallas Leland and she is a sweet child, fair-haired and blue-eyed, not yet fifteen—far too young for a man my age, but her family is extremely eager for the match and my father and the King are insistent that I marry—I am the last of my line and it is imperative that I have a son to carry on the title. We are to be married sometime in the spring. . . .*

It gave Nicolas a strange feeling to read his grandfather's words and an even more peculiar feeling to realize that their situations had been remarkably similar—just as Benedict had been under pressure from his family to marry and produce an heir, so had he. He glanced across at Tess, her little face serious and intent as she watched him, and he was suddenly conscious of a great rush of gratitude toward Lady Halliwell. . . . Because of her, he had found the bride of *his* choice—not a bride chosen for him by someone else, but a bride, he admitted slowly as an inordinately tender smile played around the corners of his mouth, that he would not trade for any other woman in the world.

"What is it?" Tess hissed in the silence, wondering why he was looking at her so oddly. "Why are you smiling like that? It is your grandfather's diary, isn't it?"

He shut the book carefully, slipping it inside his jacket. "Oh yes, it is Benedict's, and I was merely smiling at the vagaries of fate, my dear—something I will explain to you at some other date. For now, let us be off from this place."

Tess managed to contain the dozens of questions that hovered on her lips and allowed Nicolas to hurry them from the room and down the stairs to the outside. It wasn't until they were mounted and riding toward the court that she asked the question uppermost in her mind.

Glancing across at him as they rode side by side through the sun-dappled woods, she inquired curiously, "Are you going to tell your grandmother?"

Nick looked thoughtful. "I don't know," he finally said. "It will depend, I suppose, on what he wrote—I know that some things will be extremely painful for her, especially anything dealing with your great-grandmother, but I'm hoping that there will be other parts that will give her a degree of comfort. I'll have to read it myself first and then decide." His jaw tightened. "I don't want her hurt any more than she has been, and if the diary contains passages that I know will wound her grievously, then I'll burn the damn thing before I'll let her see it."

They talked of little else but the diary for the remainder of their ride back to the court. It was only when the stables came into view that Nick halted the horses and said, "If anyone asks, we were just out for a morning ride. The discovery of the diary should remain a secret between the two of us until I decide what to do about it. And God knows I wouldn't want my grandmother to learn of its existence from anyone but me."

Tess nodded, agreeing wholeheartedly with him. "Oh, absolutely! She should be the first to know of it."

Upon their return to the stables, they found the place bustling. A pair of grooms rushed forward to take their horses the instant they approached the stables, and others were seen busily flitting in and out of the various stalls. As soon as they had dismounted, Nick and Tess sought out the stable master.

They found the fellow hurrying to meet them. When Nicolas explained that he wanted a word in private, the stable master, Nate Langford, a burly, ruddy-faced individual, with much bowing and scraping, immediately ushered them into his office. It was a comfortable room, not too large but spacious enough for a desk and several chairs. There were several horse prints upon the rough walls, and bits and pieces of saddlery were scattered about.

Nick declined the offer of a seat, and Tess remained standing also. Nate, gratified, and not a little worried, by this early morning visit by the earl, stood uncertainly behind the desk, fidgeting from foot to foot.

"There is a small chestnut gelding with a white star and one hind white foot in the stall next to one of my new driving blacks. When and where did you get him?"

Nate appeared flummoxed by Nick's question. "A chestnut gelding with a white star and hind," he muttered, scratching his head in perplexity. He thought for a moment, then his face cleared. "Oh, I know the one you mean—spirited little devil! Can't say where he came from, but he showed up one morning last week in the very stall you mentioned." He looked at Nicolas uneasily. "We think that the owlers left him here by mistake—you know how they are always borrowing stock whenever they please—I figured they forgot where they got him and just stuck him here. I asked if anyone knew the horse and then waited a day or two before I had one of the boys put up a notice in the village, describing the animal. So far no one has come to claim him."

Nick looked at Tess and cocked a brow. She wrinkled her nose at him. Langford's explanation was perfectly logical, and she felt a little silly over her earlier suspicions.

Nick turned back to Langford and smiled charmingly. "You may take the notices down. It seems the animal—his name, by the way, is Fireball—belongs to my bride. She recognized him immediately. The smugglers, er, appropriated him from her one evening last week. It is most fortunate," Nick ended dryly, "that he ended up in my stables."

Having solved the puzzle of Fireball's presence to their satisfaction, Nick and Tess returned to the main house.

By the time the newlyweds had finished their breakfast, Lord Rockwell and Alexander and the aunts had made their appearances; Pallas's maid brought word that Lady Sherbourne was still rather worn out from the strain of the previous day and wouldn't be joining them until much later. Meg and Hetty had already eaten from trays in their rooms, and since the hour was already approaching noon, Nick decided with obvious regret that it was time for the gentlemen to begin anew their explorations of the tunnels. They departed shortly thereafter, leaving the ladies to amuse themselves.

The hours dragged for Tess, but the time did pass. The gentlemen returned early, as Nick found it hard to stay away from his bride. That evening at dinner, the men regaled the ladies with stories of their fruitless explorations.

Having all but abandoned his bride the day before; Nick gave up any ideas that evening of beginning to read his grandfather's diary and devoted himself to the far more agreeable task of making love to his new wife. He did so with such intensity and enthusiasm that it was not surprising that Tess woke the next morning with a dreamy, satisfied smile on her face. The smile threatened to remain permanently fixed on her lips when, after joining the others, Nick declared that the men would refrain from their labors today and spend the time with the ladies.

It was a fine fall day, and after a leisurely breakfast, they all decided upon a stroll around the immaculate grounds of the estate. Eventually they found themselves in the extensive rose garden at the side of the house. The ladies were admiring the last few lingering blooms when the approach of a swiftly driven vehicle caught their attention.

Nick stiffened slightly. It had to be Athena returning, and in a damned big hurry from the sound of it. Which could only

mean one thing, he thought gloomily: the announcement of
his marriage to Tess must have appeared in this morning's
Times.

The stylish rig pulled by four beautifully matched chestnuts
suddenly came into view and swept regally around the wide,
circular carriageway at the front of the house. Snorting and
stamping, the horses were reined to a halt by the coachman,
and a second later a liveried servant leaped down from the
back and with a flourish opened the door to the vehicle.

By this time everyone had gravitated from the rose garden
to the front of the house. As Athena's dark head appeared and
she impatiently stepped down from the carriage, Nick found
his arm sliding protectively around Tess's narrow waist. If
Athena's vexed expression was anything to go by, this was
going to be unpleasant.

As she started up the broad steps, Athena caught sight of
them and stopped abruptly, her fine nostrils flaring when she
spied Tess standing next to Nick. "My God!" she exclaimed
furiously. "It *is* true! I couldn't believe my eyes when I read
the announcement in the paper this morning." Her lips lifted
in a sneer. "*Such* a hasty wedding, dear brother. Why? Is she
breeding already?"

Having fired that ugly salvo, she turned away and stormed
up the steps, her bishop's blue skirts billowing out behind her,
leaving a stunned silence in her wake. It was Rockwell who
broke it. "You know," he said confidingly, "a lot of people
don't think I'm very observant, but I'll tell you what—that
sister of yours ain't best pleased by your marriage, old fellow!"

Chapter Twenty-two

*I*n spite of the unpleasantness of the moment, Nick felt his lips twitch. "Yes, I suppose that you could say that," he murmured as he ushered his guests up the steps that Athena had taken. He made no apologies for his sister. He had known his marriage to Tess was going to cause difficulties, and he had suspected that the most outspoken critic of the match would be Athena. He hadn't, however, expected such open, outright venom. Along with the very natural anger he felt at the insult given his wife, he was also a little taken aback.

It was true that the Talmages had no reason to love the Mandevilles—besides the old tragedy of Benedict and Theresa, there was the more recent and unfortunate fact that Tess's uncle, another Baron Mandeville, had been the cause of Randal's death. Nick's lips twisted. If what he had heard about that infamous duel was true, one might say that Randal had gotten precisely what he deserved for deliberately provoking a man well known for his lack of interest or skill with weaponry to issue a challenge! Facing Sidney Mandeville on the dueling field should have been like shooting fish in a barrel for someone like Randal, and Nicolas suspected that no one had been more astonished than his brother when Sidney's bullet had actually found its mark. He sighed. Of course, Athena wouldn't look at it that way. In her eyes their brother could do no wrong—she had been, he admitted, inordinately fond of Randal. . . . But if Pallas, who had suffered far more greatly from the actions of the Mandevilles, could accept his marriage, what the hell difference did it make to his sister? he thought in sudden fury.

Athena's arrival had shattered the relaxed air of the group. Once they were inside, they all scattered, as if realizing that Nick needed time alone. The aunts retired to the library to browse and the gentlemen hastened to the game room to amuse themselves. Only Tess remained with him.

When they were alone in his office, Tess said softly, "Lady Athena is very angry about our marriage, isn't she?"

Nick grimaced. "I knew she would be, but I didn't expect her to be so openly venomous about it." He met her troubled gaze and asked, "I trust you were not too insulted by her words?"

Tess smiled wryly. "Why should I be, when we both know that it might be true?"

"Do you think you might be breeding?" he demanded abruptly.

"I couldn't possibly know this soon," Tess returned tartly. "It has been barely ten days since the night at the Black Pig."

His face softened. Bringing her hand to his lips, he pressed a warm kiss against the palm. His eyes locked with hers, and he said huskily, "I sometimes forget how briefly we have known each other—it has been a whirlwind time for us, hasn't it, sweetheart?"

Drowning in his gaze, Tess nodded slowly, a lump forming in her throat. It didn't matter if she had known him ten days or ten years, she doubted that she could have loved him more than she did. He was in many ways the embodiment of a maiden's most cherished dream—charming and one of the most wickedly attractive men she had ever met in her life. There were some who might even have found the manner of their meeting and marriage vastly exciting and would have had no qualms about spending the rest of their lives married

to a man like Nick Talmage—even if he never said one word
of love. He had proven himself to be an honorable, considerate man, even indulgent, and Tess couldn't pretend that he had
been anything but kind to her and her aunts. But while she had
accepted her marriage to him, she couldn't help wishing that
they had come together under different circumstances. Their
marriage, she thought wistfully, would be so much sweeter if
she knew that he cared deeply for her and that he hadn't been
forced to marry her.

She had tried to tell herself these past few days that she was
being greedy, wanting him to love her as well as desire her,
but it didn't do any good. She *was* greedy, she admitted
fiercely. And she wanted more than just his name and body—
above all else, she wanted his heart. . . .

When she didn't reply immediately, his hand tightened on
hers. "You don't regret our marriage, do you?"

She smiled and shook her head. "No. I was just wondering
how things might have been if we had met otherwise. . . ."

He grinned wickedly and pulled her into his arms. "You
mean if I had spied you at Almack's one night?"

She nodded. Her eyes wide, she searched his beloved features. Her breathing became erratic at what she saw in those
teasing eyes, and she asked, "What would you have done?"

"Well," he said slowly, brushing his mouth against hers,
"once I had determined the identity of the beguiling little
witch with the fiery hair, I would no doubt have gone off in a
high dudgeon!"

"Why?" she asked in slight trepidation.

"Because it would have infuriated me," he said softly,
laughter quirking the corner of his mouth, "to discover that
the one woman in all of England who had finally captured my
attention was one of *those* Mandevilles! I would have been
thoroughly enraged at the trick fate had played me."

Despite the teasing quality of his words, they did not ease
the leaden feeling in her heart. She bent her head, seemingly
fascinated by the buttons on the front of his waistcoat. "Do

you hate me and my family so very much?" she finally whispered.

Nick groaned, crushing her next to him. "Tess, you little fool! I'm half mad for you, and when I hold you in my arms, hatred is the *last* thing on my mind!"

He kissed her then, his mouth taking fierce possession of hers, and for a little while Tess forgot about the fact that being half mad for someone wasn't quite the same as being in love. When he finally lifted his mouth from hers, her eyes were shining. Slipping her arms around his neck, she said impishly, "I wonder . . . do you think we should send Avery a note, telling him how much we appreciate his sending me fleeing from his advances?"

Nick shot her a look. "No," he said firmly. "Avery Mandeville will never get any thanks from me." He looked thoughtful for a moment. "Writing him a note, however, requesting that all of your personal belongings as well as whatever belongs to your aunts be sent over immediately to Sherbourne Court would be a very good idea."

Tess looked impressed. "Oh, my. He's going to be absolutely furious!"

Nick smiled. "I know." Then, reluctantly, he released Tess and asked, "Would you mind joining your aunts for a while? I'd like to begin reading the diary and"—he frowned—"I need to speak with Athena."

Tess looked anxious. "Oh, Nick . . . don't fight with her! There has been enough tension lately with all that has occurred. Please, couldn't you just let it alone? Give her time to get used to me? . . . It has been a great shock to her, and I'm sure that she'll eventually see reason."

Nick snorted, his features grim. "I don't think we're talking about the same person. Athena *never* sees reason. And she's disliked me practically since birth. She's made it clear that she resents my standing in Randal's shoes, and if she had her way, *she'd* have inherited the title and all that goes with it." Bitterly he added, "My marriage to you is just another example to her of how utterly unworthy I am to be the earl of Sherbourne." He smiled tightly at her. "Believe me—Athena will not change her mind no matter how much time I give her. The situation needs to be settled now—I won't allow it to fester, and I don't want you insulted again. Nor do I want my grandmother or my guests put in the uncomfortable position of being subjected to one of Athena's vicious tirades."

"I see," Tess said slowly, wishing there were an amicable solution. Having been an only child and, except for her great-grandfather, having been surrounded by loving relatives all her life, she found it distressing that Nick and his only surviving sibling were at daggers drawn—and over her!

Sending him an uncertain little smile, she murmured, "I suppose, in this case, that you know best. I'll leave you then and go see what my aunts are doing." At the door she hesitated and looked back over her shoulder at him. "Perhaps, now that she's had a moment or two to calm down, she won't be so angry."

"Again, I don't think we're talking about the same person," Nick replied. "Athena's rages, both in magnitude and longevity, are legendary, and she can hold a grudge longer than anyone I know. You can wager your next quarter's allowance on the fact that our marriage, accomplished so quickly and clandestinely, is something that she is not going to forgive or forget any time soon." His jaw hardened. "She'll be furious about it twenty years from now. *That,* my dear, I can guarantee!"

His words did nothing to reassure Tess, and it was with a deepening unease that she left him and went in search of her aunts. She found them happily examining the fine library at the rear of the house. Though she tried to show proper enthusiasm and interest in the magnificent collection of leather-bound volumes that lined the walls of the spacious room, her thoughts kept straying to her husband and the confrontation with his sister.

After Tess had left, Nicolas immediately rang for Bellingham and requested the butler to inform Lady Athena that he wished to speak to her in his office—at once. Not at all looking forward to the meeting with his sister, Nick paced the confines of the room, wondering if Tess had been right. Would time soften Athena's hostility to the match? Should he be more understanding? Once the first shock of his marriage was over, would Athena relent and accept the inevitable? He didn't think so.

He hadn't known precisely how he was going to settle the situation, but as he paced, he happened to stop before one of the tall windows that overlooked the expanse of wood to the west of the house, and he caught sight of the towers of the Dowager House soaring above the trees. A grim smile crossed his face. Of course. The perfect solution.

There was a sharp rap on the door, and at his command, Athena surged into the room, slamming the door behind her, the purplish blue skirts of her gown flowing wildly about her ankles. With a haughty expression on her beautiful face, her black eyes full of malice, she halted in the middle of the room and demanded, "Well? What is it? Have you ordered me here to throw me out of my own home?"

Nick seated himself behind his desk. Meeting his sister's angry eyes, he said calmly, "Perhaps nothing quite as dramatic as that, but I am going to ask you to treat my wife and her relatives with the respect they deserve and to restrain yourself from putting on any more scenes like the one you displayed for us when you arrived, or . . ." His voice grew cool. "Or, you can remove yourself to the Dowager House. The choice is yours."

Athena's face darkened, and she leaned forward, her hands gripping the front of his desk. "You would *dare*?" she breathed furiously, hardly able to believe her ears.

Nick met her wrathful gaze unflinchingly. "You don't leave me much choice. But yes, I would dare. I'll not have my wife insulted by anyone—and particularly not by my own sister!" His voice softened. "Athena, I don't want to fight with you . . . I know that things have not always been easy between us, but can't you put your dislike of the situation behind you? I know that you are shocked by my sudden marriage, and I apologize for not giving you any warning—there were reasons. . . ." Athena's lip was curling contemptuously, and he realized she was indifferent to his words. Wearily he said, "Very well, then, this is my final word on the subject: Either apologize to my wife and give her the respect she is due or plan on living in the Dowager House. I won't," he added somberly, "prevent you from visiting our grandmother whenever you choose, provided you don't use your visits as an opportunity to create trouble for my wife. I will not have either Tess or our grandmother distressed. Do you understand me?"

Athena dramatically flung herself away from the desk. Standing before him, her magnificent bosom heaving, she said with loathing, "I always knew that you would act this way! Behind your charming smile and fine manners lie a domineering despot. I knew it was only a matter of time until you showed your true colors." She took an agitated step around the room and glared at him. With black eyes glittering feverishly, her delicate nostrils flaring, she spat, "Oh, God! If only I'd been born a male!" Her hand swept out to encompass the room. "This should all have been *mine*. I was born *before* Randal—in a fairer world, I would have been the heir! You're the youngest son—I should have inherited everything, not you!" She took a deep, angry breath and said harshly, "And now, instead of enjoying the wealth and power of the Sherbournes, I am reduced to living on the pittance you give me—being banished to the Dowager House." An expression of utter loathing on her face, she added tightly, "I've always resented you, you know, but it wasn't until now that I *hated* you. By God, but I wish it were you instead of Randal who had died!"

Nicolas remained unfazed in the midst of Athena's rage. When she took another deep breath in preparation for the next volley, he said flatly, "That's quite enough. I've heard all of this little speech that I want to, and believe me, you've made your opinion of me quite, *quite* clear. I'm sorry you feel the way you do, but it changes nothing." His eyes as hard and unyielding as steel, he said grimly, "Either I have your word for no more scenes such as this one or the one earlier or you remove yourself to the Dowager House . . . tonight, before dinner."

Athena drew herself up proudly. "Don't worry, dear brother, you won't have to put up with my presence a moment longer. I assume that you will allow me time to pack and that you will allow an adequate staff to accompany me to the Dowager House?"

"Of course," Nick replied tiredly, suddenly weary of the entire situation. "Whatever you want." Why, he wondered, had he ever thought that Athena would prove reasonable? With a brooding gaze, he watched as she marched from the room, stopping at the door only long enough to say over her shoulder, "And of course you'll pay for any repairs or refurbishing of the Dowager House?" He nodded, and with a challenging gleam in her eyes, she added, "I'll also want my horses and carriages removed to the stables at the Dowager House, along with the appropriate staff."

"Of course," he answered dryly, his expression wry. "Whatever it takes to make you happy in your new home."

She gave a harsh laugh. "There is only one thing that would make me happy—to see you lying in your grave!"

The door shut with a resounding bang behind her, and Nick didn't know whether to laugh or swear. One thing about Athena, he thought acidly, she didn't try to hide her feelings.

Nicolas sat behind his desk for some time, wondering if he had done the right thing or if there might have been some other way of handling his sister. He doubted it. The problem had begun even before he had entered the picture—if left to their own devices, Randal and Athena would have run gaily through the family fortune until there was nothing left—or damn little! They had been two of a kind, bent on their own pleasure at any cost. Nicolas had known that Athena resented his attempts to slow down her wild ride to folly, and if Randal had ever exerted the *least* authority over her, his task would have been much easier. The uneasy relationship with his sister looked to be irreparably damaged, but if any good could be said to have come from the confrontation, it would be the fact that at least they both knew where they stood.

The scene with Athena had left a nasty taste in his mouth. With some reluctance he retrieved the diary from the locked drawer in his desk and stared at it moodily. Even under the best of circumstances, he hadn't been looking forward to reading about his grandfather's obsessive, adulterous love for another woman. With the ugly exchange with Athena so fresh in his mind, Benedict's diary was the last thing he wanted to read. What he wanted was to find Tess and spirit her away so that he could spend the remainder of the day making love to her.

Just thinking of Tess lightened his mood somewhat, and with a bit more enthusiasm, he picked up the small black book. What dire truths would it hold for him? Would it explain how Benedict could turn his back on his young wife and his infant son to run away with another man's wife? Desert his title, lands, and great wealth? And what of the Sherbourne diamonds? Did he write of those?

Suppressing the urge to start at the end of the diary, where his grandfather had no doubt written of his plans to run away with Theresa, Nicolas idly thumbed through the beginning of the book. With a sinking heart he read of Benedict's joy the day his betrothal to Theresa Dalby had been announced. It was clear from every word that his grandfather had been deeply, profoundly in love with Theresa and that she had returned his love equally. Nick had never thought too much about Tess's great-grandmother, except as the woman who had stolen his grandfather away from Pallas. But as he read Benedict's glowing words, another picture of her emerged. She sounded, he thought with surprise, very much like Tess.

She had the same spirit. The same slender beauty. And the same passionate nature. . . .

Uneasy with his conclusions, he flipped through several pages, stopping to read of his grandfather's great rage and terrible anguish when the black perfidy of Gregory Mandeville had been discovered and Benedict had learned that his love had been abducted and would be forcibly married to another man—a man Benedict had once called "friend." Equally tragic, Benedict had written several pages about his great despair upon learning that Theresa was to bear her new husband a child.

Nicolas had often wondered why Benedict had never challenged Gregory to a duel, and he found the answer in the diary. The king. The king had expressly forbidden it, wishing to avoid, no matter how serious the offense, a lethal squabble between two of his favorite nobles. Benedict's parents, too, had added their weight to the king's. They had been desperate not to have Benedict risk his life in a duel over a woman who was already pregnant with another man's get. He was their only child, the last of the Talmages. It was his duty to survive and sire the next generation. There was such despair in those words that Nick's sympathy for his grandfather increased.

Benedict had bowed to his duty, but his hatred of Gregory Mandeville fairly scorched the pages of his diary, and Nicolas read with growing understanding of his grandfather's rages against the other man, the plots he dreamed up to kill him. Plots that came to nothing, for Benedict Talmage was not a cold-blooded murderer, even if murder was in his heart.

Eventually Nicolas put the book aside long enough to pour himself a glass of hock. Drinking his wine, he settled more comfortably on his chair and picked up the diary. Soon he was once more engrossed in a tragic tale nearly seventy years old. But it wasn't all tragic, he found to his surprise as his gaze randomly fell upon the page dated October 17, 1744:

*What a magically happy day! My sweet, glorious
little bride has presented me with a fine healthy
son. We have named him Francis, and like most
proud parents, believe him to be most handsome.
It is strange, but I never thought to be happy
again, and yet, today I am full of joy. I have a
loving wife and a strong, lusty heir. I was so
certain that my life had ended when Gregory
abducted Theresa, but I find that dear Pallas has
brought me great pleasure. Not only has she given
me a son, but with her gentleness and sweetness,
she has chased out most of the shadows from my
heart, and has replaced them with sunlight. . . .*

Nick closed the little book and stared off into space, unaware of the silly little smile that quirked at the corners of his mouth. His grandmother should read this passage, he thought fondly. It would please her enormously to know the depth of feeling that she had engendered in Benedict's breast. Then he frowned, thinking back over what his grandfather had written. They did not sound like the words of a man who would, not two months later, coolly abandon that same glorious little wife and newborn son and run away with another woman.

He was on the point of picking up the book and reading farther when there was a knock on the door. Nick stiffened. He seriously hoped that it wasn't Athena. Cautiously he bade the person to enter, and a smile curved his lips when Baron Rockwell came into the room.

After putting away the diary in the drawer and locking it, he looked quizzically at his friend. "I know I have not been the best host. Have you grown unbearably bored, Thomas?"

"Oh, no, it ain't that," the baron was quick to assure him. "It's just that I don't care to view all those fusty portraits of your ancestors. Your grandmother offered to give the ladies a tour of the gallery, and you know women—they thought it was a treat of the first water!" He added proudly, "Nearly

snaffled me into joining them, but said I had business with
you. Here I am!"

After offering the baron some hock, which was accepted
with alacrity, Nicolas indicated that they should sit on a pair
of high-backed oxblood red leather chairs near a window that
overlooked the formally laid-out gardens. It was by now late
afternoon, and the garden was glowing softly golden in the
slowly fading fall sunlight. Nick took a sip of his wine. Then,
smiling, he asked, "And Alexander? Did you just callously
leave him to the mercy of the ladies?"

The baron looked aggrieved. "Didn't desert him. Silly fool
wanted to join 'em—would do anything that gave him a
chance to moon over Hetty Mandeville. Why the devil he
don't just marry that chit out of hand and be done with it is
beyond me!"

Nick nearly choked on his wine. Marry the chit out of
hand? It seemed his friend had reckless depths he'd never
plumbed before.

Hiding his amusement, Nick said dryly, "I had noticed that
your brother seemed inordinately fond of the lady."

The baron snorted. "Been head over heels in love with her
for years!"

Nick frowned. "Then why hasn't he offered for her? Surely
there can be no impediment?"

"Well, you see, it's like this," the baron began eagerly.
"Hetty's two years older than m'brother, and when he first
came up to London and spied her, she'd already been out for
a year or two and there was some rich duke or other who was
dangling after her. Her grandfather was dead set on the match
and was forever going on about what a grand duchess his
granddaughter would make. Everyone was positive she'd
marry the fellow, so Alexander never made a push to fix her
interest, figuring it was hopeless. Think that was why he
joined the army with you." Rockwell paused, taking a drink
of his wine. Then he continued with relish, "But the match
with the duke never came about. Heard it told that when she

refused, her grandfather nearly went off in a fit of apoplexy. Threatened to lock her up in a nunnery for the rest of her life. Mean-hearted old devil. Alexander grew most encouraged after that—soon as he could, he sold his commission and came home, but you see, there was Tess."

"Tess?"

Rockwell nodded portentously. "Orphaned, you know. Gregory swore he needed Hetty to help him with Tess. Made her feel she'd be abandoning her little niece if she even considered marrying. Of course, Meg was there, too, but the old bastard insisted, and Hetty believed him, that Tess needed someone younger around her, so he pressured Hetty into the job. Never let her go to London again—at least not until Tess was older."

"You seem extremely well acquainted with the workings of the Mandeville family," Nick commented lightly.

"Well, naturally!" Rockwell exclaimed, almost offended. "Tess is m'sister's only child. And if Alexander don't marry and provide some new Rockwells, my heir." He looked thoughtful. "Alexander's too!"

Nick shrugged. "You could marry yourself and get your own heirs, you know."

The baron's fine blue eyes nearly started from his handsome face. "Married? *Me?*" he gasped in horrified tones. "Oh, my dear boy! Ain't in the petticoat line!" He hesitated and added fairly, "Except, of course, for the occasional bit of muslin I keep. But marriage?" He shuddered. "No. Never. All those twittering respectable little females and their matchmaking mamas terrify me. It ain't for me. Made up m'mind to it."

"But Alexander doesn't share your views, I take it?"

"No, he don't—at least not if we're speaking about him marrying Hetty. Talks of nothing else."

"Then why doesn't he just offer for her and have done with it?" Nick asked again. "Hetty is long past her majority, and since Gregory and her brother are dead, she doesn't even have a real guardian to gainsay the match. I could understand, although not entirely, Alexander not wanting to take Hetty away from Tess when she was a young child, but surely he could have made his intentions clear any time in the past several years?"

"Did," the baron replied gloomily.

"Are you telling me that Alexander offered for Hetty and she *refused* him?" Nick demanded incredulously.

The baron nodded. "Offered for her not two months after the old baron died. Did it again yesterday."

"And she turned him down? For what earthly reason?"

"Gel has too much pride," Rockwell answered moodily. "First time, didn't want to come to Alexander empty-handed. Had been hoping that when that old devil of a grandfather of hers died that he'd have provided for her—not a fortune, mind you, but a tidy little sum. Turns out, wasn't even enough money for Sidney to settle some on her—he was hanging out for an heiress to pull them all out of the River Tick when he had that duel with your brother. Very little ready at all—that's why she and Meg had to stay on when Avery inherited. Left penniless. No place else to go."

Nick frowned. "But why didn't you or your brother discreetly make some arrangements for her? Couldn't Tess?"

Rockwell was shaking his blond head. "No, she couldn't," he said exasperatedly. "Told you that Hetty had pride. She and Meg wouldn't let any of us lift a finger to help them. Tried. Said it wouldn't be right. Wouldn't budge. That's why Tess wouldn't leave when Avery stepped into her great-grand-father's shoes. Didn't want to desert the aunts. Fond of 'em!"

"Are you telling me that Hetty won't marry Alexander because she hasn't any money?"

The baron nodded glumly.

Nick took a deep breath. "But surely now that it is obvious that they can no longer stay at Mandeville Manor and are virtually dependent upon my wife and me for everything, Hetty has had second thoughts?"

"No, she hasn't—feels that now, even more, it wouldn't be right to marry Alexander. Afraid he'll think she's accepting him just because her situation is so desperate. Doesn't want that."

"Of all the—" Nick broke off, aggravated. "This is ridiculous! Penniless women marry men of great fortunes all the time. There is no shame in it."

Nodding, Rockwell said sagely, "Lot of women do. But not Hetty!"

Nick had never given Tess's fortune a moment's thought, but he was suddenly grateful that she *was* a great heiress. Knowing his bride as he did, he was certain that if she had been penniless like her aunt, he might well have found himself in the same situation as Alexander. He smiled grimly. Of course, if she hadn't been an heiress, Avery wouldn't have tried to compromise her and she wouldn't have run away and ended up in his arms, so the situation became moot. But it didn't help Alexander's suit, and he stared soberly at his wine, revolving different schemes to bring the two lovers together. When he realized what he was actually doing, the uneasy thought crossed his mind that being married to Tess must have addled his wits! Since when had he spared a minute to consider anyone's rocky path to love?

While Nick remained lost in his thoughts, the baron took another swallow of his wine and, putting down his glass, leaned forward. With a bright gleam in his brilliant blue eyes, he said confidingly, "Been thinking about the situation a lot. Know I ain't got any brains, everyone knows it! But you and Tess gave me an idea how to make things right for Alexander and Hetty. Got a plan."

With something between amusement and trepidation, Nick stared at his friend. Warily he asked, "And your plan is?"

"Compromise 'em! Same as you and Tess!"

Chapter Twenty-three

Uncertain whether to laugh or swear, Nick stared at Rockwell. What his friend had just suggested was both shocking and deplorable—and typically Rockwell! Harebrained and outrageous. But it just might work.... "Are you," Nick asked, amused, "proposing what I think you are?"

The baron nodded eagerly. "Only way. We do it right, and by this time next week, Alexander will be leg-shackled to Hetty!"

Nick, who had been considering a much more mundane solution such as a mysterious inheritance, could only look at his friend in growing awe. "My dear fellow," he finally said in a voice that quivered with laughter, "there are times when your intelligence is definitely underrated!"

"Don't know about that," the baron said thoughtfully, "but I do know that Alexander is going to be the very devil to be around if he don't marry Hetty in the near future. Be dashed uncomfortable. Don't like being uncomfortable."

Affectionate amusement dancing in his eyes, Nick asked, "Well, since you came up with this brilliant solution, how do you propose that we put it into motion?"

Rockwell looked thoroughly alarmed. "Uh, thought, p'rhaps, *you* could figure out the details." At Nick's fascinated stare, he muttered feebly, "No brains, remember? Much better if you take over from here."

Nick continued to look at him until the baron squirmed on his chair. "Now why," Nick drawled, "do I have the distinct impression that I am being expertly maneuvered into doing your planning for you?"

"Now, Nick, old fellow, it ain't that way at all," Rockwell protested earnestly. "You know that you are much better at this sort of thing than I am. Always were!"

"I am, am I?" Nick commented dryly. "This has been a most revealing conversation, my friend, and I'm just beginning to wonder how many of our harum-scarum adventures in the past were put into my brain by you!"

"Now, Nick," Rockwell said placatingly, a glimmer of laughter in his own eyes, "you know that I ain't got any brains—had to have been your idea."

At that, Nick did laugh out loud. Rising, he said, "That's all very well and good, but if you expect me to come up with an idea that will solve Alexander's difficulties with Hetty, you're going to have to leave me alone for a while to think."

The baron protested, but Nick would have none of it. "Yes, yes, I know you don't want to look at any of the portraits of my illustrious ancestors, but I do have one or two things to take care of and I can't accomplish anything with you hovering over my shoulder demanding to know every two minutes if I've come up with a solution. Go find something to amuse yourself—look at the new hunter I bought last month at Tattersall's or chase one of the parlor maids about the house."

With much muttering about disloyal friends who deserted one in a moment of need, Rockwell eventually left the sanctuary of Nick's study. Shutting the door behind him, Nick smiled, then turned and walked back to his desk. The diary called to him, but the hour was growing late and shortly it would be time to dress for dinner and join the others. Rockwell had distracted him, and before he pondered various plots to unite Hetty and Alexander, there was something he wanted to do.

Nick hadn't been jesting when he had mentioned to Tess about writing to Avery and demanding that her belongings and those of her aunts be sent to Sherbourne Court. They had all left behind several personal items, and Nick saw no reason why Avery shouldn't send them to the court. After all, he was only asking for what belonged to the ladies.

The note that he eventually composed and sent to Mandeville Manor was brief and to the point. He wasted no time on explanations or politeness, merely stated that he wished that *all* the belongings of *his wife* and her aunts be sent over immediately to Sherbourne Court. Not giving Avery any room to wiggle around, he also sent several servants and two carts along with his note.

Nicolas's curt note sent Avery reeling. Understanding now why he had found no trace of Tess or her aunts, he was so stunned by the news that Tess was married to Nick Talmage that he numbly ordered the rooms of the three ladies cleared and loaded in the carts. Alone in his study, he stared blankly at the scrap of paper that lay in the center of his desk, drinking glass after glass of wine.

All was lost, he thought grimly, his hand curling into a fist. That bastard Talmage had stolen the march on him and married the heiress, leaving him to scramble wildly in the wreckage left behind. It seemed that the earl of Sherbourne had beaten him and that his golden future, becoming one of the leaders of the ton and living lavishly on Tess's fortune, lay in ruins. His arrangement with Mr. Brown was profitable, but not *that* profitable!

As the hours passed, Avery remained sequestered in his study, drinking heavily, brooding on all the wrongs done to him by one man: Nick Talmage. From their first days in the army, they'd been rivals. Bitterness grew within Avery as he recalled every time Nick had bested him during those days.

Whether it had been a game of cards, the favors of a woman, fighting, or athletic abilities, it hadn't mattered: Nick had usually managed to vanquish him. The rivalry had been intense, and somewhere along the line it had become a deep, abiding hatred. Avery scowled. He didn't know when the rivalry had turned ugly, or when he had first started to hate Talmage, but he knew that he had hated Nick a long time before the other man had begun to hate him. Suddenly he smiled. He knew exactly when Nick had begun to hate him. . . .

Her name had been Catherine, and she had been the daughter of a sergeant in Nick's regiment, one whose family had served on the Sherbourne estate for decades. Nick had been uncommonly friendly with his sergeant, and he and several fellow officers stopped occasionally to visit with Compton and his wife and their only child, when off duty and other pursuits had not called. Now and then Avery and a few of his friends had also found themselves at the jovial quarters of the Compton family. Mrs. Compton had possessed the knack of turning any place into a pleasant home, be it a leaky tent in India or a mud hovel in Portugal. She was also a marvelous cook, and for men far from home, the scent of plum pudding wafting in the air or the aroma of kidney pie was more powerful than any siren's call. It became the habit of several young officers to bring to the plump, genial Mrs. Compton for cooking any delicacies that came their way.

In fact, the Compton home, wherever it might have been, had been a gathering place for many officers even before Catherine began to grow into a beauty. And of course, once she had blossomed into a golden-haired, angel-faced creature with a merry smile, the younger officers fairly haunted the Compton household. It had all been very innocent, Avery recalled, the sergeant and his wife too well liked for anyone even to think of seducing their only child. . . .

Avery's mouth thinned. He hadn't *meant* to seduce the silly chit! He had merely been playing with her, flirting with her in a lighthearted manner, much as the others did, and she had been stupid enough to fall in love with him. Well, perhaps he *had* led her on a bit after Nick had warned him off. Oh, all right—he'd deliberately set out to seduce her, to show the mighty Nick Talmage that his wishes carried little weight with *him*. Nick had always been protective of her, Avery remembered with a sneer, almost like à brother.

For a while Avery had enjoyed making seventeen-year-old Catherine Compton fall in love with him. She had been a beauty, a doe-eyed, long-stemmed rose, and he had clandestinely wooed her with kisses and promises of undying love. When she'd finally given in to his passionate entreaties and given him her virginity, he had been triumphant.

His mouth twisted. The feeling hadn't lasted long, just five short weeks. The stupid little slut had gotten pregnant and then had had the audacity to expect him to marry her! He snorted. As if he would have aligned himself with the daughter of a mere sergeant!

He took another long swallow of his wine, his mind on those last days in Portugal. They had been extremely uncomfortable, knowing as he did that sooner or later Catherine was going to tell someone of her condition and that he was going to have to bluff his way through her accusations, flatly denying them. It was going to be difficult, though, since the Comptons were so well liked, and he had steeled himself to be the object of open dislike among many of the officers and men. But he would continue to protest his innocence, and in time the gossip would die away.

Avery had had it all figured out, but he hadn't taken into account the extent of Catherine's wild desperation or the disagreeable fact that she would kill herself by throwing herself into the river . . . or that her mother would try frantically to save her and drown in the attempt. More tragedy was to follow—not twenty-four hours later, after seeing his wife and child laid in their common grave, in a frenzy of grief, the sergeant had taken his best pistol and blown his brains out.

At first Avery had thought that he had managed to escape

unscathed from the horrible tragedy. But within a week the reason for Catherine's suicide became known. It had been very ugly. It turned out that he hadn't been as discreet as he had thought—there had been those who had seen him now and then with Catherine, and worse, Catherine had confided in a friend not only that she was pregnant, but the name of the father of her unborn child.

Drinking his wine and glancing around the fine room in which he sat, Avery conceded that it had all been a near thing—thank God Sidney had died when he had. Otherwise he might have had to endure the contempt of his fellow officers as well as fight a deadly duel with his hated rival. Avery had known that Nick wouldn't have been satisfied with merely wounding him—he'd have wanted to kill him. Fortunately, Talmage had been away at the time of the tragedy, so Avery had escaped, or postponed, as the case may be, retribution at the hands of his rival. But there had been another stroke of luck—not two days after his involvement with Catherine became known, word of Sidney Mandeville's death and his unexpected inheritance had reached him. Before he'd found himself facing a furious Nick Talmage on a dueling field, he'd resigned from the army, left the continent, and returned to England. It seemed, however, that he hadn't been able to completely escape from Nick Talmage. . . .

Avery scowled again. It hadn't pleased him to learn that the duel that had killed Sidney had also killed Nick's brother and that Talmage was now the earl of Sherbourne—and his neighbor. All these months he'd half expected Nick to show up on his doorstep demanding satisfaction, and he'd begun to breathe a sigh of relief as time had passed and that hadn't happened. In fact, their paths had not crossed since they'd been in England, even though they frequented many of the same circles. But Avery had known that sooner or later Nick was going to become a problem that would have to be dealt with—he just hadn't expected it to happen so soon or in such a devastating way.

His clenched fist suddenly banged on the polished surface of his desk. *Goddamn* Nick Talmage! He'd ruined everything. Tess would be married to *him* by now if it weren't for that bastard Talmage. By God! He was the wronged one in this case—Tess had been under his protection here at Mandeville Manor. He'd been, he told himself firmly, coolly ignoring reality, *almost* been like a guardian to her. It was clear to him that there was something smoky about this sudden, unexpected marriage, and it was obvious, too, since to his knowledge Tess had never even met her new husband prior to her marrying him, that Talmage must have compromised her and married her out of hand. He dismissed whatever part her uncles may have played in the sudden marriage. They were such fops and cake-brained fools that they'd never even realized Tess's honor had been tarnished. It was up to him to make Talmage pay for taking advantage of an innocent miss! He was of a fair mind to ride over to Sherbourne Court and challenge Nick to a duel this very night. If he had his way, Tess would be a widow before she'd celebrate her first week of marriage. . . .

Avery sat up in his chair. If Tess were a widow . . . If Nick were to die . . . He frowned. Of course, she wouldn't be able to remarry immediately, and he'd have to keep her sequestered here at the manor until the proper time. Assuming he could wrest her away from Sherbourne Court. His eyes narrowed. She could be breeding already, but that didn't matter—there were ways of seeing to it that an infant didn't survive.

Suddenly hopeful about the situation, Avery continued to turn over in his mind the idea of making Tess a widow. There were several obstacles, and rather large ones at that, in his way. Nick would have to die. Killing his rival was not going to be easy, and it occurred to him that it might not be wise for him to be a party to his death—a duel was not the answer. Much better if he were not involved in any way. Then he could present himself as the young widow's sympathetic relative, genuinely grieved by the tragedy that had overtaken

her, wanting only to put the past behind them and to comfort
her in her hour of need. Avery smiled. Yes, that was much better. He looked thoughtful. There were always all sorts of
tragic happenings that could cut a man down in his prime. He
would talk to his friend in London. Perhaps something could
be arranged. . . .

Pleased with himself, he considered the other obstacles in
front of him, and some of his pleasure ebbed. Removing Tess
from Sherbourne Court, he admitted sourly, was going to be
more difficult than making certain her husband died. The first
step must be that the aunts returned home. It was highly unlikely that Tess would return to Mandeville Manor, under any
circumstances, without her aunts. But suppose he could convince the aunts that he'd been wild with love for Tess and that
passion for her had driven him mad, crazed him? And that
half insane with despair by Tess's cold treatment of him, he
had dared to act so deplorably? He would have to grovel and
beg their forgiveness, but since he'd always had a mostly
pleasant relationship with the aunts, he didn't doubt his ability to win them over.

It wasn't going to be easy, he'd be the first to admit it, but
it was certainly worth a try. Especially if he started wooing
the aunts before Nick died. Perhaps, if he were lucky, the
aunts would be safe under his roof prior to Nick's tragic
death. His eyes gleamed. And then, of course, grieving and
heartbroken, Tess would want to return to her ancestral home
and to the bosom of her family—her aunts. The Rockwells
might throw a rub his way, but he was certain he could deal
with them.

Avery took another long swallow of his wine, viewing his
plan from all angles. There was undeniably the possibility of
failure every step of the way, he wasn't stupid enough to pretend otherwise, but what did he have to lose? Nothing. And he
had everything to gain by trying.

His mind made up, he reached for his quill and a sheet of
paper. Some time later he read the appropriately abject note

that he had composed. Tess would no doubt reject his profuse apologies and pleas for forgiveness out of hand, but he was confident that the aunts would view his words more kindly. And that was what he was after . . . for now.

He had barely signed his name with a flourish at the bottom of the missive and folded the note before the door to his office was flung open and a tall, willowy figure in a form-fitting dark blue jacket and breeches, a curly-brimmed beaver hat pulled low across his face, entered the room. Avery didn't seem surprised to see him—or that he had not been announced by Lowell. He merely lifted one slim blond brow and said, "Ah, Mr. Brown. What an unexpected pleasure. Do you have good news for us? I certainly hope so—there has been a slight miscalculation on my part, and I must admit that my coffers have begun to run low again."

Mr. Brown made no reply but angrily flung aside his fashionable hat, revealing a wealth of thick black hair. Almost ignoring his host, he boldly helped himself to a glass of wine, pulled up a chair in front of Avery's desk, and coolly placed his highly polished boots on one corner. He took a deep gulp of his wine.

"I know all about your 'slight miscalculation,' and I intend to do something about it," Mr. Brown said tightly. "Furthermore. I've decided that mere money is no longer enough to suit me. I want more. I want it all. Everything. And you're going to help me get it."

Avery leaned back on his chair. Sipping his own wine, he stared uneasily at his visitor. "And how," he asked, "am I to do that?"

Holding a half-empty glass in a slim white hand, her black eyes glittering dangerously, Athena Talmage said, "Simply by killing the earl of Sherbourne. . . ." And at his stunned expression, she gave an ugly laugh. "I thought that would make you happy. First, though, you have to understand your position in my plans." She took another gulp of her wine and then began coolly, "Despite my reservations about you and the way you blackmailed us into making you a partner, our arrangement—or partnership, if you like—has worked very well for the three of us these past months. Your connections in London have provided us with extremely salable information we might not have obtained otherwise and has added to our profit." She paused and finished off the remainder of her wine. Pouring herself another glass, she went on, "But Frampton and I were doing very well without you. Aside from the information you provided us, you've actually done very little but step into a lucrative operation and cut yourself a share of the profits." Her voice grew grim, as his actions obviously still rankled. "And the *only* reason you were allowed to do that is because you had discovered our identities and had threatened to expose us." She swallowed more wine. "But the situation is different now—you're as guilty as we are—you're the one who has passed on the military secrets, and you've certainly never been backward in taking your share of the profits. You cannot betray us without your own part coming out. And I should warn you that I've made arrangements for just that to happen should something, ah, *unhealthy* befall me." She smiled into Avery's suddenly wary features. "But you have nothing to fear as long as we all understand each other. Frampton and I have always run the greatest risk. You've done nothing but collect a few interesting bits and pieces for us while in London and then sat here and collected your gold. I've decided that's unfair, that you should prove yourself. What I'm trying to say, my dear fellow, is that the time has come for you to, ah, branch out a little. . . ."

Her eyes suddenly diamond hard, she said bluntly, "I want you to talk to your people in London and make arrangements for my dear, *dear* brother to suffer an unfortunate accident. A fatal one." She smiled when she saw Avery's lips twitch in amusement. "Yes," Athena said softly, "you will have your heiress—I will see to it—provided she first relinquishes *any* interest in her soon-to-be late husband's estate and you take

care of any other claimant who might appear within the next
nine months. . . . Do you understand me?"

Avery nodded, rather amazed at how much they thought
alike. The future was looking very bright indeed. With Athena
on his side, getting Tess and the aunts to return to Mandeville
Manor was going to be child's play. And once Tess stepped
foot into the manor . . . she'd never leave it again until she
was his legally wedded and bedded bride, even if he had to re-
open those damned dungeons Gregory had ordered bricked up
years ago and lock her in there until she agreed!

Athena gave him a second to absorb her words and then
said cheerfully, "Frampton has nearly replenished the fortune
depleted by his father and is ready to, er, retire from the smuggling business—we never intended it to go on indefinitely.
You shall have Tess and her fortune, and with Nick gone, as
the last of the line, feminine though it be, Sherbourne Court
and all the wealth of the Talmages will be *mine*—as it should
have been in the first place! If all goes well, in a matter of
days, weeks at the most, Mr. Brown will disappear forever
and our venture will be ended." She lifted her wineglass.
"Shall we drink a toast to our success?"

Some time before the conversation between Athena and
Avery, Nick had left his study and gone in search of Tess.
Rockwell's comments on Alexander's courtship difficulties
and the reading of his grandfather's thwarted love for another
woman suddenly made it imperative that he hold Tess in his
arms, that he reassure himself that at least *he* had captured the
bride of his choice.

It was simple to find Tess, since the carts from Mandeville
Manor had arrived and a small army of servants was carrying
armloads of various, decidedly feminine objects up the stairs.
He found his bride standing in the center of her bedroom, staring dazed at the array of silks and laces, muslins and cam-
brics, velvets and satins, that were scattered across the room.
She glanced at Nick as he propped himself against the

doorjamb and amusedly surveyed the multitude of stylish garments and fripperies piled haphazardly on every available surface. Almost guiltily Tess said, "I didn't realize that I owned so many things! You must think me woefully extravagant."

What Nick thought was that he was the luckiest man in the world, and he was conscious of an odd feeling in the region of his heart. His bride looked very fetching standing there in the middle of the room, wearing a high-waisted gown of willow green muslin, her red gold hair slipping free of the confines of the matching ribbon with which she had tied it back and tumbling attractively around her lovely face. Her violet eyes were shining, her skin was glowing, and staring at her, particularly at the hint of her sweet breasts, which rose above the laced-edge neckline of her gown, Nick felt a warm heaviness pool between his thighs. Despite their long, intoxicating nights of mutual exploration and passionate lovemaking, he was surprised to discover that he still had only to look at her and his body stirred violently, his blood heating, his breathing deepening, and his sex swelling prodigiously in his breeches.

Half amused by his reaction, he pushed away from the doorjamb and walked over to her. Pulling her into his arms, he dropped a kiss on her nose. "What I think," he said huskily, "is that you are absolutely *adorable*."

Tess blushed rosily, her eyes shyly meeting his. "Do you really?" she asked. "In spite of the way our marriage came about?"

He pulled her closer, unable to tear his gaze away from the soft outline of her lips. "Perhaps," he murmured, "*because* of the way it happened."

"What do you mean?" she asked with a slight frown, her fingers unconsciously caressing his shoulders and neck.

With her tempting body resting against his, the last thing that Nick wanted was to think rationally, but her question was fair. His own hands wandered irresistibly here and there, and he said softly, "We met under most unusual circumstances—

we were not hemmed in by the dictates of society, and in a short time we learned more about each other than our contemporaries would learn in months about their intended spouses." His voice deepened, his eyes holding hers. "Because of the events leading up to our marriage, I learned that you are brave and valiant and that when faced with adversity you do not whine and mope—you take action." His lips quirked. "Perhaps not the wisest action, but nonetheless you did not let yourself become daunted by what lay ahead of you."

Tess made a face at him, and he laughed. But as they stayed there, their bodies tantalizingly close, his laughter slowly faded. His gaze probing hers, he said softly, "But those are not the only qualities that I learned you possess—you are capable of great loyalty and affection—your bond and manner with your aunts is proof of that. Another thing, you don't hold grudges—compelled to marry me, you could have made life miserable for both of us, but you didn't." He brushed his mouth warmly across hers. "You're also generous, sweetheart, generous in your affection and so wonderfully generous to me with that delectable little body of yours. . . . Every time we make love, I know that I am indeed a lucky husband."

Despite having shared his bed several times now, Tess still couldn't help the faint pinkening of her cheeks. Her eyes dropped and she stared hard at his starched, neatly tied cravat, mulling over what he had said. She couldn't help but be flattered and pleased that he thought her brave and valiant and all those other nice things. But while his words warmed her, they also filled her with a strange hurtful ache. She didn't want just to be admired, she thought fiercely, she wanted to be *loved*!

Not meeting his gaze, hiding the pain in her heart, she said in a stilted little voice, "You're very kind to me. Most men finding themselves in your position wouldn't have been."

Nick frowned, uneasily aware that in some indefinable way he had hurt Tess. He stared at her downbent head, trying to figure out where he had gone wrong. Speaking of his feelings for her hadn't come easily to him—he was thoroughly astonished at how openly he had spoken. He certainly hadn't planned this conversation—it had just happened, the words welling up inside of him and pouring forth before he could stop them or think about what he was actually admitting. And having practically laid bare his heart, he was irritated that Tess had not responded more encouragingly to his words. Didn't the little minx realize, he thought with annoyance, that in his own ham-fisted way, he'd been trying to tell her that he loved—

Nick's eyes widened, enlightenment exploding across his brain. Involuntarily he crushed her to him. With his lips buried in her hair, he said in decidedly unloverlike accents, "You silly little fool! I am *not* kind to you—I'm in love with you!"

Chapter Twenty-four

*A*fraid that her unspoken yearnings had made her misunderstand his words, Tess gaped at him. Nick merely smiled back at her, a smile of such warmth, of such tenderness, that her heart lurched in her breast. Perhaps she hadn't misheard him.... Her gaze fixed painfully on his, she demanded breathlessly, "What did you just say?"

Nick laughed, a fierce, exultant joy sweeping through him at the naked hope in her lovely eyes. Pulling her even closer to him, he said clearly, "I love you. I've been in love with you practically from the first second I laid eyes on you at the Black Pig—only I didn't realize it until this very moment."

He smiled down into her stunned features, watching the soft glow that spread slowly across her face as the meaning and heartfelt tones of his words gradually impinged upon her senses. "Do I dare hope," he asked carefully, "that my very sincere sentiments are returned?"

Tess made a sound, half laugh, half sob, and threw her arms around his neck, hugging him ardently. "Oh, *yes!*" she cried. "Oh, very definitely, yes! It seems I've loved you forever, and I feared that you would *never* love me!"

"*Sweetheart.*"

Nick had kissed her before, many times and many different

ways, but this time the touch of his hungry, yearning lips against hers was undoubtedly the sweetest of all kisses. . . .

It was some time later before either one of them drifted back to reality, and then they could only stare at each other, a bemused, delightfully silly smile on their faces. Oblivious of Bellingham, who had deigned to help with the unloading of the carts and who had started to walk into the room with another armload of clothing, Nick and Tess continued to stare dazedly at each other, their features utterly radiant. Spying them, Bellingham froze. Observing their wondering, moon-struck expressions, he spun on his heel and quietly shut the door behind him. Unaware of the equally silly smile upon his usually stern features, he hurried from the room to spread the word that love had once more returned to Sherbourne Court. . . .

As if gradually becoming aware of his surroundings, Nick glanced around at the disordered room and his lips quirked. "You'd think," he said with amusement, "that I would have found a more romantic spot in which to declare myself, wouldn't you?"

"Hmm," Tess fairly purred, her eyes dreamy and unfocused. Like a kitten, she rubbed her cheek against his chest and added softly, "At this very minute, I think that this is the *most* romantic spot in the world. . . ."

Nick tipped her face up toward him. He kissed her warmly and murmured, "And you are a darling! I am a most fortunate man." With a finger that almost trembled, he delicately traced her features. "Do you know," he said huskily, "I think that I just might have to thank Avery for being such a black-hearted scoundrel. . . ."

Tess giggled, and Nick was thoroughly charmed and of course had to kiss her again. At the feel of her soft lips beneath his, the sensation of her slender body pressing against his, desire, made all the more powerful and intense by the knowledge that he loved and was loved in return, surged up through him. His kiss deepened, his tongue boldly seeking the warm haven of her mouth.

Tess sighed as his tongue petted and stroked hers, her body filling with a languid heat, her nipples tingling, and low in her belly, she felt the now familiar stirring of passion. She pressed nearer, her body offering itself unconsciously.

Nick groaned. His mouth never left off its increasingly hungry exploration as he picked her up. With his arms full of warm, yielding femininity, he strode toward his own bed-chamber. Kicking the door shut behind them, he laid her gently on his bed and his lips slipped from her mouth down to that spot where the blood beat strongly at the base of her neck. He said thickly, "I've never felt this way before—I *do* love you, Tess. I will always love you."

His words were far more seductive than any kisses, and her arms clutched him even more tightly. "Forever," she murmured fervently. "I will love you forever."

There was reverence and passion in his touch as he slowly removed her gown, his lips immediately following the path his hands took, lingering hotly here and there. He was in no hurry, wanting to savor this delicious moment, wanting to show her how much he adored her. By the time Tess was nude, her entire body was burning, aching for him, as his wicked, knowing mouth had explored and caressed nearly every inch of her soft flesh.

Reluctantly he tore his hungry mouth from her fascinating body, stood up, and ripped off his garments. He was gone from her side but a moment, and then she was hauled once more into his arms, crushed against his lean, hard body, her mouth being sweetly ravished.

They had made love many times since their paths had first crossed that night at the Black Pig, but this time was different; the emotions and sensations aroused by each other's caresses were deeper, more intense, and more powerful than ever before. Each touch, each kiss, sent a thousand shimmering, burning, lightning shocks of pleasure flashing through them. Everything seemed more sharply felt, from the gentle rasp of his teeth on her breast to the drugging quality of their kisses. And love made the difference.

Nick drank greedily of her sweetness, his tongue filling her mouth, leaving her in no doubt of his carnal intentions, his hands roaming feverishly over her, his fingers teasing her nipples into hard little buds. He did not want to hurry, he wanted to linger, to prolong this joining, but his need to sink deeply into her slick heat was nearly overpowering.

His member was so tightly swollen, so rigidly erect, that he feared one touch would set him off, and when Tess's exploring fingers closed around him, he groaned, part pleasure, part pain. Trying desperately to ignore the incredibly arousing sliding motions of her warm palm up and down his near-to-bursting shaft, Nick plunged his tongue more frantically into Tess's mouth, his hands cupping her breasts more urgently.

Tess sighed, relishing the obvious signs of how very aroused her husband was, her own body already anticipating the exquisite pleasure of his taking. When his lips left her mouth and closed around her nipple, she gasped with delight and arched up, heat spiraling wildly outward from her breast. Feeling his hands on her thighs, parting them, his fingers tangling in the wiry hair he found there, she grew breathless with anticipation. When he parted the tender flesh and first one finger, then two, slid deeply within her, she cried out, the sensation so sweetly carnal that she could not help herself.

Hearing her cry, Nick smiled tightly and his mouth pulled more hungrily at her breast; the movement of his fingers between her legs became swifter, deeper, demanding a response. She was like silk, he thought dizzily, silk heated until it was ready to burst into flame, and he wanted nothing more than to lose himself in that silken warmth, to feel her inner muscles clamp tightly around his sex and draw them both into a vortex of fire.

Afraid to wait a second longer, he caught her caressing hands and pulled them above her head. Holding her an eager, adoring prisoner, he slid between her thighs and lowered himself onto her. A fluid movement of his hips and his aching shaft found its mark. Slowly he sank within her narrow channel, nearly losing control as he felt that hot, silken flesh close snugly around him. Releasing her hands, he bent his head and kissed her welcoming mouth passionately. It was so very sweet to slake his hunger for her kisses, to revel in the sensation of being buried deep within her, to know that at this moment they were one, that she loved him, and that she was his love . . . and yet the frankly primitive demands of his body would not let him enjoy what he had won. Catching her bottom lip in his teeth, he bit down gently as his body began its elemental movements, his shaft sliding slickly in and out of her wet heat, his hips rising and falling against her as they both sought paradise.

There was magic between them. Such powerful magic that it seemed as if they were the only ones who had ever shared this earthshaking emotion. . . . When it was over, when that final, explosive summit had been reached, when the last tremor of rapture had faded, there was the exquisite ecstasy of finding themselves in each other's arms with the realization that what they had shared together was unique and precious and that they could find it again only in each other's arms.

They lay abed for hours, Tess cradled against him, her head resting on his shoulder, Nick's arm holding her close, the world forgotten. In between gentle kisses and warm caresses, they spoke in soft murmurings, in a language understood only by lovers. . . .

Eventually Nick roused himself to light a candle. Looking at the clock ticking on the black marble mantel, he laughed. Glancing back at Tess, he said, "I wonder what sort of excuse we can offer for missing dinner tonight."

Tess made a face and stretched, reveling in the way Nick's eyes seemed riveted by the inherently sensuous movement of her body. "Does it matter?"

"God, no!" he burst out, brushing a kiss across the crest of her nipple. Her breath caught in her throat, and he smiled. "If I had my way," he murmured, "I would keep you in bed a fortnight or two and we would do nothing but this. . . ."

His hands cupped her breasts, his mouth found hers, and Tess's thoughts went spinning away. They made love again, slower this time, less frantically, yet in the end there was the same blinding ecstasy they had experienced earlier.

As pleasure gradually ebbed and she could think coherently again, Tess turned her head and kissed his shoulder. Dreamily she asked, "Do you think that a fortnight or two would be long enough?"

"Probably not," he replied with a tender smile on his chiseled lips, "but at least it would slake my most *immediate* needs." His stomach grumbled just then, and he added, "Although, I think that before we continue these extremely gratifying activities we should feed ourselves." He sent her a lecherous look. "You have caught me in a weakened state—I shall show much more stamina after I have eaten."

Tess laughed, her eyes dancing. "If you show much more stamina, I shall surely expire before the night is over."

An inordinately pleased expression crossed his handsome face. "Good! I would not want to have my bride complaining of my prowess in the marriage bed so soon after the wedding!"

Tess smiled giddily, certain that she had never been so happy in her life. It was wonderful to tease with him, to know that her love was fully and equally reciprocated. As she lay there in his bed, her body still limp and sated from his passionate lovemaking, the future, with Nick at her side, seemed to stretch out before her like an endless golden ray of summer sunshine. . . .

She was so lucky. Luckier, she thought abruptly, than Theresa had been. Unexpectedly a shiver passed through her, and she was suddenly aware of being afraid, as if a cold, dark, menacing shadow had passed over her.

Nick had gotten out of bed and was shrugging into his clothes. She sat up and asked anxiously, "What are you doing?"

He grinned at her as he fastened his breeches. "I'm getting dressed so that I may make a raid on the kitchens and find us some sustenance. You stay right there—I won't be gone very long, and then we shall enjoy a midnight feast." A gleam entered his black eyes. "And then," he said huskily, "I shall feast again. . . ."

Nick did not, however, have to go to the kitchens. He opened the door to his room, and almost immediately his gaze fell upon the mahogany cart sitting there—a cart littered with several covered dishes and various oddments. Lifting one lid, he discovered a roast chicken, lightly browned little potatoes artfully arranged around it, and under another, several dainty, golden brown pastries. Guessing even more delicacies were to be found under the other lids, he smiled, an amused smile that spread slowly across his face. It seemed someone had anticipated their needs and had already provided the midnight feast.

He started to roll the cart into his room when he spied two bottles of wine and a folded slip of paper lodged between them. Unfolding the note, he read:

> *These, along with several others, were laid down*
> *on the day that I married your grandfather. . . .*
> *I've been saving them for some extraordinary*
> *event. This seems to be it—at least until my first*
> *grandchild is born! Pallas.*

A rueful grin lurking at the corners of his mouth, Nick shook his head, marveling at the effectiveness of the household news-vine—he and Tess had barely discovered the state of their own hearts, and already it was known throughout the court. At least, he thought as he rolled the cart forward, we won't have to make any excuses for our absence tonight—obviously everyone knows what we were doing!

Aside from a little embarrassment about the circumstances, Tess was deeply touched by Pallas's note. Reading it for a second time, after they had enjoyed a thoroughly splendid meal, she said thoughtfully, "She really is impatient for a grandchild, is she not?"

She was sitting in the middle of the bed, the sheet draped across her lower body, her firm little breasts gleaming in the candlelight. Nick lounged beside her with his arms behind his head. His eyes were roving caressingly over those same little breasts, but at her words he glanced at her face and cocked an eyebrow. "You're displeased at the idea of a child?"

"Oh, no! It isn't that," Tess answered quickly, the thought of his child growing within her making her feel giddy. "I just meant that having a grandchild seems to be of paramount importance to her, and if I do not conceive immediately, I shall feel as if I have failed her."

A boldly sensual smile curved his bottom lip as he reached for her. Gently kissing her collarbone, he said, "Then we shall just have to do our best to see that you become pregnant as quickly as possible, won't we?"

Her eyes glowing softly, she caressed his dark head. "Oh, yes!"

They made love again, and not long afterward Tess fell asleep cradled in her husband's arms. Sleep eluded Nick, however, and he lay awake in the darkened room for some time, listening to Tess's even breathing. He was far luckier than his grandfather had been, he mused somberly. Not only would he have his love, but he wouldn't have to leave home and hearth and travel halfway across the world to have her, leaving scandal and shame in his wake. His arm tightened around Tess. With his heart full of love for her, he again felt a stirring of sympathy for his grandfather. Would I have made a different choice if I had been faced with the same circumstances Benedict had been? he wondered. He moved uneasily in the bed, knowing the answer, guiltily aware that he would have allowed *nothing* to come between himself and Tess. If he admitted that, how could he continue to blame his grandfather for following his own heart? He scowled, not liking the path of his thoughts, especially when all he wanted to think about was his happy future with Tess.

But thoughts of his grandfather would not go away, and finally he slipped his arm from beneath Tess's head and got out of bed. After dragging on his dressing robe, he lit a candle and left the room.

Traversing the dark and silent house, he went directly to his study. A few minutes later, the diary in his hand, he returned to his bedchamber. After setting the candle by the bedside, he rejoined Tess, smiling faintly as she mumbled slightly in her sleep when he climbed back into bed.

For a long moment he stared at her averted profile, at the straight little nose and soft mouth. His heart felt as if it would burst inside his chest from all the love he felt for her. Almost reverently he touched the heavy mass of thick curly hair that cascaded wildly across his pillow. No, he swore fiercely, nothing would ever come between *them*.

Reluctantly he turned away from her and, settling back against the pillows, picked up the diary. Avoiding the last few pages, not wanting to know the precise end of the tale just yet—he *already* knew it ended tragically for his grandmother—he thumbed back toward the middle of the diary until a notation caught his eye: Benedict's emotions on first learning that Pallas was pregnant. Since having read of the birth of his own father earlier in the day, Nick found it interesting to discover his grandfather's musings on the probable sex of the child—and how much he was looking forward to its arrival, be it girl or boy. With Tess sleeping peacefully at his side, the candlelight flickering softly in the darkness, Nick read for quite some time, following the course of Pallas's pregnancy and his grandfather's growing delight, not only in his coming child, but in his young wife as well. The diary was full of Pallas's doings, the way she smiled, her kindness, her sweet laughter, and the increasing pleasure it gave Benedict to be with her, to watch her, to tease her and cosset her, and how very much she had come to mean to him. . . .

A frown grew between Nick's brows. It was plainly evident, to him, at least, that Benedict had fallen headlong in love with his young wife. Nick started as something suddenly dawned on him. For pages now, pages that covered the early months of Pallas's pregnancy, there had been not one word of Theresa, not even *one* reference, and he was puzzled by that glaring omission. Had he skipped over it? It was true that previously he had been reading the diary randomly, jumping backward and forward, skipping pages at a time, following no particular order. But not tonight. Tonight he had started with Pallas's announcement of her pregnancy, and he had read right through the first seven or eight months of her pregnancy . . . and all during that time there had been no mention of Theresa. Had Benedict simply stopped writing of his assignations with Theresa?

His frown increased, and he backtracked, skimming quickly over the heavy black strokes of Benedict's handwriting. The early months of his marriage to Pallas. The wedding itself. Nothing about his love for another woman. No mention of Theresa. It was as if she had never existed. The diary was full of day-to-day happenings, his grandfather's deepest thoughts and emotions, but nothing about Theresa. How could that be? His fingers turned the pages more swiftly, his eyes flying across the written words. And then he found it.

> *February 26, 1743:*
> *I just made the most agonizing decision of my life, and though it grieves me unmercifully, I know that it is only right and just. Theresa, her lovely face pale and set, those purple-jeweled eyes of hers full of tears, broached the topic—with my wedding set for two months hence, we cannot*

*continue as we are. We cannot meet again
privately and continue our intimacies. Ever.*

*And why? Because of Pallas. None of this is
any of her doing, and while Theresa and I can
ignore the vows that Gregory forced upon her,
neither of us can pretend the same situation exists
in connection with my impending marriage. It is
true that it was at the urging of my parents and
the prodding of the King that I asked for Pallas's
hand, but the fact remains, I did ask her to
become my wife.*

*Pallas is an innocent. She is young and
beautiful and, as Theresa said, she does not
deserve to have a husband who sneaks out at
night to lie in the arms of another woman. I am
very fond of Pallas and she is to be my bride, my
wife, even if my heart is given to another. I must,
at the very least, give her the respect and honor
due her.*

*I do not know how I am to face the future
without Theresa, but she was right when she said
that if we continued to meet clandestinely and
ignored my marriage, we would destroy ourselves,
that our love would become sullied and tainted. I
argued fiercely to the contrary, but eventually she
made me see the wisdom in what she was
saying—bitter, bitter, though it was.*

*My heart aches for Theresa, not only because
she is my dearest love and I will never be able to
hold her in my arms again, but also because,
while I go to a gentle, sweet bride, she is still
chained to that black-hearted monster who ruined
our lives. She hates him so, but she also fears
him. He has beaten her—she did not tell me, but
to my helpless rage, I have seen the bruises upon
her lovely body—and he has threatened*

*repeatedly to send their child, a mere babe, to
some distant relatives of his if she does not please
him. She seldom speaks of their life together, but I
hear of his petty viciousness from others. Only
once did she tell me of the nights during which
she must suffer his rutting upon her and how she
lies there, her body shaking with revulsion. To her
relief, he has not touched her for months now,
choosing instead to taunt her with his many
women, to let her know that he has found her a
poor, wanting thing in his bed. We have smiled
over this, knowing how she turns to fire in my
arms and how joyous our coupling has been. But
no more. Tonight was our last meeting at the
gatekeeper's cottage. And while she shall never
again lie in my arms, I cannot help but fear what
the future will hold for her, married to that
monstrous creature. I am helpless to rescue her—
since the King forbade me to kill Gregory in a
duel, I can do nothing to alleviate her suffering.*

*I am full of guilt that my life with Pallas will be
so very different—I know that Pallas will make me
happy—as happy as I can be under the
circumstances. Guilt smites me every time I catch
myself smiling at some amusing thing Pallas has
said or every time she makes me laugh with her
lively antics. I should not be able to laugh, or
smile, or take any pleasure in the sweetness of my
bride-to-be, and though my heart yearns for
Theresa, I find that I do and damn myself a
thousand times because of it. . . .*

Keeping the place with his finger, Nick closed the book for
a moment and leaned back against the pillows. At least now
he knew why there had been no mention of Theresa. Benedict
and Theresa had stopped meeting. But if that were so, he

thought with a scowl, and most of what he had read tonight confirmed it, then how was it that Benedict and Theresa, some nineteen or twenty months later, had run away together—taking the Sherbourne diamonds with them?

The first clue to what must have happened leaped out at him as he came to the entry dated October 1, 1744—about two weeks before Pallas's child was born.

> *I am the most ignoble and wretched of men. I have betrayed not only myself, but my dear wife as well.*
>
> *God knows that I did not mean for it to happen . . . but when the note from Theresa came, begging, imploring me to meet with her once more at the gatekeeper's cottage, I could not deny her. I swear upon all that I hold dear that I did not meet with her to taste the forbidden sweetness of her body—that was not in my mind, nor in hers. Theresa was desperate—her face thin, her eyes dark and shadowed—she cannot bear the situation any longer and turned to me to help her escape from her husband. What else could I do, but agree?*
>
> *I will travel to London at the first opportunity and purchase passage for her and her child to the Colonies. She should be safe there—and beyond Gregory's reach! She did not ask it of me, but I shall also make the necessary arrangements for her to have a generous sum of money at her disposal. She will need it once she reaches the New World—I could not bear the thought of her alone and far away and in need of any sort. It is terrible enough for me to think of her making that uncertain, dangerous journey across the ocean and then forging her way alone in an unknown*

world, without my making some monetary provisions for her.

We had settled all this and handled ourselves as we should. It was only as we prepared to part that disaster overtook us. Though I longed to do it, I had not touched her, I did not mean to allow desire to rear its soul-destroying head, but it happened. She looked so sad, so forlorn, that I could not control an urge to hold her in my arms and give her what solace I could. I swear that only giving comfort was in my mind, but once I touched her, once she raised her face to mine, we were lost. . . . Afterward, there was such remorse between us, such horror that we had betrayed ourselves and Pallas and had basely given in to the despised weaknesses of our flesh. When we finally parted, for the first time, there was guilt and deep shame between us.

And now I cannot look my dear, sweet Pallas in the face without pain and remorse surging through me. Her body is greatly swollen with my child, and I damn myself for a craven lecher and writhe inside at the ugly knowledge that I have broken my vows, have blackened my honor and lain with another—no matter what the circumstances. . . . I am the basest of men, but I shall dedicate my life to proving myself worthy of being married to an angel like Pallas. I shall never betray her, nor cause her a moment's pain, again. On my life, I swear it. . . .

Chapter Twenty-five

*N*ick stared blackly at the diary, almost as if he suspected the book were playing a trick on him. He *knew* that Benedict and Theresa had run away together, yet Benedict's words seemed sincere.

Impatiently Nick quickly skimmed over the following pages. The trip to London had been delayed because of bad weather and the birth of his son, and it was nearly a month after that meeting with Theresa before he could travel to London. Obtaining passage to the Colonies was difficult this time of year—it was nearly November, and few ships were putting out to sea for such a long journey. But one vessel had been delayed because of refitting and was sailing just after the first of the year. It was the earliest date that Benedict could arrange—any other ships that might have been departing he had deemed unsafe, or he had not cared for the captain or the crews. He was in London for the better part of two weeks, and he had barely returned home and greeted his wife and newborn son when another even more frantic and desperate note from Theresa was handed to him furtively by an anxious maidservant.

The meeting took place once again in the gatekeeper's cottage, and Benedict was both stunned and appalled, not only by the marked deterioration of Theresa's spirits and health, but by the news she gave him. *She was pregnant.* With his child! It could not possibly be Gregory's child—they had not been intimate for nearly six months. She was almost out of her mind, nearly hysterical and terrified that her husband suspected—he had caught her throwing up twice now, and just last night he had commented in an icy voice on her lack of appetite. She had to get away from him *immediately*! If he knew for certain that she was with child, he would kill her. She had to leave now. She could not wait until January.

Aware of a tenseness creeping through his body, Nick glanced at the next entry. Dated two days after Benedict's return from London, November 24, 1744, the entry read:

> *I have made arrangements with a smuggler I know and trust to transport Theresa and her two-year-old son, Richard, to France. There has been no time to make any other arrangements. She is terrified of Gregory, and I must get her to safety immediately. There was not even time for me to obtain adequate funds for her, and I am going to have to give her the Sherbourne diamonds, to ensure that she does not go to the continent nearly penniless. In France she can sell the diamonds, and from there she can obtain passage to the Colonies. I will make further arrangements for other monies for her, once I know she is safely away.*
>
> *I hesitated about the diamonds, they have been in the family for generations, but I shall buy Pallas an even lovelier and more expensive set and present them to her with my love . . . and I do love her. Just as I love Theresa. I love them both, each in different ways, and it seems that all I am capable of doing is wounding both of them. I am not worthy of either one of them, but I shall spend the rest of my life trying to make amends.*

I cannot desert Theresa—especially not knowing that she carries my child. I intend to acknowledge the child, and eventually I shall have to tell Pallas. Yet I would do everything within my power not to cause her pain—perhaps in time she will forgive me. . . .

Though it pains me to write these words, it is best that Theresa goes to America. Our love can never be—my life is with Pallas now, and Theresa's life here is a hellish misery. She deserves her chance for happiness, and mayhap in the New World she will find it. I can only pray for that to happen.

I am most anxious—time has fled since I began to write these words. Theresa was to meet me at the gatekeeper's cottage as soon after dark as she could, and from there I was to escort her to the coast and the meeting with the smuggler. It is now after ten o'clock and I fear the worst. I have the diamonds with me, a pair of my fastest horses, and a small, light vehicle standing ready. All is prepared. Except that Theresa has not arrived.

I know the way she was to come—the way she came to me so many times in the past—through the dungeons underneath Mandeville Manor. A long time ago, another lifetime, it seems, when Gregory and I were boys together, we discovered a secret entrance to the dungeons from the outside of the manor. After Theresa and I became lovers, I showed her where it was and she used it, slipping in and out of the manor at will. She was to come that very same way tonight. But she has not.

I must go to her. I must find out what has delayed her. I will wait another ten minutes and then if she has not arrived, I leave to look for her in the dungeons of Mandeville Manor. . . .

It was the last entry in the diary, and Nick closed the book with a snap, his eyes as cold and hard as obsidian daggers.

Silently Tess sat up. She touched him on the cheek, and he turned to look at her, the fierce expression on his face making her heart drop.

"They never left England," he said thickly. "And Benedict had no intention of abandoning my grandmother—he was going to help Theresa escape and then he was coming back to Pallas."

"You mean Gregory found them . . . and murdered them?" she asked in dawning horror.

"I'm certain of it. Benedict's last entry states that he was going to Mandeville Manor and that he was going to go into the dungeons to find her."

Tess gasped, her pupils dilated. In a voice barely above a whisper, she said, "He had them bricked up."

"When?"

Tess shook her head. "I don't know. A long time ago. Long before I was born or even Hetty was born." She gave another gasp. "Oh, my God! I just remembered—Meg used to talk about my grandfather having horrible nightmares, of being somewhere dark and cold. He must have been with them when Gregory found them. She was taking her son away with her, but Gregory discovered her. . . ."

They stared at each other for a long time, envisioning what must have happened. . . . Tearing her thoughts away from the ugly pictures in her mind, she said unhappily, "He used to terrorize me when I was little by telling me that perhaps he'd open up the dungeons just to put me in there and then brick them up again. Hetty said he even did the same thing to her when she displeased him as a child—although she indicated that he seemed to take particular delight in using that threat on me."

"I have to get in there," Nick said urgently. "I'll either have to find the entrance Benedict used or I'll have to smash through the bricks from inside the manor, but one way or another, I'm getting into those dungeons. I *know* that's where they are—all I have to do is prove it!"

"You're not going to do any such thing," Tess said vehemently, "and if you don't swear to me right now that you'll attempt no such foolishness, I'm marching right out of here this very minute and going directly to your grandmother—I'll tell her the entire tale."

Nick eyed her consideringly. Her chin was set at a stubborn angle, and he knew that she wasn't jesting. She would tell his grandmother.

"She'll have to know eventually," he said carefully. "Once I've found his body—and Theresa's—I intend to give her the diary and explain everything."

Tess snorted. "Yes, I'd guessed as much, but you don't want her, or anybody else, to know right *now,* and I'm going to tell everything if you don't give me your word that you won't go anywhere near Mandeville Manor by yourself." Terror peeked out of her eyes. "Avery would kill you if he got the chance—you know he would!" Then she murmured, "Nick, I don't want anything to happen to you—I love you, and I especially don't want history repeating itself."

Nick sighed. There was enough truth in what she said to give him pause. While every instinct cried out for an immediate resolution of his grandfather's fate, he realized that he couldn't just leap on a horse and go storming over to Mandeville Manor.

"I'd have to wait until Avery leaves for London again anyway—or goes away to visit with friends," he said thoughtfully. "And to placate you, when we actually break into the dungeons, I'll need help from your aunts and your uncles. . . . The day we plan to storm the dungeons, your aunt Meg can keep my grandmother company while the rest of us return to the manor, ostensibly to retrieve a few personal items that Avery did not send over." He paused, obviously turning over the various aspects of his hasty plan, looking for flaws. "The servants at the manor," he began again slowly, "shouldn't give us any trouble—not with you and Hetty along. After all, until a week or so ago, it was your home. At any rate, the only two we'd have to worry about would be Lowell and Coleman, and I'm certain that between your uncles and myself, we can handle them. The other servants will no doubt be pleased to see you." Nick grinned at her. "They all might think we've gone mad, however, when we decide to open and explore the old dungeons, but they won't prove an obstacle. If they do, I'm sure that you and Hetty can talk them round. As for the bricked-up portion, your uncles and I should be able to make short work of the barrier—we might even enlist one or two of the manor's servants to help us if need be. I doubt the dungeons are very extensive, probably not more than a half dozens cells, if that. It shouldn't take us very long to find what we're looking for." He cocked a brow at her. "Well, what do you think? Will it work? And will it meet with your approval, Madame Wife?"

"Suppose Avery were to return unexpectedly? Suppose the absolutely worst thing were to happen and he caught us in the dungeons?"

Nick snorted. "Tess, there will be several people who will know where we are, and though he might consider it, he could hardly murder the *five* of us!"

Tess made a face. Nick was right, and she liked the sound of this plan far better, but she was troubled by one aspect of it. "You're going to tell everyone else about the diary before your grandmother?"

Nick shook his head. "No. But I'll have to let the others know what I suspect. They don't have to know precisely *why* I have concluded that Benedict and Theresa never left Mandeville Manor, only that I think it would be a good idea for us to open up those dungeons and discover for ourselves what they contain."

They discussed the situation for a long time, refining and looking for weaknesses in Nick's plan. Only when the clock on the mantel struck three and Tess had smothered half a dozen yawns did their words gradually dwindle off. A short while later both were sound asleep, wrapped securely in each other's arms.

Freshly bathed and appropriately garbed, they emerged from their bedrooms the next morning just before eleven. As they came down the long, majestic staircase, they found the house bustling with activity. Servants were hurrying in and out of the house, carrying trunks and bags and boxes, and Nick stared mystified after them. What the devil was going on?

Rockwell appeared just then from the morning room. Spying the pair of them, he grinned. "Your grandmother has decided that we're all to go to Cornwall and leave the pair of you alone here. She says that while you might not have gone on a honeymoon, you don't need a bunch of relatives underfoot. Said that she'd like to visit Rockwell Hall again—hasn't been there in years. Good thing you're up—she intends for us to leave within the hour!"

Nick and Tess exchanged a glance of dismay. Under different circumstances they would have appreciated the privacy, but discovering what had happened to Benedict and Theresa was uppermost in their minds. Nick might have wished them all at Coventry a dozen times recently, but right now he needed them. Here—not in bloody Cornwall!

Leaving Tess in Rockwell's company, Nick went in search of his grandmother. He found her in her room, happily supervising the last trunk of clothing she planned to take with her. She looked to be in excellent spirits, her eyes sparkling and her face dimpling with smiles.

"I don't know why I didn't think of this earlier," she exclaimed once they had greeted each other and he had thanked her for last night's feast. "You and Tess need time by yourselves, and you certainly don't need all of us underfoot right now. It's all decided—the pair of you can join us at Rockwell Hall for Christmas, and then sometime after the first of the year we shall all return home."

Nick had forgotten that, for all her frailness and small size, when Pallas got an idea into her head it would be easier to stop an invading army than to sway her from her path. He tried. At his most winning, he charmed, he teased, he cajoled, but she just smiled at him and patted him fondly on the cheek. "Oh, what nonsense! You know that I am right. It will be much better for you and Tess to have the court to yourselves for the first several weeks of you marriage. You'll have to put up with me and her aunts long enough when we all return."

Momentarily diverted, he asked, "You don't mind the aunts living with us here at Sherbourne?"

"Of course not! Hetty is a dear—always so cheerful and helpful—and Meg and I have much in common. Until she arrived I never realized how much I missed having a companion nearer my own age. Athena did her best, but . . ." Her smile faded, and her eyes clouded with pain.

Nick's heart sank. "Does it distress you that Athena and I cannot share the same house?"

She shook her head. "I was greatly troubled yesterday evening when she told me what had happened between the two of you. I had always hoped that you two would resolve your differences, but I see that there is too wide a chasm between you." She gave him a twisted smile. "I think that having Athena live in the Dowager House will probably be best for all of us." A flicker of hope entered her eyes. "Who knows, without having to rub shoulders with each other all the time, you still might learn to live amiably together!"

Nick didn't want to disillusion her, so he dropped a kiss on her soft, lined cheek and murmured, "Perhaps. One never knows."

It was apparent that nothing short of telling her of the discovery of the diary was going to sway Pallas from leaving. Having decided to keep the diary a secret until he knew whether or not his suspicions were correct, Nick didn't have much choice but to give in gracefully. He told himself it didn't really matter—they would have had to wait until Avery had left the area anyway, and who knew when that might be. Nick had been considering having an urgent summons sent to Avery from London, demanding the baron's appearance in the City to speed things up a bit, but regretfully he laid that idea away for a while. His grandfather had disappeared nearly seventy years ago, and except for Pallas, all the principals were dead—waiting a short while longer wasn't going to hurt anything. Avery was, no doubt, home for the winter now, and it would be after the first of the year before they'd be able to explore the dungeons anyway, so what did it matter if the others went off to Cornwall? He didn't want to wait, but he forced himself to be patient.

Nick did make one last attempt. Cornering Rockwell in the gaming room, he said with deceptive indifference, "Well, since you are deserting me so cavalierly, I guess I'll have to finish exploring those tunnels at the gatekeeper's cottage by myself. I only hope I don't run into any returning smugglers. . . ."

Rockwell looked alarmed. "Now, Nick," he began agitatedly, "that ain't such a good idea. Better wait until we come back after the first of the year." Inspiration struck, and with blue eyes gleaming he said triumphantly, "Besides, you said that we had to desert the place for a while to give them time to decide to use it again. Need to wait—you said so yourself!"

Nick smiled ruefully. Rockwell was right. He had said just that very thing, and while he had been thinking in short terms, he knew that he had lost the argument. He and Tess were being deserted and going to be in solitary possession of Sherbourne Court—whether they liked it or not. Which, the more he thought about it, didn't seem like such a bad idea after all. . . .

He was able to steal a moment alone with Tess and bring her up-to-date. While, like him, she wanted an immediate resolution, she realized that they were just going to have to wait. She certainly wasn't going to let him go poking around in the dungeons of Mandeville Manor by himself!

Having been informed of her grandmother's imminent departure, Athena appeared at the court to say good-bye. She and Nick greeted each other stiffly, but under Pallas's eye they were exceedingly polite to each other. When the plan had first been concocted the previous evening, Athena had been invited to come with the others, but she had declined. She needed, she said, to get more settled in her new home before dashing off for an extended visit to Cornwall.

Pallas had been a little uneasy about leaving Athena behind, particularly considering the situation with Nicolas— who knew what might transpire between them without her around to keep the peace? But she decided that the pair of them would just have to work it out themselves.

And so it was that at precisely one o'clock that afternoon, Nick, Tess, and Athena waved farewell to the others. Watching them disappear down the driveway, the coach and wagon piled high with luggage and half the staff and the Rockwells riding a pair of striking black thoroughbreds, Tess felt a pang. Should they have revealed what they knew? She was suddenly conscious that she and Nick were on their own with a secret that had remained hidden for nearly seventy years and that if something were to happen to them . . .

Athena sailed up to them just then. She felt Nick stiffen at Athena's approach, but keeping her hand firmly on his arm, she said in friendly tones to her sister-in-law, "What upheavals you have been faced with lately! Are you very much vexed by it all?"

Athena smiled. Something in her black eyes, so like Nick's, increased Tess's uneasiness. "Vexed?" Athena asked softly. "Oh, no, my dear, I am not upset at all." Her smile deepened. "Actually things couldn't have worked out better! Just think, you and I shall be able to get to know each other without everyone else hovering about. It'll be just the two of us. . . . I'm so looking forward to entertaining you at the Dowager House. We shall have *such* a wonderful time together!"

"Can it be," Nick asked dryly, his eyes watchful, "that you are resigned to living at the Dowager House?"

"Oh, my, yes!" Athena fairly purred. "It really is for the best—I've always liked my privacy, and having an entire house to myself is just so exciting." She hesitated, looking contrite. Then she said in a rush, "Nick, I hope you'll overlook my outburst last night. I said some things that I shouldn't have, and upon calmer reflection, I'm very sorry for them." She gave him a winning smile. "Will you forgive me? I really don't want to be at daggers drawn with you and certainly not with your bride! Shall we try to do better? And perhaps, if we work diligently at it while grandmother is gone, we can settle our differences."

It was a handsome apology, and Nick could do nothing but accept it. He muttered something polite in return and even managed to keep a smile on his face when Tess innocently invited Athena to go riding with them tomorrow afternoon. All smiles, Athena departed a few minutes later. Watching her ride away on the raking chestnut gelding she had arrived on, Nick was suspicious. His eyes narrowed. He didn't trust this sudden about-face of hers. Despite all her avowals of friendship and goodwill, Athena was up to something.

Chapter Twenty-six

*D*espite his suspicions, in the days that followed Nick could not fault Athena's behavior—or her warm manner with Tess. She seemed fairly to dote upon Tess, cheerfully pointing out some of her favorite aspects of Tess's new home and inviting her to come visit at the Dowager House. Since the Dowager House was a scant mile down the road, Nick could hardly raise any objections. But those infrequent afternoons when Tess would ride through the extensive woods to spend some time with Athena always made him particularly uneasy. Unable to explain himself, he insisted that Tess take a pair of grooms with her, and they had strict orders from the master that they were never to return to Sherbourne Court without their mistress. Tess thought him silly and teased him, but then he reminded her of the near fatal attack she had suffered and she did not tease him anymore.

Fine weather prevailed into November except for the random stormy day, and for Nick and Tess it was a wondrous time. Though they saw Athena frequently, there were hours and hours of pure magic that they spent by themselves. By the time a month had passed and December was drawing near, Nick had come to the conclusion that his grandmother had been right in departing from Sherbourne. It wasn't precisely a honeymoon, but they had only to please themselves, and

please themselves they did. There were long, passion-filled
nights as they explored and discovered every facet of each
other's bodies, and there were lazy afternoons, weather per-
mitting, spent wandering over the vast lands amassed by earlier earls of Sherbourne. There were intimate dinners for two
and happy meals eaten al fresco as they roamed the estate on
brisk but pleasant days—or, on inclement days, hours spent in
the library before the roaring fire, reading and talking and
falling more and more deeply in love with each other with
every passing moment.

As news of their marriage spread, there was the occasional
local caller. Squire Frampton came to visit and offer congratulations, Dickerson having returned to London. Admiral
Brownell and his wife and Lord and Lady Spencer also called
briefly, and cards and letters began to trickle in, but beyond
that, the newlyweds were left to their own devices, and they
were quite happy that it was so.

While he delighted in his bride and fell more fully under
her sweet spell every day, Nick could not forget about the terrible secret that might lie waiting to be revealed in the dungeons of Mandeville Manor. He wanted to get in those
dungeons so desperately that he even rashly considered slipping away from Tess and doing some reconnoitering on his
own, but common sense prevailed—that and the certain
knowledge that he would be confronted by a raging violet-
eyed virago upon his return. There was the added fact that he
seemed unable to be away from her for any length of time.
Those occasions when she visited with Athena, he found himself pacing the floor, longing for her return and waiting impatiently for the moment he heard her voice and step in the hall.
He was, he admitted, thoroughly besotted and no doubt firmly
under the cat's paw, but it bothered him not a whit.

Thoughts of the elusive Mr. Brown also nagged at him, but
until the smugglers returned to their haunts at the gatekeeper's cottage there was not much he could do. In his

darker moments he feared that they had heard the last of Mr. Brown.

The diary and the dungeons occupied a great deal of both his and Tess's thoughts. They discussed them endlessly, and both became increasingly impatient with the waiting.

One good thing grew out of their semi-isolation—Nick and Athena came to know each other in a way that had not been possible before. To his surprise, Nick found his sister a charming companion. They had seemed to work out a truce that boded well for the future, and seeing the two siblings together, no one would ever have guessed of the deep hostility that had once lain between them. In the beginning, they had been scrupulously polite to one another. But as the days passed, both had become more relaxed in each other's company, and Nick began to see some of the more admirable qualities in his sister that his grandmother had alluded to on several occasions. He actually found himself appreciating Athena's sharp wit and, to his astonishment, enjoying himself—even if a part of him still held warily aloof from her.

The move to the Dowager House appeared to have lessened Athena's bitter resentment, and she seemed to have come to grips with her rancor against him; the fact that she got along so well with his wife made him look at her more kindly and made him more willingly to extend the hand of friendship. She respected their privacy, and while she did not run tame through the house, she did visit with them frequently. It was inevitable that she learn of the diary.

It happened by accident. One rainy Monday afternoon when Athena came to call, Tess and Nick had been going over the diary, clarifying for the hundredth time the sequence of events that had led up to Benedict's disappearance with Theresa. Athena found them in the library, the little black leather book lying between them on the burgundy silk sofa upon which they sat.

She had entered the room unannounced, as was her habit, and the obvious look of dismay that crossed their faces made her halt halfway across the room and look at them with open curiosity. "What is it?" she asked slowly. "Has something happened?" Anxiety etched her handsome features. "You have not heard bad news from Grandmother?"

Nick shook his head quickly and rose. "No, nothing like that! We were just having a . . . uh, intense conversation."

Athena looked arch. "A lovers' quarrel?"

Nick smiled and, turning back to the sofa, reached over and casually lifted the diary and placed it inside his jacket. "No, we weren't quarreling—just discussing something."

Athena's eyes narrowed. "Something in that little black book that you are at such pains to hide from me?"

There was such an expression of guilt on Tess's lively face that Athena burst out laughing. "Oh, come now, what is it? If you don't tell me, I shall think the worst."

Nick and Tess exchanged glances. "Perhaps we should tell her," Tess said slowly. "She has as much right as any of us—only your grandmother has more right."

Nick sighed and looked back at Athena. "Swear that what I am about to tell you goes no further until I say so."

Athena's smile faded and her features became serious. "What *is* it? You both look so solemn."

"Swear it," Nick said grimly.

Athena sat on a chair near the fire that was leaping in the fireplace. After arranging the skirts of her fine ruby red merino wool gown to her satisfaction, she studied each of their faces. "Oh, very well," she said finally when it became obvious that they would not budge. "I swear it. I shall not let a word of what you tell me escape my lips."

Reluctantly, and with great misgivings, Nick told her of the diary and what they suspected. Athena was stunned, excited, and appalled. For several moments the room was quiet as she digested the enormous discovery that had been made. Her face softened. "Grandmother will be so pleased, so thrilled to learn that he loved her and that he had not left her. She *always* believed in him. Always protested when our father spoke ill of him. This will make her deliriously happy." Tears gleamed in her eyes. "She will be devastated to learn of his fate, but in the end, she will have the knowledge that he had not deserted her."

"Provided," Nick said somberly, "we can get inside those dungeons and prove what we suspect. Until then, I don't want her to know about the diary. It would plague her unmercifully not knowing if his body really does lie in those dungeons or if he did indeed leave with Theresa. Only after I have managed to explore those dungeons and have determined his fate will I tell her about the diary. Until then, this information goes no farther—it remains amongst us three."

An odd expression crossed Athena's face, and Nick found himself trying to interpret it. Triumph? Or regret? He couldn't tell. It seemed a mixture of both, and it troubled him, and the feeling returned to him almost instantly that Athena was up to something. Something, he felt instinctively, that boded ill for him and Tess. . . .

Athena looked away from him. Staring into the fire, she asked, "How do you intend to get into those dungeons? Avery is in residence, and I doubt he would allow you to drive up to his house and boldly march in and start demolishing the brick wall that Tess has said exists."

"We intend to wait until Avery has gone back to London or is away visiting. We plan to strike after the first of the year, when Rockwell and the others return from Cornwall—provided Avery is gone from the manor."

"Do Rockwell and the others know of this plan?" Athena asked idly.

"No," Nick answered. "At the moment, no one except the three of us even know of the diary's existence, let alone what we suspect."

Her eyes fixed on the fire, Athena said slowly, "The first of the year is an awfully long time to wait to find out the truth."

"We know," Tess said regretfully. "We have discussed nothing else these past weeks, but we can think of no other way to do it."

"Suppose Avery were to leave—to go to spend the holidays with friends. . . . Would you still insist upon waiting for the return of the others?"

Nick rubbed his chin. "It would be very tempting, but Tess and I have agreed to wait for the others." He smiled at Tess. "She has this fear of Avery returning unexpectedly and trapping me in the dungeons."

"But if we all *three* went in together," Athena began excitedly, her fine black eyes gleaming, "there would be no danger." She looked at Tess. "You don't really believe that once Avery has departed, he would return so unprovidentially, do you?"

Tess wiggled uncomfortably on the sofa. "I don't know—I just know that I don't want to give Avery any chance to hurt Nick—and he would, if he caught him at Mandeville Manor."

"But not if we all were there," Athena said soothingly. She smiled brightly at Tess. "After all, he could hardly murder all three of us!"

Nick laughed. "I said much the same thing to her some time ago, only then it was five of us."

Even Tess laughed, albeit reluctantly. "I know that I am being silly, but I just don't trust Avery."

"Oh, pooh on Avery," Athena said gaily. "The three of us will outsmart him."

"Yes, no doubt we could," Nick said, "but before we can do anything, Avery has to go away."

"Hmm, yes, that *is* a problem, isn't it?" Athena purred. "But who knows, he might just take it in his head to go away—or he might already be planning to do so. Shall I find out for you?"

"*You?*" questioned Nick with astonishment. "How do you know him?"

Athena smiled serenely. "Oh, the new baron and I have often met in London. Considering who he is, we are not friends by any means, but I know him well enough to exchange polite conversation with him when our paths cross."

She looked thoughtful. "Now where did I hear that he goes riding every morning? . . . Ah, yes, I remember. It was from Squire Frampton. He said something about the two of them often meeting on the marsh road. I think I shall ask the squire to escort me upon that same ride tomorrow morning." She looked mischievous. "Who knows whom we may meet?"

Neither Nick nor Tess was completely won over by Athena's scheme, but they could find no fault with her discreetly questioning Avery about his plans for the holidays, even though something about Athena's feverish enthusiasm for the project struck a jarring note with Nick.

They had left the subject at that, but that night as Nick and Tess lay abed together, their arms entwined, Nick said slowly, "I hope we haven't made a mistake by including Athena in our plans—although under the circumstances we could hardly have avoided doing it. I know things have been easier between us of late, but I just don't quite trust her. . . ." His lips twisted. "Yet I cannot think of what harm she could do, and if there is one thing I do know, it is that she genuinely cares for Grandmother and would want to help solve the mystery of Benedict's disappearance."

Tess angled her head upward to look at his dark face. "You don't believe that she would betray us, do you? Somehow be in collusion with Avery?"

Nick's first instinct was to deny such an ugly idea, but he hesitated. Finally he muttered, "I don't think so, but I cannot pretend that I trust her completely. I have the feeling that she is up to something, but I cannot even wager a guess as to what it might be!"

"Perhaps because you have been at odds with her for so long, you find it hard to accept that she has changed toward you?"

Nick made a face. "Perhaps. And until she does something that makes me *more* suspicious, I shall simply have to take her actions at face value."

"Wouldn't it be wonderful if Avery *was* going away for the holidays and the three of us could get into the dungeons before your grandmother came back?" Tess's face glowed with enthusiasm. "Just think, we might be able to take the news of our discovery to her at Rockwell Hall."

Nick grunted, not quite as enamored of the idea as his wife. The idea once planted would not go away, however, and Nick found himself hoping that Athena would bring them good news when next she came to call. She did.

The very next afternoon Athena rode up just as Tess and Nick were preparing to take their horses out for a pleasant gambol. The excited expression on Athena's face told them that she had been successful and that she had good news for them. They halted their horses, and as she drew her own mount to a stop, she said gaily, "I had a *most* eventful morning, my dears. I will tell you all. . . ." She glanced meaningfully at the grooms who were busy around the stables and said softly, "But first let us ride a bit farther away from listening ears."

The three of them quickly rode away, and only when the stables were out of sight did Athena speak. Her black eyes glittering like diamond-polished obsidian, she said breathlessly, "Frampton and I went riding this morning along the marsh road, and whom do you think we happened to meet?" She smiled broadly. "Yes, of course! Baron Mandeville. We had a most pleasant little chat, and he happened to mention that he leaves this Thursday to spend the holidays with friends in Yorkshire. I was thrilled! He must have thought me mad by my open elation about his trip."

"You didn't make him suspicious, did you?" Nick asked sharply.

Athena shook her head. "No, no, of course not! I am not a fool." She looked at them, speculation rampant on her face. "Well? Are we going to do it?"

Nick hesitated; he glanced at Tess, and seeing the flush of excitement across her cheeks and the sparkling enthusiasm in her violet eyes, he nodded slowly. "Yes, I think we shall . . . but we're going to need a reason to visit the manor—we can't just boldly ride up and demand entrance."

Tess looked thoughtful. "What if I claimed that a favorite brooch or necklace had been left behind? Something that had been my mother's? Wouldn't that be reason enough? None of the servants would question my words."

"Excellent!" exclaimed Athena. "It gives us a perfectly valid reason to call at the manor."

Nick was less enthusiastic, but he finally agreed it was probably the best excuse they were going to come up with. It was decided that Athena would employ Squire Frampton to make certain Avery had in fact left for Yorkshire—and, if possible, to discover how many servants were in residence.

His brow furrowed, Nick stared hard at his sister. "You can get him to do this without arousing his curiosity?"

Athena smiled demurely. "John is quite taken with me, you know—he believes everything I tell him. I shall stick as close to our tale as possible and tell him that Tess desperately wants to retrieve a brooch, which belonged to her mother and which she is particularly fond of, and she doesn't want to run the risk of meeting Avery. He will easily find out exactly when Avery left and just how many servants remain in residence."

Nick could not fault the plan, nor could he come up with a better one, and yet . . . Pushing aside his feeling of unease, he committed himself to the undertaking.

If they had been impatient before, the days between Tuesday and Friday dragged endlessly for Tess and Nick as they waited for events to fall into place. When Athena came riding over Friday morning, a smile on her face, they knew that Avery had left.

When the trio were alone in the library, Athena took off her riding gloves and her saucy brimmed black velvet hat. She warmed her hands before the fire as she said, "He's gone. He left yesterday afternoon. His valet went with him, and he has given his butler and most of the staff a holiday until after the first of the year. Only a few old retainers remain. Just enough to keep the place in order until his return."

Tess let her breath out in a rush. Her eyes sparkling, she said eagerly, "Then we can go ahead. This afternoon we shall set the plan in motion."

Athena nodded slowly, and for the first time Nick noticed a subdued air about her. Her jaw was set in resolute lines, and he wondered at the faint expression of regret he glimpsed in her eyes. "What is it?" he asked quietly. "Have you changed your mind?"

Athena took a deep breath and glanced, not at him, but at the richly furnished room in which they stood. Her eyes finally came back to him. Looking him squarely in the face, she said steadily, "No, I haven't changed my mind. Events will go as planned."

Athena did not linger. Promising to return at the appointed hour, two o'clock that afternoon, she departed soon afterward.

Tess was bubbling over with excitement. She said teasingly to her husband, "This is far more thrilling than exploring the cellars beneath the gatekeeper's cottage. I can hardly wait to find out if your suspicions are correct!" A little of her excitement ebbed as she added quietly, "I know it will be grisly and sad, but I am so glad that I can be with you when we discover what really happened to them." She shook off her somber thought and smiled impishly. "You shall not have all the adventures!"

His thoughts elsewhere, Nick made some casual reply and excused himself to have a word with Lovejoy, who was upstairs in Nick's room. Shutting the door carefully behind him, Nick said bluntly, "I may be doing a damn foolish thing, old fellow. I don't believe so and I wouldn't dare risk a hair of Tess's head, but I would feel so much better if I knew that you were aware of what I was about."

Lovejoy glanced sharply at him, laying aside the jacket he had been brushing. "Now what sorts of tricks are you up to today?" he demanded.

Nick smiled faintly. "I'm not certain. There should be no danger, and if I seriously thought that there was any real danger, I certainly would not be taking my wife with me. I am, I find, growing more cautious the older I get." He reached inside his jacket and withdrew the diary. Handing it to Lovejoy, he said slowly, "Keep this for me. And if something untoward should happen to me, see that you place it in, and *only* in, my grandmother's hands. My wife and I are going to be visiting Mandeville Manor this afternoon with Athena." At Lovejoy's start of surprise, Nick added grimly, "Oh, don't worry—the baron is not supposed to be in residence. We intend to solve a mystery and plan on exploring the old dungeons beneath the manor itself." Their eyes met, and his voice hard, Nick said, "Should your mistress and I not return by, say, seven o'clock this evening—I do not know how long our task may take—I want you and several of the strongest men to come to Mandeville Manor and demand our presence." Nick smiled thinly. "No matter what you are told, or by whom, do not leave that accursed place without both of us."

Lovejoy looked greatly disturbed. "You suspect a trap?"

Nick shook his head. "Not necessarily. I'm just not taking any chances." He grinned.

"You could cry off," Lovejoy answered quietly.

Nick's jaw set. "No. I have to know the truth about . . . several things."

Leaving his servant standing there, Nick walked over to one of the massive mahogany wardrobes that lined the north wall of his bedchamber. Rummaging round in it, he eventually found what he was looking for—a small, easily hidden pistol and a deadly-looking knife. Expertly, he slid the knife into the top of his boot, where it was concealed but readily accessible, and hid the little pistol carefully within his waistcoat pocket. "There," he said grimly, "just in case there are any surprises—I'll have a few of my own."

Chapter Twenty-seven

As the hours passed, Nick's feeling of unease did not abate, and he made one last attempt to dissuade Tess from accompanying him to Mandeville Manor. She listened to him in silence before saying calmly, "Do you really believe that you will be able to gain access to Mandeville Manor without me? Or that I would let you, *especially* since you have grave reservations about Athena's trustworthiness?"

Nick rubbed the back of his neck. "It's not that I don't trust her, exactly," he said in exasperated tones. "I just feel that everything worked out a little too conveniently. Everything has been arranged by her, and we have only her word for it." He sent Tess a rueful smile. "You have to remember, these past weeks have been the only time in my memory that she and I have managed to get along for any length of time. I've told myself a dozen times that she has changed—perhaps I have changed, too, but it doesn't reassure me very much." He sighed. "And yet, unless I am willing to believe that my own sister has my demise in mind—as well as yours—I can offer no solid reason for my feelings."

Tess touched his cheek. "Well, I do believe that Athena has finally decided to make the best of a situation she can't alter. She is genuinely fond of having her own household. Surely you see that?"

Nick stifled a curse and pulled her urgently against him. "Yes, Athena does seem to be far happier living apart from us. I pray you are right and that she has accepted her new position."

At the appointed hour Athena arrived, and with no sign of reservation, Tess and Nick rode away with her. For a trio embarking upon a great adventure, they were all oddly subdued as they traveled toward Mandeville Manor. Nick supposed it was because they knew that, at best, the most they were going to find was a sad little pile of bones—all that remained of Benedict and Theresa after these many years.

Nick had brought the tools they would need to break through the brick wall—two picks, a heavy maul, a pair of shovels, and several thatch torches for light. They were all in the two bulky canvas bags tied across the back of his saddle.

There wasn't much conversation among the three of them as they approached their destination, and even Athena was curiously silent. What little speech they had exchanged came to an abrupt halt when Tess's former home finally came into view. Instinctively they pulled their horses to a halt and stared at the manor. The place looked harmless, just a charming old manor house, drowsing in the weak afternoon sunlight.

Remembering her terror the night she had fled from her home, Tess took a deep breath and said brightly, "Well, shall we?"

The others nodded. The die was cast.

Everything went as planned. An old retainer, Henry Barnes, answered their knock on the door, his seamed face warming as his eyes fell upon Tess's countenance. "Miss!" he exclaimed happily. "You've come back!"

Tess spoke with him a few minutes, introducing her husband and his sister. After he had offered fond congratulations on her marriage and Tess has reassured him that the aunts were fine, Henry confirmed all that Athena had said: the master was gone to Yorkshire until after the first of the year and, except for himself and the cook and a young scullery maid, all the other servants were away, having been given another unexpected holiday.

Leading them into the house, Henry shook his grizzled head and said softly to Tess, "I never would have thought that the new baron would prove so generous to the staff. But he has been most kind in allowing all of us time to spend with our families."

While Tess urged him to return to his favorite spot near the fire in the kitchen, Nick and Athena went to get the bags of tools. By the time they came back inside, Tess greeted them with the news that Henry had returned to the kitchen, where he would no doubt remain until they rang for him when they were ready to leave. Now they had only to find the bricked wall to the dungeons.

They followed Tess down several narrow, convoluted hallways at the rear of the building, and after a few false starts they finally found themselves walking down a hallway that was obviously very old and seldom used. As Tess explained, the present manor house had been built partially on top of and connected to a much older dwelling—a small stone keep constructed in Norman times. The dungeons had been part of the previous building, and it was unlikely, since they had been bricked up for decades, that anyone ever came to this part of the house. Except for the family and an old servant or two, it was doubtful anyone knew that the dungeons even existed.

They had lit two of the torches some time ago. Tess and Nick were each carrying one, and when they suddenly rounded a corner, the flickering light revealed a most astonishing sight: a brick wall with a huge black gaping hole in the middle of it, mortar and broken bricks lying in a heap near the base.

As soon as he saw the hole, Nick knew it was a trap. Dropping the bags of tools he carried, he was already grabbing for Tess, his first thought to get her away, when Athena said smoothly, "I wouldn't if I were you."

He glanced at his sister and found himself looking into the double barrel of a pistol. He understood now why she had not wanted to carry a torch and had claimed that the tools were too heavy for her. She was smiling slightly, a mirthless smile that sent chills down his spine. She motioned toward the opening in the brick wall. "Well, go ahead, you wanted to know what happened to them."

His fingers digging into Tess's arm, Nick said levelly, "Why don't you just tell us what you've found."

Athena shrugged. "You were right. They *are* here—what is left of them. We found the bodies, bones mostly, in the middle cell on the right. The diamonds, too."

Tess had known what they would find, but hearing Athena confirm their suspicions sent a stab of pain through her.

Never taking his eyes off Athena's face, Nick asked quietly, "So what happens now? History repeats itself?"

Athena's grimaced. "Yes, I'm rather afraid that's exactly what is going to happen. Now get moving through that opening."

Nick's eyes met Tess's, and she sent him such a look of love and confidence that his breath caught in his throat. They were *not* going to die!

For a second he considered refusing, but he discarded that option rather swiftly—he had no doubt that Athena would shoot them where they stood. Hoping that a way out of this deadly tangle would occur to him, he released Tess's arm and climbed over the rubble to the other side. Tess followed closely behind him, and Athena, keeping the barrel of the pistol fixed on him, scrambled on their heels, allowing them no chance for escape.

On the other side, they found themselves in a large, dank, stone room, about twelve feet by thirty. The torchlight danced eerily off the dark, smoke-stained walls. Glancing around, Nick saw that several small doorways opened off the main chamber. Cells, he suspected, where poor unfortunates were simply left to die. His eyes lingered on the middle cell on the right, knowing that his grandfather and Theresa's remains rested there—had rested there for nearly seventy long years. . . . Pray God they had been dead when Gregory sealed them in their tomb.

As she had come through the rubble, Athena had motioned them farther into the chamber, and reluctantly they obeyed, skirting carefully around the menacing black hole that yawned in the center of the stone floor. Only when they were nearly at the far wall of the chamber did Athena let them stop. For a second Nick's gaze rested on that ominous black hole, guessing that it was an old well that had probably served the original building—or a cesspit.

Athena noticed the direction of his gaze and smiled. "No, I don't intend to throw you down there—although that idea did occur to me. I'll be kind enough to shoot you dead before I leave you."

"How generous of you," Nick said dryly. "Always the considerate hostess."

Athena laughed. "Do you know," she said lightly, "there are times that I almost like you? And regret, perhaps just a tiny bit, that I have to kill you?"

"You don't, you know. You could let us go. No one has been harmed yet."

Athena gave him a smile and shook her head. "No. I'm afraid you stand between me and what I want." Her voice hardened. "What *should* have been mine!" She looked sadly at Tess. "As for you, I truly regret the need for your death, but with Nick dead, you would be his heir, which wouldn't do *me* any good. And of course, you could be breeding already. Sorry, my dear, I really have grown rather fond of you this past month."

The figure of a man suddenly appeared in the shadows behind Athena, and Tess gasped, instinctively moving closer to Nick. Athena seemed not at all surprised by his appearance. As he stepped into the flickering light of the torches held by Tess and Nick, she asked, "Did he give you any trouble?"

John Frampton shook his head. "No. He never even suspected, until it was too late."

"You're certain he's dead?"

Frampton nodded. "Quite."

Nick's brows snapped together in a frown. Why the devil was Frampton here? Who was dead? And how in the bloody hell was he to get Tess to safety?

His furiously churning thoughts were jerked back to Athena as she said, "I suppose it's only fair to tell you what we're talking about. . . ." She inclined her head toward the doorway where Frampton had first appeared. "You'll be pleased to know that Avery isn't going to be enjoying a long life. I'm sure you'll dislike sharing eternity down here with him, but there wasn't any other way."

If Nick had been puzzled before, he was thoroughly confused now. "You had Frampton kill Avery? Why, in God's name? I know the man was a bastard and I'd have liked to kill him myself, but what the devil did he ever do to you?"

Athena seemed to be enjoying herself, and Nick was thankful that she also seemed willing to talk. Smiling faintly, she said, "Well, you see, Avery has been a bit of a problem for us for some time now—perhaps the last eight to ten months. I just decided that since I was going to get rid of you, I might as well take care of him while I was at it."

Nick frowned. "What sort of problem? Don't tell me that he tried to seduce you?"

Athena laughed aloud at that. "Avery? Oh, heavens, no!"

She hesitated and looked questioningly at Frampton. He made a face and shrugged. "They're never leaving here alive, tell them if you want to."

"Well, you see, I wasn't quite truthful when I said that Randal was always generous with me," Athena began carefully. "He could be as tight-fisted as you have been lately, so some time ago—when John inherited his father's estates and discovered that they were sadly to let—he and I put our heads together to bolster up our sagging fortunes. The solution was simple, particularly when you consider the area—and its, ah, natural resources."

Nick's eyes narrowed. "You turned to smuggling."

Athena nodded. "Yes, dear brother, we did. We were very successful at it, too—we were on the verge of abandoning our lucrative little operation when John suffered a slight setback, a bad investment, and Randal and Sidney died. You became the new earl and Avery inherited Mandeville." She sighed regretfully. "After that, we hesitated to end our illegal activities just then—I did not want to walk away from the smuggling until I knew precisely where my position would be in your household, and John wanted to recoup and expand the size of his holdings. Still, we had intended to continue only for a few more months. But then Avery discovered what we were about, and that changed everything."

Nick nodded, "It would, knowing Avery," he said dryly. "I assume that he blackmailed you both into giving him a share of the profits?"

John Frampton spoke up, his tone bitter. "Cut himself in a for a full third, when Athena and I had already done all the work. We'd set up everything—even the horses and carts for transport—and then that bastard Avery just calmly demands a third of our operation. He threatened to expose us. We had no choice."

"And perhaps it was Avery who suggested a way to expand the operation?" Nick asked with deceptive idleness, the identity of Roxbury's spy suddenly occurring to him.

Frampton looked amazed at the accuracy of his guess, and Athena smiled admiringly. "You always were quick," she said. "And yes, you're right. Avery turned us into spies. He had connections with Whitehall and the Horse Guards, and soon enough he was using our operation as a way to send and receive information from the French. It did increase our revenue dramatically, but neither one of us liked being under Avery's thumb. He acted as if it were *his* operation and we were mere underlings carrying out his orders."

"So you decided to kill him."

Athena nodded. "But not until very recently. For a while everything was just fine, and of course, once we started passing information to the French, Avery was as deeply involved in the smuggling as we were—he could not expose us without exposing himself. But John and I wanted out and Avery didn't." She glanced at Tess. "If he had married you, no doubt he would have been content and would have been willing for the partnership to end. But there was always the danger that eventually he'd run through even your fortune and at some time in the future would come whining back to us, either demanding we restart the smuggling business or for just plain blackmail. We couldn't let him live."

"But what does all that have to do with us?" demanded Tess, her violet eyes stormy. "Why kill us? We've done nothing to you!"

"Well, you're wrong there," Frampton said suddenly. "Your presence at the old gatekeeper's cottage was dashed inconvenient for us! We needed you out of there, although neither Athena nor I realized who you were at the time—we thought you were just some little fancy piece of Nick's."

Nick's free hand clenched into a fist. Harshly he said, "And tried to kill her so that I would abandon the place."

Ignoring Tess's gasp, Athena nodded. "As I said, you always were quick."

Tess stared in horror from Athena to Frampton. "It was *you* who tried to strangle me?" she asked in a squeak. "And fought with Alexander?"

"You've had several near escapes lately, my dear," Athena said coolly. "If that fool had done as I'd told him, you'd have died the night you met the smugglers and . . . Mr. Brown." She sketched them a bow. "At your service—passing myself off as a man proved exceedingly useful, but I'm afraid that it is time for Mr. Brown to disappear forever. And to answer the question hovering on your lips, little brother, yes, I was the one who hit you in the cellars that night." Her fingers tight-

ened on the pistol. "As for your bride, it might have been better for her if Frampton had succeeded that afternoon." Her
face hardened, and there was a feverish glow in her eyes.
"Now there is no escape—you stand between me and something far more valuable—Sherbourne Court. I want what
should have been mine, if I'd been born a male—Sherbourne
Court and the fortune that goes with it! With Nick dead, the
title ends, but everything else will be *mine*—as it should have
been in the first place!"

"Your brother is not an ungenerous man," Tess said urgently. "He would, I'm sure, increase your allowance and
funds to an amount you thought suitable . . . you don't have to
kill us in order to gain what you want." It was a desperate
ploy, and Tess didn't really believe that Athena would even
consider it, but she had to do something. Time was running
out for them.

Athena gave a bitter laugh. "And how, dear sister-in-law,
do you explain away Mandeville's death? Would that just be
our little secret? And the smuggling? Will you and Nick just
pretend it never happened?"

Tess had already considered those things, and she'd known
that Athena would throw them in her face, but it was necessary to keep Athena talking—about anything! Once she
stopped talking . . . Tess swallowed painfully. She didn't want
to end up like Benedict and Theresa. Gamely trying another
tack, she asked quietly, "How did you get Avery to go along
with your plan to lure us here? He must have cooperated with
you—otherwise the servants wouldn't have been sent away
and you wouldn't have had a chance to open the brick wall."

Athena's lips twisted. "He fell over himself in agreeing
with my plan when I presented it to him, thought it was splendid. He was also very interested in finding out if Nick's idea
about Benedict and Theresa was correct, and as for the
other . . . he assumed that Nick would be the only one dying
today—that in due course he could try his hand at marrying
you again—which I encouraged him to think might be possi-

ble. I told him that I would distract you long enough for Nick to enter the dungeons alone. The plan was for Avery and Frampton to have hidden themselves earlier in one of the cells, and when Nick arrived they would catch him by surprise and tip him down the well. Once I estimated that they'd had enough time to kill Nick and hide themselves, then you and I would come into the dungeons and discover that there had been another terrible tragedy. When we left, heartsick and shattered, to spread the word, they would leave the dungeons after us and slip away—John for his home and Avery immediately for Yorkshire. No one would ever know that he'd had anything to do with Nick's demise."

"And the diary?" Nick asked grimly. "What about it? Are you so cruel that you will keep the truth about Benedict from Pallas?"

Athena sighed. "I intend for Grandmother to read it . . . after I have carefully edited it. With your bodies down here, I cannot let her know what really happened to him, but I do want her to know that he loved her and that he wasn't planning on leaving with Theresa. From what you've said, he wrote often enough of it, and if I obliterate any reference to the dungeons, it should be safe enough for her to read."

"If you can find it," Nick drawled, playing desperately for time.

Athena smiled tiredly. "I'll find it. I suspect that you've either given it to Lovejoy or Laidlaw to keep for you. After everything I've done so far, one more murder won't make any difference."

"Is Sherbourne really that important to you?" Tess demanded fiercely. "So important that you'll kill your own brother to possess it? What about Pallas? You claim to love her, but how can you do something that is going to cause her such grief? She loves Nick!"

Athena's mouth thinned. "There is nothing that you can say to change my mind!"

Despite her earlier feeling of calm, when Tess glanced at

Nick her face was full of despair. Were they going to die like Benedict and Theresa after all? She didn't want to believe it, not for a moment, and yet, though she could almost feel Theresa's presence, feel her great-grandmother urging her to fight, not to give up hope, fear coiled in her belly.

His eyes grave, Nick met her stare, his free hand curling warmly around hers. Their gazes held for a moment, and then Nick looked swiftly at the torch in her other hand before meeting her eyes again. Tess's heart leaped. His eyes shifted again to the torch, and there was an imperceptible nod of his head in Frampton's direction.

The interplay between them had taken mere seconds, but Tess had understood instantly what he wanted of her. They were not totally defenseless, after all—*they* held the torches! *The only light in the dungeons.* Her heart banging painfully in her chest, she took a deep breath, and when Nick's hand suddenly tightened savagely on hers, she swiftly threw the torch at Frampton.

Nick's torch had gone flying toward Athena's head at the same instant, and it had hardly left his hand before he was ruthlessly shoving Tess to the floor out of the line of fire and reaching for his own pistol. There was a horrified yelp from Frampton as Tess's torch hit him full on the chest, and he staggered backward. Athena spared not a glance for him, lithely dodging Nick's torch, which tumbled down the well. Dashing into the nearest cell, she fired blindly in Nick's direction, their end of the dungeon now plunged into murky, indistinct shadows. Her leap to avoid the torch had thrown off her aim, and the sound of her bullet smashing into the rear wall where Nick had been standing a moment before echoed deafeningly in the stone chamber.

Crouched protectively above Tess, the pistol held firmly in his hand, Nick waited in the shadowy darkness, his eyes trying to pierce the gloom. He couldn't see Athena, but Frampton was clearly revealed, his clothes on fire. Tess's torch, having served its purpose, had rolled across the floor to lie burning fitfully off to the side of the chamber.

"For God's sake, Athena," screamed Frampton, "help me! I'm on fire!" He was beating frenziedly at the front of his shirt and jacket, the scent of smoldering cloth mixing unpleasantly with the lingering odor of gunpowder. Frampton was beyond reason as he danced wildly about the dungeon, yelling and pleading for Athena to come to his aid. In a fit of terror he threw himself down on the floor and began to roll about frenetically, heedless of how near he came to the gaping hole of the well.

From her position on the floor, Tess watched with horrified eyes as Frampton writhed dangerously near the edge of the well. Then it happened—one second he was there and the next his body had given a frantic jerk and he was tumbling wildly down the well, his terrified cries seeming to linger for endless moments in the air.

It was very quiet after Frampton's dying scream ebbed away. Very dark, too, with only Tess's smoldering torch giving any light in the dense blackness of the dungeon. Nick listened intently for any sound from Athena, but only an eerie silence met his straining ears.

Tess slowly sat up. She could sense a presence, a comforting presence, definitely not Athena's. . . . Her breath caught. It was mad, she knew, but she was suddenly certain that she and Nick were the only ones alive in the dungeon. . . .

Something cool caressed her cheek, and she gave a startled cry, but she wasn't really frightened—that touch, so fleeting and brief, had held such tenderness, such yearning affection, that tears inexplicably came to her eyes.

Nick was gripped by the same sensation that held Tess in thrall. He couldn't explain it, but instinctively he knew that Athena was no longer a danger and that something else, some unnamed force, moved in the shadows around them. Earlier, when Athena had disappeared into the cell, he could have sworn that a second later he'd heard the faintest clank of a sword, but he was certain that he'd been imagining things. Yet the sensation would not go away. Someone else was here with them, a presence that meant no harm. . . .

Cautiously he stood up, his pistol held ready, and helped Tess to her feet. They remained there for several moments, the dying torch casting wildly dancing shadows on the stone walls of the dungeon. Motioning for Tess to follow him, they slowly edged along the wall, carefully passing the well where Frampton had vanished.

Nick hesitated a moment, and then he stepped forward and picked up Tess's torch. The chamber was utterly empty. He and Tess exchanged baffled glances. If she was still here, why didn't Athena shoot? Had she escaped in the confusion?

Intuitively Tess knew that Athena hadn't left the dungeons. She was still down here with them. "She's in the cell . . . with them," she said softly, shocking herself. How had she known that?

Moving with great stealth, Nick approached the middle cell. Despite motioning for her to remain where she was, Tess was right behind him. Together they peered inside, the torch-light flowing gently over the grim, stark interior.

It was the pitiful pile of bones, scraps of satin and velvet still clinging to the limbs they had clothed in life, that first riveted their gaze. There was no doubt that they were looking at the remains of Benedict and Theresa. Staring at the fragile skeletons, Tess choked back a sob. It was obvious from the position of the bones that they had died in each other's arms, Theresa sitting upright on the stone bench against the back wall, Benedict kneeling at her side, his head resting in her lap. Near Benedict's feet, winking like stars in the flickering light, were the Sherbourne diamonds. . . .

Tess began to weep, and Nick's arms closed fiercely around her. "Don't mourn, sweetheart. They died a long time ago. Even Gregory is beyond our vengeance." Words failed him, and they clung to each other.

They had been so intent upon their grief and sadness that it was only as they turned to go that the torchlight revealed the other occupant of that dank, depressing cell. In the corner, as far away from the sad little pile of bones as she could get, was Athena . . . or rather Athena's body. It took Nick but a moment to discover that she was quite, quite dead. There wasn't a mark on her, but her eyes were wide open, her face the picture of abject terror, and on the floor at her feet was the pistol, an old-fashioned sword lying across it. . . .

Epilogue

She is coming, my own, my sweet;
Were it ever so airy a tread,
My heart would hear her and beat,
Were it earth in an earthy bed;
My dust would hear her and beat,
Had I lain for a century dead;
Would start and tremble under her feet,
And blossom in purple and red.

Maud, Part I, St. II
Alfred, Lord Tennyson

Chapter Twenty-eight

*S*eptember had been lovely so far in this year of our Lord 1812. In fact, Tess thought dreamily as she stared down at the babe sleeping peacefully in her arms, the entire year had been most lovely. The news from the continent was even good; in June Sir Arthur Wellesley and his troops had stormed Salamanca in Spain, giving the allies a tremendous victory. The news was not all good—that same June the Americans had declared war on the British, but those events were far away from Tess this particular golden afternoon as she sat beneath the spreading branches of a great oak tree watching her son, Benedict, just six weeks old today, slumber soundly.

Her contentment faded a little as she recalled those awful moments in the dungeons, and a faint shudder rippled over her slender frame. The passage of time had erased most of the terror of that afternoon, but occasionally Tess remembered how close to death she and Nick had come.

They had lingered in that place of tragedy and death only long enough to discover Avery's body in one of the other cells; Frampton had at least killed him quickly—his neck had been broken. With three prominent people dead, they had realized that they were in a most troubling predicament: did they tell the truth or did they wrap it in clean linen? After a painfully brief discussion, they had decided that telling the bare truth would serve nothing. The others were beyond justice, and revealing all that had happened would only cause a huge scandal—and bring more pain to Pallas. Nick felt strongly that a bit of judicious editing was definitely called for. The story they concocted before leaving the dungeons was weak, but it answered their needs, and all it took to make it hang together was the distasteful task of dropping Avery's body down the well to join Frampton's—and the removal of Athena's pistol.

Some hours after they had climbed out of the dungeons, Nick told his tale to the local magistrate, Sir Charles Wetherby, smoothly explaining about finding the diary and why he had suspected that his grandfather had never left Mandeville Manor. His face as bland and unreadable as porridge, Nick had told Wetherby that he and Athena had met with Avery a few days ago to enlist his help; he skipped lightly over Avery's excitement at the possibility of solving the mystery of the long-ago disappearance of Lord Sherbourne and Lady Mandeville. Never hesitating, he went directly to how earlier in the day they all—Avery, Athena, Frampton, Tess, and himself—had found the bricked passage and smashed a hole in it. After that the story became a bit trickier, but Nick carried on gamely.

As they'd entered the chamber, disaster had struck almost at once: one of the torches they had carried, Nick couldn't tell the rapt-faced Wetherby *precisely* how, had inexplicably set Frampton's clothes on fire. In his terror Frampton had thrown himself on the floor and rolled around in great agitation. Avery and Nick had gone immediately to his aid, Avery bravely throwing himself on the screaming Frampton, and somehow, again Nick couldn't *exactly* explain it, in the wild thrashing about, Avery and Frampton had tragically fallen down the well. It had been a ghastly accident, just ghastly. But there was worse to come.

His poor sister, Athena, had been in a state of stunned shock, and with her delicate sensibilities completely overwrought, she had inadvertently stumbled into the very cell containing the bodies of Benedict and Theresa. Coming instantly after the unspeakable horror of seeing the man she loved, Frampton, and his friend, Lord Mandeville, die in such an appalling manner, the sight of those pale, ghostly bones had been the final blow in a series of tragic events. She had given a terrified shriek, and Nick had rushed in to find her lying dead on the floor. Her poor heart must have simply stopped.

Nick had told his tale to Sir Charles in the library at Mandeville Manor—Tess, according to her husband, had been too distraught to talk about the horrific events just then, and she had been sent home to Sherbourne Court. When Nick had finished speaking, Wetherby, rather more shrewd and astute than many would believe, looking at his bluff features and mild blue eyes, had stared at him for a long time.

Just when Nick had been certain all was lost, Wetherby had slowly nodded his balding head and said, "Tragic story. So very sad." Wetherby's lids had lowered, and looking at nothing in particular, he'd murmured, "Known Frampton for years. Rum sort of fellow . . . sailed rather close to the wind. Heard quite a bit about you—good things. People think you'll do well, and well by them. Think it's not a bad thing that the reins of Sherbourne are in your hands these days." He'd finished the glass of port Nick had poured earlier and, after setting it down, cleared his throat and added gravely, "I have always held dear Lady Sherbourne in the highest regard. Fine woman. She's suffered enough scandal and grief. Wouldn't want to add to it."

Nick's heart had begun to beat again, and with suspect haste he had escorted Wetherby to the door. But Sir Charles had stopped at the threshold and, fixing Nick with those mild blue eyes, said dryly, "Come to my home, Rosewood Manor, one day next week. I'd like to hear what *really* happened down there today. . . ."

Lying to Sir Charles had been the easiest hurdle for them to cross; lying to Pallas had not been so simple. But lied they had, and remembering the way Pallas's fragile features had crumpled upon learning of Athena's death when they had finally arrived at Rockwell Hall three days later and had broken the terrible news, Tess felt tears crowd behind her lids. She bent and kissed her son's downy cheek, her heart aching for Pallas's anguish.

Nick knew that his grandmother did not completely believe his story: something in the way she had looked at him made his heart heavy, but he stuck to the tale. Did she really need to know about Mr. Brown? Was it important that she learn that Athena had planned to murder him and Tess in cold blood? He didn't think so.

The news of finding Benedict's body in the dungeons had brought Pallas great joy and deep, abiding sorrow. Her beautiful eyes full of tears, she had said to Nick, "I always believed. I always knew that he had not left me. That he loved me. . . ."

It had been a grim Christmas. In late December Nick had written to Roxbury, telling him only that "Mr. Brown" would not be selling any more secrets to the French. . . . Tragedy behind them, they had viewed the new year with hopeful hearts. The news that Tess would give birth to a child in the summer provided just the distraction that Pallas had needed from her grieving. There was a spring to her step these days, a sparkle in her gaze, and a soft glow about her.

Hetty's laugh, followed by Alexander's deeper tones, floated on the warm air toward Tess; Meg's voice and Rockwell's hearty chuckle were also heard. A smile curved Tess's lips. She watched as the four of them slowly walked her way, Alexander hovering solicitously over an obviously pregnant Hetty—their child would be born in December. It *had* been an eventful year.

With Avery's death, Hetty and Meg had inherited the estate. The title had died with Avery, but the estate had been divided between the two women. Able at last to come to him with a small dowry, Hetty had not hesitated to accept Alexander's offer, and they had married in February. After a brief honeymoon they had taken up permanent residence at Mandeville Manor with Meg. Alexander's fortune was more than adequate to keep the manor and his lovely wife in grand style, and they had settled down to wedded bliss. To their immense joy, Hetty had gotten pregnant almost immediately. Lord Rockwell had been most pleased.

"Oh, here you are, my dear!" exclaimed Hetty as she spied Tess and the baby beneath the tree. "Bellingham said that you and the others were out here enjoying the fine day." She glanced around. "Where is your husband and his grandmother? Have they abandoned you?"

Rising, Tess shook her head. She picked up her son and said, "They are just over there . . . Pallas wanted to lay flowers on Benedict's grave."

The disposal of Benedict's earthly remains had posed no problem; it was his right to be buried with his ancestors at Sherbourne. But Theresa . . . it was out of the question that she be buried near her hateful, murdering husband, and Tess had been adamant in not even wanting Theresa to lie in the Mandeville family plot. Theresa had never been a Mandeville, not in her heart.

For a moment Tess's eyes blurred with tears. Had she not already fallen under Pallas's gentle spell she would have come to adore Nick's grandmother when Pallas had overheard them discussing the situation and had unexpectedly provided a solution. Her once lovely features worn and tired, lines of grief scoring her pale cheeks, she had said one night after they had returned to Sherbourne from Rockwell Hall, "I hated your great-grandmother for a long time—I felt that she had taken my husband from me . . . and in a way she did. But knowing the truth about them, I can find it in my heart to pity her. Having read the diary, I know how she suffered at Gregory's hands and I know that she and Benedict tried so very hard to do what was right. . . ." Her voice had quavered slightly, making it obvious that though she had forgiven the past, it still had the power to hurt—unbearably. Pallas had looked away from Tess's strained features and then, drawing upon resources deep within herself, she had glanced back at her and smiled, albeit shakily. "Your great-grandmother was his first love, but in the end, I was the one who had his heart. . . . Benedict loved us both, and he could no more have deserted Theresa than he could have stopped breathing—I would not have loved him so greatly if he had been any different. One day I will be with him again, and my grave shall lie by his. . . ." Tears had suspended her voice, and she'd gallantly brought her emotions under control before saying huskily, "The events that tore my life apart and took my husband from me happened a very long time ago. Now my husband is returned to me, and for that I shall always be grateful. As for Theresa . . ." She'd swallowed painfully and then said in a rush, as if she'd had to get the words out before she changed her mind, "When I die, I shall lie on one side of him . . . it is only fitting that she should lie on the other. . . ."

Tess had been utterly stunned by Pallas's magnanimous gesture. Few women would have reacted so generously to a rival—even a dead rival. Consequently, lying next to the magnificent stone edifice that marked Benedict's grave, and that one day Pallas would share with him, was a smaller one, a little off to the side, with Theresa's name and birth and date of death engraved on it. It seemed appropriate.

Carrying her sleeping baby in her arms, Tess led the others the short distance through the dappled woods to the Talmage graveyard, where they found Pallas rearranging a huge bouquet of roses, Nick standing ready with another armful. As Tess caught sight of his tall form, a slight breeze riffling that thick black hair, as always, her heart gave a leap. Her face luminous with all the love she felt for him, she quickly crossed to his side.

After greetings were exchanged and Pallas finished her task, she turned and imperiously reached out her arms for baby Benedict. "Here, let me hold him awhile."

Tess gently shifted her precious burden into Pallas's arms and watched the soft glow that spread over the older woman's face as she stared down into her great-grandson's sleeping features. Pallas openly adored the baby, certain that he was the grandest little fellow ever born and that he looked even more like his great-grandsire than did Nick.

Amid laughter, the small group gradually began to walk toward the house. They had not gone very far before Nick caught Tess's hand and pulled her off the path, letting the others continue on their way.

Hidden from view by the concealing foliage, Nick pressed Tess against the trunk of a towering oak and kissed her thoroughly. His black eyes were glittering with hungry passion when he finally lifted his mouth from hers and murmured, "I think that we should go away for that honeymoon we never took. What do you think?"

Her arms wrapped around his neck, her breathing erratic, she asked softly, "But what about Benedict? I am still nursing him part of the time." She made a little face. "You were the one who wanted a nursemaid for him, and while she is wonderful and has plenty of milk for him, I miss having him nuzzling at my breast."

Nick smiled at her tenderly, one hand brushing back a fiery tendril of hair that caressed her cheek. "I know, sweetheart, and I am a selfish bastard, wanting you all to myself. If you don't want the nursemaid, then let the damned wench go— you know that I can deny you nothing."

"You really wouldn't mind?"

He shook his head, a whimsical expression on his handsome face. "No. I thought you would like having her . . . and of course there is the fact that *I* wanted to be the one nuzzling at your breast!"

Tess's breath caught and heat pooled deep in her belly. The latter months of her pregnancy had not been easy, and the birth, while not difficult, had been hard on her. Consequently it had been almost four months since they had last made love, and Tess had been increasingly aware these past few weeks of the frank hunger in her husband's stare and the swelling needs stirring deep within her own body.

She toyed with one of the intricate folds of his cravat and said huskily, "Perhaps the nursemaid isn't such a bad idea after all. . . . Uh, where did you think to go on this honeymoon?"

A carnal smile curved his lips, and his hands tightened on her waist. Brushing a kiss against the side of her neck, he murmured, "I thought that we might spend a few weeks alone at the gatekeeper's cottage. . . . I could show you, Madame Wife, how very much I adore you and how utterly fascinating I find this tantalizing little body of yours. We could spend the days and nights doing nothing but making love. . . ." Suddenly he pulled her against him, his arms crushing her to him. "Oh, God, Tess," he muttered in a shaky voice, "I do love you! More than life! You have changed everything for me . . . for Sherbourne, my grandmother, everyone." Pushing her back a little from him, he gazed down warmly into her face. A faint, wry smile lurked at the corners of his lips. "Do you know, I have begun to believe that old fool Bellingham is right when he says that love has returned to Sherbourne Court?" His voice deepened. "It has, and it is all wrapped up in your sweet form."

She smiled up at him mistily, her arms tightening around him. "Oh, Nick! You couldn't love me more than I love you!"

Their absence had finally been noticed by Lord Rockwell, and while Nick and Tess lost themselves in the impossibly sweet argument about who loved whom the most, Rockwell stopped and looked back. Spying their entwined forms through a break in the concealing woods, he said to no one in particular, "You mark my words, by this time next year, I'll have *another* grandnevvy!"

THROUGHOUT THE NEXT YEAR, LOOK FOR OTHER
FABULOUS BOOKS FROM YOUR FAVORITE WRITERS
IN THE WARNER ROMANCE GUARANTEED PROGRAM